THE LANGUAGE OF STARS

Also by Louise Hawes

Anteaters Don't Dream and Other Stories

Black Pearls: A Faerie Strand

Muti's Necklace

Nelson Malone Saves Flight 942

Rosey in the Present Tense

The Vanishing Point

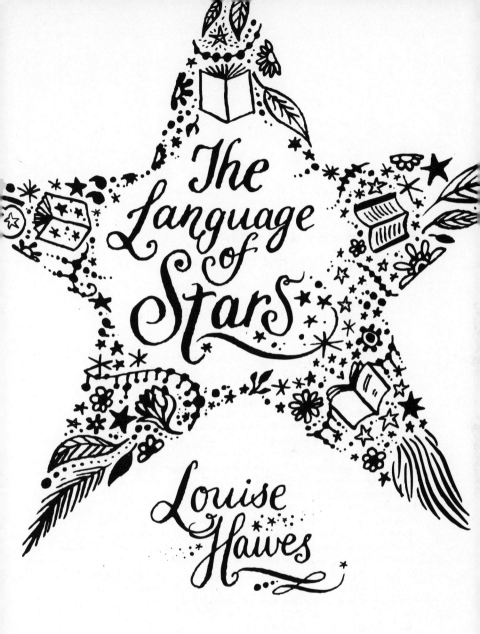

The Language of Stars

Louise Hawes

MARGARET K. MCELDERRY BOOKS
NEW YORK LONDON TORONTO SYDNEY NEW DELHI

For Indi and Owen,
last but far from least

MARGARET K. McELDERRY BOOKS
An imprint of Simon & Schuster Children's Publishing Division
1230 Avenue of the Americas, New York, New York 10020

The text for this book is set in Adobe Jenson Pro.
Manufactured in the United States of America
10 9 8 7 6 5 4 3 2 1
CIP data is available from the Library of Congress.
ISBN 978-1-4814-6241-9 (hardcover)
ISBN 978-1-4814-6243-3 (eBook)
FIRST EDITION

I dwell in a lonely house I know
That vanished many a summer ago. . . .

—Robert Frost, "Ghost House"

Whale Point Watch

APRIL 12

HIGH TIDE: 11:07 A.M., 11:22 P.M. • LOW TIDE: 5:23 A.M., 5:00 P.M.

Letters to the Editor

The Baylor Break-In

I hope someone has the guts to teach those kids a lesson. I've heard bleeding hearts talk about building a rec center so our children have a place to go at night. Hold the phone! Why should we reward a bunch of inconsiderate, destructive delinquents for trashing a historic landmark? Why should taxpayers pay to babysit the junior felons that urinated on valuable photographs, smashed priceless antiques, and played drinking games in the former home of our nation's greatest poet? If they were a year or two older, those punks would be thrown in jail. I say give them a preview of coming attractions!

Harold Lloyd, Wilmington

Most things have two sides, but the kind of desecration that went on in that house last week is just plain wrong. "Shameful" is another word for it. If we're raising boys and girls who trample on everything we hold precious, what hope is there for the future? Fishing isn't going to keep this town alive, but we have other things to offer; or we *did*. In a single night, those hooligans didn't just set off every fire alarm in the place; they didn't just burn all the furniture and heirlooms; they didn't just destroy $50,000 worth of public property. Something else went up in flames that night—our hopes to put Whale Point on the map.

Melissa Slaytor, Whale Point

I work with kids. I like kids. But kids and booze and drugs spell disaster. Until we pass legislation to make this a dry town, we're just asking for more of what happened at the Baylor house. I know everybody is petrified that going dry would cost us summer rentals, but which do we want: Safe kids? Or tourists who can't go on vacation without Johnnie Walker? That break-in was a wake-up call. It's time to join the other family resort towns that play it safe; it's time for Whale Point to sober up.

Jesse H. Cornblatt, Whale Point

I really didn't think it was possible that a bunch of teenagers, regular high school students, some of them kids of my neighbors, could deliberately destroy an old man's past. And not just any old man, but the greatest poetic voice this country has ever known. "I forgive the wind," Rufus Baylor wrote in *Southern Autumn*. "I know why it rattles the gate." Well, maybe *he* can forgive the rowdies who spilled beer all over his family photos and left their excrement streaked across his manuscripts. But as someone who has loved his poetry ever since I could speak, I can't. I won't.

Bessie Lavender, Sea Crest

A Home Away from Home

When you are the planet's Worst of All Waitresses, your only hope is to be its newest, too. Drop a plate on some poor diner who didn't even order it? Widen your eyes in horror, then put your hand to your mouth. "Oh, I am *so* sorry!" Breathe deeply, tragically. "I'm new here." Screw up the orders, so the haddock goes to the table that wanted the veal—half an hour ago? "I can't believe I did that!" Pause. Sigh. Whisper, "It's my first day."

It was my first day at Mamselle's for over a year. I went to work there as soon as I turned fifteen. I couldn't serve drinks, but I could wait on tables. And since Shepherd needed all the help he could get, and my mother wanted me to save for college, it was pretty much decided without me. I'd never seen my father in his element before, and trust me, it was nothing like Take Your Kid to Work Day. No fancy office, no quiet hum of printers or doors you can close and keep closed. Only the glare and blare of the kitchen at full tilt, the steam and the tension. And it wasn't just a once-a-year visit, either. From then on, it happened every weekend—hell on Fridays and Saturdays.

I never really learned to pace myself, never got used to the rush and the heat and the yelling. I trailed two waitresses, one after the other, for weeks on end. But nothing took. I couldn't get the graceful balancing act going that the others managed. I felt more like a clown juggler in shoes the size of boats. Cut to thirteen months later: I was still dropping plates, still making the same newbie mistakes—I placed too many orders at once, I cleared from the left, I brought the salad last. But I guess I should be glad I was there, messing up like always, when Shepherd fired the new hire. Otherwise, I might never have found Baylor's cottage. It's tied together in my mind, somehow: first the steam and the noise, and then that little house that helped me forget all about them.

It was only a few days after Christmas. The silver wreaths were still hanging over each table in the dining room, but it was business as usual in the kitchen. I was cutting bread for Chef Manny, focusing on keeping the slices thin enough so I could get three baskets out of one loaf, when Mamselle's brand-new busboy pushed into the kitchen at the same time Shepherd was going out. The sound that made me look up, that made everyone in the room stop what they were doing, was like a train wreck. Only this train was made of silver and china and glass. When the tray of leftover food hit the tile floor, it bounced and clattered halfway across the room, and by the time the flatware and dishes had stopped spinning and smashing, we were all staring at the kid, holding our breath.

For a few seconds, everything was quiet—no talking, no cupboards closing, no pots slamming; only the low sputter from something on the grill and the skittering of a single plate, spinning and wobbling like a one-legged ballerina:

KITCHEN AND WAITSTAFF
(*Silent, watching*)

GRILL
S-S-S-S-S-S-S-S-s-s-s-s-s-s-s-s-s-s-s-s-s.

PLATE
Winn-WINN-winn-WINN-winn, WANG, WANG,
wannn, tannn, t-chang,
TUNK-TUN-t-ccchin,
tang, pang,
wiiiinNN
tuuNNN
DANNNCK-k-k-k.

SHEPHERD
Son of a bitch!

There was a sort of music in what was happening. Until that last sour note. Shepherd's voice was a yell and a snarl at once. It was a tone I'd heard more times than I could count, the one he saved for anyone who screwed up. And, of course, I screwed up more than most. "I thought you said you'd worked tables before?"

The boy was my age, maybe younger. He stood over his fallen bus tray, staring in disbelief at how the six half-eaten meals he'd been carrying a minute ago had flown through the air and landed . . . well, everywhere. There were soggy rolls, smashed veggies, and lumps of who knew what smeared across the tiles; gravy had splattered onto the pass-through, and béchamel sauce was oozing like an alien life form down the counter's metal sides; sprigs of parsley and bits of carrot had shot as far as the baseboard heater, and I'm pretty sure the lemon curl I pulled out of the bread basket wasn't one of Manny's "innovations."

Shepherd was in his maître d' monkey suit, but he'd lost his dining-room manners. "Pick up this shit, and get out," he told the boy, who was still entranced with the food collage he'd made. "And don't forget to take off that cummerbund before you go." *Merry Christmas,* Shepherd-style.

"You're firing him?" I spoke up before I realized that *my* support was the last thing this kid needed. Some fathers might give their daughters slack, and others might bend over backward to pretend there's no difference at all. But ever since he'd given me this job, Shepherd had gone out of his way to be harder on me than on anyone else. My station was the last to be filled, my tables were always small parties, and I never, ever did anything right. So sticking up for the new busboy was probably giving him the kiss of death.

"Shut up, Sarah."

See what I mean? Nice father-daughter dialogue, right?

"Shepherd, I'm just saying—"

"You're just saying *nothing,* Sarah. And as for *you*"—Shepherd turned back to the boy, who'd sunk to his knees and was making sloppy passes through the mess with a sponge—"you're lucky I'm not charging you for those dishes. Now get lost." *Happy holidays, from our place to yours.*

The kid stood slowly, his face flushed and damp, then fumbled with his satin belt. You could see he was way too nervous for fine motor movements.

"Shit!" Shepherd grabbed one end of the cummerbund and yanked it off so hard the boy's shirttails got pulled out of his pants and hung from his waist like a collapsed parachute. A parachute that hadn't saved anyone.

Then the kitchen doors were swinging silently and Shepherd was back in the dining room, making nice. Out front, Mamselle's was *très élégant,* as they say in France. Those giant padded doors were like a border between two countries, locking out the heat and the earsplitting noise from the kitchen and opening into climate-controlled comfort, old-fashioned butter churns, tablecloths made from antique grain sacks, and Shepherd in a tux. He called everyone "sir" or "madam," remembered their names and their favorite desserts, and generally split a gut to make sure they came back. (Which meant, of course, he also made sure only the older waitresses served the regulars—a good thing for my first-day routine, but a pretty lousy thing for my self-esteem.)

I had watched my father work that room weekend after weekend. And tonight was no different. In between orders, I studied the way he glided when he walked, the way he almost whispered when he spoke, the way he soothed and calmed and sweet-talked. "That little noise, Mrs. Hazen? Why, that was just some high spirits in the kitchen. It's one of the staff's birthday."

He bowed at the waist, leaned into the table. "I certainly will, Mrs. Hazen. Why don't you let me freshen that drink? I won't forget the extra olive." And then he was on to the next table, with more smiles, more little touches that made customers feel pampered and special. Mr. Congeniality—that was my dining-room dad.

My kitchen dad? Let's just say he deserved a different award. "I'm sorry," I told our newest ex-busboy on my next pass through Hell's

Kitchen. The kid was tall and skinny and looked seconds away from tears. "My dad's a jerk."

"That's your *father?*" He sounded like I'd told him I had cancer. I walked with him to the staff-room door, watched him take his jacket off the hook.

"Sort of," I said. It was too hard, too complicated, to explain. I didn't go around announcing to strangers that my mother had once had a thing with Shepherd. That she never wanted to marry him. That now, she didn't even want to speak to him.

I wished I could tell this boy not to let Shepherd get to him. But he'd just lost what was probably his first job, and words wouldn't change that. Besides, it had taken me forever to learn to roll with the punches. So all I said was good-bye, and then I watched him and his starched shirttails disappear out the back door.

As for me, I wanted to make a statement. My shift was over, not that Shepherd had seated anyone at my tables in the last half hour, anyway. So I decided to leave, too. But not by the staff door—that would have been following the rules. Instead, I kept my apron on and walked, head high, right through the dining room, right past everybody's favorite maître d' cracking jokes with a party of eight. I moved the way I did onstage, even when I only had a supporting role. Calm and steady, I fell right into my part, a girl who belonged in that elegance and cool, a girl who could barely feel Shepherd's eyes burning holes in her back.

I knew he wouldn't call after me, not with everyone in the room watching. Not with Mrs. What's-Her-Name waiting for her drink. Not with that jolly make-believe birthday party under way in the kitchen. And Shepherd sure wasn't about to rat me out to Mom. He would never dare tell her he hadn't given me a ride home.

So I just kept going. Straight through the front door and out onto the patio, where lights were strung in the potted trees, and where in six months, summer diners would be eating at wrought-iron tables under giant blue umbrellas embroidered with a silver *M*. I stopped when I hit the fresh air, but only for a minute. I didn't know where I was going next; I only knew it wasn't home.

The dirt path took you so far off the main road that, until the sign was put up the year before, not a whole lot of tourists ever found the place. That night, I almost walked past the turn myself. I was still fuming over the way Shepherd had treated the new kid. And yes, over the way he hadn't put anyone at my tables until Marsha's and Laynelle's diners were eating butt to butt. I had replayed every one of his curses, every snide comment, until I was pretty near liftoff. That was when I saw the streetlight bouncing off the gold letters by the drive: RUFUS H. BAYLOR SUMMER COTTAGE: 1.5 MILES.

I knew the house existed. Everybody did. But even though a few of my friends had hiked up there and taken the tour, I'd always wondered what all the fuss was about. A famous poet, who'd lived lots of places, had rented a regulation beach cottage here for a few summers. Big deal, right? Now, though, I decided anywhere was better than home: one and a half miles up. And back. That would give me time to cool down. Maybe.

It was midwinter, but on the Carolina shore, that doesn't exactly look like a holiday card. There's no snow. No red cheeks. Sure, you'll usually want a sweater or jacket at night. But I was carrying more than enough heat with me—from the steamy kitchen, from Shepherd's abuse, from getting up the nerve to parade through the dining room like that. So I slipped out of my sweatshirt, tied the sleeves around my waist, and followed the winding trail through the pines and scrub brush. The farther up the path I got, the less Shepherd mattered and the more I felt like myself again. By the time I saw another light winking at me through the trees, my heart was settling, and the whole bad day was righting itself, turning over like one of Manny's crepes, light and lacy and good enough to eat right out of the pan.

That second streetlight, when I reached the end of the drive, lit up a row of white fence pickets, made them rise up out of the shadows. Long, spindly fingers of spicebush waved from behind them, still summer yellow, still smelling like something you wished you could keep in a bottle and spill all over yourself when things got bad.

Sure enough, once I got close, the house was no different from most of the cottages that dotted the woods on the bay side of town. It had a porch out back so renters could finish their day sitting in the breeze that came off the water when the sun went down. The front was plain, no-nonsense, and except for the metal plaque on the siding by the door, you'd never know it was anything special:

RUFUS H. BAYLOR SUMMER COTTAGE—FOR TEN YEARS, THE RENOWNED POET BROUGHT HIS FAMILY HERE EACH SUMMER, DRAWING PEACE AND INSPIRATION FROM WHALE POINT'S PICTURESQUE STREETS AND FRIENDLY RESIDENTS.

I laughed when I read the words. Because the only way I could find my own brand of peace and inspiration was to get as far away as possible from those very same picturesque streets and friendly residents. All I wanted was to forget that my mother had my life mapped out for me, including rest stops, attractions, and shortcuts to success; and that my father . . . well, you already know about my father.

I went around to the back of the house, stepped onto the porch, and put my face up to one of the windows. A security light on the roof threw part of the room into a sort of spotlight, and made the rest disappear in gloom. In the center of the spotlight, a group of photo frames glinted from the top of an old rolltop desk. Rufus Baylor was a household name, a National Treasure, someone we all had to learn about in school. Which is why it was hard to imagine him sitting at that ordinary desk, walking through the rooms of this ordinary house, and going to the beach with all the ordinary kids in those photos. Ordinary, except for one.

I had leaned so close to the window that I felt the glass on my forehead when I picked out her picture, set in a silver oval, right in the middle. There were other photos around hers, but you knew this girl was the main attraction. She was about my age, only more together—face it, there are sixteen-year-olds . . . and then there are sixteen-year-olds.

Her hair was lighter than mine, nearly white, and much curlier. She had friendly, safe eyes and a holdback smile that told you if she opened her mouth, poetry would come out. I didn't know if she was the Great One's daughter or maybe granddaughter, but she was clearly special to him, sitting center front like that.

I'm not sure why I decided to call her Nella. Maybe because the name sounds like water. She looked the way light does when it shines on waves—glittery, but peaceful. The next time I went back, on the way to work, I named the other kids. The ones in all the frames I could see through the windows in the daytime. Some of them were thinner or prettier than Nella. Some sat beside dogs or wore graduation caps and broad, smug grins. But none of them made me feel the way she did: Like if I walked up to her, I wouldn't have to introduce myself. Like this was my house, too.

It wasn't, of course. Yes, I made a habit, from then on, of stopping by the Baylor cottage on my way to the restaurant. As winter turned to spring, I watched the red allspice berries and sumac fruit give way to tiny grape hyacinths and daffodils. And I found myself imagining the lives of the family that used to live in that picture-perfect dollhouse. But no, I never thought of going inside, not even on visiting days, when the rooms downstairs were open to the public.

For one thing, the place was always closed by five, which was when Mamselle's prepped for dinner and I walked to work. For another, being inside a dollhouse isn't the same as looking at it from the outside, and who wants to find out the whole thing is held together with glue and Scotch tape? Trust me, the diners at Mamselle's were better off in their air-conditioned never-never land, where everyone wore jackets and no one threw pots or economy-size tantrums.

Looking in from the outside was good enough for me. The truth is, spying through the windows of the Baylor place gave me another life, one I didn't want to lose by walking inside. For just a few minutes, I lived there, too. I spoke in rhyme, I read just for fun, and I had a fancy celebrity father instead of Shepherd, who was, now that I'd gotten to know him up close and personal, worse than none at all.

Prince Charming

Sarah is a name from the Bible, right up front, in Genesis. Sarah was Abraham's wife, and she had a baby when she was ninety years old. Considering that everyone lived a lot longer in those days, and that burning bushes talked and seas parted for the right people, this was probably only a minor miracle. But still. My mother was forty-five years old when I was born, which is why, after her brain unfroze from the shock, she named me Sarah. (She couldn't name me after Sarah's baby because he was a boy. And my life was definitely going to be hard enough without being called Isaac.)

So two days after Thanksgiving, Mom had a kid no one was particularly thankful for: Sarah, the Surprise. Sarah, the Slipup. Sarah, the Last Thing Anybody in My Family Needed. As legend had it, Katherine Wheeler, a.k.a. my mother, enjoyed a sweet setup before she made the mistake of going out with Shepherd Ryan. She and Aunt Jocelyn shared a small condo on the best side of Whale Point, the ocean side. Mom had a good job with *Her*, which boasted the biggest circulation of any magazine in North Carolina. She had respect, independence, and just enough money to pretend that she was almost as rich as her neighbors.

Until her boss turned fifty, and she volunteered to manage the birthday party. They celebrated at a small but pricey restaurant called Mamselle's, where the maître d' fell all over himself to make Mom sit up and take notice. That was when my father was good looking—in a gray-temples, shave-three-times-a-day kind of way. So all he had to do back then was smile and keep his sleaze factor on low. I can just picture Shepherd, leaning like a parenthesis or a broken lamp over her chair. I can hear him whispering, "May I help you?" "May I get that for you?" "Let me." "PURR-PURRR-PURRRRRR."

"How could I know every line out of that man's mouth was scripted?" Mom asked the same question whenever she told the story of their "relationship." By the time she got to the part where her crush had turned into a semiliterate deadbeat who wouldn't even split the cost of my braces in sixth grade, she was steaming.

"Let that be a lesson, Sarah." Lately, she always finished her story the same way. "Weak knees do not a grand amour make." Her fake smile was a warning. The future she saw for me was like the beach at low tide, studded with pebbles, driftwood splinters, and bits of broken glass.

What she really meant was, *Don't fall in love.* A love story didn't fit in with my mother's plans: She had decided, you see, that I was going to med school. And according to this grand scheme, hatched before I was even born, I would become a doctor—someone with talent, money, and influence. Someone who'd never have to wonder where next month's car payment was coming from. And someone who would never, ever date anyone without initials after his name.

Both of us made sacrifices for this rosy future, but only one of us understood why. Remember those shortcuts to success? I was five years old when my mother browbeat the school board into letting me skip kindergarten. Which meant I was always a year younger than most of the kids in my class. But it also meant Mom could call me "gifted."

If romance didn't have any place in my mother's version of my future, neither did the stage. Whether I got the lead in a play or landed Prince Charming, it was all the same to her—bad. Plays were fine, she'd conceded when I first tried out for parts in junior high and began to plaster my room with Sarah Bernhardt posters. Theater was a good creative outlet, but acting wasn't a career. No ifs, ands, or buts.

So no, she never came to my performances, and no, she never invited any of my friends, especially those of the male persuasion, past the front door. She seemed convinced that if she didn't encourage what she called "distractions," I'd forget about them. But of course, what she didn't realize was they weren't distractions, they were my life. So I kept going out with my friends. And I kept watching films of Sarah Bernhardt, papering my wall with posters of her most famous roles, and wishing I could make people cry and throw roses onstage the way she had.

If I didn't end up with roses from the audience, I did manage to catch the attention of the boy who came as close to Prince Charming as you could get at Whale Point High. When we met, Fry Reynolds and I were both juniors at WPH. Even though we'd had a lot of the same classes since freshman year, I don't think he'd even noticed me before the fall play. He had a smile you couldn't read, and he turned it, like a floodlight, on everyone. He was always surrounded by other kids, guys in goth black or wife-beaters under their wide-open shirts, girls with long legs, perfect lashes, and the kind of hair that would set off an alarm if it fell out of place.

So the love story I might have told Mom, if she'd been interested enough to ask, was a lot more romantic than hers. It featured me as a lonely stand-in for a bit part in the first production of the year. And my prince? He wasn't in the play at all—he and his friends had only joined the lighting crew so they could go to the cast party.

By the last night of rehearsals, it was pretty clear that Stephanie Semple, who had the part I was understudying, was not going to get a fatal disease or even a cold. I was never going to play the Parisian flower girl who helps the hero win the French Revolution. But there was a consolation prize: He had finger-deep curls and dark chocolate eyes, and he could bounce a Ping-Pong ball from one bicep to the other. Really.

"You would have been way better than Semple." That's what Fry told me after our final run-through. I was picking my way over the wires backstage and heading for the exit. I still carried my script with me, though I don't know why I bothered. I never got to read a single line from it.

"How do you know I'd be better?" I asked him. "You've never even seen me act." I didn't have time to be surprised that one of the coolest guys in the school was talking to me as though I were one of the coolest girls. All that registered was his lanky, heat-emitting body, much too close for breathing room.

"Oh, I've watched you act, all right," Fry assured me. "Every rehearsal, I hear you tell Semple how great she was."

He waited just long enough for all the blood to rush to my face. "Besides," he added, "you're twice as hot."

I turned on him, half angry at the way he'd seen through my runner-up's faint praise, half dizzy with the compliment he'd tagged on at the end. "Look," I told him, "you—"

"Okay, okay." He backed away, hands in front of those eyes and that smile. "*Three* times as hot." He folded his arms, which he *must* have known showed off his muscles. "Now prove it."

"What?" I looked toward the orange eye of the exit sign. This guy had a reputation. Maybe there were worse things about him than fast talk.

"Prove it," he repeated. "Read me the scene." He nodded at the copy of the play in my hand.

I stared at my script, as if it were a mango or a porcupine. As if I were totally shocked to find it there.

"Go on, read it." I should have hated the look Fry gave me then, because it had nothing to do with my being hot. It was more like he was laughing at me, daring me to jump off a cliff. So I opened the script to the scene. Or, actually, it fell open to the place I'd dog-eared and mauled a million times. "André," I read, embarrassed and angry at once, "you can't give up." But soon I was falling into my character, a dying girl saying good-bye. At first, I looked up at Fry between the lines I knew by heart. And then? I wasn't looking at the lines at all. "Don't you realize, my dear, that the children of tomorrow, of next year, and of centuries after that, are watching what we do now?"

Fry unfolded his arms, and his eyes lost their challenge, focused on my face. The gym disappeared, and we were sitting in the shadow of an old stone house on a street in Paris. "We have seen our friends killed today," I told him. "And we will see more of them killed tomorrow." I coughed, spit invisible blood. "But you will survive, André, and you will give our sons and daughters what we died for." It wasn't hard to see the boy in front of me as a fighter, a sturdy champion who could take hold of the future and change it for all of us. "If you have no faith in yourself, learn from me, my love. I believe in all you can be."

When the scene ended, I stood for a minute, breathless, empty. I woke from one dream into another when Fry started clapping. "I'm not sure what you said," he told me, still staring with those intense, dizzy-making eyes. "But I loved the way your lips moved when you said it." He stood closer now, then clapped again. His applause was so loud it echoed out across the empty seats and then came back to us, louder still. As if he'd tossed a single ball into the dark, and dozens had bouncd back. Or maybe an empty stage just makes everything you say and do bigger than it is.

Which might explain why our first kiss—my first kiss ever—felt like the universe was coming unglued. Why two kids, alone onstage, kissing like stars in a ghost play, trumped every romance movie I'd ever seen, from *Cinderella* and *Snow White*, right up to the films with subtitles Aunt Jocelyn used to sneak me into. I didn't see fireworks under my closed eyes, not exactly. It was more like things were growing there, wild things, soft but pushy, sweet but rude. Tiger lilies that roared:

FRY

(*Laughing softly*)

You can open your eyes now.

TIGER LILIES

Rrrrr-RRRRR—RRRRRRR.

ME

Huh?

GYM EXIT SIGN

Bzzzz. . . . Bzzzz. . . . Bzzzz. . . .

FRY

Open your eyes. What do you see?

ME

Huh?

GYM EXIT SIGN

Bzzzz. . . . Bzzzz. . . .

FRY

Let's do that again.

TIGER LILIES

RRRRRR-RRRRRRRRR.

That night was the start of something I never expected—a love life. Not only had no guy ever kissed me, no guy had ever walked me home (which Fry did, after a few more kisses, when it finally dawned on him that I'd lost both the power of speech and my inner GPS). No guy had ever called me hot, and in fact, no guy had ever even called me. (Which Fry did, the very next night. And the next. And the next after that.)

I wasn't sure "love" was the word for what he made me feel. But then, I wasn't sure of anything when I was around Fry.

It's not that I didn't know any boys. But my friends and I had always gone to dinner or to the movies in one big herd, the same way we went to dances and parties. It got so when I told my mother or Aunt Jocelyn I was going out, they didn't even ask where or with whom. They knew: Alicia and Thea and Eli and George and Wanda and Marcia and Brett.

My mother called us the Pack; Wanda usually referred to us as the Chosen; and Eli, more realistic in terms of our social standing at school, preferred the Untouchables. The popular kids didn't know we existed, which was fine with us. "It makes them feel better to pretend we're not here," Eli explained. "That way, they don't have to stretch."

Since Fry, though, everything was different; all bets were off. Suddenly, nonsensically, I was "dating." Not just anyone, but a magnificent, dreamy specimen of the Upper Caste: a Popular Guy. It was like landing a role I hadn't even read for. I kept wondering if there hadn't been a mistake, if somewhere in another dimension, a popular girl was waiting for the boy who was supposed to be hers. She must have wondered, that poor thing, why she'd suddenly become invisible to all her sparkly, wrinkle-free girlfriends; why they were rushing past her in the halls and cornering me, instead, to ask what kind of lip balm I used. Or whether I had time to "approve" the playlist for their next party. Can you imagine what that *felt* like? Not really. Not unless you've won the Powerball. And the Mega Millions. Twice each.

I started making excuses to my friends, and went out with Fry instead. It took a couple of weeks before Mom caught on that there were just two of us at the movies now. And that the movies were usually at Fry's house, if his mother was still at work. We didn't watch foreign films like my friends and I did, and we didn't talk about them afterward. Mostly, we lay beside each other in the light from the TV while Fry tried to take my clothes off. We turned the sound down so the only dialogue was Fry saying yes and me saying no. Because, even though being within lip's reach of my fairy-tale boyfriend felt more exciting than almost anything I'd ever done, I always had a third voice, a much louder one, in my head: *Let that be a lesson, Sarah.*

So far, my mother's voice was winning. You know what they say about the squeaky wheel. A yelling wheel doesn't even give you time to think. You just do what it says. And frankly? That was a lot easier than wondering whether, once he'd gotten what he was begging for, I'd join the ranks of all those girls Fry didn't even talk to after he'd dumped them. According to Whale Point legend, they were legion. But according to Fry, I was different. "You're like this tricky wave," he told me on our second date. "If you catch it right, it takes you places you've never been." (Did I mention the prince liked surfing even more than pool or beer? And that when he wasn't riding waves, he was talking about them?)

When she finally figured things out, my mother made Fry pick me up at the door. She let him stand outside under the bug light, grilling him with questions straight out of a black-and-white sitcom. She used standards like "Where will you go after the movie?" or "Are parents going to be at this party?"

Fry always came to the door by himself, so my mother never guessed how little time we actually spent alone. She would have felt much better knowing that Hector Losada was usually waiting for us, curbside, in his car. Most people called Fry's best friend and head groupie H, and more often than not, it was the three of us—H, Fry, and me—who did things together after school and even on weekends. We formed a new, condensed Pack, less inclined to vintage clothes and old novels, and more drawn to designer sneakers and pool. I can't say I found H's constant need to prove how much macho and Latin suave could be packed into one short, skinny seventeen-year-old very convincing. Or that I liked the way he always took Fry's side against me in any argument. But he was a senior and he had a car (a junkyard special, but still). He was, quite simply, part of the package. If I wanted Fry, then H came with him.

H probably felt the same way about me: In order to get his Fry fix, soaking up his friend's every word, chuckling low and slow so he slid right under Mr. Cool's easy, open laugh, he had to put up with me. I guess that's why I used to catch him looking at me sideways, why he went all quiet when I spoke, as if he were trying to figure out how I'd happened, what made me special enough for his hero.

But if Hector Losada clung to his *jefe* like Velcro, I'm ashamed to admit that once Fry and I were a thing, I let my old friends slip away. It wasn't something that happened all at once. I mean, I didn't wake up one day and decide to dump the Untouchables. It was more like when you find a new street that cuts right to the beach. Gradually you forget how to get there any other way. Sure, you remember you used to walk by an open field, and there was a stray cat that always followed you for blocks. But the new road is quicker and faster, and the sun and the dunes can't wait.

It was sometime in March when Wanda, my used-to-be best friend and conspirator, cornered me in the girls' room at school. It was probably the only place she could find me without the crowd that hung out around Fry, and if it was a peculiar spot to have a reunion, well, Wanda always operated from her heart, not her head. That's just what she'd done the one and only time I tried to mix my old friends with my new ones. You'd think I'd know better, right? But I actually introduced her to H because he said she was hot. Which was when, in front of Fry's whole crew, she turned down the chance to go to a concert with us. She told H she didn't like rock, and why didn't we all go to a Kabuki ballet, instead? A freaking Kabuki freaking ballet.

The girls who'd been eating lunch with us looked at her, silent for once. They just sat there, their fake lashes blinking and their glossy lips parted in astonishment. Or confusion. "What's Caboosey?" one asked.

That had been only a few months ago, but already my former sidekick looked different to me—standing in the middle of that ammonia-drenched bathroom, wearing striped suspenders she must have found at the PTA thrift shop, Wanda seemed delicate and out of place. She was someone who'd guarded my secrets once, secrets that felt a little immature and a lot inconsequential next to the sweet rush of lying close to Fry in the dark.

"We've missed you at homework theater." Wanda got right to the point, just the way we always had. We'd never done the "How are you?" or "What's new?" thing, but always rushed, like bats with radar, straight to what mattered.

I pictured my old friends acting out quadratic equations and world history, imagined them laughing helplessly at jokes that Fry and H couldn't get and wouldn't want to. "Sorry," I told her. "I've been really busy."

"I know." And of course, she did. She knew who was with me all the time now, who had taken over my life. And why. After all, if you'd been working in the kitchen with the palace servants, how often would you visit them after you married the prince? Oh, sure, maybe you'd climb down those stairs into the warmth and the gossip a few times, but after a while? Your visits would get shorter, and you'd go less often. And pretty soon? Well, there's so much to do when you're helping to run a castle.

"It's my birthday Friday."

I felt a rush of something. Was it guilt? I had the date circled somewhere. With a heart around it.

"We're celebrating at the cove." Wanda didn't invite me, she just assumed I'd be there. She shrugged a long coil of red hair off her shoulder, smiled at me, open, waiting. As if we always met in the girls' room. As if I hadn't stopped calling her back, and didn't walk right by her in the halls without waving.

The cove. It was the Untouchables' meeting place at the beach. It was where we put on ridiculous pageants that involved Esther Williams choreography and a lot of splashing. It was where Thea brought picnics that featured food from all the books she loved (James's giant peach, honey from *Winnie-the-Pooh*, roasted potatoes from *The Secret Garden*), and where Eli and Marcia divided us into debate teams to wrestle with burning issues like, Daylight saving time: boon or bust?

Not exactly the sort of party Fry and I were invited to almost every weekend now: Music too loud to talk. Food that came in microwavable bags. Couples wrapped around each other in the pitch black.

"I can't come." I said it before I even knew it was true. Instinctively, like kicking your leg when the doctor taps your knee with that little silver hammer. Only in this case the hammer was Wanda's brave smile, her standing there as if Fry had never happened. As if I hadn't already left her world behind, hadn't traded the comfort of the Untouchables for a heady, scary realm where cool came first, and beer and sex trumped brains and costumes from the thrift shop.

I went on to make an excuse so lame it needed crutches, something about studying and working for my mother. I think I even threw in a low-grade fever. It doesn't matter what I said, because when I watched her smile melt away, I knew Wanda didn't believe a single word. Her new expression was halfway between embarrassment and dismay. "I'm sorry," she told me finally. "I was hoping you'd be there."

We talked a little bit more, but you could tell she'd decided to stop hoping. "Alicia's putting real rose petals on the cake," she told me just before the bell rang. "And Brett's finished the blueprint for his biggest sand castle yet."

See what I mean? Would you trade an ergonomically designed sand castle for being at the top of the social ladder? A place where you helped plan what everyone else (except maybe a few holdouts like the Untouchables) thought and wore and did? Would you give up the blood rushing to your head as the prince touched you in places you didn't even know you had for a slice of birthday cake, roses or no roses?

Not that I didn't sometimes think about the laughs my Pack and I had shared, and the whispering, and yes, the crazy, brainy fun. But it was like hearing talk from that kitchen way, way downstairs. So far down that it felt harder and harder to go there. Instead, I drowned out the distant noise, the background hum of missing. I kept busy, I kept moving. In fact, between the AP science courses my mother insisted I needed for premed, and my weekend job at Mamselle's, there was barely enough time for my most important concentration of all—kissing Fry.

Mistake with a Capital *M*

Old-fashioned princesses had it easy. They just clasped their hands to their silky bosoms whenever their princes jousted in a tournament. They sat in the bleachers on pillows and waved their handkerchiefs and said things like, "Forsooth, methinks Prince Harold is taking a beating."

But the thing about Fry was, he liked his women wading into battle right alongside him. Helpless damsels weren't his style, which was why he'd dared me to read that script the night we kissed. And why he always chose girls who could match him step for step, sip for sip.

I guess that's what I was trying to do when Fry talked H and me into the escapade that landed us in court and made us loathsome bottom-feeders in the eyes of our families, our town, and people all over the country who'd never even met us. The three of us were sitting on H's porch—Mom and Fry's mother were both home, but H's parents worked the night shift. We spent a lot of time there now, after school, sprawled in the peeling wicker chairs or balancing drinks on the porch rails. It was the end of March, and the afternoons were getting warmer; you could smell the ocean, inhale it as you talked.

So when Fry suggested a party during spring break, it sounded like just the kind of fun to carry us through the wet, weary transition to summer. "We all need this," he said, helping himself to a chip from the bowl in my lap. "Surf's no good, and hurricane season is still months away. Gotta shake things up, right?"

I loved the idea. Why wouldn't I? After years of spending most parties in the basement with a small, earnest group who shared how superior we felt to the shallow people with dates having noisy, drunken fun in the rest of the house, I was more than ready to have my own shallow fun. And to be part of the group that planned it.

But when Fry announced the site of our bash, I suddenly felt like someone designing my own funeral. I would rather he had picked any other place on Earth. I would never have smiled and nodded, never agreed to spread the word to the theater kids, if I'd known what he had in mind. But that was before I learned the Fry Entertainment Formula. When it came to parties, he said, you had to consider three things: location, location, and location.

"The Baylor house is perfect," he told H and me. I loved the way he sat, one sneaker braced against the rails, the other side by side with my own sandaled foot. "It's off a long road behind trees. Plus, it's on the right side of town. The side no one goes to."

It was true. On the bay side, Whale Point had sort of given up on tourists. In the summer, it was full of mosquitoes, and most of the stores sold stuff like auto parts and plumbing supplies, not the bikinis, surfboards, and shell sculptures that filled the windows in shops on the ocean side. Except for Mamselle's, there wasn't much to draw people to Plantation Drive. Not even Rufus Baylor. Sure, everyone knew the People's Poet was from North Carolina, but not many guessed that he used to spend summers in this town when his kids were little.

"Isn't that cottage sort of . . . small?" I asked it like I was seriously considering Fry's idea, not fighting the impulse to stand up and scream, *No! No!* I'd been hiking up to the place for months now, and it felt like my own personal secret, one I didn't want to share. One I was pretty sure my prince and his friend would never understand, even if I tried to explain it.

H pulled his usual satellite routine, totally agreeing with his *jefe*, shutting me out. "*That* is high and sly," he told Fry, yes-man enthusiasm nearly sending him off the railing where he was perched. "Raising hell in the woods in the dark. *Chido!*"

Not that Hector Losada needed to worry about the size of that little house, anyway. Unless you counted Fry and me, and maybe one or two other kids, he didn't really have any close friends. He was like a stray Fry had picked up and taken in, a stray that pretended he'd been part of the in crowd all along. I gave him a withering, what-do-you-know stare, and appealed to Fry. "Don't we need some place the whole class can fit?"

"You mean herds of nerds?" Fry tilted his chair back and laughed at the thought. Even though he was talking about most of the kids I'd hung out with until this year, I couldn't help smiling. He simply had no idea I wasn't prom queen material. Which was one reason I'd fallen so hard for him. That and how awful he was at karaoke. And oh, yes, the way his kiss sucked all the air out of me.

"This party's only for brave hearts who know how to get down." Some people are inspired by a painting or a view from a mountaintop, but Fry was on fire with a different vision—a picture of kids and kegs packed into Baylor's cottage, *my* cottage. "What do you say, Sar?"

I wanted to say yes. I wanted to say, *Sure, my prince, my one and only.* I wanted to tell him, *No problem.* That's what the love interest in the action films Fry favored always said—"no problem." "No problem, I'll go check out the bad guy's apartment." Or "No problem, I'll act as bait for the serial maniac." But I couldn't get the words out. It would be like drinking in church to hold a bash in that little house.

"It depends on how many names are on your guest list," I told him, *no* still thumping away in my chest. "It's not like a mansion or anything." The cottage wasn't really big enough for a party, but it was just small enough to feel safe. Special.

"Perfect. Because this will be a very select gathering." Fry sounded as if the invitations had already been sent. Invitations that, of course, would not go to any of the Untouchables. Wanda and George were major poetry fans, anyway, and would have been furious if they'd gotten wind of my boyfriend's plans. Not to mention, Wanda had dealt herself a socially fatal blow with her preference for soft ballet over hard rock. So I never even suggested including them.

"H and I will scope the place out tomorrow. Hell, we may even take the tour." Fry smiled his badass smile at H, which was sort of like using a blowtorch to light a cigarette.

"For sure, *ése*." Hector, whose parents were from Costa Rica, but who couldn't roll an *R* if his life depended on it, fell right into line. "That way, we can figure where to put stuff, find out if there's an alarm system."

Fry nodded. "You can come with us, right, Sar?"

I loved that he wanted me along, that I was part of the plan, that the blowtorch was turned on me now. Fry's smile wasn't secret and shy, like Nella's. He could have used it to sell lakefront property in the desert.

"Plus, we could bring back some brochures and stuff." Fry was full steam ahead, scheming. "That should get us out of at least one English class, right?"

H and I didn't understand, so Fry let his chair fall forward, leaned toward the two of us, and used his fingers to count it out. "One: The Baylor house is where Rufus H. Baylor wrote. Two: We will be *in* the Baylor house. Three: We will bring back talking points. Four: Miss Kinney is in total love with Baylor, which means, five, she will spend the entire period telling us how much."

He snapped his counting fingers and grinned at me. "See?"

I nodded. I still wanted to say yes to this craziness. I loved making Fry happy, setting off the sort of growl/cheer thing he did in his throat, watching him high-five H, then grab my hand like it was the most natural thing in the world. "Well, I—"

"That is way past gross!" H was not saving me from a tough spot; it was just that he had this unrequited thing going with our English teacher. "Kinney is completely hot. But Mr. Iambic Whatever must be at least a million years old." He stopped, tried to remember. "Or maybe he's dead. Is he dead?"

"I can't take the tour," I said. "I have stuff to do." My head was glad I'd bowed out, but my heart wasn't sure. I watched the car lights winking on along Shore Drive and told myself I hadn't exactly lied. How could

I explain that visiting my dollhouse with somebody else would spoil everything? Even if that somebody set off little electric charges everywhere he touched me.

"Tours mean the place is sort of in the public eye, right?" With any luck, H would keep asking questions, and Fry would give up on the whole idea. "Isn't it, like, historically reserved?"

"Historically *pre*served," I told H. "And yes, it definitely is." The house had a tiny, polite sign on the door to prove it: THIS LANDMARK IS MAINTAINED BY THE NONPROFIT FRIENDS OF HISTORIC WHALE POINT. THANK YOU FOR YOUR DONATION.

"But there's nobody around at night." Fry was not letting go. Giving up wasn't in his DNA. "If we're careful, no one will even know we were there." He lowered his voice to a whisper, but grinned fiendishly. "Without a trace!"

If he hadn't put his arm around me as he said this, I might have mentioned a few pertinent details. Including the fact that Fry was not exactly famous for being careful. And the fact that the last full-scale WPH (go, Whales!) party had ended with one kid walking out a window and being taken to the hospital.

But I guess it was the casual tenderness, the way Fry curled around me as if we were family, that froze me. That kept me, in the end, from fighting the bash. You see, if Katherine Wheeler's daughter knew anything, it was the difference between a fairy tale and real life. In a fairy tale, the prince holds you and stares deeply into your eyes. In real life, you have to keep his hands out of your pants.

"There are only two things a man wants from you," Mom used to tell me from so early on, I'm not sure that, in the beginning, I had any idea what she was talking about. "One of them is to get you to listen to his nonsense. And the other is to knock your feet off the floor."

So far, my limited experience had proved her right. Fry loved me hanging on his every word. And he also loved trying to push me into sex. Which is why, when it wasn't about that, when his arm around me felt like love, not pressure, I wanted it to last. *Don't move. Don't talk. Stay.*

Besides, even if I'd taken the time to explain what a bad idea the party was, H would just have jumped into devoted-hound-dog mode and disagreed with everything I said. His goal in life was to cover Fry's back, front, and sides. So, no, I never really tried to stop them. No, I never dreamed H would be dumb enough to put directions to the old Baylor place on his Facebook page. Or that word would get out on the Net and people I didn't even know would be telling me about the bash. And yes, after all that happened, things definitely got out of hand. Way out of hand.

Four of us headed to the Baylor place over an hour before the party was supposed to start. We weren't the first ones there, though. By the time we'd followed the road up to the cottage, there were several dozen kids already standing by the front gate, waiting like they were behind the velvet rope of some big-city club. It felt different, my secret house, with so many people clustered around it.

"I don't like everyone out here while it's still light." Fry surveyed the group, some with bottles in not-very-discreet brown paper bags. "Let's get them inside." You could see he hated the thought of a party stopped before it got started. He didn't play a single sport. He never got As. But he was a born leader when it came to having a good time.

H's brother, Span, who was home from college and who'd bought beer for us, reached over and opened the latch on the gate the way I showed him. I went through first, then H and Span and Fry. Everyone else trooped in behind us. Each step I took, the whole group followed—their shadows, their feet, their laughter strung out across the yard.

Even from the beginning, then, something felt wrong. But the way Fry treated me? That felt way beyond right: He looked at me as though I was the most important person there, the Resident Expert on All Things Baylor. He kept checking in, consulting me every few minutes: "Sarah, what's that shack out back?" (He and H hadn't been able to prowl around the yard on the tour, but my nocturnal visits gave me free roaming privileges.) I told him the Great One's summer quarters included a tiny toolshed, filled with old rakes and mowers and shovels. "Hey, Sar, how far to the water? Is there a dock out there?" (All the trees had leafed out and fattened up with spring. You couldn't see the strip of sand a few hundred yards past the stand of pines behind the porch.) And yes, there was a string of wood planks that ventured into the water, though they looked more like kindling than anything you'd want to trust your weight on. "Got the keys to the kingdom, Sar?" That last was a joke, since the plan had been to pick the lock all along.

H had come prepared. He pulled a coat hanger out of his backpack and started wiggling it in the keyhole on the front door. I hated the way he brandished that hanger, the way he flexed his fingers like a movie burglar limbering up before a heist. He knew from the tour that there was no burglar alarm, so he spent a good fifteen minutes fiddling, fiddling. Pretty soon, the kids who'd been waiting for us had company, and as the crowd got bigger, it got restless. People closed in, standing right behind H, baiting him, cracking themselves up with their own lame remarks.

"What?" someone I'd never seen before asked. "It doesn't work like on TV?" Lots of kids laughed.

"No wonder the crime rate in this town is so low." That was a girl I sort of knew from U.S. history. More laughter, more people crowding in on the house.

"Are we loitering?" That was the girl's boyfriend, or at least someone she didn't mind crushing her in the leather armpit of his bomber jacket. The two of them were joined at the hip. They even held their cigarettes in opposite hands, so they could take drags and hug at the same time.

H ignored everyone around him and kept trying to jimmy the lock.

"Three to the left." A big kid, almost as broad as Span, and a lot taller, stepped out of the crowd to look over H's shoulder. "Forty-four to the right, then break the mutha down."

It was pretty clear by now that H's low-profile B and E wasn't going to happen. And it was also clear that if somebody didn't do something fast, the breaking and entering would be a lot messier than we'd planned. For one heartbeat, one dumb in-your-dreams second, I hoped Fry would call a halt to the whole bash. That he'd tell everybody to give it up and go home. But of course, he didn't.

What he did was grab H's arm just as his friend had dropped the hanger and was about to take Smart-Mouth's advice about breaking down the door. "C'mon, man," he said. "Let's do this the easy way. Sarah, what's out back?"

One part of me led the two of them around behind the cottage, while the other part, the part that sometimes dreamed of living inside with the Great One and his family, wanted to turn around and run from the scene of our crime. But Fry had taken my hand now, and the warm feeling was spreading right to my heart. I couldn't hear a single thing over all that happy thumping. *Stay.*

When I stopped in front of my favorite window, the one by Rufus Baylor's desk, the make-believe me who lived in the cottage got very quiet. She shrank, too. She turned as tiny as a dollhouse daughter, a girl with bendable arms and legs. And no voice at all.

Fry peered in the window with me. "Remember this, H?" he asked.

H said nothing, just stood back to case the joint, hands on hips.

"That tour lady said Baylor liked to write by this window, she said he loved the view." Fry grinned at me, as if I had all the answers. "Maybe he left it unlocked, huh?"

If I'd known they were going to break it, I would have tried to stop them. But it happened so fast: One minute H was grunting and pushing his pencil-thin shoulders against the window frame, trying to lift it up. The next minute, Fry told him to hold his coat across the bottom pane and then kicked it, karate-style, with his foot. The glass shattered as easily as an eggshell, and no one got hurt.

At first, the window held its old shape, and the shattered pane looked like a spider's web, an intricate pattern of fits and starts, zigs and zags. Then Fry covered his fist with the jacket and punched a hole in the middle of the web, just above the window lock. Shards of glass spilled out of the window and clinked against each other on the ground; more rained down as H lifted the bottom half of the window and crawled in.

When he'd walked through and opened the front door, I heard a yell go up from the kids out front. "They're in!" Fry took my hand again to pull me around the side of the house. And I mean *pull.* He must have thought I'd dropped something, because I kept turning my head to look back at the broken web window, shattered and sparkling.

I was nearly the last one in. Maybe it was all those times I'd imagined being in that living room by a fire, or sitting with the Great One's photogenic kids at the dining-room table. I let almost everyone who'd been waiting go ahead of me. They were the ones hot to gate-crash a dollhouse, after all.

"So, Sarah. You going to stand out there all night?" Fry held a beer through Rufus Baylor's front door. Behind him, I saw someone stacking one keg on top of another in the hall. And behind him, five kids more were squeezed onto the couch in the living room. I recognized one of them, a boy perched on the arm, popping open a beer can and passing it to the girl next to him. He had long legs and the same nervous expression he'd worn the last time I'd seen him. When he looked up, it took him a moment to recognize me. It had been last winter, after all, and maybe I looked different without my apron and uniform. When he finally gave me a shy wave, I stepped inside, took the beer from Fry, and waved back at the boy Shepherd had fired from Mamselle's.

The Wages of Sin

It was chilly and gloomy inside, even though the sun outside hadn't gone down yet. It had never occurred to me that the Friends of Historic Whale Point might cut off the electric when they went home. A lot of our "guests" must have been used to B and E, though; they'd brought flashlights with them. Some had already turned them on and were waving them around, like little kids who zip open their light sticks too early on the Fourth of July.

By the time Fry and I had fought our way through the crowd to the couch, it was filled with people none of us knew, and the boy from Mamselle's had disappeared. That was when, even though I knew better, I found myself scanning the crowd, looking for other faces I'd hardly seen all year. For Wanda and George, intense in a corner, arguing over which silent-movie star could have made the transition to talkies. Or Eli, working his way toward me through the press of bodies, eager to share his latest insight about Egyptian astronomy.

But of course, there wasn't a single member of the Pack in attendance.

Instead, the front room was filled to overflowing with my new "friends," none of whom seemed likely to be fans of either silent films or Egyptology. There was no room to sit down anywhere, and Fry and Span and a guy I'd never seen before had fallen into an intense and boring discussion about the lyrics to Arcade's worst-ever song. (I never exactly lied to Fry, but I did a lot of smiling and high-fiving whenever he asked me if I liked the latest MP3 he'd downloaded from the site with black roses and dead baby birds.) When four of the perfect-hair girls surrounded me, asking where I'd gotten my jeans (PTA thrift shop) and my "darling little key earrings" (I'd hooked my mom's old luggage keys onto ear loops), I decided I'd rather check out the house than share fashion secrets.

There was still enough light to recognize all the things I'd spent hours studying through the windows. The setting sun was glinting off pieces of furniture, a chair here, a table there. The light traveled from thing to thing, touching, patting, as if it knew it was saying good-bye to the silver tea set in the breakfront, to the lace runner on the table, to the parade of china dogs on the coffee table. And to the photos. Especially to the photos.

Light pooled on the glass, glimmered in the frames, and it wasn't just a beer buzz. I felt high walking toward all those pictures, knowing who was who. I wasn't usually crazy about the taste of beer. Mostly, I just drank when Fry was looking. (He liked me sharing sips from his can, and I liked the way he kissed my ear while I did.) Now, though, I kept sipping as I studied the photos on the desk. After I'd downed half a can, the dollhouse girl wasn't so nervous; she figured the party would be over soon and no one would ever know. Meantime, I felt a fuzzy, sleepwalker kind of happiness, drifting from one familiar face to another.

Up close, "my" family wasn't as perfect as they'd seemed from outside. There were toddlers with missing teeth, swimsuit beauties with thighs that looked like ads for liposuction, and the baby girl I'd named Farah Ann turned out to be a baby boy. Someone had written a caption in neat block letters under the picture: NATHAN, AGE 4 MONTHS.

But Nella looked just the same. She was bathed in light, a finger of dying sun that had slipped through the venetian blinds H had smashed as he climbed through the window. To set the record straight, Nella was no pageant queen when I spied on her from the backyard, and she still wasn't what you'd call beautiful now that we'd met "face-to-face." But she had that same smart, funny look in her eyes, the same smile that made me know we were sisters. Not soul sisters exactly, more like big sister–little sister. She was someone I would have liked to be, a place I wanted to go.

"She's kind of hot." A boy came to stand beside me, waving the beam of his flashlight across Nella's photo. Like I said, it was still light enough to see just fine, but maybe this kid had finished two beers in the time it had taken me to drink one? Or maybe he just liked PowerPoint?

It took a few seconds. Like the micro lag between your first laugh at a lousy joke and your understanding how bad it truly is. He was the kid with the tray, or rather without it; the busboy my dad had fired after Christmas. He was just as tall as I remembered, but even skinnier, and the light he was holding hollowed his cheeks like a jack-o'-lantern's.

"She looks thirsty, dontcha think?" He was already slurring his words. And truthfully? The last thing Nella, who was staring at him with that soft fraction of a smile, looked was thirsty.

"I bet she could use a drink," the boy added, taking a swig from his bottle. I knew where he was going with this, and it was strange how steamed it made me. As if he were making fun of someone in my own family. My sister.

"I think she's on the wagon," I told him. But he was already reaching across the desk, raising the bottle to the glass on Nella's picture, pressing it right up against her half-open lips.

I didn't even stop to think, I just swatted his arm away from her. Of course, that knocked some of the smaller pictures off the desk and spilled pale ale all over their frames. Across the desk, too. And onto the floor.

I stood there as the boy laughed and walked away. I thought about watching him leave Mamselle's last year, about how sorry I'd felt for him. Then I remembered that Shepherd had a word for people like that, people who bend silverware as a joke or write on the ladies' room mirror in lipstick. He called them assholes. If the shoe fits, right?

I'm not sure when Fry brought me the second beer. Or the third. All I know is that by the third, I'd stopped following people around, picking stuff up, straightening frames, and emptying ashtrays. I'd forgotten whose house this was or that I'd ever wanted it to be mine. All I remember is that, as it got later, it grew darker. And colder.

You'd think with nearly fifty kids crowded into those small rooms, we would have been warm. But the temperature kept dropping, even with all the booze and body heat going for us. A Southern cold snap in April—who figured?

I'd stopped counting *Fry's* beers, too. But his voice had found the deep purr that usually meant at least four. "Wish we had something to burn." He looked longingly at the fireplace, waved his empty bottle toward the hearth. He slipped his arm around my waist, and I snuggled up fast. "How about your bra?" he suggested, unhooking it through my shirt. (He was good at that. Too good.)

I swiveled around in his arms, pretending to be mad, then turned back to the empty fireplace. Three beers back, I might have imagined a family of healthy, sun-drunk summer people gathered around a crackling fire, marshmallows turning brown and gooey on the ends of their pine twig skewers. Two beers back, I might have pictured them all listening, cozy and rapt, to a father-poet reading them stories by the rosy embers. But now? All I felt was freezing. All I said was, "We need a fire."

I guess Fry meant well, then, when he sent someone out to the shed for the can of gasoline the Friends kept there for their lawn mower. And when he pulled the curtains down from the dining-room window. I guess he was just too drunk by that time to worry about how he made me happy. Or kept us all from freezing. One thing I know for sure: My sleepy daze had turned into a nightmare numbness. The only thing I cared about was the glow those curtains made when he threw them into the fireplace, dribbled the last of the gasoline left in the can on top, and lit them with a match.

Curtains, ultimately, are not what you'd call fuel-efficient. So a few minutes later, someone else threw in the living-room curtains, too. After that, others fed the fire with braided rugs, shelves, chair legs, anything they could pick up and hurl into the fireplace. I don't remember actually throwing in anything myself, but I remember not stopping the kids who did. And I remember the brisk, almost loving way the fire talked to all of us:

FIRE

Pkk. Pkkkcckkk. Chhhh . . . chhhhhhh. Chew?

FRY

Here you go, here's a basket.

FIRE

Crkk, crkkkk. CHE-EE-EEEEEEEEEEWWWWW!

FRY

And three phone books. Look, one's for L.A. Why'd they need that?

FIRE

Chhhhhh. Chhh. Chew?

H (*Or maybe* SPAN?)

It's died down. What about those wood shutters?

FIRE

Crrrrr. CRRRR. CH-E-E-EWWWWWWWWW!!

It turns out kids stripped the spreads off the beds and carried in the bedroom curtains, too. I'm still not sure when or how the other things, the nonflammable stuff like the gold mantel clock or the glass candy dishes or those little coffee-table dogs, got smashed. But they did. Along with a whole list of other antiques that filled three pages when the district attorney's office added it all up. It turns out, that shoe? The asshole one? It was a pretty good fit for all of us.

Poor little house. Poor happy family. Poor Princess Sarah, who couldn't save them. Didn't save them. Who was too numb, too dumb, too head over heels. Who didn't remember anything after her fourth beer and her seventh kiss: Not how all three fire extinguishers got set off. Not who peed on the walls like a dog at a hydrant. Not who took the books off the shelves and tore out all their pages. Not even how, sometime before it turned light, she got home from what was left of the Rufus H. Baylor Summer Cottage.

I found the picture folded up in the back pocket of my jeans. It was the day after the bash, and once the world stopped spinning, I realized I'd better get my incriminating, beer-soaked clothes into the wash before my mother conducted one of her OCD room sweeps. When I unfolded the photo and laid it flat, Nella had a crease down the middle of her face and another that cut right across her neck, like someone had tried to decapitate her. And of course, no matter how hard I tried, I couldn't remember taking that photo out of its frame or putting it in my pocket.

But I was glad I had. Nothing else about that night felt good. I flashed back to everyone packed tight, to the noise and the smoke. Now, after the crowd had thinned to one, all I felt was a hole, a mile-wide emptiness where something important was supposed to be. Each time I tried to smooth away her creases, Nella smiled sadly at me from between my fingers, as if . . . well, as if we'd survived a major disaster together. A disaster that had changed us both. Only, her changes had already happened, and mine were just beginning. . . .

It was only a few days later that the police found a car abandoned one street over from the Baylor place. The fenderless heap didn't belong to anyone we knew, but it did belong to someone who knew someone who had been at the bash. And that someone knew someone else. It wasn't long before twenty-five of us from Whale Point and ten students from two other towns were invited downtown for fingerprinting and mug shots. I never did figure out why some of the kids at the party weren't picked up. But like Shepherd always said, "Who told you life is fair? Life is life."

So I should have known this was going to happen. In fact, when the two policemen showed up at our door, I felt something like relief, a breath let out that I'd been holding in for days. You can't make that big a mess without people finding out about it. And once I'd woken up and sobered up, I knew we'd have to pay. Nella might have forgiven me, but I was sure no one else would.

Which was why I hadn't mentioned our little gathering to anyone in my family. "Are you certain you've got the right address?" Mom asked the older cop. He was close to her age, and she smiled at him as if he would understand the mistake they'd made. My mother, even at sixty-one, was a pretty woman, when she tried. And she was trying . . . hard. "My daughter is an honor student. She's going to medical school when she graduates."

"Mom!" I'd been an accessory to breaking and entering, vandalism, pyromania, and God knew what else, but my mother was still putting on airs, still pretending. "It's *PRE*med, and I haven't even applied yet."

Like I told you, I'd been destined for medical school since forever. Every birthday after my fourth, every Christmas, and sometimes even

Easter, I'd get a present with a for-the-future-doctor theme. Once it was a little see-through plastic man with all his bright blue and red organs on display. Once it was *The Junior Book of Anatomy* in two volumes. I owned the biographies of every famous physician and medical scientist who'd ever lived, from Hippocrates to Galen to Marie Curie to Jonas Salk. For my sixteenth birthday, which happened right after I met Fry, I truly hit the jackpot: a T-shirt from my new boyfriend and a copy of the *Physicians' Desk Reference* with my very own name engraved in gold on the cover. Guess which one I never opened?

The officer checked the paper he held in his hand. "This is the right address, ma'am," he told my mother. "Says so right here." Then he looked at me. "Are you Sarah Wheeler?" He sounded almost sorry he had to ask.

"Yes, sir." I was definitely sorry I had to answer.

"And were you at the Rufus Baylor house on the night of April sixth?"

"Yes, sir," I said again. And then all hell broke loose.

My mother, who sits on the Whale Point Town Council, was horrified. Not just by my trip downtown for booking and fingerprinting. Or the newspaper articles (because we were minors, our names weren't mentioned, but within hours, the whole town knew who we were, anyway). It wasn't only the way the story went viral on the Internet or the way curiosity seekers drove into town to look at the ruined cottage (where were all those people when we needed tourists?).

Talk dies down. Newspapers get thrown out. Even Internet gossip eventually gets buried under the next new thing. For Mom, though, the shock went a lot deeper and lasted a lot longer. She'd counted on something solid, and ended up in a muddy salt marsh: I wasn't the model student and future physician she'd thought I was. I wasn't a hard worker, a team player, a good girl. Sometimes now, I caught her looking at me when she didn't think I'd notice. Sure, she was angry, but she seemed curious, too. As if she was trying to figure out who I really was.

My aunt Jocelyn, who's always acted more like my mother's daughter than her sister, jumped at the chance to prove that I was a true degenerate and a total flop in the respect-your-elders department. "You need help," she told me in front of Mom. When Jocelyn was outraged, all the blood in her face went to her nose. Which always made me smile. Which always made her more outraged. "You are truly a pervert, and you've trampled on an old man's grave."

"He's not dead yet," I pointed out. Which was true, because they'd quoted the Great One in two of the newspaper articles. He lived all the way at the other end of the state, in Asheville, probably in some nursing home. Where he'd sat up in bed long enough to say that he had donated family belongings to furnish the cottage, and he was sorry to see them destroyed.

The only person who didn't act like I'd helped burglarize a church was Shepherd. He was the first one to read about the bash in the paper, but the last one to blame me for what happened. Of course, he had his own reasons for playing it cool.

There's a *Whale Point Watch* stand right outside Mamselle's. We were heading for his car the night he spotted that first article in the morning edition. He put in three quarters and unfolded the front page under my nose. "It's hit the papers," he told me, in a voice that sounded like he'd just swallowed a bag of canaries. "Your mother will be so proud."

* * * *

"It's not that I didn't *want* you." That's what my mother always told me. "It's more that I didn't *need* you." Which pretty much said it all—not just for Mom, but for Jocelyn, who was raised by Mom after my grandparents died in a plane crash, and who thought she'd be the baby in the family forever. Even Shepherd, who figured at first that a kid might help convince Mom to marry him, realized soon enough that making a home for me was a lot lower on her to-do list than keeping her magazine job and not getting saddled with a scumbag.

Something else nobody needed was to have their nearest and dearest arraigned and tried for criminal vandalism and destruction of property. Even though the sergeant who booked us downtown told us we probably wouldn't go to prison since we were minors, the next few weeks were hard on us all. Especially my mother. Who specialized in Caring What Everyone Thinks. Who always wore makeup, even to the mailbox. Who now barely left home, slinking between her office and our house, afraid people would spot the Mother of the Criminal. Would point. Whisper. Judge.

To be honest? I suppose my mother wasn't the only one who was ashamed. Once the papers came out, I felt more cut off from my old friends than ever. For all I knew, they still called themselves the Untouchables. But it was me who felt like one. When I passed George or Wanda in the hall, I looked away. When I saw Wanda's number on my cell phone, I didn't even concoct an excuse not to call back. I just erased it. I was sure, you see, what she and the rest of them were thinking; I was certain they'd filed me under *L* for "Lost Cause." *D* for "Degenerate." Or *T* for "Terminator of Poetry, Art, Friendship, and All Things Sacred."

The judgment that mattered, of course, came at the trial, which was over in a single day. The judge told us the same thing the sergeant had, that we were too young to go to jail. But she said she wanted us to understand what we'd done. She talked about how Rufus H. Baylor was an institution. How we should respect the way he loved our state, the gifts he'd given us all. Then she sentenced us to clean up the cottage we'd nearly burned to the ground. *And* to take a course in Baylor's poetry at the community college. That last part surprised everyone, and except for the judge and maybe the college prof who was supposed to teach the course, it didn't make anybody happy.

People in town? They thought we deserved way worse. The *Watch* printed a whole new series of letters to the editor, most of them insisting we should do community work, hang in effigy, or spend the rest of our lives with red letters on our chests. And in case you think I'm exaggerating, one writer actually suggested we wear armbands "so everyone will know these kids for the lowlifes they are."

So I suppose you could say we got off easy. Or *some* of us did. I don't know how many other parents decided they needed to go the court one better, but my mother couldn't leave bad enough alone. She decided I needed to learn what I'd put at risk that night, and sentenced me to an endless and hideously boring lecture series at the library. It was called Women in Medicine, and it was only slightly preferable to being grounded for the rest of my life. Which, Mom made clear, was the alternative.

In the end, then, none of us had to wear armbands or paint park benches. But if we didn't do hard time, our way out and up wasn't exactly a get-out-of-jail-free card, either. Even Fry and H, whose parents didn't pile more punishments on top of the court's, were still saddled with summer poetry school. And given how they felt about school of any kind, maybe that was enough.

Me? When I wasn't enduring Shepherd's jokes about juvenile delinquents or watching the less-than-enthralling cinematic reenactment of the first surgery performed by a female physician, I kind of looked forward to learning more about Nella's father. I knew that, under different circumstances, my old nerdy friends would probably be jealous of my chance to study Baylor's poems with an expert. And then, just a few days after the sentencing, I decided they'd probably want to trade places with me, even if they had to wear armbands to do it. Because that's when we found out the Great One had decided to teach the course himself!

Things Take a Poetic Turn

POETIC JUSTICE FOR WAYWARD TEENS. That was the headline. RENOWNED POET TO TEACH DELINQUENTS. And there he was, Rufus H. Baylor himself, in a blurry photo right underneath. His eyes were narrowed to slits and his mouth was open in what could have been a smile but was more likely, given his age, a grin-and-bear-it stab of arthritis, lumbago, or whatever senior citizens get. Smiling or not, though, that photo and the announcement that came with it were the beginning of our little town feeling like a very big deal.

No one could figure out why a world-famous celebrity had volunteered to teach us himself. The mayor and town council were sure it was fond memories that were bringing him back. They said so in as many interviews and articles as they could. (Their speeches were definitely written by the same person who'd boasted, in the plaque at the cottage, about "picturesque streets and friendly residents.")

My personal theory was that Baylor had simply gotten tired of being an institution. Of being filed away in encyclopedias and anthologies and left to die. In fact, after listening to the way my teachers, the judge, and the newspapers all talked about him, I decided the Great One and I might have something in common: Nobody needed him, either.

Baylor's problem wasn't getting born, of course; it was hanging around too long afterward. His poems, the really big ones, had all been written decades ago. He'd been invited to read one at the White House a few years ago, but he'd lost his glasses and stumbled over the lines. That's when the world decided he was too old to count, and more or less forgot about him.

Fry thought I was right. "The guy's gotta be bored. And helping us sure beats working puzzles at the old folks' home." But that was the end of Fry's empathy. Mostly, he wanted nothing to do with Baylor. And H, no surprise there, felt the same way. Which, of course, was not at all how the good residents of Whale Point reacted. Yes, there were more letters to the editor, this time praising the Great One, his charity, his generosity, his ability to forgive. And the chamber of commerce? Let's just say they appreciated the timing of Baylor's gesture, which would focus national attention on our town just as the summer season got under way. Like sunscreen and beach towels, WELCOME, RUFUS BAYLOR signs and "poetry specials" began cropping up everywhere. Even at the supermarket.

I'm sorry to say that my prince had learned very little about the perils of buying alcohol before you reach drinking age. Even though I'd switched to ginger ale (under threat of eternal grounding), Fry and H were determined to stock up on beer. As soon as Span got home from college for the summer, H drove us all to Save More, and while the three of them debated the merits of lager versus ale, I cruised the snack aisle. I was halfway down when a large, handwritten shelf sign caught my eye: "THE SKY LIKE CHIPS OF SAPPHIRE, THE WATER DIPPED IN DARK." CHIPS AND DIPS AT POETIC PRICES!

But when I went back to get the others, to ask them to come see the sign, Span just smiled and pointed to another one over the wine rack: "EVERY VINTAGE BRINGS ITS HARVEST, AND THIS YEAR WE'VE REAPED JOY." LYRICAL WINES AT PROFOUND DISCOUNTS! Clearly, Whale Point's biggest supermarket had a poetry fan among its employees. Specifically, a Rufus Baylor fan, since those quoted lines, it turned out, were all from our visiting poet's work. Before we left, we read more verse in nearly every aisle, so we weren't surprised when the cashier told us (after squinting at Span's ID for what seemed like an eternity) that the assistant store manager was a major poetry buff, and that he'd matched up products and poems all over the store.

And there were other Baylor groupies, too. The Oceanside Motel was already advertising "Laureate Suites." The local radio station read sponsored poems instead of ads. And everyone, from the clerks in stores to the staff in restaurants to the policeman who directed traffic where a signal had gone dark, was wearing yellow buttons: WELCOME TO WHALE POINT, THE SUMMER OF POETRY.

"What is the big deal?" Fry was not the least bit impressed. In fact, he sounded outraged. "So the guy can rhyme. So what?"

"Well, for one, his rhymes are beyond famous." Span grinned at my prince and me from the passenger seat. "As in, *world* famous. Hell, I'd like to meet him, just to tell the kids at school I shook his hand, you know?"

"Maybe I can help you out with that big dream, Spano." Fry was not smiling back. "How about you go to class for me? And I'll stay home for you?"

I was surprised at how angry he was, how . . . well, almost jealous. And his mood didn't improve even after H and Span dropped us off at his house. Of course, that may have been because (a) his mother was home, so (b) we didn't have the place to ourselves, which meant (c) he couldn't try to talk me out of my underwear. Plus, (d) that was the day the letter came from court.

When she handed him the envelope, Fry's mother wore this sorry, shamed expression—as if it were her fault we were going to summer school. Fry took one look at the return address and groaned, then passed the letter on to me. After I made small talk with Mrs. Reynolds (she liked my sweater, I liked the smell of whatever she had in the oven), Fry and I took our bad news into the den. We had to ramp up the volume on the TV so his mom wouldn't hear what we were saying. She was a friendly woman, who told me she'd always wanted a daughter and apologized every time I visited for the dog hair on the couch. But she was also one of the chattiest people I'd ever met, so Fry and I usually ended up excusing ourselves and telling her we had homework to do. Which meant we had to whisper if we wanted to talk about anything besides constitutional amendments or logarithms.

The letter said our first cleanup was scheduled in two weeks, and that poetry classes would start before that, in less than a week. Fry, who loved working with cars and was always fixing things around the house for his mother, didn't seem to mind the idea of the cleanup. But he was still having trouble cultivating the appropriate attitude for poetry school.

"Screw this!" he said when I read him the dates. "I've got driver's ed on Thursdays." He reached for the letter, double-checked the class day, then threw it onto a pile of papers and magazines by the TV. There was a movie on, but we weren't really watching it.

Even though Fry had turned the volume up, I tried to whisper. If I could hear Mrs. Reynolds chopping in the kitchen, why couldn't she hear me talking in the den? "Baylor doesn't *have* to do this, you know," I told Fry. "He could stay in Asheville and rest on his laurels."

"His what?"

Once in a while, I forgot myself and talked to Fry like he was one of my old nerdy friends. "Put yourself in his place," I told him. "If you were very old and very famous, would you make a special trip to teach us the error of our ways?" I pulled that week's *Watch*, along with Fearless Fosdick's rubber dog bone, from under the couch cushion. (I was getting tired of crinkling and squeaking every time I moved.) I threw the bone into the middle of the room and watched Fry's ancient setter amble toward it.

"I'd feel a whole lot better if everyone who played paid, that's all." Fry nodded at his dog, who had reached the bone and was looking back, as if to check with us before he picked it up.

"What do you mean?" I asked.

"I mean there were plenty of kids at that party who never made it to court." Fry held out his hands for the slobbery trophy Fosdick carried back. "Money talks." He shook his head. "And pigeons fly."

"Huh?"

"Look. If the cops offered you a chance to walk, wouldn't you give them names?"

I wasn't sure how these things worked. I stared at the TV, where people were lined up, waving their arms and singing. Could you plea-bargain your way out of being drunk and teenage? "I most certainly would not!" I was taking the moral high ground here. Of course, no one had offered me an alternative. And what if I didn't go to Whale Point? What if I recognized some of the kids at the bash, but didn't really know them? Didn't care?

And then I was back at the cottage. And he was beside me again, the tall, lanky kid from Mamselle's. He was trying to give Nella a drink, and his face was a mask. He didn't look angry, but he didn't look like he was having fun, either. He just had it in for pretty girls, pretty girls who probably wouldn't even talk to him unless they were drunk. *She looks thirsty, dontcha think?*

When Fry put his arm around me, I didn't respond. "Earth to Sar." My prince wasn't used to chilly princesses. "What's up? Where'd you go?"

"There was this boy at the bash," I told him, easing out of flashback mode, turning in his arms. "My dad fired him from the restaurant."

"And?"

"And maybe he called the police?"

Fry nodded. "Come to think of it," he told me, "there were plenty of people there with their attitudes on wrong." He was smiling. Finally. "Including three girls I've broken up with." Pulling me close. "Three girls who'd love to be where you are right now." He ran his tongue along the crease between my ear and my cheek. I'm not sure whether I shivered because it felt so good. Or because Mrs. Reynolds's blender had stopped and someone on TV was suddenly singing very loudly. I sat up straight and proper, nodded toward the kitchen. I grabbed the dog toy from Fry's lap and threw it to Fosdick for cover.

But the blender started up again and Fry moved on. "Hey," he said, throwing himself into a new scheme, "maybe we can get the old fart to teach us poetry *and* parking." He was still not happy about missing the only course he was likely to pass without cracking a book. "That way, we'd actually learn something we can use."

"I don't think Baylor drives anymore," I told him. The woman on TV was singing from the deck of a sinking ship. I ignored her, remembering parallel parking. Shepherd had tried to teach me once after he'd driven me home. Once was enough:

FEARLESS FOSDICK

Fhluuuumph, stchuuuumph, chuuuumph.

RUBBER BONE

WhhhhEET. WhhhEEEET.

SHEPHERD

(*In my head*)

Turn the lousy wheel, for Chrissake!

WOMAN ON TV

(*Singing*)

I'll never give up, up, up! This won't get me down, down, down!

FRY'S MOM'S BLENDER

CHRRRRRRRRR . . . CHRRRRRRRR . . . CHRRRRRRRRRRRRRRRRRR.

SHEPHERD

(In my head, louder)

I said "sharp"! Are you freakin' deaf?

I was doing it again. Tuning in to the crazy, busy dialogue that filled up every day, like a script that never ended. But Fosdick decided it was time I quit listening and started throwing again. He looked up at me, huge eyes pooled with dog tears, then laid his squeaky toy, coated with drool, in my lap. As Aunt Jocelyn used to say when things in the refrigerator collected mold, *Quadruple yuck!*

Fry stroked his old dog's head, a reward Fosdick probably figured he'd earned for leaving that slime trail on my jeans. He waited for more pats, but Fry was focused on Baylor, instead, and on dissing poets, poetry, and words in general. "Writing seems like not living to me." He got all flushed and worked up when he was on a riff. It made him seem deep and sensitive. So I didn't mind that he was talking complete trash. I mean, he'd never written a poem in his life.

"It's worse than wanking." Fry grabbed the newspaper from between us and tossed it toward the paper pile. "That's at least *doing* something."

"Shhhhh!" I couldn't believe Fry was talking like this only one room away from his mother, blender or no blender. The *Watch* had fallen short, landing to one side of Fry's weight bench, and the page with the Great One's picture had spilled out. The way it landed, the poet was standing on that white head of his. "If he's too old to drive," I whispered to Fry, "he's too old for that stuff, too." I didn't want him making fun of someone he didn't even know. Someone who'd roasted marshmallows with Nella. "Miss Kinney says he's over eighty."

Fry processed that factoid from our English teacher, something he'd obviously missed, probably due to an incoming text. (He could blind text, and since he hid his cell in his hoodie or a binder, even I couldn't always tell when he was using it.) Now he seemed genuinely stunned that anyone, anywhere, could live as long as Baylor had. "I don't want to get *that* old," he said. "Ever. I'd rather go out with all my engines revved full speed."

"I hope he's got some family around." I let Fry take my hand now, because the couch had stopped squeaking and I could hear his mom's blender purring like a lawn mower. "I mean, who's glad he's alive? Who really cares?"

"Not me, that's for sure." Fry leveled a laser death-beam at the *Watch*, which stubbornly refused to disintegrate. "There must be a thousand celebrities I'd rather get the chance to meet.

"On the other hand," he said, pulling me close, "let's look on the bright side. If he's as old as Miss Kinney says, he might croak before the class starts."

"They'd just find someone else to take his place." I pushed his hands away from places I knew Mrs. R. wouldn't want to find them, then snuggled against his chest. "Some runner-up poet." I could feel Fry's heart pump against my cheek. *Stay*.

"Yeah," he admitted. "At least we'll get bored by the best, Mr. Big League himself: 'You are my dear compass.' Gag me with ten spoons!"

"What?" If I separated the words from Fry's sarcasm, they felt pretty good. I sat up, turned his face toward me. "Say that again."

"Where were *you*? Kinney spent half of last class talking about that one." A frown at the memory. "Then kept us past the bell so she could recite it."

"Don't *you* remember?" I asked him. "I wasn't there." Nothing's free, that's what Shepherd always says, and although I hated to admit it, I guessed he was right. I mean, leaving school early for Women in Medicine was a small price to pay for my mother not grounding me until I was ninety. But it turned out, I'd missed more than clock-watching. Apparently, Miss Kinney was using the end of class to read her favorites.

"I can tell she knows all his stuff by heart," Fry explained. "She closes her eyes through almost every line." He leaned across me on the couch, and for a minute I thought I was going to have to fight him off again. But then he dug our English book out from behind the cushions, and suddenly he was doing something I'd never dreamed of, even in my most far-fetched Cinderella and Prince Fry fantasies—he was reading me poetry!

He thumbed through the book and found the page he wanted. Then he put one hand across his chest, and spoke so high I wondered if he'd break something. "You are my dear compass, / who knows no way but true," he said in a pathetic imitation of our English teacher's voice. "So when I'm lost and drifting, / I find myself in you."

In spite of his hideous delivery, I loved the sound of what he'd read. The sound and the meaning, too. "I like it," I said, hoping I wouldn't scare him off, hoping he'd read more. "It feels like it's about two people in love. They don't even need to talk, just look at each other."

"You mean like this?" Fry let the book drop and leaned close, crossing his eyes and breathing in stereo like a nearsighted Darth Vader.

"Yeah," I told him, pushing him backward, onto the arm of the couch. Couldn't he be serious even once in his life? "*Just* like that."

Bearings

You are my dear compass,
who knows no way but true,
so when I'm lost and drifting,
I find myself in you.

Yet when I ask you, fearful,
if I should set you free,
imagine my surprise to hear
you take your north from me.

The First Class

After the rich kids' parents hired lawyers and all the special-ed students got excused, there were seventeen of us mainstreamers who couldn't buy or talk our way out of the poetry course. It was held after school, so we all had to drive down to the community college the second Thursday in June. It didn't seem like a whole lot of planning had gone into our reform; the college was already on break and there was no air-conditioning. But really, how could we complain? Our instructor was going to be one of the most famous people in the world. (Which late-breaking development inspired five of the rich kids' families to suggest, oops, they didn't mean it and they were willing take their punishment after all. But the judge told their lawyers that if their reasons for *not* taking the course were good, then their reasons *for* taking it had to be bad. Score one for the huddled masses.)

We still couldn't figure out why the Great One had decided to teach us. We all knew why *we* were there—too young to serve time, too old not to be punished for $50,000 worth of property damage. But why would a legend leave the security of the nursing home where he was comfortably decaying, to teach a bunch of incorrigibles who had set his house on fire about iambic pentameter?

"He's got it all," H acknowledged. "Fame, money, a zillion books." He looked around the small cinder-block room. "There's not a single person here who hasn't heard of Rufus H. Baylor." Despite the fact that he'd complained about being here, and moaned every time Fry did, my prince's second-in-command sounded just the tiniest bit starstruck.

And what he'd said about people knowing who Baylor was? It was true. Not only for the kids in that room. But for their parents, their friends, and just about everyone on the planet. "You're right," I told him, surprised to be agreeing with the guy I usually went out of my way to pick fights with. "Baylor sure doesn't need to come all the way out here to teach a roomful of . . ."

I paused, trying to think of a way to describe the unbrilliance that filled that classroom. I took a quick survey: three people openly on cell phones, two undercover; four guys talking in the corner; two girls reading the same magazine; and one doing her nails. (Throw in the three of us holding a conversation about all this, and that left only two—count them, two—kids who sat up straight and looked expectantly at the classroom door. As if they couldn't wait to get started.)

"Think about it," I said. "If you were a celebrity, would you want to hang out with kids like us?"

Fry, who was not inclined to speculation about anything except microbrews, shrugged. "Maybe he just wants to see how the other half lives."

He had a point. Sure, Baylor's work was required reading (in the case of a few really famous poems, required memorizing). And he got wheeled out in front of reporters once a year to read a sonnet, to smile for the cameras, to say something dripping with metaphors. But then he was supposed to go back to sleep and let the world go on without him. Maybe he was just plain curious about that world?

At first, when a thin, nervous man walked into class and looked at us like we might bite, I thought he could be our famous teacher. But he was much too young, and after he took roll, he pointed to his name tag, as if he were teaching us to read. "Dr. Fenshaw, English Literature," he said. Me Dick, you Jane. If we weren't all so hot and sweaty, it would have been funny.

After that, our fearless leader, who was probably the prof who'd been scheduled to teach us before Baylor decided to do it himself, launched into what sounded like a speech he had practiced over and over. In fact, Fenshaw was so busy talking to himself, he never even heard the old man come in. The visitor had to listen to the speech right along with the rest of us. Together, we learned everything we never wanted to know about "Southern pastoral." Rufus H. Baylor wasn't just the *People's* Poet, Fenshaw told us, he was the *place's*, too. His poems had made Carolina wrens, fence lizards, redbuds, wisteria—all of it—famous, even poison ivy. He'd turned pieces of our state into household words, scattering them across the country from his office at the Library of Congress or wherever Poets Laureate worked.

Meanwhile, Baylor (who else could it be?!) stood quietly beside the door, hands folded over the handle of a walking stick. He smiled and sized us up while we did the same. The Great One, it turned out, was much taller than I'd imagined. He didn't seem to fit the dainty rolltop desk I'd seen at the House That Was No More, and he made Fenshaw look like a skinny miniature. But it wasn't just his size that was a surprise; Baylor seemed brighter, more alive than I'd expected.

Maybe it was all the black-and-white news photos I'd seen, or the fact that he was older than anyone I knew. I'd pictured him in a wheelchair, with white hair, pale skin, and a tweed jacket he probably couldn't put on by himself. The only thing I'd gotten right was the white hair.

Under that famous, snowy mop, Baylor's cheeks were flushed and his eyes were sharp blue, deep and twisty like the middle of a cat's-eye marble. He didn't wear glasses, so when he looked at you, there was nothing between you and those marble eyes. He wore comfort clothes, a bright orange tee, the writing on it nearly illegible, and jeans—an *octogenarian* in jeans.

Finally, either because he realized we were looking past him, or because he got that tingly feeling you sometimes do when a person's watching you from behind, Professor Hot Air turned around and spotted our guest of honor. That's when the poet left his stick in a corner and walked to the center of the room with both hands open, holding them out for the prof's. Flustered, the smaller man stuck his out, too, and let Baylor grab him in a double handshake.

Then, while Fenshaw was pulling file cards out of his pocket, looking for the introduction he finally located and began to read, the Great One took off down the aisles between our seats. He came over to each one of us in turn, waiting beside our desks, holding out those open hands. One by one, we stood up, and did the double-handshake thing. It was the oddest feeling, having your hands trapped in that old man's. Up close, the peeled letters on his tee announced, I THINK, THEREFORE

I RHYME. He didn't say anything, just beamed a smile on you, a huge, open grin no one could possibly fake.

When the prof had finished his introduction and Baylor had shaken the last hands and ambled back up to the front of the room, our celebrity teacher started class. He didn't introduce himself; he didn't say, "Hi, how are you?" Or even, "How could you have done this dastardly deed?" Instead, he talked a poem—right out of the gate, just like that. He hadn't written it down because he knew it by heart. His voice wasn't exactly old, but it was comfortable like his clothes, with just enough Southern in it, to make him sound like home. He didn't stop at the ends of the lines and breathe heavy, the way Miss Kinney always did when she read poetry. It was like he was having a conversation with us, only we weren't talking back. Not even Coral Ann Levin, whose father was the soccer coach, and who had the biggest mouth in the entire school. And not Hector Losada, who had the second biggest. Even the mule-size kid who'd answered roll as Thatcher, and whom I recognized as the bully who'd wanted H to break down the cottage door, had stopped talking to his friends. He just smiled patiently, as if Baylor were telling a joke and he were waiting for the punch line.

The poem wasn't very long; in fact, it stopped just when I'd gotten used to the song it was making. It rhymed, but not in a "rose" / "nose" kind of way. It could have been a love poem, but I wasn't sure. All I knew was that it was about trying to make good things last. Almost as if Baylor had heard me wish it every time Fry put his arms around me: *Stay*.

When he'd finished, Baylor turned and looked at Fenshaw, who was definitely on the spot. The prof hugged his chest, shook his head. "I thought I knew your work, sir." The tighter he hugged, the more he showed off the perspiration moons under his arms. "But I'm afraid I've never read that poem before."

"That's because I just wrote it, Dr. Fenshaw." Baylor looked pointedly at our intrepid mentor's name tag. "Do you have a first name, young man?"

"Charles," the teacher said, glad to know something. "It's Charles."

"Well, Charles," Baylor told him, "that's part of the reason I'm here. I wanted to thank these folks for the first poem I've written in years."

"Sir?" Fenshaw was back to knowing nothing.

But Baylor wasn't looking at him anymore. He'd turned to us, instead. "You see, if y'all hadn't broken into that old summer place of mine, I might not have gotten to thinking about the good times, the sweet times I had there."

I'm sure I wasn't the only one in that stuffy, bile-colored room who was surprised that Baylor was thanking us for anything. It made what we'd done seem worse, like we'd run over a puppy with a Mack truck. A puppy who had stumbled to its feet and was licking our faces.

"And if I hadn't thought about those times," Baylor told us, "and realized they were over and that I could never get them back, I don't suppose I would have written a poem about them." The way he *looked* at you! It wasn't like being under a microscope. It was more like he thought you were special, one of a kind. Like there was nowhere else he'd rather be, no one else he'd rather see.

"I'm not saying what you did was right, mind you. In fact, it was much closer to dead wrong. But I am saying the longer I live, the easier it gets to believe that our darkest moments have lessons hiding in them. And if that lesson is a poem? Well, for a fossil like me, that's pretty close to a miracle."

He wasn't handing us a line, you could see that. He wasn't talking down to us; he was telling us the simple truth: We'd trashed his house. And we'd helped him write a poem. How long had it been between poems? Maybe it felt like forever. Maybe that's why he was here.

Now he asked us to take his new poem apart. He said it again, line by line, and told us he wanted to know how it made us feel. "I don't give a rat's rear end what you think it *means*," he warned us before anyone had time to raise their hand. I thought of Miss Kinney telling us that every poem had a message, that it was our job to read between the lines.

"I want to know what the sound of the words does to your gut," Baylor told us. "I want to know what pictures it puts in your head."

Even after Fry took his hand down, I kept seeing it up in the air. It was that hard to believe. But Baylor called on him like he was just anyone, not the Absolute Last Person in the Universe Who Would Ever Under Any Circumstances Be Expected to Volunteer in Class.

"That line about the girl's neck bones?" Fry asked. "Maybe the poet wants to choke her?"

Fry grinned at me then. I couldn't figure out if he was teasing our famous teacher, or if he really meant what he'd said. (Lately, the way he'd been acting, it could have gone either way.) H, Faithful Shadow and Sucker Up, was sitting on the other side of Fry, the way he always did. He started to smile, then took it back. Just like me, he wasn't sure if his *jefe* was serious or not.

But Baylor? Baylor laughed right out loud. "That's a pretty drastic way to get the last word." He shook his head. "Frankly? This poet hadn't considered that." He stopped then, ducked his white head, and brushed his lips with one hand. "But you know what, young man? A lot of tenderness is very close to violence, isn't it? We take the best care of things we could easily crush.

"Yes," he said, looking at Fry as if Mr. Laid-Back had just shown him how to solve a really tough quadratic equation. "Yes, that's in there, too."

Baylor didn't know it, of course, but Fry had just done him an even bigger favor. Because once the coolest guy in that room, possibly in the whole school, had answered his question, it was like dominoes falling. A mini forest of hands shot up, and Baylor beamed. He nodded toward a girl I recognized from Miss Kinney's class, a girl I couldn't remember saying a single word in school. But here she was, telling Baylor how she understood the line about eyes giving you away. "My mother knows whenever I'm lying," she said. "She says she can read it in my eyes."

"And that's because she loves you." Baylor was thinking it through, what the girl had said. "How about you?" he asked. "You know when *she's* not telling the truth?"

"Yes," said the girl. "Every time, even when she says nothing's wrong."

"Eye language, right?"

"Yeah. I guess I speak it, too." The girl was smiling, proud of herself. She was sitting in this class to avoid going to jail, and she was actually proud. I didn't know if anyone else thought this was as preposterous as I did. I looked around the room: Two kids were texting, and Thatcher the Moose had put on a serious mask, but you could tell he was sleeping behind it. Which meant Rufus Baylor had achieved a minor miracle, a response way better than the usual half-listening–half-out-to-lunch ratio in most classes at WPH.

And if more kids than usual were paying attention, a whole lot more were actually taking part. Pretty soon, most of the kids in that room had talked about Baylor's poem. Sometimes they said interesting stuff, sometimes not. But he listened, thought about everything, and never made anyone feel stupid or wrong. He always found something in what we said, something that grew the poem, made it even bigger.

Of course, no one had talked about the *sound* of the words yet. And *sound* was what he'd asked us about, what I'd noticed right away. What I always noticed if I stopped to listen: the grill in the kitchen at work, leaves whispering to each other in the rain, furniture breathing at night—voices everywhere. Yeah, I know what you're thinking. And you're right. I raised my hand.

"Name and serial number," Baylor said.

"Sarah," I told him. "My name is Sarah Wheeler." I kept going while I still had the nerve. "It felt like your poem didn't really end," I said. "That last line?"

Baylor nodded.

"It sounded like a bell or an echo, something that should keep going and going."

As soon as I heard myself say it, I wanted to take it back. Baylor stared at me, and for a minute, I thought he didn't understand. I wanted to explain that the words repeated in my head, not in a bad way, not like leaf blowers on Sunday. More like a prayer or a heartbeat.

"Going and going." The poet put his head to one side, the way Fry sometimes did when he wasn't sure about something, when he needed to check it out.

"Yes," Baylor said now. "That's just what I wanted it to do." He sounded as if he and I were talking about hanging a picture frame or planning a garden. Something we were doing together, just the two of us. "I had in mind that the reader would keep hearing it over and over in his brain or his heart, or wherever things stay." Head still cocked, he pointed a trigger finger at me. "Is that what you mean?"

It was my turn to nod. To wonder if he could read minds. And to feel very relieved I hadn't made a total jerk of myself.

Now Baylor pointed the finger gun at his own head. "Of course! Why can't it be out loud?" He seemed to be asking himself more than us. "Why can't *we* be the bell?"

And believe it or not, we were. He took the two words in the poem's last line, and he split them apart. He helped all the boys get a slow, steady drumbeat going. He even had the prof reciting it with them. "Don't, don't, don't," they said, over and over. Or most of them did. I was amazed to see H start in before Fry. He didn't even check with the boss before he was tapping his foot and repeating the word, over and over. And the hard cases like Thatcher? They just sat there, no laughter, no talking. I guess they were trying to figure out what the old man was up to.

Next, Baylor asked the girls to jump in just behind the guys, with the same beat, different word. "Try," we chimed, "try, try, try."

After we got going, it was just like I'd imagined it, only better. The guys' deep thrumming wove in and out of our higher, softer sound. "Don't," they rumbled; "Try," we answered. Those two sad words, over and over. But together like that, they weren't sad at all. They were voice music. Water words rushing, brushing, tumbling over each other.

Each time I joined in, I got this thrill, like I was doing something too loud and too much fun. I was three years old again, and I'd found this giant pot I couldn't lift off the kitchen floor. I took a spoon and a smaller pot, and slammed them both against its fat sides. The spoon made a high, silver sound. The little pot made a dull, hollow thud. I slammed harder and harder till the sounds vibrated inside me. A whole world opened up then—a world where everything talked. Not just people, but pots and spoons and floors and the fat, stolid sides of cupboards:

SPOON AND BIG POT

Tiiiiinnnnng! Tiiiiiiiinnng!

BIG POT AND LITTLE POT

WHUUMP! WHUUUUUMP!

SPOON AND FLOOR

Phat, phat, phat.

HIGH HEELS AND STAIRS

Tlik, tlik, tlik, tlik, tlik, tlik, tlik.

I heard my mother's anger before I saw it. But by the time she and Auntie J. appeared at the kitchen door, I had three more pots and their lids out, along with a ladle, a fork, and a corkscrew with silver curls that whispered and crunched instead of banged. I kept laughing and beating and thumping, even while Mom knelt down and started picking everything up off the floor. She didn't say a word to me, just turned to my aunt beside her. "We're going to have to childproof that cabinet door," she said.

Now whenever I jumped in to sing-talk the end of Baylor's poem, my adrenaline rushed, as if any second someone was going to walk into the classroom and make us all stop bamming and whamming. In fact, right up until the very last minute, when Rufus Baylor looked at his watch and said he'd kept us too long and we could leave, I kept wondering when our punishment was going to start. Was being bad supposed to make you feel this good?

Safe Deposit

I thought that I could keep it—
the light on the running tide,
how your eyes give you away
no matter what you hide.

I thought that I could hold it—
the forest along the sand,
your neck bones like pearls
underneath my hand.

But time's school has taught me
how petals brown and die.
There's no saving pleasure.
Don't try. Don't try.

Star Pupils

If you'd been in that first class with Baylor, you'd understand the high we felt afterward. I don't mean it was like some syrupy teacher-knows-best movie, where we sat around talking about how much we'd learned. Or that we walked out of that oven-temperature classroom spouting poetry and determined never to throw another party as long as we lived. But the truth is we'd each expected a sermon, or worse. Our families, the town, everyone, had hammered and hammered and hammered, till most of us were feeling bad to the core. Sure, there were some kids who still laughed about it, but they were the ones who laughed at everything, the ones so dense or so drugged you'd have to drill their skulls to get a thought out.

But here the rest of us were feeling more alive after class than we had before. That wasn't supposed to happen. The one person who had a right to hate us apparently didn't. In fact, he'd shared something with us that the finger pointers would have given anything to be in on.

A new poem by Rufus Baylor! My old friends, the ones I'd let slip away after Fry filled up my life, would never have believed it. Wanda and George, in particular, were Baylor groupies. They'd memorized most of his poems, and were always quoting pieces of them, fitting them into conversations even where they didn't belong.

And Fry? He was excited about the poem, too, though probably not for the same reasons Wanda or George would have been. "We have to be the first people on the planet to hear that poem," he told H and me now. He was in scheme mode, walking and talking double time. "Wait till we tell Kinney, she'll go into orbit." He headed toward the parking lot, but kept turning back to us. "I bet she'll give us extra credit." Walking. "She'll put our names on a plaque and give us all As." Turning. "Hell, she may just decide to graduate us right now. No pain, all gain!"

Graduation was a sensitive subject for H. The school had decided that he and the three other WPH seniors who'd been at the bash could graduate. I mean, they'd get their diplomas. But they couldn't attend the ceremony. Which meant that H's mother and father, who held down three jobs to keep him in books and gas, would never get to see him walk across the football field in a cap and gown.

Fry must have realized why his friend had gone suddenly silent. He waited for us to catch up to him, then put his arm around H. "I think you should give the news to Kinney, little buddy," he said. "You're about to move to the head of the class."

"*Chingón*." You could see two impulses at war in H—his massive crush on our English teacher and the whole Hispanic gangsta thing. The crush won; his smile was as wide and open as a little kid's. "I'll tell her that me and my compadre, Rufus?" Two skinny fingers high and tight. "We're like this!"

The three of us stood in the lot now, while H hunted for his car key. (The rust-covered wreck he insisted on calling "vintage" had once had two keys, but Shore Salvage didn't include luxury extras like duplicate keys.) It wasn't long before the gangsta and the grin both disappeared, and the Three Stooges routine started. After Fry and I each assured him that he hadn't given the key to us, H emptied both pockets, squatted on the asphalt to turn his backpack inside out, then stood up again and finally spotted the key right where he'd left it—in the ignition of his once-proud '93 Taurus.

A light rain had started up, a summer sprinkle that actually felt good after the heat in the classroom. (Dr. Fenshaw, English Literature, had tried to budge the thermostat and start up the AC, but apparently the whole system shut down at 5 p.m.) So the fact that, for once in his life, H had locked the car didn't really upset anyone but him. He slapped his forehead about a thousand times and ran through his whole repertoire of Spanish swearwords. None of us, H included, understood what they meant. Still, they sounded authentic and passionate, and added to the romantic nature of the whole experience.

We were feeling slightly less romantic ten minutes later. All the other kids were gone, even the ones who'd been waiting for rides. Because it was so hot that he'd left the window open a crack, and because he had his mother's dry cleaning in the trunk (in true vintage fashion, chronically unlocked), H was convinced he could snag the door lock with a clothes hanger. It was like watching him try to pick the lock the night we'd broken into the Baylor cottage. And he wasn't having any better luck now than he had then.

"Why do I have the feeling we've been here before, man?" Fry's patience was wearing thin. The rain was coming down harder now. "Let's just call Triple A."

Watching H manhandle that hanger brought it all back. The fumbling at the cottage door, the crowd and the cold, the way things had curled and turned brown in the flames. I lost my poetry high and began to feel the way I did at the hearing. ("Don't call it a *trial,*" my mother had insisted. "It's not going on your record, thank God.") The district attorney had rubbed our noses in all the details, so we wouldn't forget. And so the judge wouldn't, either, I guess. He made a point of reading the entire police report out loud, including the long list of what we couldn't make right.

"Item," he'd recited in a voice that carried the whole room. "Six porcelain dogs, heads and/or tails broken off. Estimated value, $3,500. If those dogs had been thrown into the fireplace, they would have been totally smashed, wouldn't they? Did someone sit on that crowded couch, instead, and snap their tiny heads off, one by one?

"Item: thirty-six family photographs, twenty 8" × 10" or larger; sixteen 4" × 6" or smaller. All frames broken and/or pictures torn. Estimated value, TBD." To be determined? How? Those photos were all taken before digital cameras, and none of the people in them would ever be young again. Didn't that make the pictures, like the credit card ads say, priceless?

I thought about the cleanup that would start the following week. Even though Fry and H had talked, in the same conspiratorial way they shared the names of their favorite NASCAR drivers, about gutters and flashing and struts, I couldn't understand the point. How would fixing up the shell of that little house bring any of those things back?

What difference would plaster and a new roof make when it was empty inside? The rain was coming down in buckets now. (Okay, summer rain doesn't actually fall in buckets in North Carolina. It's more like a high-pressure hose that some poor, heat-crazed homeowner turns away from the parched grass and blasts into his own face. Full bore.)

Still, H wouldn't give up. "Have faith, *ése*," he told Fry. "I'm close, I know it." He crouched beside the window, fishing with his clumsy hook and resorting to some of the same mysterious curses he'd already used. At least, they sounded the same.

"Having trouble?"

All three of us turned to find Rufus Baylor himself walking toward the stranded Taurus. He'd left his green beater—what was a famous poet doing driving a wreck as old as H's?—at the back of the lot. His was the only other car there, and whether he understood Spanish or not, it wouldn't have been hard to figure out we needed help. Swearing probably sounds the same in any language.

H paused in mid-tirade. His mouth stayed open, but the stream of musical obscenities stopped pouring out. Deserted by every last bit of macho he'd mustered a few minutes before, he stared at his famous "compadre." "I—uh . . . ," he said. "I . . ."

"We've locked the key in the car, sir." Fry took charge; Fry always took charge. He dug into his pocket for his cell. "We'll just call Triple A, no problem." He nodded at the old man, whose white hair had been flattened against his head by the rain. "Thanks for stopping, but we've got it licked." Behind him, H smiled and nodded, too, as if that had been his plan all along.

"Before you call," the poet asked, "why not let me take a look?"

H hesitated, glanced at Fry, then stepped back so Baylor could stare through the Taurus's window. A second later, he tapped the poet on the back and offered him the clothes hanger, like an OR nurse passing a surgeon his scalpel.

"Won't need that," Baylor said, without looking at the tear-shaped hook H had made at the end of the hanger. Instead he took a Swiss Army knife from his pocket and turned his cane upside down. He opened the knife and sank the blade deep into the business end of the stick. Next, he opened the corkscrew on the knife, and left it sticking out like a broken wing. Finally, he worked the whole thing through the top of the window.

It was so fast I missed it, but I saw the results. Baylor managed to snag H's key ring with the corkscrew and slip the key out of the ignition. In less than a minute, he had pulled the stick, knife, and key ring back through the window. "You could have been fooling with that lock all night, young man," he told H. "Myself? I prefer the direct route." He unhooked the keyring from the corkscrew and handed it to H.

Who was, once again, speechless.

"You want the key, go after the key." Baylor pulled his knife from the cane and pocketed it, then turned to Fry and me. "See y'all next week?"

The rainy curls pressed against his forehead made him look younger. Or maybe it was just that between his smile and that wet-baby-duck look, you didn't even think about his age.

"Yes, sir," H said for all of us. "We'll be here." He unlocked the Taurus, and Fry took my arm, tried to lead us to the car.

But I stood there in the rain, needing to tell Baylor. How we'd never meant to set fire to his dollhouse. My dollhouse. Our dollhouse. How a trillion "sorrys" could never make up for what we'd done.

What came out, though, was a lot shorter, a lot easier to say. "Thank you," I said.

Fry gave up, ran for the car, and got in. Baylor lifted his cane to eye level, smiled again. "Sometimes it pays to have three legs," he told me.

"No, I don't mean the key." I felt my own hair streaming down my face, sticking to my cheeks. "I mean for coming today. For writing the poem." Didn't he know? "For everything."

Now his grin ate up the space between us, and he took my hand. "Thank *you*," he said, "for ringing my poem like a bell. It made all the difference, didn't it, Miss . . . ?"

"Sarah," I told him. "My name's Sarah Wheeler."

"You shall not call her name Sarai," Baylor quoted the Bible passage I knew, "but Sarah shall her name be."

I saw H roll down his window, and heard Fry calling me.

"God wanted to make sure Abraham got it right," Baylor explained.

H rolled the window back up, and all I heard now was the rain's tinny drumming on the roof of the Taurus. "I read that part," I said. In fact, because it was all about me, I'd read that section of Genesis over and over, ever since I was little. "But I don't really get it." (My mom didn't, either. "Biblical splitting of hairs, that's all," she always said.)

"'Sarai' means '*my* princess,'" the Great One explained. "But 'Sarah' means just plain 'princess.' No one owns her, she belongs to herself."

I gasped. It felt like something important, something secret, had suddenly come clear. Maybe I gasped out loud, because now Baylor's smile opened like a happy seam, ragged and wide. "Makes all the difference, doesn't it?" he asked.

Then he knocked on the car's back door, Fry opened it, and I got in. I shook the drops from my hair, then slipped my soggy book bag under the front seat. I felt content, full of a secret I couldn't even name.

"So what was that all about, teacher's pet?" Fry was grinning. But not in a good way.

"What?"

"First, the old man looks at you like you're the only one in class. And now?" He nodded out the window at Baylor, who waved as we pulled away. "An after-school special."

I sat up, looked out the back window, saw the Great One growing smaller and smaller behind us. "That?" I said it light as air, as if it were nothing, as if it didn't matter at all. "He just wanted to make sure he knew how to spell my name."

Even though it rained all night, next morning the sun felt the way it does on the best summer days at the shore: warm, but not blazing. Toasty, but open to what the wind has to say. In short, it was *not* the sort of day anyone wanted to waste on school. So it was only because vacation started in one more week, and because we'd get to report the new poem to Miss Kinney, that any of us settled for watching a perfect beach day through the window.

In the end, though, it wasn't H, or me or Fry, who delivered the glad tidings. It was the shy girl who'd talked with Baylor about the language of eyes. She must have left her seventh-period class early to beat us all into the room. By the time we got there, the deed was done. And yes, Miss Kinney's eyes were doing that melting, sparkly thing they did whenever anyone mentioned Rufus Baylor.

But no, we didn't get As. Or a plaque. What the four of us, who were taking both Baylor's class and English 3C, got from our very happy teacher was an invitation to stay after school. Miss Kinney wanted to hear all about the new poem; in fact, she wanted us to reconstruct the whole thing. Not something we were eager to do while everyone else headed for the waves.

"I can't believe it. I just can't believe it!" Julie Kinney was a tiny woman, and her enthusiasm looked way too big for her. "I honestly thought there'd be no more after 'Sparrow.' I thought that was the last poem we'd ever have."

Earlier in the year, she'd told us about the poem she called Baylor's "epitaph." How she was sure that "The Sparrow" was what he wanted to leave us with, the way he wanted us to remember him and his work. It was about a father's love, and maybe about something bigger, something you can't see when you're caught up in every day. It ended with the words she wrote on the board in pink chalk: "I've been mostly wrong, / and God was mostly right." (She didn't erase those words for three days straight, not until someone crossed out "God" and wrote in "Kinney.")

Today, she was wearing one of her peasant/hippie skirts and sandals. "Do you suppose," she asked us, once the rest of the class had left and the four of us had moved to desks in the front row, "I mean, do you think you could get a copy of the poem?"

Fry, who was already looking at his watch, calculating lost surfing time, wasn't going to make things easy for her. He turned to the rest of us, then sighed. "I don't know," he told her. "Rufus Baylor is a very busy man, and we only see him once a week, and—"

The shy girl who wasn't actually, and whose name turned out to be Margaret, interrupted him with the truth: "I'm sure we can, Julie," she said. (Miss Kinney was a Yankee, and she'd asked the class to call her by her first name, but most of us didn't. In the South, manners die hard, and my mother would have had a shame stroke if I'd slipped up, even at home, and called my teacher Julie.)

"Mr. Baylor is just about the sweetest person in the entire world." Margaret had obviously contracted a serious case of Miss Kinney's Baylor worship. "And if you wrote us a note to take with us . . ."

"Really?" Our teacher's gypsy bracelets jangled as she brought both hands to her chest.

"If you explained how you love his work," Margaret told her. "If you told him you want to use the poem in class . . ."

"And won't publish it somewhere," H added. "Rufus is pretty touchy about things like that."

"He is?" Margaret turned, stared at H. So did I. This was a total Mad Lib, and yet he seemed convinced it was true.

Margaret's worldview was being crushed. You could see it in the way she stopped talking, pulled into herself. "I didn't think he was like that at all."

"Well, see, I kinda talked to him after class." H sounded casual, humble. "You know, he helped me get my car started."

"Maybe if *you* took him my note." Unfortunately, the look Miss Kinney gave H now, the way she touched his wrist, was probably enough to keep him lying for the rest of his life, even if he lived to be as old as Baylor.

H's powers of speech were temporarily short-circuited, and he wore an expression that made him look afraid of how happy he was. "I—I mean . . ."

"Of course he can take Mr. Baylor your note, Miss Kinney." Fry knew just the words to put in his friend's mouth. "As close as they are, I'll bet Hector could make sure you get copies of any other new stuff he writes, too."

Between H's paralysis and Julie Kinney's rapture, there wasn't much sense coming out of either of them. "New poetry?" More bracelets jangling, more chest hugging. "Other poems?"

Every time our teacher spoke, H turned toward her, as if she were his own private sun. Even though the whole thing was ridiculous, I couldn't help wondering what it would be like to have someone that crazy in love with you. Someone who wanted to hear you talk, someone who thought you were too good to be true. Too good to touch . . .

It must have been because she had taken her hand off his wrist. H suddenly regained his ability to talk. "Sure," he promised. "Why not? You see, Rufus is full of poetry, full of feelings about what happened." He went on to assure our teacher that the Great One had essentially sworn an oath to come up with a new book of poems, based on his life-changing encounter with the amazing students of Whale Point High. Or at least, with the outstanding sample that had nearly burned down his former home.

By the time we left school, H's confidence level had soared so high that he asked Margaret and Miss Kinney to come to the beach with us. Margaret said yes, but mercifully, Miss Kinney said no. Still, she stood in the faculty lot, loading her not-so-secret admirer with enough last-minute instructions and attention that he hardly minded. Armed with the note she'd written for the poet and the near certainty of another meeting with his teacher if he coaxed a poem from Baylor, H was tripping. His dream machine kept hatching plans all the way to the student lot.

"I'm thinking *I'll* write a poem for her," he told us as we piled into the Taurus. (He never locked it at school, so we didn't have to go through the Great Key Hunt until we were all safe inside the car.) "Maybe Julie will like it even better than Baylor's." He rifled through his pockets while he spoke, then started pulling his backpack inside out. "Hey, she might decide to read it in class." He stopped his search long enough to turn to Margaret and me in the back. "You know, like a model?" Hard as it is to believe, the boy was dead serious.

"It's *Julie* now?" I asked him. "What happened to *Miss Kinney?*" Fry and I traded wise smiles across the front seat. Which felt sweet and private, even though we weren't touching.

"You mean you're going to try to compete with Rufus Baylor?" Margaret didn't seem like the cynical type, but the snort-laugh that followed her question did not exactly convey optimism about H's chances.

H flicked open the glove compartment, found his key, and started the car. He was much too excited to care about anything we said. Our sarcasm must have sounded like a dim and distant rain falling somewhere outside his private Happy Land.

"She likes love poems, right?" He turned to Fry now, but didn't wait for an answer. "Maybe I'll leave one on her desk, unsigned. Make her wonder whose spell she's under, whose words are driving her *loca*."

"A fine plan, my man." Fry was wearing his riff look. "Let's swing by and pick up my board. Then we'll help you write the greatest love poem of all time. *On the beach*." He turned to me and Margaret for support. "Kinney's eyes will be shining like stars, right? And her lips? Her lips will be like two—"

"Halves of a clamshell?" Margaret actually had a sense of humor. Who knew?

"Dead herring?" I suggested. "Two dead herring dropped by seagulls and rotting in the sun."

Margaret laughed, not a snort-laugh this time, but a sort of triple-header, like she couldn't stop. I was beginning to like this girl. Besides, her hair was almost as red as Wanda's.

"See, my man?" Fry leaned back, buckled himself into his seat. "A few hours under an umbrella, sipping and sunning, and we'll have a poem that cannot fail."

"I wish I could contribute more than dead fish," I told them. "But I can't go with you. I'm on early at Mamselle's tonight."

Even though I'd joked about H's poem, I began to feel pretty sorry for myself, knowing what I'd be doing while the others were chilling on beach towels and camp chairs, watching Fry try for the kick-flip surf stunt he claimed he'd already achieved last fall, when no one was looking. Whether he made it official or not, there would still be plenty of wading and splashing. Tanning, wisecracks, and the salty pretzels we hadn't tasted since Surf Snacks closed last fall.

"Come for an hour." I loved it that Fry sounded disappointed. "First day without wet suits. You can't miss *that*!"

"No can do." I tried not to picture Shepherd, tapping his polished Italian dress shoe. "My dad wants me to set up and help type the menu."

Of course, even if I got there early, I'd do something wrong, something he could yell at me for.

So I told Margaret I'd see her next week at school, said good-bye to Fry and H, then walked to Mamselle's, right past the driveway that led to the Baylor place. The little house was so deep in the woods, though, and the trees had leafed out so much, you couldn't tell anything had changed at all. I wasn't sorry I was late, didn't mind that I had no time to follow the path to where you could see the boards the police had put across all the windows and doors. Smell charcoal, like old campfires. And stare past the barricade to where dozens of hardened footprints crisscrossed mud that used to be grass.

The Sparrow

"Not one of them will fall to the ground
outside your Father's care."

Once I nursed a feverish child,
as the moon climbed up the sky.
Morning came, his head still burned,
and I cursed God who did not
care if he lived or died.

That night's boy is grown to man,
who says he's lost the words.
"But I still know the story, Dad,
you told when I was sick, about
a giant and a fallen bird."

I'd forgot the tale I dreamed,
half told, half sung till it grew light.
So it's only now I see from here to
there, that I've been mostly wrong,
and God was mostly right.

An Explosion at Mamselle's, But My Bacon Is Saved

Maybe it was not making the pilgrimage up that driveway (if only to remember the way things used to be). Or maybe it was trading the beach and Fry for Mamselle's and Shepherd. One thing was sure: By the time I got to the restaurant, my afternoon felt like an old balloon, with hardly any color or air left in it. I didn't worry about folding the emerald-green napkins into neat swans, and I hardly noticed whether I spelled "foie gras" right. It would all lead to the same place, no matter how fast or slow I went, no matter how careful I was. Shepherd would get that tight, angry look and then explode. Sooner or later.

Tonight I guessed it would be sooner. Marsha had called in sick, and she was just about the only one who could replace the tape in the bar register when it ran out. Shepherd, leaning over the coil of paper, had already used some of his best swearwords, and since my station was right next to the bar, I figured it was only a matter of time before I gave him an excuse to practice the rest.

It was early and only a few tables had been filled, so mine were all empty. (I got customers only when Shepherd was desperate.) So yes, I was almost relieved when he sent me into the kitchen to wash dishes. I knew he didn't have time to stand around in there, waiting for me to break something. The bad part of kitchen duty, though, was that now he could conveniently forget where I was and never seat anyone at my tables at all.

Still, Manny was glad to see me; and he knew I was better than pushing soap around a plate. "Would you help with the Caesar, sugar?" he asked as soon as I walked in the room, which was already steamy from the sauces and reductions he was heating up. He must have come to work late again, because I could see he was way behind on prep. He was stirring two concoctions in frying pans and racing among three chopping boards full of half-sliced veggies. He was a big man, but he could move gracefully when he had to. Now he wore the inspired, sweaty look he always got when he was under pressure.

I took my apron off so it wouldn't get dirty, and sat by the long metal counter, mixing oil and mayo, the base for Manny's low-rent salad dressing. "Eggs are too expensive," he always said. "We don't use anchovies, so why not go fake all the way?"

When one of the busboys came to tell me I had a party, I was just pouring what I'd made into a pitcher. I stopped it up, then rushed into the dining room and headed for the white-haired gentleman Shepherd had seated all by himself in the middle of my empty station.

At first, I couldn't believe Shepherd had actually given me a customer before filling up the other stations. So what if this diner was a senior citizen who probably hadn't changed his tipping rate in forty years? So what if it was a party of one? But then I realized that, like all my father's favors, this one was helping him, not me: Since Marsha was out sick (or home free, depending on how you looked at things), that left just me and Laynelle. And if he'd put this old guy at one of Laynelle's tables, it would have slowed her down with the four- and six-tops.

Still, a customer was a customer. I was halfway to the table when Shepherd's high-voltage snarl made me turn around. "Where's your apron?" He was on me in seconds, covering the distance between us so fast, I barely had time to look down and realize I'd left my apron in the kitchen.

It wasn't even seven, and there were only a few diners in the whole place. But naturally, each one of them looked up. Wouldn't you? I mean, here's a man in a tuxedo, the same man who spoke in a soft, perfume-ad voice when he showed you to your table, who's now going postal. Yelling. Screaming, actually. "How many fucking servers are in here without a uniform, Sarah?"

I didn't answer. What was there to say?

"How many times have I told you? How many times are you gonna come in here disrespecting me, the staff, and the customers?" Shepherd seemed to have completely forgotten the customers himself. It wasn't like him to make a scene in public, not at work, anyway.

Manny coming in late had probably set him off. And Marsha waiting until five o'clock to tell him she wasn't coming in at all. In the end, though, it didn't matter who had stoked his fire. It was still *me* taking the heat.

"You got nothing to say?"

Once he was under way, there was no stopping Shepherd. But I didn't have to stand there, did I? All hot and hurt, like that busboy with dropsy?

"Get out of here, for crying out loud." He grabbed my wrist and pushed me toward the kitchen. "Just get out of my sight."

Which is exactly what I decided to do. If he could fire his waitress, I could fire my father.

"*I* have something to say." My lone customer stood up now and came toward us. "And I'd like to say it to you in private, young man."

When I tell you that the diner who took Shepherd by the arm and walked with him out of earshot was Rufus Baylor, you won't be half as surprised as I was. Somehow, I'd never dreamed our famous poet would hang around Whale Point any longer than he had to. But there he was, the day after our class, rising up out of his seat and turning those eyes on Shepherd. Leaning down to him, into him, as if they had secrets to share.

In that moment, Baylor looked like a knight in shining armor to me. He was an old man, yes, and his jacket was a little short in the sleeves. He had left his cane by his chair, and I worried about whether I should get it for him. But none of that changed the fact that, when he led Shepherd off toward the front door, when the two of them disappeared, arm in arm, behind a giant potted fern, Rufus Baylor was most definitely and undeniably the Greatest One of All.

When Shepherd came back, he was different somehow. Sure, he was extra polite to my party of one, totally stealing my thunder and waiting on the man himself. But even after Rufus Baylor left me a 50 percent tip and drove off in that weird jalopy of his, our new poetry teacher's influence lingered on. For one thing, the talk he'd had with my father definitely lowered the decibel level. How else could you explain that, for the rest of the night, Shepherd barely yelled at me or anyone else? Unless you count the incident over the dropped soufflé, but since that was only a six on the Richter, I don't think you should.

"What do you know?" All the way home, Shepherd couldn't stop talking about his new celebrity BFF. As soon as he'd closed both registers and carefully nosed his precious, polished-until-it-looked-like-it-was-covered-in-plastic Mustang out of the employee lot, he was off and running. "I just chatted up the most important guy in town!"

I guessed it wasn't the time to point out that said chatting was thanks to me, so I just listened. "He's staying up at the Hendricks'. They're in Montreal or some damn place for the summer."

Rufus Baylor, Poet Laureate, was living in town! Now that I thought about it, that made sense. He couldn't magically appear out of nowhere for each class, then disappear again until the next. He had to eat and sleep and laugh and talk somewhere between classes, and as it turned out, that somewhere was right around the corner.

The Hendricks were an elderly couple who both used to teach at UNC. *Her* had once done a feature on student life in North Carolina, so my mother had been assigned to interview them. She'd taken me along, but I was too young then to remember the visit. What I did remember, though, is that we walked over. *Walked!*

"I think Rufus went to school with them. Something like that. Says he doesn't want to stay in a hotel."

"Rufus?!"

"Yeah." My father sounded smug, proud. "He asked me to call him that. Said it made him feel like home." We pulled up in front of my house, but Shepherd was still on fast-forward. "He said we have stuff in common, stuff we didn't even know about.

"He's quite a guy, that poet of yours." He didn't turn off the ignition, but he didn't reach over and unlock my door, either. "He's got it upstairs, for sure. And not in a show-off, book kind of way, either. He's had a life."

I figured it was a safe bet that anyone who'd made it into their eighties had had a life. Still, it was best to let Shepherd circle around whatever he wanted to say until he decided to say it.

"How about you and me talk some more tomorrow after work?" He glanced at the house, as if my mother were watching. Shepherd had a strict policy: Avoid Katherine Wheeler if you owe her money. And he always owed her money.

"What do you say? I'll take you for ice cream after we close up?"

Whoa! What? Maybe you can imagine the internal double take I did when Shepherd invited me for ice cream, the mental WTF that boomeranged in my chest. I mean, if you overlooked the fact that my father had forgotten I was allergic to milk, didn't that invitation sound almost friendly? Almost like someone who cared?

I was too stunned to talk, too tired to process what had happened. So I just nodded. Then I unlocked my own car door and ran for the house. As soon as I got inside, I went straight to my room. Without checking my cell and without stopping in the kitchen to see if Aunt J. had left me something from dinner. Upstairs, I didn't take my tip money out of my pocket or even brush my teeth. I just fell into bed. I wasn't sure why Shepherd wanted to talk. Or what we could possibly have to say to each other. But as I drifted to sleep, one thing was certain. I was the newest member of the ever-expanding Whale Point chapter of the Rufus H. Baylor Admiration Society.

You would have been, too. Especially if the next night, your father managed to get through an entire Saturday dinner service without blowing a gasket. Well, almost. He kind of lost it when a deuce Laynelle was supposed to serve walked out. He knew their long wait wasn't her fault, though, and he couldn't blame Manny or me, either, since it was Shepherd himself who'd sent the wrong customers to the bar while he seated a couple who'd just arrived.

Instead, he had a private meltdown, like a volcano rumbling and steaming away all by itself without hurting anyone. I watched him from across the dining room, looking out over the sea of diners talking and eating, oblivious to the explosion brewing. I watched him slam his fist against the stack of recycled wine barrels he used as a host stand. Hard. But miracle of miracles, the wood didn't split or fly across the room. And after that? Shepherd shook his head, rubbed his sore knuckles, and simply carried on for the rest of the night. No yelling, no dumping on his favorite victim. Just, "Sarah, that four-top needs a refill." Or, "Don't forget to wipe those tables down." Nearly normal.

And believe me, I knew normal—I'd studied it. When I was little and spent the night at other kids' houses, I used to watch daddies. As if they were an exotic species, some sort of strange bird whose habits and plumage needed to be listed, memorized, saved for future reference. When I visited Sandy Lee Mercer, and her daddy teased her about liking red, when he hugged her and told her she'd grow up to live in a house with a red roof, drive a red car, and dress all her children in red, I took notes. At Maryann Woods's house, when her daddy came home and pretended he was too hungry to wait for dinner, when he said he'd have to eat her, instead, and the two of them play-wrestled on the living-room rug, I filed it away.

Daddies were live-in, fathers not necessarily so. Shepherd, as my mother made repeatedly clear, was a biological accident that had happened to me and her. We had to live with the consequences, but we didn't have to like them. And we certainly didn't have to like *him*. If there had been an Olympic event for speed swearing, Shepherd would have won a gold medal. Most Feelings Hurt in a Single Day? Shepherd had set records that would stand for years. Snarkiest Remark? Lowest Blow? Cheapest Trick? Shepherd was the titleholder, hands down. But when it came to nice, he wasn't even on the field.

I'd learned a long time ago, then, not to want my father around, not to confuse him with someone who might tickle, or hug, or play. But guess what? A few minutes after the staff had left and Mamselle's went dark, there we were, Shepherd and me, in a booth at Shake It Baby. Just like a regular, everyday, *normal* father and daughter. Except that Shepherd wasn't looking at me. Which was okay, because I wasn't sure I wanted him to see me not looking at him. Baylor might have written a poem about us, another one that could go on and on: Shepherd not looking at me, not looking at him, not looking at . . . You get the idea.

I'd ordered a soy smoothie and Shepherd had something in front of him that was about three feet high, smothered in pistachios and whipped cream. Not that he'd eaten any of it. "Did you know he ran a farm once?" he asked.

"Baylor?" I unwrapped a straw. "You mean with horses and cows, stuff like that?"

"Yeah." Shepherd caught my eye for a second, then looked down again. "What? You think poets are born that way?" He stirred the goop at the bottom of his bowl, but didn't lift his spoon. "You think his parents took one look at their baby, and said, 'Well, I'll be damned. We got ourselves a poet!'?"

This was the Shepherd I was used to, the Shepherd who made me feel like a jerk. What were we doing here, anyway? Besides forcing two sleepy waitresses in grass skirts to leave their conversation every few minutes and ask us if we needed anything? When Shepherd ordered coffee, one of them carried it over while the other sat down in a corner and rubbed her feet. (Which would have cost her her job at Mamselle's, for sure.)

"So he had this farm," I told him. "So what?"

"He had this one particular horse, see." Shepherd was careful now, trying to remember what Baylor had told him. He stared at the hula girl painted on the wall above our table. She was wearing a grass skirt like our waitresses, shaking a milk shake and her booty at the same time. "Actually, it was more like a pony," my father corrected himself. "Some pretty little white-footed thing that was running with a herd of wild horses he penned."

"And?"

"And nothing. Just that little pony horse presented certain problems that only a guy who knew what he was doing could work through.

"You couldn't be too gentle, otherwise she'd never learn." He was actually looking at me now. "But on the other hand, you needed to go easy, let her have her head sometimes."

I shook my own head, and would have laughed out loud if I hadn't been so surprised. "Oh, my God, I don't believe it," I told Shepherd. "Now I'm a metaphor?!"

"You're a what?"

"I'm a horse! I'm a freaking horse!" Finally I did laugh. But Shepherd was dead serious.

"Baylor says you got spirit, in a good way. He says you need someone smart enough to see how to bring it along." His ice cream had started to melt, but he didn't seem to notice. He leaned across the table and lowered his voice—another surprise, since I'd never heard him whisper to anyone but big tippers.

"You know, I wasn't always easy to handle when I was a kid. And coming down hard on me just made me fight back more." He took his first bite, buying time. "My old man came down so hard, I left home when I was fifteen." Another bite, a quick look at me. "Frankly? I think your mother can be a little too rough on you." I checked his eyes, before I looked back at my straw. Shepherd was for real.

"All this med-school stuff? It's not about you, Sarah; it's about her."

ME

(*Speechless*)

MY STRAW

Tssthththssssss. TssthssssSSSSSSSSSSSSSSSS.

SHEPHERD'S SPOON AND DISH

Crreeen. Currreeen. Citcitcit.

SHEPHERD

Did you know she was dating a doctor when she met me?

ME

(*Still speechless*)

HULA GIRL ON THE WALL

There's an island across the sea, beautiful Kauai, beautiful Kauai. . . .

SHEPHERD

Yeah. Some big deal-cancer doc.

HULA GIRL

Where my true love is waiting for me, beautiful Kauai, beautiful Kauai . . .

I felt cold all over, and it wasn't just the smoothie. I already knew I'd ruined Mom's life, but I didn't know that life had included a romance, one that might have lasted more than a few months.

"Or heart, something like that." Shepherd made eye contact again. "She never told you?"

No, she never told me.

"She said he was no fun, said he didn't know how to make her laugh."

"And you did?"

"Hey, your mother and me? We had something going. We were good for each other, you know what I mean? We were okay until . . ."

I knew what he meant: until Sarah the Surprise.

"Mr. MD? He was the happy ending that got away. 'I could have been a doctor's wife.' She must have said it a thousand times. 'I could have had respect.'

"Respect? What is it with your mother and respect? That and a nickel, right?"

One of the waitresses, her skirt rustling, brought the check now, and the coffeepot. Shepherd grabbed the bill from her hand and waved the coffee away. "Anyway, between a high school dropout for an ex and a JD for a daughter, it doesn't seem like respect is in the cards, does it?"

I guess it was the sly smile he gave me. The way he lumped us together as fellow failures, out to rain on Mom's parade. Suddenly I'd reached my Shepherd quota—for the day, for the week, for the foreseeable future. "Look," I told him. "I'm really glad we had this talk and all. But there's still another week of school, and I've got homework."

"So, Sarah." Shepherd leaned across the table again, missing a hint no one else could have ignored. "Do you ever write poetry in school? Rufus says you have a real ear."

He let that compliment hang in the air for a while. *A world-famous poet thought I had an ear?!*

"He also says he's jealous of me." The whisper was back: "Between you and me, Sarah? I think there's such a thing as being too famous. Rufus is, like, Exhibit A. Here he is, a household name, and he's jealous of a nobody like me."

"Rufus Baylor is jealous of *you*?!!"

"That's what the man said." Shepherd shrugged. "The point is, this classy, world-famous guy tells me he's made mistakes, lots of them.

"I tell him he hasn't exactly got a monopoly on screwing up, but he says the difference between him and me is I can still fix things."

I tried to remember what I knew about Baylor's life, but it wasn't much. I wished I'd been curious enough to research the real family that had once lived in "my" cottage. But I'd preferred the made-up one I'd put there, instead.

"Listen, what I'm trying to say is, I only got one kid and it's you. I can't give you the stuff your mother wants me to, but I can give you stuff she can't."

"Have you just found out you've got three months to live?" I was only half joking, but Shepherd ignored me.

"Baylor—er, Rufus says you're too smart to do what other people tell you. He says I'm the same way. And when we dig in our heels, we may have a real good reason, you know?"

"What on earth are you talking about, Shepherd?" I looked straight at him now. And guess what? He was looking straight back.

Mea Culpa

I forgive the wind, I know why it rattles the gate.
I love the lunging owl, the lance-eyed hawk,
whose flights bring death and pain.
In downward spirals, fits and starts,
all of us fall because we're alive
and rise to stay that way.

Distance grows the heart, not fonder, but too late.
I've missed the hurt, the heft of your wounds,
your blood is dried to crusts of shame.
In comings and goings, ins and outs,
each of us moves toward a home we miss
but that we cannot name.

A Manuscript Consultation

"I gave you a present for your seventh birthday. A present you never got."

It was still true confessions time at Shake It Baby. And if I could believe him, Shepherd had actually tried to be a father to Sarah the Surprise. Trouble is, I wasn't sure I could believe him. "If it came with a card," I said, "I didn't get that, either." *Not any card for any birthday. But who's counting?*

Shepherd, apparently, wasn't one for formalities. "I leave cards and stuff to your mother. Wrapping, too." His face turned harder now, his jaw as stiff as if it were wired. "But Kate never even bothered to wrap the pajamas I bought. She said you were a girl, and cowboys were all wrong."

"Cowboys?" Had Shepherd walked into a store? Compared patterns? Chosen one for me?

"But what's new? Everything I do is wrong." He rolled his napkin into a tight ball, pitched it onto the table. "Hey, that wasn't the only gift that didn't make the cut. I just don't shop at the right stores, you know?"

I knew about doing everything wrong. About giving up on trying to get it right. "Well," I told Shepherd, standing, wrestling into my sweater, "it's the thought that counts. But like I said, I've got—"

"Baylor says you helped him see one of his poems in a whole new way."

I sat back down. "I did?"

"Yeah. Says he's rewriting it."

More news. But this news sounded good. I looked down as soon as I felt myself smiling.

"Point is, if you decide you want to study something besides medicine? I've got your back."

"Did Rufus Baylor tell you to say this?"

"No, this is my idea. If somebody's good at something, they should do it, you know?

"Look at Manny. As much as he drinks and as many times as he's fucked up, I should have fired the guy years ago."

It was true. Since I'd been working at Mamselle's, I'd seen Chef Manny start grease fires, screw up orders, and not show up for work. In the Kingdom of Shepherd, anyone else who slipped up the way Manny did would have been long gone. "Why *don't* you can him?" I asked.

"Because," Shepherd told the wall, "he's good." He studied the bare feet of the painted hula girl. "In fact, when he's sober, Manny is the best."

I didn't know Shepherd looked up to anyone. I didn't know he cared about anything. I didn't know I had a choice about med school. Apparently, there was a lot I didn't know.

"Look, Sarah"—he turned back to me now—"sometimes I got a mouth on me."

Did he expect me to disagree with him?

"But I got a brain, too. If you have a chance to be the best at something—anything—you should grab it. I can help."

I didn't ask how. I didn't say "Thanks." Or, "No, thanks." Or, "What planet is this?" I just let Shepherd leave the waitress a too-big tip, pay the check, and drive me home. He didn't come into the house; some things hadn't changed. So when Mom asked me what had taken so long, I wasn't sure what to say. Finally, I settled for the truth. "We were talking," I told her.

"Who was talking?" she asked.

"Me and Shepherd," I said. I didn't blame her for the look on her face. I wouldn't have believed it, either.

Before I fell asleep, I must have replayed that scene at Shake It Baby a dozen times. All weekend, I thought about Shepherd wanting to give me cowboy pajamas, about Shepherd as a kid who ran away from home and tried to make it without an education. And I thought about the mistakes he said he and Rufus Baylor had made. Especially about those mistakes. Somewhere, in the middle of all that thinking, I stumbled on a brand-new question: Could fathers grow up?

I had questions about the Great One, too. I Googled "Rufus H. Baylor," and my laptop practically exploded. He'd done everything, been everywhere. But when I Googled "Rufus H. Baylor" and "mistakes," I didn't find any articles at all. First thing Monday, I took two books out from the school library and put a hold on a third. Unfortunately, someone had already checked out the one I really wanted, a biography of our new teacher, four-time Pulitzer winner and former Poet Laureate. But now that his visit had made the papers, I wasn't the only one in school interested in our poet. Still, Whale Point's never-say-die librarian, Ms. Sawyer, hated to let a possible book junkie leave empty handed, so she found me copies of *Poems for Sale*, Baylor's first published work, and *The Wait-a-Minute Bush*, his last volume of poems.

I didn't have much time after school, but before I went to sleep that night, I opened *Poems for Sale*. I lay in bed and pretended Baylor was reading to me out loud. I heard every poem I read in that deep, slow drawl of his, and all the words made a sort of music that, instead of putting me to sleep, kept me awake, trying to figure out how he did it. How could he talk and sing at the same time? How could he start out saying one thing and leave me thinking another? Why did it feel like he was right inside my head when he looked at the world? Why did I feel smarter, bigger, better, after every poem?

Women in Medicine was finally over, I didn't have to sit through those boring videos after school, and Tuesday was my first trip to the beach with Fry and H. It was also the first chance I'd had to watch Fry surf, except for my pre-princess days, when I'd followed his exploits from a distance. Even the Untouchables were grudging fans. I remembered Eli, the Pack's resident skeptic, pausing construction on a Victorian sand castle the summer before. He'd raised his ever-present binoculars and studied the handsome boy who was riding waves no one else even tried. "You have to admit," he'd told the rest of us, "that kid knows what he's doing out there. It's like he's got water for brains."

But today the water lay as smooth and shiny as a snakeskin . . . and just as flat. "How come I caught a million monsters yesterday, and now?" Fry looked at the ocean as if it had calmed on purpose just to spite him. "Nothing but ankle busters." After H and I had watched him float his board on the water, waiting not very patiently for anything that resembled a wave, we all settled for moving back up the beach, spreading our towels out by the cooler, and listening to our budding poet's new ode to Miss Kinney. H told me he was anxious to get a response from someone who hadn't been present at his poem's creation.

"I want a totally objective opinion." He unfolded the piece of paper he'd put in a plastic baggie, presumably because it was too precious to get sand on. He lifted his sunglasses to look me in the eyes. "This has to be perfect before I take it to Julie. I need you to be honest."

Oh. Oh. I'd just spent the night before poring over Rufus Baylor's book, so I knew what good poetry was. Now, as I listened to H, sighing after every adjective, shaking the paper for emphasis, I also knew what it wasn't.

When he'd finished, I answered slowly, taking my time. "Don't you think that fourth line is a little bit long?" I didn't want to hurt his feelings, not in front of Fry, anyway. Not here, tucked into the sandy underbelly of a giant dune. Not with one thigh pressed against Fry's sun-warmed leg and the lazy shimmer of summer all around us.

"My man and Margaret think it's great." H, already defensive, looked at Fry. "Right?" He folded the paper up again and stowed it carefully inside his backpack, then wedged the pack behind the ancient cooler that held melting ice, leftover chips, half a container of pineapple salsa, and naturally, beer. I'd bought the salsa and chips (as well as ginger ale for me, the only reformed drinker in our trio), and the guys had managed the beer. It was a pale lager, not Fry's favorite, but underage beggars can't be choosers.

"That poem has heart," Fry assured me. "It's sexy without being rude." He looked proud enough that I was suddenly afraid he'd had more than a little to do with creating this monster. "It kind of sneaks up on what the poet's thinking, you know? It's got a beat you can dance to." He studied the foam in the paper cup that camouflaged his beer. "Plus it rhymes," he added, as if this were the clincher.

I remembered Fry's face the night he'd listened to me read the role I never played. The way he'd studied my mouth without listening to the words I said. We'd hit the Great Divide again, the place Fry and I always ended up. My prince saw things one way, and except for a few basics (pizza, hugs, and sleeping late), I usually saw them another. The Great Divide made talking hard, kissing easy.

"Can you let me see it again, H?" I offered. "Maybe listening to it went too fast." I sat up and watched him sigh, retrieve the pack, unfold the poem, and hand it to me.

I felt two pairs of eyes burning hopeful holes in me while I studied the page. I was sure that if I read the lines over, I'd find something special, something I could honestly say I liked in at least one of them. But the poem was actually worse the second time around. If those lines had been part of a script, no one could have said them with a straight face.

Desperate, I read the poem one last time, the silence heavy as the heat. I wished we were back in that surf, even though it was nothing but a placid skim of white lace. I wished H had decided to win Miss Kinney with flowers or a kitten or good grades. I wished he and Fry would stop staring and start breathing.

I looked up from the page now, determined to lie. I scanned the horizon, following the shoreline. I waited for inspiration, but none came.

BEACH

(*Quiet in a waiting way*)

OCEAN

Shloooom, shhhh, shloooom, shhhh, shlooom.

Why did it matter, anyway? What were these phony Valentine words next to what Rufus Baylor had told us about the fire? No wonder we couldn't write the kind of poetry he did. Which of us had hearts big enough to forgive the things he'd forgiven?

GULLS

KREEE! KREEE! KREEEEEEEE! KREE!

ME

(*Quiet in a stalling way*)

MY PRINCE

HOLY SHIT!

Saved by whatever had made Fry leap up from our towel and start digging through the cooler, I jumped up, too. "What's wrong?" I asked, not really caring, just glad I could stop thinking about poetry, good or bad.

"Beach patrol!" Fry grabbed our paper cups and, forgetting I wasn't drinking beer, emptied all three of them onto the sand under our blanket. Then he pulled three soda cans from the cooler and passed one to H and one to me. "Don't look back," he growled when the two of us turned to check the stretch of beach behind us.

I handed the piece of paper with the poem to H, who stashed it quickly as if poetry, like beer, might be something the beach patrol was on the lookout for. By the time the orange dune buggy with the leaping swordfish on its side had reached us, we were model, if nervous, beach bums. H high-fived the driver, who was a friend of Span's, and I small-talked with the girl beside him, who had been president of the drama club when I was a freshman. (She'd gone to acting school in New York, and came back every summer to do open-air theater.)

It turned out the two lifeguards had just a few minutes before they went off duty, and were simply killing time with us. Weekdays were slow, they told us, especially when the water was this calm. Today's excitement had consisted of one sick kid and a souvenir hunter who'd tried to rip off a NO SWIMMING PAST JETTIES sign. They were definitely not looking for drama at 5 p.m. Thank goodness.

Once the all-terrain had rumbled off on its puffed-up tires, both H and Fry had forgotten all about the poem. The two of them fist-bumped and chortled, and generally congratulated themselves on how cool they'd been and on how narrowly we'd all avoided a very unpleasant second date with the Whale Point police.

"I do not want to see that no-lips DA ever again." Fry was already packing up, shaking out our towels and folding them into sloppy squares. For what it's worth? That wasn't actually true about the DA having no lips. It's just that whenever he'd made a point to the judge at our hearing, he had stopped and looked at her with his eyebrows joined and his lips sucked in.

And, let's face it, he had lots of points to make. All the things we'd destroyed. All the bad choices we'd made. "Party animals," he'd called us. Hardly human. Thugs who didn't know any better than to throw up or pee on someone else's life.

"Got to give the Whale Point Beach Patrol props, man," H told Fry. "They have a nose for trouble. Remember when we took your cousin's Jeep out on the dunes at North Beach?"

"Yeah." Fry looked positively nostalgic. "We just missed a thousand-dollar fine that night. Who knew they used undercover SUVs, huh?"

And then they were off, talking about the glory days. It was as if the fire had never happened. As if the trial were a movie they'd seen and already forgotten. What counted more, what totally absorbed them, were the days they had courted disaster, just the two of them. The days Fry now labeled BS, Before Sarah. All the way home, even though I was in the backseat beside Fry, I might as well have stayed at the beach. All the near misses, all the hilarious comebacks, and the sly moves—they were all BS.

Which made me wonder why I was the only one who couldn't put the trial behind us. Who kept playing the days before the bash over in my head every chance I got: What if I'd said, loud and clear, "I don't want to do this"? What if I'd told Fry how much that little house meant to me?

"What's up, Sarah?" Fry had finally noticed I was staring out the window instead of waiting breathlessly for the next adventure of Fry Man and Lieutenant H.

And that's when I thought of it. "I'm not really the best judge of poetry," I told them now. "Why don't we take H's poem to the source?"

They both looked at me, waiting.

"I know where Rufus Baylor is staying. The house is right on the next block." It sounded so logical. It made such sense. "Let's show *him* H's poem."

"Are you kidding?" Fry stifled a laugh. "Go see the teacher when school's out?" He let his laugh go now, but it came out more like a growl. "The court can order me to see that old man during class, but nothing's going to make me kiss up to him in my free time."

H, for once, felt differently. "Do you really think he'd look at it?"

I remembered Baylor's marble eyes, his smile. I pictured the four of us sitting in a living room, instead of a classroom. "I'm sure he would," I told H.

H checked out his *jefe* in the rearview. "We could just drop it off, man. It would only take a second." He turned to look at us now, full face, and delivered the clincher: "It's for love."

The four of us, sitting in a beach cottage: wicker furniture, a straw rug, a fishnet or a pod of tin dolphins on the wall. Wouldn't it be easier to tell our poet there? To slip it into conversation? To say, "I didn't mean it. I'm sorry. I'm so sorry."

It took some negotiation. And it took promising that H and I would leave the poem with Baylor while Fry stayed in the car. It wasn't hard at all to find the place. The walk there with my mother came back easily, since it was probably the longest continuous hand-holding we'd ever done. (She couldn't find a sitter, the interview was important, and I was much too young to leave at home.) A few minutes later, then, H pulled up in front of the bungalow that was now the temporary home of the world's most famous bard. On the outside, it didn't look very different from the cottages on each side of it; its only distinction, and the only memory I had of the place, was a giant magnolia tree that nearly dwarfed the little house and that shed pale-pink petals all over the walk to the front door.

But when Baylor opened that door, nothing looked like I'd expected: There were no fishnets or tin dolphins, no rattan carpet. Instead, there were flowers everywhere . . . and a very angry guard cat. Our poet smiled when he saw us, but the calico that had wrapped itself around his feet was a lot less friendly. It was one of the biggest cats I'd ever seen, and it hissed and whined so loudly that both H and I stepped back. "Allow me to introduce Carmen," Baylor told us. "She comes with the house."

The orange monster continued to spit at us until Baylor stooped down and scooped it up in his arms, scratching its ears in a fearless, roughhouse caress I would never have dared. "Her bark is much worse than her bite." He stroked the cat again, which started up a rumble that sounded like an outboard but was probably a purr. "In fact, she has almost no teeth."

Our teacher seemed glad to see us. But then, Baylor seemed glad to see everyone. "I wish you could stay," he told us. "But they've invited me to a boat launch. I'm afraid I have to leave in a few minutes." He was wearing the jacket I'd seen him in at Mamselle's, but underneath it, his jeans and T-shirt announced he wasn't big on dressing up, even for special occasions.

"I've been to so many ribbon cuttings and grand openings in the last few days," he told us, "I'm getting handshake blisters." Which didn't stop him from shaking *our* hands, from offering us seats on an overstuffed sofa surrounded by souvenirs from his hosts' world travels (masks from Bali, he explained, tapestries from Guatemala, kimono belts from Japan). But overwhelming everything, filling half the room and forcing us to push them aside to see each other, were dozens of floral arrangements. There were vases of peonies and irises on the coffee table and end tables, pots of tulips and begonias on the mantel and floor and bookcases, not to mention a cluster of small fruit trees wearing WELCOME TO WHALE POINT ribbons on their trunks. Our teacher caught us staring at the plant life that had taken over the place. "Y'all live in an extremely friendly town," he acknowledged. "They say hello with flowers."

"Everybody's glad you're here," I told him. I remembered the poetic signs at the supermarket, the Baylor specials all over town. "Very glad."

"Even us," H added before he realized what he'd said. "I mean, it's a pleasure to be punished by you." He heard himself again, and knew he hadn't made things better. "That is, I—"

"I think I understand, Mr. . . . who are you, young man? I'm ashamed to say I remember your Taurus, but not your name." Rufus Baylor leaned back in the armchair he'd pulled up to face us, and Carmen the Cat That Ate Cleveland jumped up to settle in his lap.

"Hector, sir. Hector Losada."

"Well, Hector and Sarah Not Sarai, how can I help before I'm off to launch that boat?" He stroked Carmen's head, and the roar-purr started up again.

"You see, sir." H reached for the precious polyethylene packet, and took out the page on which he'd written his opus to Miss Kinney. "I've created a poem." He held it out, as if it were an offering.

I've created a poem?! He made it sound like he'd just finished the *Mona Lisa*. Or carved those faces on Mount Rushmore.

"For me?" Baylor leaned forward, ready for more flowers, another welcome-to-Whale-Point tribute.

Latin toughs might not blush, but H sure looked embarrassed. "Not exactly, sir. You see, I wrote this for someone special." More embarrassment. "I mean, someone *else* special." He watched Baylor unwrap the paper, and I swear I smelled sea salt and beer as those hammy, overblown words, hit the air. "It's just that I'd like to make sure it's good enough before she sees it."

Baylor looked up from the page, smiled. "You'd like a manuscript consultation?"

H looked uncertain. "I think so, sir."

Our poet folded the poem up again, stood, and deposited Carmen on the floor. The cat looked surprised, but preserved her dignity by pretending she had somewhere better to be. She shook herself, then ambled slowly toward the kitchen we could see behind a counter that ran along the back of the room.

Meantime, Baylor had wrestled his way between the Welcome trees to a sleek teak desk across the room. It didn't look anything like the rolltop he'd worked on at the cottage, but it was obviously what he was using now. It was piled high with papers and letters and two old tin cups bristling with pens and pencils. He laid H's poem on top of one of the paper piles. "I'd be glad to look this over, Hector. But I'm afraid I can't do it justice right now."

H was clearly unhappy about leaving his sacred poem with anyone, even Rufus Baylor. To give him credit, though, he shook our host's hand again and walked beside him to the door. All with only one worried glance at the desk where his masterpiece lay.

Baylor must have caught the look. (Did the man miss anything?) "I'll give your poem back in class Thursday," he assured H. "That will give me time to live with it, soak it in."

H seemed satisfied, even excited. So we said good-bye, walked out of the cottage with our poet, then watched him get into his mess of a car and drive off. As he did, I couldn't help wondering how Rufus Baylor would hold up under the strain of keeping his promise. How could anyone bear, even for a few days, to live with Hector Losada's poetry?

For JK from HL

Your nearness makes everyone sigh
Your beauty makes class fly
Your hair makes an honest man lie
Your gentle touch makes me want to just curl up and die.

So please take pity on me, sighing and poor
because my heart is yearning to soar
to that faraway heaven behind your locked door
where we two will be happy forevermore.

I Miss Old Friends and Visit a New Neighbor

Fry had spent the time, while we were visiting Baylor, doing what he loved. He'd listened to music, and now he was ready to listen to more. "Let's go back to H's," he proposed, pulling out his earbuds and wrapping his arm around me. "I feel a retrospective coming on."

Which could only mean Millennial Carolina Funk: little-known bands that he and H had discovered when they were both in junior high. It wasn't music that I knew or, truth be told, cared about. And it was sure to lead to more reminiscences about times and fun that were all Before Sarah. But of course, when I settled into the nest his arms made and Fry whispered that he couldn't wait to share the next song with me (passing me half his headset so that the cord was stretched like a heart between us), I knew I'd ride along. Go along. Tag along.

That song, it turned out, was one Fry and H had first heard live at a club two towns over. A club that had never carded and, not surprisingly, no longer existed. So even before we got to H's place, the two of them were in full nostalgia mode. And I was left out. Again. I had no one to talk to about my adventures Before Fry, such as they were. My BF days had gone up in flames, right along with Rufus Baylor's memories. There was no way my old friends would want to talk to me now. And the truth was, even before I became convinced they were ashamed of me, I had acted as if I were ashamed of them. Who knows? Fry might have learned to like them, even if he wouldn't get all their jokes. Even if he didn't share their love of art films, or '60s TV, or fantasy games. But I never took a chance. One awkward moment between Wanda and H, and I'd given up.

While Fry and H were going down memory lane, then, I was feeling pretty sorry for myself. And missing the friends I'd never even told good-bye: Alicia, who loved Middle-earth and all things orange, especially her apricot-colored granny shawl. Brett, who along with Marcia, Thea, Eli, and me made up our homework theater, where we acted out assignments. (Eli had worn a beard and glasses when he was Pythagoras for geometry, even though we explained that glasses weren't invented before right triangles.) And Wanda and George, who both had red hair and who liked poetry almost as much as Miss Kinney did, who still waved when they saw me in the hall. I sometimes waved back, unless I was with Fry, who usually had his arm around me, so I didn't want to move. *Stay.*

It wasn't just my friends I missed. I was in theater withdrawal, too. Since my understudy's role last fall, I hadn't tried out for a single production. But I still remembered that jumped-up, scrambled feeling in my stomach just before the curtain went up. And the way the shabby, one-sided sets and thrift-store furniture suddenly became real, while relatives and friends in the audience faded into a hazy, underexposed photo behind the lights.

"Coast is clear, *cuates*." H pulled his car into the empty driveway. Both his parents were still at work. "Let's finish that beer."

We lugged the cooler inside, and sat in the immaculate living room to unpack the drinks and salsa on a light wood coffee table that was practically begging for a stain. (I hoped Mrs. Losada didn't feel the way my mother did about chips and sweaty cans.) Fry and I took the sofa, and H corralled the recliner, tilting himself and his beer as far back as he could go. "Here's to the last three days of school," he announced, taking a long sip, then sighing and belching at once as he settled into the chair.

"Whoa! I just saw a ghost." Fry shook his head at H, not a slow, that's-amazing shake, but fast and hard, as if he were trying to knock something loose. "My dad used to fall into his chair exactly like that." Fry's father had died when he was twelve, and he hardly ever talked about him. Now I felt his body tense up beside me. It made the whole room tighter, more uncomfortable, as if the walls had just moved in on us.

"Whenever he was well enough, he'd come downstairs." It wasn't even Fry's voice we were hearing. It was smaller, quieter, and not at all cool. "Then he'd call me over to sit on the arm of his chair. 'Small Fry,' he'd say, 'how was your day?'"

He was staring straight ahead. I thought of Shepherd not looking at me not looking at him. Fry was seeing someone, all right. But it wasn't H or me. "Of course, I never got to tell him. The phone was always ringing. Sometimes he'd talk straight through dinner."

"Hey, man," H jumped right in, fearless. "Your dad? He did what he had to, you know?"

For once, I was glad it was H's full-time job to put Fry first, to keep him happy. Fry downed half his can now, and I felt the tension melt away. "Yeah, I guess," he said. "Making book is the perfect job for someone who can't get out of bed."

It was my strict policy not to ask my prince about his dad, because whenever anyone else did, it put him on edge. But I was father-hungry enough to have pieced together the story, the story of a miner who'd retired to the shore on disability, then wasted away from lung disease. Someone who took sports bets out of his home until the day he collapsed and died. "It was a good day," Fry told me once. "Everyone went heavy for the Vikings, but the Redskins won."

Now he scooped the last of the salsa up with a chip. "So let's talk about something else," he said. "Something with a little more flavor."

He grinned at H. "It's your house, your call. Pepperoni, or meatballs with anchovies?"

I hoped H would opt out of anchovies (I always picked them off, anyway), and I also hoped that, someday, I wouldn't have to learn about Fry secondhand. I'd never known, for instance, that his nickname came from his dad calling him Small Fry. Any more than I'd guessed what missing there must have been behind that smart remark about the Vikings. Knowing that Fry dreamed of daddies, too, made me want to put my arms around him.

I knew some guys weren't good at showing their feelings, and my own life certainly wasn't loaded with people of either gender who did. But wasn't that part of being in love? Weren't you supposed to confide things to your girlfriend? Things you wouldn't tell anyone else, not even your second-in-command, who never left your side and who might as well have been your brother since you spent so much time together, more even than you devoted to said girlfriend? What if Fry had been able to let me in?

Soul baring and pizza aren't really a good fit, though. Once the pie arrived, the safest topic of conversation was, once again, ancient history. H remembered the time he and Fry were in seventh and eighth grades, and too young to know that the "haunted house" three seniors dared them to visit was actually a funeral home. And Fry recalled the night he, H, and two blind dates found a giant dead shark on the beach.

Me? I let them talk, while I remembered, too. Once, after I'd landed a small part in our junior high spring play, Alicia and Marcia knew how nervous I was. They came to my house every day after school to feed me my two lines. By the time the play started, they knew them as well as I did. Long after the show, we used them as codes: "Alas! I have been poorly used in this affair" meant we didn't get the test grade we thought we should have. And "I foreswear your proposal, Sir Edgar" meant we didn't want to do what someone asked us to.

I didn't mention these memories, of course. Play rehearsals weren't likely to compete with funeral homes for Fry's attention. But I couldn't help thinking what fun it had been for the three of us girls to have our own secret language. It was just as thrilling, and lots more useful, than finding a dead shark. Even now, I was sure that if I'd walked up to either Alicia or Marcia that very minute and told her, "I foreswear your proposal, Sir Edgar," she would have known exactly what I meant. And I was afraid, in a way I had no words for, that this made me closer to both those old friends than I could ever get to Fry.

* * * *

There was only one more day until poetry school. I could have waited. But I found myself walking to Rufus Baylor's home away from home the very next afternoon. I took his first book of poems with me because I wanted to ask him about the one that was already my favorite. I told myself the reason I didn't let Fry or H know where I was going, was that I didn't want H pestering our resident celebrity about returning his pathetic poem.

The truth, though, was that I needed the chance to tell our poet what I'd been trying to all along: I wanted to make sure he knew how sorry I was about what we'd done to his long-ago cottage by the bay. I hadn't managed to apologize on that last visit with H, and I wanted another chance. It was an apology that wasn't really meant for witnesses, anyway. It was just between Rufus Baylor and me.

I probably should have called first, the Hendricks' number was sure to be in the Whale Point directory. But something told me Baylor was home. And something told me he wouldn't mind company.

"Sarah!" I loved the way he said my name. As if he'd just opened his door on the best possible surprise. As if there were no one else he'd rather invite in. And offer tea. (I said, "No, thank you.") And ask about school. (I stalled.)

"It's all right, I guess." I kept my eyes on Carmen while I answered. She was just as puffed-up and scary as I remembered, but she didn't hiss at me this time. Instead, she kept her distance, sitting by Baylor's chair, not like a normal cat, all cuddly and drowsy, but bolt upright, as if she figured she might have to fight off an attack any second.

I didn't have the heart to tell our poet that the last week of school was almost always a wash. Both teachers and students knew we'd get nothing done, but, for very different reasons, we agreed to put in the time, anyway. I told him, instead, about Miss Kinney and how she adored every word he'd ever written. "She wrote a note to you," I said, "and we're bringing it to class tomorrow. I think it's sort of a love letter." I remembered the time (okay, the endless minutes that passed like hours while our beach day got shorter and shorter) our teacher had taken over her letter. "Only checked four thousand times for grammar and spelling."

Baylor laughed. "I hope she doesn't think poets use red pencils. I'm afraid I'd disappoint her in that regard, Sarah. I'm inclined to dangle participles, you know."

He sounded as if he'd just confessed to teasing babies or stealing flowers, so I laughed, too.

It wasn't long, though, before he figured out that school was far from my favorite topic. That was when he nodded at the book I was clutching like some sort of talisman, something that would help me say and do the right thing. "Would you like me to sign that for you?" he asked.

"You can't, sir," I said. "It's a library book."

He smiled. He did that a lot. And then he waited.

"It's just, well, I had a question, Mr. Baylor."

"Call me Rufus." Still smiling. Still waiting.

I wanted to, really I did. But like I told you, I'd been raised to believe first names between adults and kids meant no holds barred, the end of civilization as we know it. "It's about one of your poems, Ruf—Mr. Baylor." I opened the book, leafed through until I found the page. "I was wondering how you made it say one thing and mean even more." I held the book so he could read the poem. "I mean, it talks about poetry, right? But it could also be about everything else, too." Was I wrong? Was I making a fool of myself? "Everything in the entire world."

There wasn't a nanosecond between my question and Rufus Baylor's answer. So I had next to no time to feel foolish before I felt wonderful. "You bet, it is!" our poet said. "Put a poem or a sunset in front of some folks, and all they'll do is try to figure out how they can own it, cut it down to size.

"Same goes for a good bottle of wine, a garden, or a friend." He stood up, then stepped carefully around Mega Cat. "Now how about you and I have that tea you turned down a minute ago? It comes with cookies?"

I remembered how Span had said his friends would be impressed to know he'd shaken hands with Rufus Baylor. I figured even fewer people could say they had drunk tea with the Great One.

But *I* did. Or I almost did. My host was in the kitchen with Carmen, putting the water on, when the doorbell rang. That first time it was a pair of reporters. They didn't look official, since they were wearing jeans, just like us. But they showed their press badges and acted way too full of themselves, so I figured they were genuine. They wanted to interview our poet about the first class he'd taught. And when they found out one of his students was visiting, they wanted to interview me, too.

"I'd be obliged if y'all would come back tomorrow," Baylor told them when he joined us. The pair looked around the room, then stared hard at me, particularly the woman reporter. It was a greedy look she gave me, but with a lot of sneer thrown in for good measure. It made me feel like I'd won a contest I'd never even entered.

Finally, though, the news snoops asked what time would be good tomorrow, and Baylor told them around five. After they'd gone, I shook my head. "Isn't five o'clock when we'll be in class?" I asked.

Baylor grinned. "I think you're right, Sarah," he told me. But his smile wasn't that much broader than usual, and his tone was so close to innocent, I couldn't be sure whether he'd just made a mistake or given the media the slip.

Tea with Rufus Baylor, Part II, didn't last much longer than Part I had. A few minutes later, the doorbell rang again. I have to admit, it was pretty annoying. Not just because our poet was so popular, but also because the sound the bell made was like an orchestra, not a normal doorbell. Baylor said he wished a whole symphony didn't start up each time someone came to visit.

This time it was a woman from the bookstore. A young woman who had a lot in common with Miss Kinney, particularly her charter membership in the Rufus Baylor Adulation Society. She had a long dark braid, an armload of books, and lots of big plans for "the most amazing author visit Whale Point Books has ever seen." (Which wasn't actually surprising, since I couldn't remember a single author ever appearing there, except a prof at the community college who'd published his own book about barnacles. No joke. *Barnacles.*)

Rufus signed and nodded, nodded and signed. By the time I had to leave, he'd agreed to a reading, a signing, and probably a dance routine. That last part *is* a joke, but from the earnest look on Book Lady's face and the way our poet kept nodding, there's no telling what he agreed to.

I should have been sorry that I didn't have the chance to say what I'd come to say. That I still hadn't apologized for my part (okay, my starring role) in the Destruction of Rufus Baylor's Historically Preserved

Summer Home. I should have been upset, too, that I didn't get more time alone with our new teacher. But the truth is, I was too excited to care. After all, I'd just almost had tea with the most famous poet on Earth. And even though I was much too nervous to do it, said famous poet had asked me to call him Rufus!

I Gave a Poem to Two Women

The first took the poem and hung
it in her closet. "How nice," she said,
leaving the door open, letting
the colors run out behind her.
"When I wear it, people will say,
'Doesntthatpoemlookgoodonher?'
Thank you."

The second woman took my poem
and sat with it, her face suspicious,
grave. At last, she poked it with one
finger, then gave it a sucker punch,
trying to catch it off guard. She
sniffed it, daring it, staring it down
nose to nose.

Suddenly, she shot out her tongue
and licked one side of the poem from
bottom to top. She took it in her arms

and squeezed it as hard as she could.
Next, she and the poem moved
around the room together, locked
like dancing bears.

After that first meeting, the poem
moved in with the woman. She set
a place for it at meals and dabbed it,
like perfume, behind her ears. She
dragged it everywhere, so it picked
up things like a sticky wrapper that
said CAREFREE SUGARLESS.

She didn't protect the poem at all.
She scratched it and dropped it
and dribbled it and chewed it. She
put it under a magnifying glass
and under her feet. She slept with it
every night. And she never said
thank you.

The Second Class

Thursday afternoon was clear and sunny. It was a perfect beach day, soft, not steamy, with just enough breeze to keep a kite up. *If* we'd had kites. And *if* we'd been at the beach. Instead, of course, we drove to the community college. But Rufus (I could call him that in my head, even if I couldn't manage it out loud yet) knew just what this weather was good for. And it wasn't talk-talk-talking inside.

We met in the classroom, then formed a straggly parade, our poet at the front and Charles Fenshaw, Celebrity Shadow, bringing up the rear. We marched down the hall, out the rear entrance, and into the gardens the ag students had planted. I'd never been farther than the patio out back, but there was a lot more. The grounds stretched for acres and acres, so Fry and I stayed close to Rufus, in case he tripped on a stone or dropped his cane. Or worse, fell and, like those helpless old people on television, couldn't get up. As it turned out, though, we didn't need to worry.

Rufus had caught fire, become someone younger, someone barely related to that old man we'd seen in newspaper photos and news footage. He still carried his walking stick, sure. But it seemed more like a stage prop than anything he actually needed. He made his way up and down winding paths, over rocks and streams, and seemed at home wherever he went: If a bird flew overhead, he could tell by its shape and the way it moved its wings what species it was. If we passed a bush, he called it by name, in English and Latin. When a butterfly landed on Margaret's shoulder, he told us not only that it was a female, but what kind of pollen it liked and how long it would probably live. He treated the whole world like a poem he knew by heart.

We followed him along a dirt path, then onto a shaded slope that overlooked the main garden. He walked straight to a giant tree, leaned his walking stick against the trunk, and, finally, sat down. The rest of us spread out in the grass around him. I counted, and yes, everyone, even Thatcher Vogel, of the perpetual smirk, was present and accounted for. Thatcher still looked like he thought this whole thing was a big joke, as though he had much better things to do than sit, his tattooed arms folded across his broad chest, in the grass under a tree, for God's sake. At first, I wondered if Dr. Fenshaw agreed with him, because the prof didn't join us on the grass, but stayed standing, one leg braced against the tree.

"I'd tell you the name of this big fellow," our poet said, patting the bark of the tree, "but I'm afraid he doesn't know it himself." He looked up into the canopy of leaves above him, then into the placid face of the CC prof. "He can't make up his mind, you see, whether he's a hickory or a pecan." A smile with some devil in it. "Just like Charles here, who can't decide whether to stand up or sit down."

The prof flushed, then took off his jacket, folded it into a neat square, and sat on it beside our poet, his back against the tree. Grass stains, apparently, scared him almost as much as Rufus Baylor did.

"Some folks call this tree a *hican*," Baylor explained. "But mixed up or not, the nuts make fine pie." Same smile, minus the devil. "Glad you could join us, Charles. And now, I'd like y'all to meet someone."

He nodded toward the mounds of tiny purple flowers that spread from under the tree to the edge of its long shadow across the grass. "Allow me to introduce *Lamium*." Our poet waved his cane toward the flowers. Their chalky, mint-green leaves had dark edges, as if a child had crayoned an outline around each one. Nestled in the leaves were pale purple blossoms, like tiny surprised mouths. "If you saw her in winter, you'd know why some folks call her dead nettle."

He reached into the hican's shadow to pick a handful of the miniature flowers, then twirled them between his fingers. "She withers away until you'd swear there was no life in her. Turns out, though"—I'm telling you he looked straight at me when he said this—"laid low doesn't mean down for the count."

He placed the flowers on the grass in front of him, then slipped a small brown notebook from his pocket. The tuft of *Lamium* he'd chosen had three small blossoms, already bedraggled and thirsty. They reminded me of Alicia, Marcia, and me, practicing my lines for that seventh-grade play. *Alas!* I wanted to tell the little flowers. *You are poorly used.*

"Let's work on another poem." Rufus opened the notebook in his lap, and I held my breath. I couldn't believe he'd already started a new poem. Had we inspired him that much?

"It isn't finished," he told us. He took a pen out of his other pocket. "In fact, it isn't even started.

"Thing is," he said, taking his time, keeping us guessing, "I was hoping y'all would help me write this one."

The class got quiet fast. Someone laughed nervously. Someone else swatted a no-see-um. (Twilight was those hungry little bugs' favorite time of day, poetry or no poetry.) "You see, I had a visit from some reporters yesterday. In fact, Miss Wheeler was there, too."

When Baylor looked at me, so did everyone else. I was half embarrassed, half thrilled. But it wasn't until Fry caught my eye that I was ashamed. I'd never told him about my visit to Baylor's house. Now I knew why.

"They want to interview me about what we're doing in this class. And I'd like to tell them we're making poetry, not just talking about it." He studied us with those marble eyes of his. "Deal?"

Finally, Margaret raised her hand and our poet nodded. So she asked what most of us were wondering: "What should we write about, sir?"

"That doesn't really matter, Miss . . . ?"

"Chasteen, sir. Margaret Chasteen." Margaret, blushing furiously, turned almost as crimson as Fenshaw.

"Anything you write will be about you, Miss Chasteen," Rufus told her. "And anything I write will be about me." He glanced at the rumpled purple blossoms in front of him. "I could write about *Lamium* here, but most every word I say will have my mark on it. One-tenth *Lamium*, nine-tenths Rufus Baylor."

He saluted Margaret now, with just a tap of his hand beside his head. "Thanks to Miss Chasteen, here, I think we've gone and found our poem's subject."

He put the notebook on the grass and leaned over those flowers as if he were going to inhale them. "I want y'all to take a good look now, up close and personal."

We obliged, each of us focusing laser eyes on the wilting leaves and the straggly, fingertip-size blooms he'd laid on the grass. I kind of liked the stubborn little face I saw in one of them. It wasn't a man in the moon, it was a girl in the flower. Under her pink, down-turned hood, two small, dark eyes peered out at me.

"What makes *Lamium* different?" our poet asked. "What words will let you take her home with you? Keep her always?"

He clicked his pen top, picked up the notebook. "Does the word 'pretty' measure her? Does 'beautiful'?"

A few hands shot up, but Baylor didn't call on anyone. "Feel before you talk," he warned us. He glanced at the grass, where some petals had already worked their way loose from one of the flowers. "Y'all get one chance apiece, so make it count."

And would you believe seventeen kids and two teachers sat, staring at a few flowers no bigger than a dime? Okay, maybe not seventeen. Maybe Thatcher Vogel and a few of his friends rolled their eyes when Baylor wasn't looking. Or stared into space, communing with their own dumbness. But the rest of us? Solemn, silent as church for almost two minutes.

It was Coral Ann Levin, of the big hair and bigger mouth, who raised her hand in a way that cut through the silence. In a way that said, *Case closed, I've got the answer and we can all go home.*

Baylor nodded, asked her for her words.

She gave him just one. "Purple," she said.

Again, our poet nodded. "What *kind* of purple?" he asked.

Coral Ann wasn't expecting another question. She looked at the rest of us. Then, when it was clear we couldn't help, she looked back at Rufus, who, without a word, pointed at the *Lamium* on the grass. Coral Ann had no choice now. She folded her arms and directed a stare at those tiny flowers that should have disintegrated them on the spot. Finally, she laughed, nervous. "You'll think I'm silly," she said.

Our poet just nodded the way he did. The way that let you know he had all the time in the world. That he wanted you to say everything you needed to.

"Well, this here *Lamium*? It's the exact same pinky purple as the fancy smocked dress my mother made me in third grade."

"She made you a dress?" Rufus smiled as if he didn't believe her. "She didn't buy it?"

"No, sir," Coral Ann told him, looking sneaky proud. "She made it herself, every stitch. It was for my birthday, and it took her three days on account of all the gathers."

Rufus didn't say anything, just wrote in his brown notebook, then read us what he'd scribbled: "The color of my first dress, gathered with love."

Coral Ann's smile was bigger than ever. And the smug look, too.

Lots more got written in that notebook. Words and memories. Small things and big ones. A friend of Margaret's told us the see-through petals made her feel scared, the same way she did around her grandmother, whose skin was so thin you could watch the pulse in her veins. "Is there a heartbeat in those purple veins?"

I could have talked about the tough little flower face I'd seen, how it felt like Sarah, not Sarai. How I planned to take my own stem of *Lamium* home and press it between the two thickest books I owned, my dictionary and the *PDR*. But I didn't think our poet could fit all that onto one of those tiny pages. So I just told about the friends who'd helped me rehearse, and he wrote, "Three blooms, three friends, alas!" "And in case it makes any difference, Sarah," he added, smiling over that magic book of his, "I would have given you the lead."

Okay, maybe it's silly. But just hearing that from someone so smart and honest and, well, famous, made me feel smarter, too. Taller, even prettier. Until I felt Fry staring at me and turned to face him. He was smiling, too, but not in the open, sunny way our poet had. His was much closer to an I-told-you-so look than a good-for-you grin. I guess Baylor noticed, too, because for the first time ever, he called on someone rather than waiting till they raised their hand. He nodded at Fry. "Do you have something you'd like to say about these flowers, young man?"

Fry looked at our poet and then at the *Lamium*. As if he hadn't even noticed them before, as if he were considering them for the first time. And maybe he was. Because even though he waited so long I thought he was stalling, it turned out he was time-traveling instead. That smile he'd hurled my way like a stealth bomber melted into a different look, the dreamy sort of face people get when they're seeing a memory. "These flowers," he told our poet at last, "are the exact same color as the bruise I got when I was six." He looked at his arm, then back at the little flowers.

"My dad had to pull me out of a riptide." He shook his head, as if he'd surprised himself. "I was so proud of that spot on my wrist, I hoped it would never go away."

"A badge of love and pain," Rufus wrote in the book. But it was hard to tell if Fry even heard the line at all. He didn't move, hardly breathed, like he didn't want to leave the beach he saw in his head. For just a minute, Mr. Cool disappeared and the boy sitting next to me seemed younger, more vulnerable. But then our poet moved on to someone else, and Fry blinked. The sly look was back in his eyes, the look that measured, locked people out.

At first, Rufus was the only one to notice someone else had something to say. "I see you've got a notebook of your own, Charles," he told Fenshaw. "Sure sign of a poet. I take it you write verse now and then?"

For the second time in less than an hour, Fenshaw blushed. He snapped the notebook no one else had spotted closed. "Yes, sir," he said. "Occasionally. I just thought . . . well, I'd like to remember the way those loose petals look." He pointed to the petals one of the flowers had dropped, then stopped, embarrassed. Our poet nodded, asked him to go on and explain what he meant.

"Well, sir, it's just the way they've fallen on the grass there. I know it's a sympathetic fallacy." He looked at the blank stares and question marks we were telegraphing him. "I mean, I know I'm attributing human emotions to a natural object that can't experience them. But"—he cleared his throat, gathering courage—"they look to me, sir, like . . ."

Rufus nodded again.

"Like tears, sir."

But Rufus didn't let Fenshaw off any easier than he had the rest of us. "What kind of tears, Charles?" he asked, though his voice was gentle, and he seemed to be asking a question the prof wanted to answer, because this time there was no hesitation at all.

"I'd say good-bye tears, sir."

"Good-bye?"

"I suppose there can be hello tears, sir. But what I think of, when I look at those petals, is a child crying. A child who's leaving home."

Our poet nodded. "Sympathetic or not, Charles," he told the prof, "that fallacy of yours took you to a good place: 'Petals small as a child's tears good-bye.'"

It felt a little like church again, and everyone got quiet. Until Baylor used his cane to stand up, then read our poem from his book. And of course, he was right. It was one-tenth *Lamium* and nine-tenths us. We had opened up, the way most people did around him. And that made the poem open up, too, wide as a flower at noon.

H started it. While the poem was still settling in our heads, he clapped. Like he'd just heard the best concert performance ever. Fry joined in, then someone else, and pretty soon we were all clapping. (Yes, even Thatcher, though he might have been brushing something off his lap, it was hard to tell.) It felt good to make noise after being quiet so long. It felt better to have heard another brand-new poem. And it felt best of all that we'd helped write it.

Rufus grinned. "I'm glad we've introduced the themes of love and pain," he said. "Because I'm about to give you some more of both. You see, ladies and gentlemen, this course includes assignments."

Normally, there would have been groans and "I told you sos." But Baylor was so full of surprises, we just sat there, waiting. One boy even got out a pencil and paper to take notes. "For next week," our poet told us, "I want y'all to write a love poem."

Now somebody *did* groan, but H reached for the sky, waving his hand. "Sir," he asked, "would it be okay to say that your sweetheart's hair makes an honest man lie?"

Our poet had a good memory, even for things he might have preferred to forget. "It would be if you hadn't already written that line, Mr. Losada." He tapped his coat pocket, and sure enough—there was H's poem sticking out like a white handkerchief. "Besides, this assignment isn't that kind of love poem."

"It's not?" H, who had probably figured his homework was aced, sounded disappointed. "Then would it be okay to compare her lips to a pair of dead herring?" He directed a smug half wink at me, and I cringed, remembering my flip suggestion. Was this H's way of getting back at me for not liking his poem?

But suddenly Rufus was laughing. Long and loud. I didn't know about the others, but by now I loved the sound of that laugh so much I would have done or said just about anything to make it happen. I guess it was the way he gave himself over to smiling and laughing, the way he seemed to forget there was anything else that needed doing.

"It's not what you think," he said at last, wiping his eyes. "You're going to need to look in the mirror for this one." He slipped the notebook back in his pocket, reached for his stick. "You see, I want you to write a love poem to yourself." I could have been wrong, but now I got the feeling I'd had a few times before, the feeling that Rufus was looking just at me. "For some of you, who are blind to your own virtues, that may prove hard to do."

Lamium

Migraine dreams, jagged seams,
A badge of love and pain.
Or dreamy eyes, sleepy eyes,
Drooping, closing, losing light.
Packages scattered under the tree,
Some torn open, some tied tight.

Is there a heartbeat in those purple veins?
Are those embryos or mouths or rosary beads?
The color of my first dress, gathered with love,
Fairy cups stirred with blades of grass,
Notes clustered on a windy score,
Three blooms, three friends, alas!

Grape flowers, cloud flowers, love flowers,
Paper parasols upside down, a butterfly herd
Stopped to rest by a deep green pool.
Petals small as a child's tears good-bye,
Dropped stitches everywhere
From a blanket the color of sky.

Poetry Versus Medicine

After class, Rufus returned H's poetry. And do you know what he said when he handed back that mind-numbing love poem? "There's a lot of strong feeling between these lines, young man, make no mistake." The two of them talked for a long time afterward, and I didn't hear most of what they said. I only know that, on the ride home, H announced he'd decided not to give his poem to Miss Kinney. Not yet, anyway. It needed, he conceded, some polishing. "There's more stuff to learn," he told us. "And I might as well learn it from the greatest poet alive." He slipped a peek at Fry in his rearview. "While he still is, I mean."

Fry, on the other hand, was not in the mood for summer school. The first full week of vacation was just ahead, the waves were finally clean, so why waste any more time? He'd show up Saturday for the first cleanup, he told us, because there'd be someone from the court there. But he'd noticed that our poet didn't take roll. "Plus," he added, in the same sarcastic tone he'd begun to adopt whenever he mentioned Baylor, "I don't feel like watching that dirty old man drool all over my girl."

I was torn between the sweet shock of being called his girl and outrage at his labeling Rufus Baylor a dirty old man. "You're kidding, right?" I turned on Fry, who just folded those gorgeous arms of his and gave me the kind of sad smile you give someone who's the last to know.

"Why didn't you tell me you were doing homework with Baylor, huh?"

That was easy. "Because I knew you'd start with this teacher's-pet craziness." I folded my arms right back, though I'm pretty sure my biceps weren't impressing anyone. "And by the way, it was all my idea. He didn't invite me or anything."

"Actually," H told the rearview, "he *did* invite me." He tried to look modest and cool at the same time, which pretty much added up to *Portrait of the Artist as a Dipstick.* He ran his fingers through his hair and gave the mirror a wink. "Yeah, Baylor says I should stop by anytime I have a question." Another wink. "He says my work in progress should be nurtured."

I could think of other things that should be done to H's poetry, but since he was sort of taking my side, I didn't mention any of them.

Fry ignored Baylor's newest poetic disciple, and turned back to me. "Craziness? What's crazy is you not noticing how that old guy looks at you when he talks. How he always calls on you first."

Was it true? For just a minute, I wondered if those times I'd felt Rufus Baylor taking his time with me, singling me out, were more than wishful thinking. But I was pretty sure that patience and attention were the same things he gave everyone.

Besides, I had a suspicion there was more to Fry's wanting to skip poetry school than trying to make vacation last. More, too, than the ridiculous notion that a world-famous poet would care about a teenage girl who'd helped set fire to his past. I decided Fry had let himself slip a little too far in that last class. His sensitive side had come out to play. Without warning. Without permission. Fry was all for fun, but he liked to be in charge.

Me? I discovered that our new teacher was right. A love poem to myself was just about the hardest assignment I'd ever worked on. And I mean *worked.* As soon as I got home, I locked myself in my room and found a little notebook in my desk. After all, Baylor had said writing in a notebook was a sign you were a poet. But this book wasn't like his ancient, abused spiral. It was completely unpoetic—brand new, bright red with a small yellow price tag that, pulling and scratching and even using spit, I couldn't get off the cover. That tag reminded me that *I* was brand new, too. That I hadn't spent years looking at things the way our poet had, filling up notebooks, finding the words that make a moment, a person, a feeling, different from any other.

Still, my father-daughter talk with Shepherd had changed things. Hadn't Rufus told Shepherd I'd helped him with his poem? Hadn't Shepherd told me he had my back? Didn't that prove beyond reasonable doubt that anything—anything at all—was possible?

If Rufus Baylor believed in me, the way Shepherd believed in Manny, I didn't want to let him down. Not again. Not any more than I already had. Besides, I'd learned for myself that the kind of word music that old man made was more exciting than anything I'd ever tried. (Not counting making out with Fry, which required outlasting H and two hovering mothers; or starring in *The Glass Menagerie,* which happened only in my dreams.)

I sat on my bed and started writing, sure of just one thing: I didn't want to go all gooey and rhymey, the way H had in his poem to Miss Kinney. Which is why I began with a sort of outline—I wrote down some of the reasons people might like me: I was a good listener; I loved animals; I was a pretty fair actress, even if seniors always got the parts I would have been perfect for; I knew how to make a hungry-wolf shadow with my hands on the bedroom wall; and I could skate backward. Listed all together, though, that stuff sounded more like a résumé than a love poem. Which is when I realized that it wasn't other people who had to like me.

I remembered how we'd stared and stared at those purple flowers. And suddenly, I also remembered what Baylor had told us we needed to do. As it turned out, swiping the oversize makeup mirror from Jocelyn's room was easy. But looking into it was hard. Really hard.

I double dog dare you. Try it: Pick up a mirror and tell yourself, eyeball to eyeball, "I love you." Mean it. Know it.

Those two quiet minutes we'd spent focused on *Lamium*? They'd flown by, compared with the eternity I spent forcing myself to study every pore and follicle I saw in my reflection.

The first thing I noticed, probably the first thing everyone who looks in a mirror sees, were my eyes. It's strange to look into your own eyes as if they were someone else's, as if you hope to see someone you like. My eyes are gray blue, and the irises looked feathery and ragged in the glass, like wet bird feathers. They were, I realized, almost exactly the same color as Florinda Dear's ball gown—after I'd left her in the yard overnight.

Florinda Dear was my best doll, and I was only four years old when I forgot her in the garden chair. Next morning, Mom wrung out her elegant dress in the sink. (It had rained all night.) But my doll was still a mess, her hair clotted with twigs, her sleeves filthy, and the colors of her skirt all run together. "Too late to be sorry now," my mother told me. And then she threw Florinda in the trash.

Did sorry always come too late? I thought of my doll's filthy dress, of our poet's house, burned from the inside out. I almost put the mirror down. I wanted to, but I didn't. Instead, I forced myself to stare into those torn irises, at the scolding mother and the girl I used to be. "I could have been a doctor's wife," the mother said. And the little girl's heart was ragged, too. It wanted to melt away.

Maybe melting was important. Because suddenly, it was easy to write about them both, the mother who knew it was too late to be sorry, and the daughter who didn't. Not yet, at least. I guessed what I was writing wasn't exactly a love poem, not in the way Rufus Baylor meant, anyway. It got all mixed up with feeling bad about Florinda Dear and worse about the beach cottage that wasn't.

Even so, writing it down felt like something I needed to do. And while I was scribbling away, I didn't worry about anyone else reading it. It was sort of like flying. I got lighter and lighter as I wrote, and I didn't ever want to come down.

Naturally, what I'd jotted in my notebook a half hour later wasn't a finished poem. I learned that the minute I read it over to myself out loud. Writing in that little book wasn't the same as working on my laptop at all. When I typed a word and it took its place on the computer screen, it looked, well, official. Right. Real.

But handwritten across the page, sounded out one by one, each word in my notebook had to earn its keep. I felt their shapes, tasted their edges, put them in different places, paired them with different neighbors. Over and over. It wasn't flying anymore. It was more like playing with those long-ago pots and pans on the kitchen floor. The big pot made one sound, the little one another. Over and over.

My mother must have had a thing about my playing with pots, real or metaphorical. Because I was in the middle of writing, saying words way too loud, rocking back and forth on my bed, when she knocked on my door. I went back years, to her brisk, impatient step, to those heels click-click-clicking on the kitchen floor. As if it were incriminating evidence, I tucked the tiny spiral under my pillow before I told her to come in.

"Are you trying out for another play?" She looked around the room, but there was no script on my bed. "You're rehearsing so loud, you missed the dinner bell."

Which, of course, was a lame remark, since we don't *have* a dinner bell. Only voices loud enough to travel from the kitchen downstairs to every room in the house. (Unless Jocelyn decides to call extra softly, so I end up coming down late and she can make her famous Sarah-is-so-irresponsible speech.)

"I'm not rehearsing," I told my mother. "I'm writing a poem for class."

"I thought school was over tomorrow." Her eyes still searched my room. What for? "Or are they giving summer homework now?"

"Not *class* class," I explained. "Rufus Baylor's poetry school."

"That!" She said it with the same disdain she reserved for Shepherd's name. "Let's not even talk about *that*. I thought your sentence was served."

"There are still four more weeks," I said. "And actually? It doesn't feel much like punishment at all." I wanted to tell her about stopping by Rufus's house, about the poem, about flying. Who knows? I might have tried, if she hadn't picked just that moment to resume her never-ending, eternally boring medical-school monologue. She leaned against the doorframe, but stayed standing in the hall. "Frankly," she said, "I can't wait till this business is behind us. Once you're in med school, people will have something else to talk about."

"That's five years away, Mom." I tried to get the mirror feeling back, the way I'd seen her just a few minutes ago. "And that's *if* I even get into med school."

"There's no if about it, missy." I mentioned my mother's pretty, right? But she can raise one eyebrow independently of the other, and when she does that, she looks sort of like Snow White's evil stepmother—hot, but not someone you'd want to spend a lot of time with.

"You've got the grades," she told me now. "And you've already taken AP chemistry and biology. We've done everything right."

We? I didn't remember my mother sweating through the four laws of thermodynamics or watching a half-sedated, half-dissected frog jump right off the lab counter.

"Of course, Harvard is still the best, but we'd be fine with UNC, too." She smiled generously, giving our home state the opportunity to provide my graduate education. "And naturally, it would mean your tuition would be one-third what you'd pay out of state."

I looked at her, really looked at her. And it didn't surprise me that she wasn't looking back. Just like Shepherd, just like Fry, just like everyone I knew, except maybe Rufus Baylor of the marble eyes, she was somewhere else—Katherine Wheeler's fantasyland, population: one.

"Mom, why is this so important to you?" *Why don't you go to med school? Why don't you settle for UNC?* After what Shepherd had told me at Shake It Baby, I thought I knew the answer, but I really, really wanted to hear it from her.

"Me?!" My part-time mother and full-time status chaser hadn't left fantasyland, even though she'd finally committed herself enough to walk inside my room. "This isn't for *me,* Sarah. It's for *you.*"

I wondered if she could have looked in a mirror then—if I'd dared hold one in front of her, whether she would have seen it. Hunger. *I could have been a doctor's wife,* the hunger said. *I could have had respect.*

Aunt Jocelyn loved to cook. She was good at it, a lot better than she was at keeping a job. She'd just lost her fourth one that year, and like always, it wasn't her fault. "They tried to save money by hiring one person to do two jobs," she told us over the grilled mahimahi with fennel marinade.

I was late to dinner, so I reserved comment, digging into the goat cheese potatoes instead. Mom, as usual, wasn't about to blame her baby sister for anything. "We'll find something, honey," she told Jocelyn, putting her fork down, patting my aunt's perfectly manicured hand. "You need a position that will tap your full potential." She sighed. "I just wish that slot at the magazine had worked out."

Jocelyn, a younger, softer version of my mother, minus the smarts, lit up. "But it did, Katie!" she told Mom. "After all, I met Kendall there."

"Kendall works in the mail room, sweetie." Mom disengaged her hand from Jocelyn's and returned her attention to the fish. "We can do much better than that."

A tiny flash of something contrary—was it pride?—narrowed Jocelyn's eyes. "At least, he has a college education," she told Mom. "At least, I'm not ashamed to be seen with him on the street."

My mother controlled herself at first, but I smelled frayed edges. "My mistakes are my mistakes, Jocelyn," she said. "I don't think this is the time or the place to discuss them."

"But Kendall isn't a mistake!" My aunt was much better at pouting than arguing. She was on the verge of a sulk, all her light snuffed out.

"A forty-eight-year-old gofer is hardly what I'd call a triumph, Jocelyn." Mom lifted her napkin to her mouth, dabbing carefully to avoid getting lipstick on the cloth. "Especially when he's so boorish he starts eating before everyone is even served."

Jocelyn put down her fork and jumped to the defense of the short, hairy guy who'd taken her to the movies a couple of times and who had managed to make it through a dinner just like the one we were having now. "Who are you to screen boyfriends, Katie?" There was a warning in her voice, a challenge I'd seldom heard. She must have really liked this one.

"What are you saying, dear?" My mother's tone was a warning, too. A warning Aunt J. either missed or ignored.

"I'm saying that if I had a choice between a handsome physician and a deadbeat, dumb waiter, I sure wouldn't pick Shepherd."

Even Jocelyn must have been surprised by what had come out of her mouth, because she sat, stunned and blinking, in the silence that followed her brave little speech. My guess is, she was willing every word back inside her mouth and down her throat.

"Mom?" I tried to wake my mother from her trance, but she didn't move. She simply sat there, staring at her sister, one hand just below the collar of her silk blouse, as if she wanted to make sure her body hadn't floated away. "Mom?"

My mother said nothing. At last, though, she took the napkin from her lap and put it gently on the table. She stood up, looked at Jocelyn with a cross between pity and outrage, then turned and left the room. We heard her go upstairs and walk down the hall toward her bedroom, but neither my aunt nor I tried to follow.

I suppose I should have relished that moment. How often was perfect Aunt J. in the doghouse? Mom had been taking care of her baby sister since she was a kid herself, and even though they were both grown-ups now, she just couldn't stop. So I should have been happy that, for once, things were Jocelyn's fault and not mine. It didn't work that way, though. Instead, all I felt was sad, like those mirror eyes.

My aunt and I sat together, awkward in the silence Mom had left behind. I was the first one to talk. "I know about the doctor," I said. If I couldn't get the truth from Mom, I was determined to pump Jocelyn. "What was he like?"

"Who knows?" Aunt J., it was clear, didn't care at all about what effect her bombshell had had on me. "He was pretty quiet. Mostly what he did was stare at Kate."

"Was he really handsome?"

"Oh, I guess so." Jocelyn shrugged, shaking off the long-ago doctor, Mom's hurt, and her own part in what had just happened. Like a child, a forty-nine-year-old kid who could turn on a dime, she beamed. "But not as handsome as Kendall."

When I was much smaller, I used to think that if I tried extra hard, I could make my mother happy. But after a while I learned happy was a place she didn't go. Which is why it was tough to imagine her in love. Satisfied. Not wanting, wanting.

If you can love a doll so much
it hurts,
if you can will her torn dress whole,
her streaked face clean,
where's the room in your new heart
for a broken mother,
a misplaced daughter,
a fresh start?

If you can weep onstage until
you ache,
for made-up love, a scripted slight,
director's loss,
where are the tears in this first poem
for a broken house,
memories trampled,
a way home?

I Lose a Doll and Gain a Poem

The first day of cleanup was mostly sweeping and bagging, not cleaning or building. Fry brought a tool belt and strapped it on as soon as we got to the cottage. But Whale Point's shop teacher, who was in charge, made him take it off. "Be sure and bring it next time, hear?" Mr. Shettle, who'd worn a belt of his own, didn't seem to notice Fry's expression, the way it changed, stiffened as if he'd been hit. "We haven't got near enough hammers. We could use hacksaws, too. You got some?"

"Yes, sir," Fry told him, those two words clipped and fast, as if it hurt to say them. It was beyond strange that he treated Mr. Shettle, who was small and short-tempered, with more respect than he gave almost anyone else at school. Thatcher was the same way. To see my confident, take-charge boyfriend and the human hulk both standing there, quietly waiting for instructions, mystified me. It was enough to conjure up a universal male club with secret rites and undercover bonding rituals involving levels, chisels, and mallets.

"Let's spread out and get some of this stuff ready for the dump." Mr.

Shettle passed around giant garbage bags and told us to fill them with "anything you can pick up or pry loose." He assigned us to teams, and my male-club theory suddenly made a lot of sense, since all the girls ended up in teams by ourselves, and the boys were split up into all-boy groups. I didn't mind; for once, I agreed with my mother about "distractions." I'd need to focus really hard to get through this day—to look at the mess, to sort through the piles of soot-black junk, without tearing up.

I had hiked out to the house a few times since the fire, but I'd never gotten past the cordons and barricades. The police had done everything but put up yellow crime-scene tape. And even if the tape wasn't there, the crime was. Everywhere you looked, you could see things that made it hard to be you. To be one of the kids who had done this.

The cottage walls were still standing, but the house was more like a hollow shell than a place you could live. You could see right through most of the rooms. In some of them, part of the roof was missing; in others, there was a giant hole in the siding, or the windows were gutted, their frames black and rotting, the glass gone. Rufus Baylor's summer place was a dollhouse for real now, the kind where you could reach inside and move the furniture around.

Only there was no furniture. Unless you counted what was underfoot. You had to walk carefully to avoid tripping over charred chair legs and mildewed couch cushions, empty drawers with crushed sides, and melted, twisty curtain rods. Every time I took a step, I heard a crunch or crackle, a squeak or a pop.

But once you got used to all that crunching? It was quiet, too quiet. It wasn't that you couldn't hear kids in other rooms, already getting to work, talking and laughing. It wasn't that Margaret and I were tiptoeing or whispering in our end of the living room. It's just that there was a silence *underneath* all the bustle and movement. A kind of missing, an emptiness. As if what used to be there wanted a voice. As if it were trying to remind us of the noisy meals, the knock-knock jokes, the kids who had come in from the beach and tracked sand on the rug. There's an old song about "the sound of silence." That's what I could hear if I stopped scooping up rusted springs and torn lampshades, if I just stood still.

So I kept busy. And there was plenty to do. I was picking my way through what looked like a whole collection of melted records when Margaret called me over.

"Look!" She was standing by the fireplace. Or by the mound of bricks that *used* to be the fireplace. She had opened her black garbage bag beside a heap of splintered two-by-fours, their sides and edges eaten away, turned black. She pointed to the jagged, random nest they made; sticking out from its center was a small arm and hand. I nodded. Gingerly, Margaret pulled it out and held up a burned doll.

I left the congealed 45s with their charred labels ("Baby, Don't Be That . . . ," one said; "How Can I . . . ," another asked), and went to look at the doll. It wasn't Florinda Dear, of course, but I couldn't help thinking of her when I saw the matted hair, the ruined dress. And even though she was a mess, a much more hopeless case than my water-soaked doll, I said it. "Don't throw her out," I told Margaret.

Where had she come from, that hopeless case? Whose had she been? Did Nella love her? Or one of the other little girls around the marshmallow fire? For no good reason, a nursery rhyme popped into my head:

London Bridge is falling down,
Falling down, falling down.
London Bridge is falling down,
My fair lady.

Margaret handed me the doll now, and I considered her broken face, one eye open, the other closed. The bottom half of her dress was burned away, an accidental miniskirt that exposed her skinny bare legs. "Nice threads," I told her, hoping Margaret didn't think I was a lost moron for talking to dolls.

Instead, my new friend smiled at me, then at the tiny figure in the torn dress. "No, really," she assured the doll. "It's not a look everyone can carry off." She narrowed her eyes, put her hands on her hips, deciding. "But it's definitely you."

Something clicked then, some thin latch that shut out worry, made me know I'd live through this cleanup. I was liking Margaret more and more. "Do we dare name her?" I asked. "Or is it like a stray you might not keep?"

"You mean we shouldn't get too attached?" Margaret studied the doll again. "She looks like she's had a rough life. What do you think about Janis?"

"For Janis Joplin?" It was perfect, actually. Those crazy eyes, the wild hair. I smoothed the doll's skirt, combed her singed curls with my finger, then sat her on top of the chimney bricks, where she could watch us work:

Build it up with wood and clay,
Wood and clay, wood and clay,

Build it up with wood and clay,
My fair lady.

The two of us had finished picking up the whole living room by the time Mr. Shettle called a break. We'd each stuffed and tied three bags, and we were ready to start sweeping. It felt good to see how much the room had changed. The charcoal smell was still everywhere, though, filling the whole house with the unmistakable scent of smoldering ashes. The party was over, but eau de stupid stunt lingered on.

Still, the floor was finally bare, and with a little soap and water, the walls and what was left of the ceiling might lose the coat of grime that covered them. It made me happy to have worked so hard, and I liked the idea of maybe showing our poet what we'd accomplished, once we'd plastered the walls and repaired the roof.

Margaret and I high-fived Janis and went outside to where the guys had been working. It was clear we weren't the only ones who'd made progress. The whole yard was cleared of the junk that had covered it when we arrived. The porch floor had been propped up, the drive had been raked, and tarps had been thrown over the worst holes in the roof. "It's going to be a tough job," Fry told us, shading his eyes to stare at the blue plastic on top of the house. He sighed after he said it, trying not to sound as if he was looking forward to it.

The guy from the county (who *did* take roll, by the way) had set up a tub of bottles and ice by the front door, and everyone kind of congregated around it, as if we didn't want to get too far from the cool. We were all panting and filthy, but there were enough self-satisfied grins and high fives going on to make it plain most of us felt pretty good about what we'd accomplished. I wanted to tell Fry about the old records I'd found, but he and H and two other boys were already deep into hard-core tool talk. I heard words like "plumb line" and "joists" and "slump" and "rebar." Margaret and I made bored faces over our ginger ale, then headed for the sandwich line. (Who knew a ham sandwich could taste so good or seem so small?)

After lunch, the girl-boy thing happened again, but this time we changed places. Most of the girls were assigned to trim hedges outside, while two teams of boys poured plaster for a project Mr. Shettle wanted finished in the dining room. Margaret and I worked with one of the perfect-hair girls Fry used to hang with in his BS days. She was a lot less perfect than I remembered, and a lot more fun than I expected. She pulled her hair into a tight bun, jammed it with a pencil so it would stay, and wielded an electric trimmer like she'd been doing it all her life. Margaret and I stuck to clippers, but called her in whenever we needed extra power. We'd almost wrestled the hedges down to eye level when somebody inside the cottage either dropped something very heavy or fell over their own feet. There was a yell, and then it got much too quiet.

Sweaty and covered with scratches, Margaret and I told Hella Hair, whose name was actually Cathi with an *i*, that we were turning in our trimmers. She waved, adjusted her protective goggles, and went back to work. We walked around to the back of the house, avoiding the boarded-up door and the sagging front steps. We peered into the dining room through a cavernous hole that had once been the back window. It turned out someone inside had dropped something, all right—a bucket of plaster . . . from a ladder. It had landed on one of Thatcher's friends, and sent him sprawling. He was a tall, quiet boy who hardly ever spoke in class, but always laughed at Thatcher's jokes. Now he sat up slowly, as if he couldn't believe what had happened. When he stood, though, he started shaking himself like a wet dog. Only this dog scattered plaster, not water drops. He wasn't quite as big as Thatcher, but he came close. Soon all the boys in the room were speckled with white goo. And all of them were laughing. So was Mr. Shettle. "It was an accident," he said, sounding a lot more relieved than angry. "The best kind." He threw the dog boy a towel. "The kind where no one gets hurt."

Margaret and I were about to move on to phase two, and trade in our trimmers for brooms and mops, when I glanced at the fireplace. It was empty. There was no sign of our doll. We walked right through the window that had become a door. "Where's Janis?" I asked.

H, who had run for the exit when the plaster started flying, shrugged.

"What?" Fry joined us.

"The doll," Margaret told him. "We left a doll right on top of those bricks." She pointed to the pile of cinders and bricks.

"Was *that* what it was?" Fry shook his head. "I threw it out."

I stared at the brick pile, at the high point where I'd perched Janis. Our really, truly, if somewhat disheveled, dollhouse doll. She was meant to watch us work. She was meant to see her house come back to life.

"Sorry, babe," Fry told me, easing his arm around me. "I thought it was just some trash someone had forgotten." He grinned at us both. "What do you think?" he asked. "Pretty good, huh?" Now it was his turn to point.

Why did I feel so angry? So hurt? It shouldn't have mattered. The doll *did* look like leftover garbage, the souvenir of a party no one wanted to remember.

"See? Right where the ceiling meets this wall?" Fry was still pointing, still waiting.

"It just looks like a bunch of plaster," Margaret told him, following his glance.

"Bunch of plaster?" H sounded outraged.

"That," Fry corrected her, "just happens to be the finest mud and tape inside corner job ever."

Both boys stared in wonder at the fresh patch of plaster that ran along the ceiling. They did everything but salute that shiny white seam.

"Do you know where you threw her?" I asked.

"Who?"

"The doll," I told Fry. "The trash you cleaned off the fireplace." *Those mismatched eyes. That crazy hair.*

He finally tore his attention from the sacred seam. "No, but it doesn't matter," he said. "Shettle already had someone drive the bags to the dump."

Tiny hands, tiny feet. I grabbed two brooms from the corner, handed one to Margaret. "Let's go," I told her.

Fry nodded toward the bucket and trowels on the floor. "We could sure use some help right here," he told us.

"We can't," I said. Did the dump compact trash or burn it? Did it matter? "We've got a lot more work to do." *Too late to be sorry now.*

I followed Margaret back out the window/door.

Wood and clay will wash away,
Wash away, wash away.

Wood and clay will wash away,
My fair lady.

Our first official day of summer vacation started with rain. And wind. Lots of both. Since the beach was definitely not in the forecast, Fry suggested we celebrate by movie hopping. There were three action films (*Fear Ride, Dillinger v. the State,* and *Don't Call Me,* all starring no one you ever heard of in scenes you'd wish you could forget) at the multiplex, and he wanted us each to buy a single ticket, then sit through all three movies. "We'll be watching crimes on screen," he told us, "while pulling one off in real life." He grinned at me, as if I'd understand. "Method acting, right?"

Which is why the first week of vacation also started with a fight. "Are you serious?" I couldn't believe how charged-up he sounded, how excited about "getting one over on the Man."

"The Man?!" Wasn't the bash enough? Did he really want to flirt with breaking more laws? "You mean the kids who work at the theater?" I asked. "Are they *the Man*?" And yes, I guess I put my hands on my hips and sounded like my own mother. "The ones who pop popcorn and check tickets? Who would lose their jobs if everyone did what you want to do?"

"Oh, come on, Sarah." Fry seemed truly perplexed. "Loosen up and get real. Those seats we'll fill in the middle of the day?" He got that patient, oh-so-tolerant look, as if he were explaining things to a very slow two-year-old. "Those seats would just go empty if we didn't do our hometown theater the favor of sneaking in." He turned to H, who, to no one's surprise, was starting his vacation with us and who liked action films as much as Fry. "Not to mention the extra popcorn they'll sell once we're into the second and third flicks, right?"

H smiled. The way he was supposed to. The same way he agreed on cue, fetched on command, and nodded yes every chance he got. Me? I stood on line three times to buy three tickets, then ended up sitting in between two movie hoppers, wondering if I was doing the wrong thing or the right thing by sharing the giant popcorn and king-size cherry Twizzlers they'd bought. One moral dilemma I was spared was whether or not to kiss the good-looking movie hopper on my left. His accomplice on my right was so busy explaining the film to me, I never had the chance! "He's not going to go with them," H would whisper. Or, "Don't worry, they don't die; I've seen this three times."

I'm not sure how many more movie marathons I could have endured, but fortunately, we'll never know—because after two days, the weather finally turned warmer and brighter. So we actually had one long beach day, one toasty, sun-dipped morning and afternoon, before it was time for poetry school again. Good as his word, though, Fry insisted he wasn't going. He refused to join what he called the "Baylor Cult."

The same way he refused my offer of SPF 30 and flew over the surf, a gorgeous, unprotected sun god, on his board. The look he wore on his face when he came out of those waves was hard not to love—he was so full of happiness, it lit him up from inside. So what if he didn't want to go to poetry school? So what if he refused to pay for movies no one else would sit through, anyway? Who could stay mad with Mr. Cool sprawled across half (okay, two-thirds) of your beach towel, his long legs pressed all along your shorter ones? Who wouldn't forget about badly filmed car chases and lousy do-or-die dialogue when his fingers found just the right places on your neck and your shoulder and your . . . ?

But no matter how many times I said I really, really wanted him to come to class; no matter how often I told him other kids all over the country would give anything to meet Rufus Baylor in person, Fry said no. And he kept saying no after the beach, too. Right through the video games he invited H and me to play. And right through H's own version of my scolding-mother routine.

"You'll just have to make it up, man," his friend warned Fry. "You can't cut like at school. This one's court-ordered."

"I told you," Fry insisted. "I've watched the old guy, and he never takes roll. Neither does the Boy Scout." In between his turns at Galactic Graveyard, he was working out, and his barbell was packed with extra weights. He grunted with every word, and frankly? I was glad I had something good to look at, because what I was hearing didn't make sense at all.

"This whole poetry-school thing?" *GRUNT.* "It's a farce. Just a chance for Whale Point to get itself on the map." *GRUNT.* "You two can go all runny every time that geezer opens his mouth. But me?" *GRUNT.* "No thanks on the Kool-Aid."

I'd never seen Fry afraid of anything. Still, that's the way he was treating poetry—like a visit to the dentist or a math final. "Hey," he told us, easing off the bench now that I'd blown my ship and all my crew to smithereens, "feeling isn't something I need to do in a group, okay? I can do that fine all by myself." He pulled me close, gave me a high-intensity grin. "Or with a significant other."

H, who had drawn the Fosdick card, threw the slobber-coated bone across the room. "Are you sure, man?" he asked. "We've got plenty of good times coming now that school's out." He studied the carpet, Fosdick's bony, retreating rear end, everything but his friend's face. "I mean, we owe the guy, don't we? Why make him look bad?"

"It's true," I said. "If you cut this class, everyone else will start cutting, too." Just because kids were going along with some of Baylor's exercises, and just because they weren't acting out the way they usually did for subs, didn't mean they'd all turned into poetry lovers. It didn't mean that, if they thought they could get away with it, they wouldn't bail on his classes.

Fry turned down the volume, then reached for the console. "How come it's my job to keep this old guy's boat afloat?" He sounded angry, but he was piloting his spaceship effortlessly through the same asteroid field where I'd met my untimely end just a few seconds ago. "Excuse me if I choose not to watch you hang on that antique's every word." A meaningful glance at me. Which I met, head-on.

"Wait a minute," I told him. "The man talks sense *and* poetry, Fry. You've heard him." I looked at H for support. "Why *shouldn't* I listen to him?"

"Sarah's right." H had accepted the squeaky toy from Fosdick again, but he held on to it. "I mean, who doesn't want to learn from the best?"

Alarms should have gone off. Confetti should have rained down and doves taken to the sky. Balloons, too. All glittery Mylar, with giant letters across their puffy faces: OMG!!! But even though none of that happened, a miracle had: For the first time since I'd known him, H had actually backed me up. He'd crossed, however timidly, the line between "Yes, sir" and "No, sir." He had disagreed with Fry.

I think Fry was as surprised as I was, because no one said anything, and H's last sentence just sort of hung there in the silence. *Who doesn't want to learn from the best?* Only Fosdick moved, backing away from H, begging him to throw the bone again. When he finally did, it was like the spell was broken, and Fry laughed.

"Okay, Mr. and Mrs. Poetry, go do your thing. But while you're *writing* about life, I'll be *living* it . . . on the beach." He turned up the game again.

H and I grinned at each other, two rebels who'd gotten off easy. In that moment, I saw a side of H I'd never known was there, a part of him that didn't care about being cool or playing second-in-command. I kind of liked it.

But the two of us didn't push our advantage. We stopped talking poetry, and spent the rest of our time at Fry's incubating a trip to the water park, wondering where H had lost his cell phone, and discussing next weekend's cleanup, which last topic devolved into a long, supremely boring debate about the best way to lay shingles.

ME

Did you see the job we did on those monster hedges?

H

Lifting that last row just weakens the shingles, man.

FRY

It's the only way to make them watertight. Trust me.

VIDEO GAME

PSwatttTTTT! INTRUDER DETONATED!

FOSDICK

WR-AWWER-RRRR?

ME

I hope they make the sandwiches bigger next time,
don't you?

FOSDICK

HHHH-HHH-HHHHAAAAAWWWW.

FRY

Besides, if you don't layer them, you'll just have to reroof.

VIDEO GAME

PHHSSSHHHTTTTT! DO NOT RESIST!

It wasn't until we were getting ready to leave that someone mentioned poetry again. And that someone was me. Fry had walked us out to H's car, where, of course, H found his cell wedged in the front seat. Our host leaned into the passenger window. "Are we okay?" He asked me like he wasn't sure. Which made me feel like a princess.

I put my hand on his. "It's just I wish you wouldn't treat this like a joke."

"Treat what like a joke?"

"The bash," I told him. "Rufus Baylor. Poetry."

"Just give me tomorrow off. You can tell everyone I'm one step from expiring."

"On the beach," I added, only half smiling. I knew how much the chance for good waves meant to him, but I also knew that where Fry went, the rest of the class would follow. "And after that?"

He stood away from the window, put his hand on his chest. "I hereby officially promise to take all that stuff seriously." I couldn't help thinking of the six-year-old he'd let show last week, the one who'd nursed a black-and-blue mark on his wrist.

"Prove it," I said, smiling up at him for real now. Did he remember the way he'd challenged me to read the play that last night of rehearsals? If he did, he didn't show it, he just smiled back. "Write a poem."

"What?!" A laugh as if I'd asked him to swim the Channel or launch himself into outer space.

"Write a poem," I said again. I glanced at H, who was checking messages on his lost-and-found phone. "Just for me," I whispered now. "A poem just for me."

The Third Class

It was just H and me on the drive to Baylor's next class. It felt strange to be going somewhere without Fry. As if Costello had suddenly decided to make a movie without Abbott. Where was the handsome straight guy when you needed him?

We were halfway to campus when my cell vibrated and I clicked on the new text message. It was from Fry, and I shivered when I read what he'd written. It was a POEM! A good one, an amazing one, so real and so full of feeling I nearly burst out crying right in front of H. There, in a few words on the backlit screen of my phone, was everything I'd hoped to hear my boyfriend say. Fry's poem was nothing like the rhyming monster he and H had concocted at the beach. It was strong and true and filled me up like a meal I'd always dreamed of but never tasted.

I read that poem over and over during the rest of the ride to the college. I kept stealing glances at my cell, and H must have thought I hadn't checked my messages all day. *Long loved, held dear past count.* I wanted to yell, to laugh, to share the poem with H. But somehow what Fry had written felt private, like a sweet secret between us. So instead, I sat and smiled dumbly through H's chatter, nodding at places I hoped it made sense, looking at my phone when I could. All the time, bubbling like a happy stream underneath, were those beautiful words. *Tear-swamped, fallen.* And the knowledge that I hadn't made it all up. That Fry really cared for me. Truly and more deeply than I'd ever imagined.

Only the man who'd stood up to my father, the wonder worker who'd turned H into a poetry reader, could have made me put my phone away when we got to class. As it was, I'd already memorized most of Fry's poem, so even while Rufus talked, even while I turned in my own homework, I kept saying Fry's words over to myself, as if I were fingering jewels in my pocket. No one could see them, but I knew they were there: *Beloved. Tender. Sigh-filled.*

Our poet told us we wouldn't be going outside, since he didn't want us sidetracked, that we had serious work to do. *Shy. Lovely. Lost.* It was already getting hot without the AC, and I guessed with no Fry Man to corral them, the herd might grow restless. One of Thatcher's friends leaned across the aisle and put his arm around H. "Where's the man?" he asked.

Before H could answer, I leaned in between them. "Fry's really sick," I said, playing the distraught girlfriend. No elaborate script required, just a worried look and a hushed whisper. "He asked me to take notes." I threw that last line in, and it may have been a little too much. The kid did a double take, but fortunately our poet had finished collecting homework and was passing out something that distracted us all.

They were sleep masks! He told us we'd probably had our fill of looking deep. "Now, it's time to *smell* deep," he said. "And *taste* deep." He put a black silky mask on every desk in the room, even the prof's. They had elastic straps like the ones Hollywood stars wore to bed in old movies. "Go on," Baylor urged us. "Put them on." He was grinning, and those eyes of his were keeping secrets.

That was the last thing I saw, our poet's eyes, before I couldn't see anything at all. Underneath my mask, though, I kept secrets of my own. *Fairest. Dancing. Soft.*

"Tight enough?" Rufus touched the back of my head, and I nodded in the dark. He slipped something into my hand, then moved on. He must have checked everyone's blindfolds, handed them all a little paper-wrapped package like mine. I heard him walking up and down the rows of desks, asking the same question.

It was candy. It had to be, I could already smell it.

"Okay," Rufus told us. "Unwrap 'em and start sniffing." I could hear his smile, even if I couldn't see it. "No tasting, mind. Right now, we're just inhaling, not ingesting."

I unwrapped a hard, round ball, put it close to my nose. Right away, I was breathing in a strong, bracing lemony smell, like the curls Chef Manny taught me to fold into roses and put on the glazed pork. I put Fry's jewel words back in my pocket and listened.

"The nose," our poet told us, "is a much maligned but truly magnificent instrument." He stopped, walked over to someone's desk, I couldn't tell whose. "No peeking," he warned. There was a shuffling sound, then an embarrassed laugh I recognized right away. It was Dr. Fenshaw. Cheating like a little kid.

"When folks say someone's nosy, they don't usually mean it as a compliment," Rufus went on. "But I *want* y'all to be nosy, and yes, I want you to rub your noses in it."

I took another whiff of my candy. It was small, but it packed a wallop. I felt both my nasal passages clear, and then a memory swamped me, and I was suddenly in the kitchen of our old house and Mom had just asked me to help her slice the lemons for lemonade. What a disaster *that* turned out to be.

"Marcel Proust, a famous French writer, knew smells and tastes hook us right up to memory. One whiff of the right aroma, and we step back in time."

Had Baylor read my mind? I smiled even more, because if he had, he already knew I couldn't make a poem out of what happened that day—me cutting myself with the knife, Mom screeching at all the blood, and the emergency-room nurse trying to calm her down. . . .

"Now in Proust's case, it was a cookie that got him remembering, thinking about his childhood. But I checked the bakery in town here, and I couldn't find the kind Proust ate." There was a crinkling sound, and I guessed our poet was putting the bag of candies away. "You know the little shop I mean? Right next to the library?"

We did. The Carousel was the only bakery in Whale Point. Unless you counted the one at the supermarket, which no one much did. Birthdays? Graduations? Promotions? They all called for one of the Carousel's triple-layers with meringue filling. They were expensive and Mom hated that you had to keep them refrigerated, but they were definitely worth it.

"Proust's madeleines were big and soft, almost like small cakes. But the only thing they had at the bakery today were those flat silver-dollar cookies my mama used to call sandies."

Rufus's voice changed now, and there was a soft, syrupy sound to his words. Was he sucking on a candy of his own? "I tasted one, but it just didn't tickle my nose. Which is why I settled on these hard candies." He paused, sucked. "Like the way they smell?"

There was a sort of murmuring, a few more crinkling sounds, and yes, lots of illegal slurping. I guess that satisfied him, because he kept going. "I see some of you have already graduated from sniffing to licking." He chuckled and slurped some more himself. "Go on, then. After you've sniffed your fill, start tasting. Tasting is ninety-nine percent smell, anyway, and it'll keep the good times rolling."

It was like the flowers in the garden all over again. A bunch of high school kids, a handful of suckers, and not a peep. "No chewing," he cautioned us. "Just hold the taste in your mouths, and let the memories come."

So we sat there, listening in the quiet to our own lips and tongues at work. We let the candy melt in our mouths, and remembered. Or at least, I did. I don't know why it worked, but it did. I was a little girl again, before my mother dreamed of med school, before I met Fry, before *whisper, wondrous, wide*. I wasn't sure how much time had passed when Baylor spoke. But when he did, it wasn't like an interruption at all. It was like that slow drawl of his slipped right into the pictures in my mind.

"So," he said, "what y'all got? Who remembered something they want to share?"

I couldn't see how many hands went up, but I knew H raised his because he was sitting right next to me. And because he made such a production out of it, banging his desk and muttering under his breath.

Mr. Desperate for the Limelight got his way, and I heard Rufus walk over to our row. "Mr. Losada," he said. "Of the poem that's still growing! Let's hear where you went."

"Not anywhere I wanted to, sir." H's voice sounded different when I couldn't see him, older, deeper. "Not at first, anyway."

Rufus Baylor's voice changed now too, shifted to something softer, more intimate as he leaned over H's desk. "What's your flavor, Hector?"

"Coffee," H told him. "This is definitely coffee. I know, even though I haven't tasted it since I was little."

"Hmmm." I could hear Baylor's smile. "So you're not a fan of my must-have beverage, eh?"

"No, sir," H told him. "I was eight the last time I drank coffee. It was the day my mom caught me smoking in my room." He stopped, waiting for us to go there. "I made sure to open the window, but I guess I was quiet for too long."

Quiet for too long? I laughed, if only to myself. No such thing in the Wheeler manse, where my mother practically jumped out of her skin every time I turned on the stereo or forgot to shut my door if I was on the phone.

"Nicotine and caffeine in one day?" Our poet sounded just a little impressed, which was all H needed.

"Yeah, that was my father's idea. My mom? She's no good at being tough, but when she called my dad, he brought home a carton of cigarettes and told her to put on a pot of coffee."

I couldn't help it. I felt that little-girl hurt, the bittersweet pinprick I used to get when I watched daddies and kids together. I'd met H's parents, sure—they were sweet and shy and couldn't pronounce their *j*'s. But here was a whole different picture: a mom and dad working together, caring about their kid.

"'You want to smoke, *hijo*?' That's what my dad tells me." H sounded like he was watching the movie of his life, giving us a blow-by-blow. "'Smoke these. Every single one.' He opens the carton, takes out a cigarette, and lights it.

"'You want to be a big man?' He has Mami pour me a cup of coffee from the pot. I can see the steam coming out of the top. 'Drink this. Every last drop.'"

Some kids were laughing now. But not Rufus. "So *did* you?" he asked.

"I tried," H told him. "But I only made it through half a cigarette and maybe six sips of coffee. Then I went to the bathroom and threw everything up."

Now practically everyone in class laughed. "So what's it like?" our poet asked, when the room was quiet again. "Tasting coffee after all this time?"

"Well, sir," H said in his deeper, older voice, "at first, I thought about spitting this candy out. But I don't know, maybe it's the sugar." He paused. "Or maybe it's the way it made me remember. They meant well, my parents."

I could hear he'd turned his head away from Rufus and faced the rest of the class. "If you don't have to swallow it whole, if you can just let it melt in your mouth . . . I don't know, it's all about love, right?"

No laughter now. No slurping. No sound at all, unless you counted a roomful of kids doing an internal *Wow*. It wasn't like Mr. Cool's first lieutenant to talk this way. And since no one, except me and Fry, really knew H that well, no one was sure whether he was serious or not.

He was.

Rufus must have leaned over H's desk then, because a shadow moved across us. I could see it, even through my blindfold. "I like that," the shadow said. "I like that a great deal.

"Myself?" Our poet straightened up again, thinking it over. "The things I've swallowed go a lot farther back. But that may be 'cause I'm closer to the end than the beginning." Was there a catch in his voice? "Less time to savor, you know?"

Suddenly, it was like being in Mamselle's dining room again, and seeing that white-haired man seated in my station. The yearning in his voice, the sadness, made him seem old.

"And you, Miss Wheeler?" I looked up, toward the sound of him, the dark shape of him, through my blindfold. "Where did you go?"

I told him, told the whole room, about my lemon cutting adventure, how it turned out to be a Sarah cutting, instead. But saying it out loud like that, it felt silly, not important like H's memory. "I guess this smell gave me a laugh, not a poem," I said when I'd finished.

"So you think that isn't serious enough for a poem?" The smile was still in Rufus's voice, but it was smaller, softer. "How did that cut feel, Sarah?"

"It hurt." Duh.

Our poet said nothing, and neither did anyone else.

"Well, it didn't really hurt too much," I added, "until my mother started screaming. Then I got scared." I remembered the blood, how it had seemed pretty at first, how it had made a shape like a dragon on the cutting board. A tiny dragon with a curly tongue.

But when Mom yelled like that? That's when I'd wanted to cry. It had frightened me, the way her hands flew to her mouth, the way she looked like she wished she could run away. "Don't be scared," I had told her. "I'm okay."

"Hurt isn't always on the outside," Rufus's shadow said. Mind reading again.

Later at the hospital, when they were giving me the tetanus shot, Mom had started scolding me. She said I wasn't old enough to help, after all. That I was still a baby she couldn't trust, a baby she had to watch every second.

"The wounds we feel when we're children last the longest of all." I felt our poet's hand on my shoulder, strong and sure, not shaky or old. "And they make the best poems. The kind I know you can write."

There were lots more memories, of course, lots more stories. And when I listened to kids, blindfolded kids who didn't have to look at each other, turn into little children as they talked, I heard poems. Maybe they weren't as perfect, as secret and profound, as the one Fry had texted me. Maybe they wouldn't all get written down, but nearly every one deserved to be. Each was different, each was important.

And I guess that was Rufus's point, "the lesson of the day," he called it. "There's nothing you feel, nothing you see or hear or taste or touch," he told us, "that can't be a poem."

So we wrote them. We all took our blindfolds off, and there he was, grinning at us, welcoming us back to the light. We kept sucking on what was left of our candy, and wrote and wrote. You realize, of course, that when I say "we," I mean the contingent that cared. Or at least felt so bad about what we'd done, we wanted to keep our poet smiling, keep him from remembering that burned-up pile of rubble he used to live in. Naturally, there were a few kids who zoned instead of wrote. Or joined Thatcher and his friends for an undercover texting fest. But most of us? We were hard at work for twenty minutes by our poet's wristwatch. (Twenty minutes that I forgot to steal a look at my cell. Twenty minutes without *near hands, dear hands.* Without *one breath, one sigh.*)

When we finished, Rufus told us anyone who wanted to share what they'd written, could. Three people did, but I wasn't one of them. I'd made so many corrections and crossed out so much, I could hardly read my own writing. Then time was up, and Rufus told us to hand him our poems on the way out. When someone asked if they had to, he said no. "If you feel uncomfortable with what you did on the spot here, you can take it home and make it better." He grinned. "Otherwise? You've already done your homework!"

Naturally, nearly the whole class handed him their poems, ready or not. I mean, there's such a thing as carrying perfectionism too far. And giving up a pass on homework is way too far. Rufus just smiled and gave everyone a patented double handshake before they filed out the door. Fry was right, of course. He hadn't taken roll, probably didn't even know he'd just taught one less felon than he had the week before.

I stayed at the end of the line. First, I wanted to see if Dr. Fenshaw would hand our poet a poem. (He did.) And second, I wanted to explain why I couldn't. (If I couldn't read my writing, how could Rufus?)

I almost lost my nerve, though. Not because I was worried about talking one-on-one with our famous teacher—I'd already done that, and found it was easy as breathing. It was the group of boys hanging around outside the classroom door that made me think twice. It was the way they were standing, the undercover insolence of their hands in their pockets, their eyes glued to me. Sure enough, Thatcher was there, leader of the rat pack. Even without Fry, that looming deadhead was saying it for him, *Teacher's pet*. Only Thatcher was pantomiming something not quite as genteel. He turned at an angle to the door, and when he was sure Baylor wasn't looking, he patted his oversize butt, then smiled and blew me a kiss.

"Ah, Sarah." Our poet swallowed my hands in both his. "I'd like to talk to you about your poem."

"It's not that I didn't write it," I explained. "It's just that it's taking longer than I thought."

"Longer?" Baylor glanced back toward the big desk at the front of the room, the one I'd never seen him stand behind. That was when I noticed our love poems from last week, our assignments, arranged in a neat pile on top. "I thought it was just the right length.

"I liked the way the two verses ended with a question, not an answer." He walked back to the desk, stacked the new poems he'd collected beside the old. "And I liked the way you didn't beat me over the head with those rhymes, just let me feel them for myself."

He wasn't talking about what I'd written today. He was talking about what I'd handed in at the beginning of class. "You read my poem already?!"

"While y'all were sniffing around, so was I." He grinned sheepishly. "I didn't get to everyone's just yet, but I knew yours would be special. And it was."

"It was?" I followed him to the desk, feeling like a little kid with something big to say. "Actually," I told him, "there's more."

"There is?" He didn't even look up from the pile of papers he was patting into shape.

I patted another pile, remembering the ragged eyes, the lost hope. "I guess," I told him, "it's something that needs saying, not writing." I willed him to look at me before I lost my nerve.

"Go ahead." He met me halfway, his eyes finding mine as if it was the most natural thing in the world. Easy as stepping into your old, comfy slippers when you slide out of bed. "Shoot."

I nodded. "I'm so sorry about what we . . . about what I did. Your house, your pictures, your—"

"Thank you, Sarah." He didn't look away, didn't pretend I hadn't started crying. Instead, he reached out with one of those big hands of his, and brushed the wet from both my cheeks, first one, then the other. "I'm sorry about what happened, too." He considered what he'd said and he smiled, just enough. "From the other end, of course. Maybe we can add up all our 'sorrys' and build something new?"

I nodded again. I thought of the cleanup. Maybe it made sense, after all. The first to look away, I busied myself, helping to stuff the rest of the poems into the canvas bag he used instead of a briefcase. As I did, a pink paper fell out. It was full of girly script, and something made me glance at the name on the bottom: Julie M. Kinney. Miss Kinney!

"You read our teacher's letter?" I stared at the page of fairy script before I gave it back. "She's so excited that you're wri—that you're here."

"I'm excited that I'm writing, too, Sarah." Baylor folded Miss Kinney's letter and slipped it back into his bag. "And I owe it to poems like this one." He reached into the pocket of his shirt, took out another piece of paper. It was typed, but I recognized it, too. He'd put my poem in his pocket.

Our poet unfolded the poem and held it close, the way people do when they need glasses to read but don't have them on. "'Where are the tears,'" he read aloud, "'in this first poem / for a broken house, / memories trampled, / a way home?'

"I sent your teacher a note." He folded the poem up again, returned it to his pocket, tapping it as if he wanted to make sure it was still there. "I've told her what an inspiration y'all have been."

I could picture Miss Kinney's face when she opened the poet's letter, her eyes misting as she read it. I wondered if she'd keep it in a diary. Put it under glass. Start a shrine?

"Shall we?" Rufus was standing by the door now, bag in hand, waiting for me. The kids by the door were gone. I floated out of the classroom, then onto the covered patio outside. Almost everyone had left, but H was waiting—not very patiently—on a bench by the entrance. I couldn't worry about H right now, though. It wasn't too late to be sorry, after all. Our poet had forgiven me. And he *liked my poem.*

Sometimes you can actually feel your own happiness. As if you were filling up like one of Aunt J.'s rain jars. Who could blame me for nearly forgetting my ride home? I would probably have been hard pressed to remember the words to Fry's poem just then. Or even my own name. Rufus had let me tell him. He'd let me cry. I'd lived through both. And on top of that, my extremely full and very proud heart kept reminding me, *The most famous poet in the world LIKED my poem.*

licks?
His tongue ~~soaks~~ the cutting board,
The dragon of blood that crawls
Out from my finger.

The half-cut lemon
Still smells like sun,
Still promises lemonade.

But then she screams and
~~Hides her eyes from my cut, hand,~~ covers her eyes,
Looks as though she'll run away.
"Don't cry," I tell her, frightened now,
"Mommy, please don't cry."
I hide my hands behind my back.

But it's too late, she's seen the blood,
She knows I'm ~~I've been~~ clumsy, wrong.
"How could you?" she asks and

~~And~~ I don't know. How could I cut
~~Cut~~ myself instead of that ~~the~~ lemon,
~~And~~ hurt her ~~like this?~~
instead of me?

Our Poet Asks for Help, and My Prince Makes an Offer

Walking into the real world outside our classroom after talking one-on-one with a legend, a legend who thought I'd written a good poem, was like taking that blindfold off. Before I was ready, there was too much light, too much noise. *And* too much H. He made a pathetic cartoon on that bench, tapping his foot like a father waiting up late for his daughter. (If any father wore black hoopers with oversize neon tongues.) As soon as he saw me, he stood and raced toward us. "My dad," he said, waving his cell. "He's called three times. He needs me home right away."

High drama, Losada-style. And Baylor played along. "You'd better hurry then," he told us, heading for his own car. The sky was flirting with sunset, and on the sidewalk I watched the poet's long shadow pull away from ours. Watched it wave good-bye with its cane. After only a few steps, though, Baylor and his shadow both turned. "Oh, before you leave," he called after us, "could you tell me where there's a good music store in town?"

It seems he wanted our class to wax poetic (or as poetic as we could) with all five senses. We'd already looked at ourselves in a mirror, and smelled and tasted candy, but we still had touch and hearing to go. "I know the kind of music I like might not fit the bill for y'all," he told us. "I thought I'd sort through some tapes, see what I can find."

"Tapes?!" H couldn't hide his surprise, his astonishment that the Great One was so far out of touch. "Do you mean CDs, sir?"

Rufus snapped his fingers. "Of course, I do," he said, then looked lost, like a kindergartner trying to keep up. "At least, I think I do?"

One glance at our faces must have told him he was in way over his head. "I guess I could use some advice. Do you suppose you might come with me to the music store, Sarah?"

"Me?" *Me and a legend at J. Z. Fab's? Me and Rufus Baylor shopping for tunes?*

"I'd be glad to give you a ride home afterward," our poet added, with a smile that brought back the kid in him. How did he *do* that?

"Well, I . . ." I glanced at H, who was torn between his father and his big chance to score with Baylor. It was painfully clear he didn't trust me as musical consultant to the stars.

"Sir," H explained, his voice low and patient. "It might be better to wait until I can go with you, too." His cell started playing "Cyclone Heartache" from inside his hip pocket, and he winced. "Listen, I gotta go, but you could call me from the store, right?" He looked at me, not Baylor, for confirmation.

"Sure," I told him as he backed toward the lot. I knew the chances of my calling were about the same as the odds of my making the Olympics. In any sport. Any year. Any lifetime.

"Nothing obvious, you know?" H was still walking backward, shouting instructions. "No metal or Dylan or DNC." You could tell he hated to leave the choice in my hands. "And absolutely no film scores, okay?"

"Don't worry," I shouted back. "I've got it covered." I waved, then turned and winked at Baylor. He looked amused, happy, I'm not sure what. But I had the definite feeling he was glad of the company, and that made two of us. I loved matching his long stride across the parking lot, loved getting into that mess of a car he drove, and I loved walking into J. Z. Fab's with the most famous poet on Earth.

Said famous poet, it was soon very clear, needed a lot of help finding music that wouldn't turn off his class. The first problem was navigating him through the bins of CDs, all with titles too tiny for him to read, in plastic cases too small for his huge hands. But after he took out the pair of glasses in his shirt pocket, and after I explained, leaning close so we could talk over the music from fifty zillion speakers around the store, how things were laid out, he was a lot more comfortable finding what he wanted. That was when things got really dicey.

I wished Fry were with us. Not just because I wanted to tell him how I felt about the poem he'd texted. And not just because he knew a lot about music. But because he knew a lot about people, too. He would have figured out just what to say, how to deflect Rufus with a funny joke or a smart remark. He would have been a lot better than I was at steering our poet away from self-destructive choices. But of course, Fry would never have agreed to come with us, even if I'd had the nerve to ask him. He would have laughed at the whole idea, then made some snide remark about old bards and young girls.

So I was in this alone. And it wasn't going well. No matter what

I said, Rufus gravitated toward show tunes. Old show tunes. Okay, ancient show tunes. And worse. *Mozart.* "The *Jupiter* Symphony might work," he told me, in all seriousness. "It has a very dramatic opening."

"I don't think . . ." I wanted to let him down easy, edge him toward something by someone alive.

"You're right, you're right," he agreed before I'd finished. He looked at the case he'd picked up, studied the cover, which showed the profile of a conductor making calligraphy in the air. "The second movement is too melancholy." He dropped the CD back in the bin and sighed as if he'd just made a very hard choice. "Perhaps something a bit more modern?"

I was glad his mind-reading skills had finally kicked in, that I didn't have to explain he was a few hundred years off the mark. But my heart sank when, instead of leading us away from the Classical section, he moved to another row in the same bin. "Ah," he said, grinning, holding up a new case. The light glanced off its face and I couldn't read the title, but I didn't need to. "Beethoven!" our poet said, triumphant. "Just the ticket!"

An hour and some tough bargaining later, we left the store with two CDs, one I hoped he'd keep to himself and the other that was perfect for our group to write to. The first was a collection of opera arias, and the second was a jumpy, jazzed-up version of *Sweet Mon,* just reggae enough to keep us grooving, but with those sad strings behind to make us stop and think.

I put the bag with the CDs on the backseat of our poet's car, then settled into the friendly clutter. I felt proud I'd helped, and proud to be where I was. To savor the warm, musty scent of ancient paper and old leather that permeated the car. The plastic Buddha who smiled at me from the middle of our poet's dashboard, the paperbacks on the floor, and the fine layer of dust everywhere. "All set," I announced, expecting to pull out of the store's lot.

But we didn't. Our poet sat for a minute, rock still, then lowered that great white mane over the steering wheel. "'Fraid not," he said.

The Buddha kept smiling, but Rufus groaned. "It seems I forgot one thing." Now he looked up, truly miserable. "How am I going to *play* this music?"

"On your CD player?" I offered.

His mane shook no.

"Your MP3?"

Another headshake.

I knew better than to ask about a computer or iPad. Rufus Baylor, Poet Laureate, owned none of the above.

"Wait!" I caught him just as he was opening the door. "I think we can solve this without buying anything else." It wasn't that I didn't think our poet had enough money to spring for a player. But he looked different than he had in class somehow. Tired, rumpled. Softer and older in a will-this-day-ever-end sort of way.

I explained that since he was taking me home, and since I owned not one but two MP3 players, I could copy the discs onto one and then show him how to use it. No problemo, as H would say.

"Thank you, Sarah." Baylor put his key back in the ignition. "I'm not good with gadgets. They break as soon as they see me coming."

He started up the car, then aimed a new smile my way, younger, more hopeful. "I'm looking forward to meeting your mother."

BAYLOR'S BEATER

Nnnurum, nnurum,
Ruuuuum—kkchu. Ruuuuuuuuumm—kkchu.
Ruuuuuuuuuuuuuuuu—KKCHU. RUUUUUUUMM.

BUDDHA

Oh, oh.

BAYLOR

Address, please, Miss Wheeler?

ME

(*Hushed, biting my tongue*)

BUDDHA

Wherever you go, there you are.
OHHHMMMMMMMMMMMMMMMMMM.

Why hadn't I thought of this? Why hadn't I driven home with H? Why had I gone and doomed Rufus to disaster? How had I managed to arrange things so that he was about to confront the one person he positively, absolutely couldn't charm into submission?

"Sarah?" The car was idling, but we had nowhere to go. "Where do you live?"

I thought of telling him I was spending the night at a friend's. I thought of having him let me out down the street because my mother was sick and couldn't stand excitement. I thought of a lot of excuses, half-truths, and downright lies. And then I told him the truth: "My address is 328 High Court Road."

"That's right around the corner from me, isn't it?"

"Yes, sir," I told him. "But my mom, Mr. Baylor? She can be a little difficult."

"Rufus."

"Rufus. She can be pretty hard to please."

Our poet took one hand off the wheel and turned to face me. "Don't you worry, Sarah," he said. He looked back to the window, drove out of the lot. "In case you hadn't noticed," he added, as we nosed onto Ocean Drive, "I like a challenge."

I held my breath all the way to my house. I answered our poet's questions in monosyllables, knowing there was nothing I could do to stop him if he was determined to go mano a mano with Katherine Wheeler, Demolition with a Smile. I braced myself for the shock waves as we pulled into the driveway and parked beside my mom's car.

Our poet rang the bell, and my mother opened the door. "Mom," I told her before we'd even come inside, "I'm sorry I'm late. This is Rufus Baylor. He's the one who . . ."

"I'm the one who's lucky enough to have your daughter in my poetry class, Mrs. Wheeler." My mother was doing her throat-holding thing, but Rufus just reached out and took both her hands in his, anyway. She got the double handshake, whether she wanted it or not.

"I hope we didn't worry you," he told her. "I'm afraid I kept Sarah after class. I admire her work, and wanted to tell her so."

"Her work?" My mother stopped, one of her newly released hands on the door, the other just where Rufus had left it in midair. She was already off balance, her expression a cross between *Has this man got the wrong house?* and *My, but isn't he polite!*

"Sarah's work in class," Baylor told her. "I mean her poetry, Mrs. Wheeler. Not many new writers, young or old, have such an instinctive feel for the sound and shape of words." He looked closely at Mom in the very short pause before he asked, "Maybe she comes by that naturally?"

Mom stepped back from the door, made a little gesture that looked like, *Come in*. But she didn't say a word, just eye-frisked our visitor from head to toe.

"Sarah tells me you work for a magazine." Rufus studied the living room while my mother studied him. "Why, that must be it, right there?" There were umptillion copies of *Her* strewn not so casually across the glass face of the coffee table by our couch, so it was hard to tell which one Baylor pointed to.

Mom smiled. Just a little, just enough. She invited us both to sit down, even though I already had. Would I have preferred to be upstairs in my room, music blaring so I couldn't hear what they said? Yes. But I had to admit things weren't going as badly as I'd figured they would.

"I do more selling than writing for this old rag," my mother told our poet, settling herself on the couch beside him. "But they do let me squeeze in an article now and then." She smiled again, shyer this time. "This one"—picking up a magazine, turning on the first try to a page she must have memorized—"is a prickly little diatribe on personal trainers and how they aren't."

Rufus, who, I was sure, knew less about personal training than he did about MP3s, said nothing. Still, the face he turned to her was curious, alive, and interest was all Mom needed. Like a little girl showing off, she jumped from one issue of *Her* to the next, from editorials she'd written to sidebars and features, to anything at all with her byline underneath. With each triumph she shoved under his nose, Baylor beamed at her like a proud parent. And with every page, every smile, my mother smiled back.

She didn't stop. She smiled when Rufus told her how much he liked headlines that spoke in a human voice. She smiled when he said how good it was to meet someone who understood the importance of writing your mind. She smiled when he read every word of her article on perfume as identity. And she smiled when she asked him—no, when she insisted—that he stay for dinner.

If I hadn't been there, I wouldn't have believed it: I sat next to our poet, and Mom and Aunt Joceyln sat across from us. We ate the same food, sat at the same table in the same stiff chairs we always did, but there was nothing stiff or same about that dinner with Rufus. (After the second time he asked me to call him by his first name, I tried to remember and sometimes managed it, even though it was really hard to do IN FRONT OF MY MOTHER.)

I wanted to leap up from the table, to call Fry. I wanted to tell him how, even with everything that had happened, I couldn't get his poem out of my heart. And because I was too excited to keep it to myself, I also wanted to share the amazing fact that I was breaking bread with The World's Most Famous Poet. I settled for excusing myself to go to the bathroom and sending a quick twofer text: *Your poem is way past wonderful. Guess who came to dinner?*

Rufus asked for seconds of everything, and told Aunt J. he had never eaten anything so heartbreaking as her stuffed squab. When Mom talked shop, Rufus listened. When she told stories about her boss, he laughed. Not polite little chuckles, but a kind of falling-apart rumble that grew and grew.

And you know what? Mom's stories were actually *funny*. They were things she'd never told me or Jocelyn before, things that had us all laughing. Like the time her whole office nearly starved to death when *Her*'s editor in chief insisted everyone go on the liquid diet she'd researched for an article on fast beauty fixes.

"And did you let your coworkers expire for fashion, Mrs. Wheeler?" Rufus asked.

"Kate, please," my mother told him, lowering her eyes over the dessert soufflé. "No, in fact. It seems *someone* posted an anonymous note above the water cooler proposing that we all meet in heaven for a postmortem weigh-in." When she looked up, she had that little-girl look back—show-off, yes, but mischievous, too.

"To rabble-rousing for the common good!" Our poet held his wine glass up in a toast.

"As you said, Rufus, there are times we simply have to write our minds." Mom clinked his glass with hers. And me? I wondered who had taken over my mother's body. Where had this funny, interesting woman come from? This woman who pulled pranks and laughed like she meant it?

After dinner, I left Mom and Rufus doing dishes. He really wanted to help, and since I had some serious copying to do, I took the CDs we'd chosen up to my room. I was halfway through the first one, when Fry's ringtone played.

"Sar," he said as soon as I answered, "you won't believe who just left here on a D-A-T-E." He spelled the word like it was X-rated.

"Your mom?"

"Yeah. It looks like Mr. Mustache is stepping up his campaign." It was clear that Fry wasn't as happy as his mother that she'd finally found someone she liked. Mr. Mustache was an insurance agent who had handled the family's claims for years, but who'd only recently become a stepfather candidate.

"Fry . . ." I wanted to tell him everything at once. "Your poem . . . your poem was—"

"But this cloud has a definite silver lining." Fry's voice dropped to a whisper, a sexy, secret sound. "The coast is clear for as long as it takes them to eat and watch a flick." He finished with a happy flourish: "I'll come get you and I can read you my poem"—he lowered his voice still further—"up close and personal."

I Call a Friend and Write a Poem by Moonlight

Even on a normal, nothing-new sort of day, a clear coast and two or three hours alone with Fry would have been hard to resist. But now that I'd read his true feelings, his proposition was practically irresistible. Notice I said "practically." After all, I had a famous poet in my house and a lesson in digital-audio technology to teach. I felt as though I were caught between fairy tales: a handsome, sexy prince on one side, and a wise and famous king on the other. "I can't, Fry," I told him. "Rufus Baylor is still here."

"The Bard of Ancient? What's *he* doing there?"

"Didn't you get my message?"

"Yeah. You said you loved the poem."

"I did. I do." Why did all the good things have to cluster together? Why couldn't I spread them out to cover the long, boring times in between? "I also said our poet is eating dinner with us. Mom's already invited him every week for the rest of the class—Thursdays with Rufus!"

"Rufus?!"

Could I tell him about the music store? "I've gotten to know him better." Without his making me feel wrong, gullible, foolish?

"A *lot* better, it sounds like." There was that tone again. The sarcasm, the anger.

"He's really nice, Fry." *Nice.* It wasn't what I meant. What I meant was brilliant, generous, astonishing.

"Nicer than you and me and no one home?"

"It's just that—"

"Nicer than you with no bra in my bed?" He paused, gave me time to picture poetry and pillows, a whole bed to ourselves. Without worrying about whether his mother might come home. His arms around me. "No farther," he purred, sealing the deal. "I promise."

"I just can't, Fry." What he was saying was so different from what he'd written, I felt dizzy, off balance. Where was *slow, love-round?* "Besides," I added, remembering the end of his poem, "I thought you were happy with my name on your lips."

"What?"

"You know. Your poem?"

"Oh, yeah. Come on, Sar, be serious. We don't get chances like this every night."

I wanted to tell him about the class he'd missed. I wanted to crow about how Rufus liked my poem. But I knew better now. Instead, I let Fry do the talking. Which meant I heard more than I wanted to about old men and young girls. "Just watch the geezer's hands under the table, okay?"

"Fry!" I was glad I couldn't see him, didn't have to look at the smirk, the tight smile he wore every time he talked about Rufus. "I thought you understood."

"I understand that kids are all talking about it. I'm not the only one who thinks the old man goes on autodrool whenever you're around."

"But—"

"And then you turn around and have the guy to dinner! What's wrong with this picture, Sarah?" Fry sounded like a father, a scolding parent. "You're in *high school,* and he's . . . he's barely alive, for Chrissake."

He paused, lowered his voice, as if finally, he could make me listen to reason. "Hey, it's not like you'll even get an A out of this."

The first CD popped out of my laptop. "I can't talk now," I told Fry. I heard my mother laugh, high and girlish, downstairs. "I have to go."

"Your choice, babe," Fry said, his voice angry again. "And your loss."

Was it? My loss? After we'd hung up, I sat down to wait for the second CD. I read the poem Fry had sent again. It *was* beautiful. Loving words strung together, a rush of passion. My head hurt from trying to figure things out, from wanting to hold Fry and listen to him say those words over and over. Still, the lightness in my neck and shoulders, as I started downstairs to show Rufus how to play the tracks, felt as much like relief as disappointment. As if half of me wanted to steal off to meet Fry, but the other half was only too glad to go on feeling the magic that always happened when Rufus Baylor was around.

As it turned out, my technology lesson was short lived. My mother just wasn't built to listen and learn, so even though our poet tried his best to follow my lead, Mom was constantly interrupting. "Rufus, if you have a moment," and "Oh, Rufus, have you seen this?" It was only when Jocelyn dragged her back into the kitchen to help pour coffee that I got to put more than two words together. So while I had the chance, I used the five that mattered most: "How do you do it?"

"I thought that's what *you* were supposed to tell *me*." Rufus, who seemed to have relaxed a little now that my mother was out of earshot, slipped off his jacket, folded it across his lap, and waited for instructions.

"No," I told him. "I mean, how do you make poetry that says so much in such a little space?"

You should have seen our poet's face then. It looked like a switch had been thrown and he'd come to life. "That's a fine question, Sarah," he said. "An astonishing one."

And then he forgot all about the player and how to work it. He almost forgot about me; in fact, he didn't seem to be looking at me at all when he answered. He was checking with something inside, something deep and sure.

"I guess the key to writing big is feeling big. You have to want and feel and taste more than you can ever get down on paper." He came up from inside and saw me. "That forces you to pay attention, take notes. And choose. Most of all it makes you choose what to put down and what to leave out."

I nodded. "Like being onstage," I told him. "There are a billion and one ways to say a line. But only one way you can say it after the lights go up."

"Exactly," Rufus said. "But everything you haven't said, everything you've left out, is still there. It echoes and thrums through a reader's heart."

"It goes on and on." I remembered the poem like a bell.

"Want to see how it's done?" Rufus smiled. "I write morning pages every day. I like to get things on paper before life gets too busy." I thought of the reporters, the librarians, the groupies.

"You're more than welcome to join me. I thought I might ask anyone in class who wants to, to try their hand." He held his head to one side in that way he had. "Though I'm not sure how many takers I'll have."

"Morning pages?" My heart sank. Was that how creative types worked? They jumped out of bed inspired? I had enough trouble waking up early for school. And it never felt like my brain turned on until after lunch.

"Eight a.m. sharp." Another smile. "After coffee, of course. I write without thinking. No editing, no second-guessing. Just notes on what's here and now, what's real."

"Would we have to read what we write?" All the crossings out, the changes I wrote in the margins of my poems before I cleaned them up and turned them in! What if Rufus had heard those lines before they were fixed? Would he still have told my mother I had a feel for poetry?

"No one has to read their morning pages," Rufus explained. "Not you, not me, not anyone." He paused. "On the other hand, if you want to share your work, you can. Unless, of course, Carmen objects."

I laughed. The picture of the Hendricks' giant feline sitting in on a poetry session was absurd. But Rufus wasn't smiling.

"It seems my Cat in Residence has an aversion to people taking themselves too seriously." Our poet sighed. "I invited a friend from Asheville to spend last weekend here, and he'd barely begun reading something from his latest book, when Carmen persuaded him to stop."

Persuasion seemed a little too subtle for a cat that size.

"We needed to get iodine and Band-Aids, you see."

"Band-Aids?!"

"I think it was the hand gestures he used while he read." Rufus shook his head. But he looked only a little sorry. "The scratches were mostly superficial."

"Don't mind us." Mom and Aunt J. arrived, with delicate, bell-shaped coffee cups arranged on a tray. Mom handed around the demitasses. "Go right on chatting."

But of course, we didn't. Our guest took one of the cups she handed him, inhaling as if he were sniffing a rose. And me? I had no intention of telling my mother and my aunt that I was considering setting an alarm to go write alongside the most famous poet in the world.

"Would you believe a Poet Laureate did our dishes?!" Mom sounded like a dizzy sixth grader with a new crush. The minute Rufus left, my player in tow, she wanted to talk about him. She had me describe every minute of every class, the same classes she hadn't even wanted mentioned a few days before. She kept me talking and talking, until Joceyln yawned and went to bed. Until I'd told her every detail, including our visit to the record store.

But that didn't satisfy her. She wanted to keep going, right into the future. She wondered if Our Famous New Friend wouldn't like to come see the magazine. Did I think she could ask him to write something for them? A few more bracelets and a peasant skirt, and Mom might as well have been Julie Kinney on one of her Rufus Baylor highs.

The difference between Mom and Miss Kinney, though, was that I was pretty sure Julie Kinney had read every poem our poet had ever written. And Mom? It was more like she was thrilled with her brush with fame, not with Rufus or his work. "Do you realize that man could boost the magazine's circulation with one little quote? A line or two!" She took my hand, something she hadn't done in a long time—something that felt good even though she was hardly in the same room with me anymore.

"Why, all this awful court business might even turn out for the best. Just imagine what a letter of recommendation from Rufus Baylor would do for your med school application!"

"Mom!"

"Oh, I know he hasn't got a science background, honey." She was in monologue mode now; she dropped my hand and paced beside the coffee table with its artfully arranged rows of magazines. "But anyone who read at the president's inauguration is someone people pay attention to." She picked up a copy of *Her*, waved it like a flag. "This man could change both our lives, Sarah."

"He's already changed mine," I told her. "Remember the poem he said he liked? I've got it upstairs." I knew I was taking a chance. I knew my poem might hurt her pride, but it was about the two of us, after all. "Want to hear it?" It was about love.

"I can't wait to get a look at it, really I can't." My mother dropped to the couch, rolled up the magazine, and propped it under her chin. "But right now we're talking about your future, Sarah. Let's get serious."

Get serious. Isn't that what Fry had just asked me to do?

The tears started up, I felt them fill the bottoms of my eyes, willed them to stay there. What had I expected? Wasn't Shepherd taking me for ice cream amazing enough? How many miracles in one family could Rufus Baylor work?

"After all"—she was wearing the focused, calculating expression that meant she wasn't interested in frivolous small talk—"Rufus is an exception. Poetry is no way to make a living, young lady."

"I'm pretty tired, Mom." I was, too. Suddenly, I felt as if I'd hiked halfway up a very steep hill and couldn't make it to the top. "I really need to go to bed."

Mom looked up from her dream, stared at me. I guess she figured my future was something she didn't really need my help to plan, because she smiled, walked with me to the foot of the stairs. "Okay, honey," she told me. "But I think I'd better do a little homework of my own tonight." A peck on my cheek.

"Before you go to bed, could you recommend a few of Rufus's poems for me to read?" She stood there, as if she were waiting for me to drop the books in her hands. "You know, some of the important ones?"

I didn't sleep, I couldn't. Not with so much hurt and anger swimming around inside me. It felt like dark shark noses circling, bumping into everything. If Mom had walked into the room then and apologized, even offered to look at my poem, I would probably have told her what she'd told me about Florinda Dear's dress: "Too late to be sorry now."

Maybe it was because I needed backup. Or because swimming behind those shark noses was some good news that I wanted to share. Whatever the reason, I did something I hadn't done in months and months: I called one of my friends. One of my old, BF friends.

Wanda's number was still stored on my cell, but guess what? I knew it, anyway. And talking to her was as easy as dialing her. She didn't make me feel guilty or apologetic for phoning; she sounded as though

I called every day, as if I'd never snubbed her in the hall, pretended she was invisible, and generally been the worst kind of ex-friend imaginable.

Best of all, she didn't mention the bash. We talked about everything else. About the other Untouchables. About school. About the months of gossip and jokes and movies I'd missed. And finally, because she made it all seem so natural, I told her the rest. About the trial. About the poetry classes. How H was writing awful poems and Fry was writing great ones. How Rufus and I had gone music shopping, how he liked my poem, how he'd turned my father almost human, and how my mother had just nominated herself regional president of the Whale Point Rufus Baylor Fan Club.

"No, no, no, a thousand nos!" Wanda had never tried out for the Players, but she was very dramatic. I pictured her pale face, the red arcs of her brows raised like a poppy-eyed emoticons. "I refuse to believe you sat at the very same, actual table as Rufus Baylor! Ate out of the same plate!"

"I didn't," I told her.

"Didn't what?"

"Eat out of the same plate. He had his own."

"Oh, Sarah, you know what I mean." Her voice was practically singing. "Imagine! Washing the actual fork he used, the actual glass, the—"

"Wan," I told her. "He's a person, like anyone else. Only smarter." I paused, realized that wasn't the extent of it. "And funnier," I added.

"And the world's most brilliant, celebrated, and truly inspired poet!" I already mentioned that Wanda loved poetry, right? "Sarah, I'm so jealous of you and happy for you at the same time. Do you know what I'd do to spend an evening with Rufus Baylor?"

"Set fire to his house?"

There was silence now, because both of us knew she wouldn't. Not ever. But I was glad I'd said it. Glad I could talk to her, even about that.

"Come to dinner next Thursday," I said. "My mother's invited him back."

"Do you mean it?" She sounded so surprised and hopeful it made me sad. Made me remember how awful I'd been to her. I thought about the way Wanda's and George's waves had gotten smaller, more dispirited each time I passed them in the hall. Smaller and smaller. And yet they'd never stopped.

"Of course," I told her. "Right after Bad Kids School lets out."

I felt looser after that call. Everything seemed easier, and tomorrow looked different, fresh. But I couldn't sleep yet. Not until I got a poem off my chest and out of my heart. This one wasn't meant for my notebook, though; I reached for my cell, instead, then curled like a fetus around the phone while I texted Fry:

> You look like a devil, but kiss like an angel.
> You skip out on class, but write deep as a well.
> It's confusing to date you, and so hard to tell,
> When we're together, if it's heaven or hell.

I hoped he'd understand. And I hoped I could find the courage to tell him in person how confused I was. How one minute, it felt as though we understood each other, not with words, but with our eyes, our bodies, with the sort of connection that makes two people laugh at the same things, reach for each other's hands at the same time. But how the next minute, I'd feel things I knew I couldn't share with him—proud of how Rufus treated me like a serious poet; happy I'd get to have dinner with him next week; glad I'd see Wanda again; and guilty I hadn't even thought of asking Fry.

Why hadn't I? Inviting Wanda to dinner had been instinctive, natural. Easy as breathing. But it was so much harder to picture Fry sitting at that table. Was it because he had called Rufus Baylor, *the* Rufus Baylor, a dirty old man? Or was it because he wrote the kind of poetry that visited you in a flash of inspiration . . . without a teacher, without talking or thinking about it? Or was it—and this was the question that gnawed and niggled at the back of my heart—was it because I was afraid?

What happens when you mix oil and water? When the prince gets off his horse and meets your friends and family? If he's still wearing his armor, if all he can talk about is jousting and all he can do is fight, you might lose the man of your dreams. You might end up, instead, with a guy who protects himself by pushing everyone away. Who tracks dirt on the carpet and smells like a stable.

Lying there, alone with a new moon at the window, I decided I had to take a chance on the person who'd made me feel like a princess. And who knew? Maybe our poet would be interested in jousting. Maybe Wanda and my mother and Aunt J. would get to know the boy I did, the one who hid his sensitive heart under cool. Best of all, maybe Fry himself would understand how very much I needed him to be a part of my life. All of it.

That's when I made a pact with the strip of moonlight that spilled across my lap: I would invite Fry to dinner on Thursday. It would be a battle to persuade my mother to add to her guest list, especially if the addition was of the boy variety. But wasn't love worth fighting for?

I got out of bed and padded over to my desk. I loved being the only one up in summer, when the floor stayed warm under my bare feet, creaking and whispering as if it had stored up gossip all day. When the monster action figures on my window seat looked like misshapen fairies huddled together for a midnight ritual. (King Kong was clearly their leader, his oversize arms raised in the moonlight, while Godzilla and the Hulk did their lurking, crouching thing beside him.) I put my cell on silent, plugged it into the charger, and was on my way back to bed when the moon found something I'd forgotten all about. Light from the window caught the white corner of a piece of paper I'd tucked under my laptop, and when I pulled it out, I found the photograph of Nella, creased but still smiling.

I needed that smile more than ever now. It persisted in the face of everything—the bash, H's bad poetry, the way shame and love were all mixed up in how I felt about Fry. None of it mattered to this girl, who insisted on liking me, and on smiling at me to prove it.

Because the moonlight was so lovely and because Nella's photo was such a sweet and sudden comfort, I opened the desk drawer and brought my notebook back to bed. I turned on the light, and in the same sort of white heat I imagined Fry wrote, I finished a poem about the girl who smiled through a fire. I wasn't sure how good it was, but I knew how good it felt. And I knew, too, that Nella belonged to Rufus, not to me. I would give him back the photo when I showed him the poem. The first was a little worn, and the second was brand new, but I was pretty sure our poet would love them both.

Your eyes are only shadows, your smile
as thin as the page in my hands.
But this ghost, your second best,
is all I know, all I need to see me through.
I have made you into something more
substantial, more abiding than a human girl:
Older guide and faithful friend,
a moonlight sage and ally, too.

Sometimes I wonder who you were
before the camera shutter clicked
(in those days that's how it worked).
Did you ever dream I'd need your help?
That I would fold your fairy face
inside my jeans to keep it from the fire?
That saving you would save
    me
        from
            myself?

How to Live a Nearly Perfect Week

I wouldn't say I thought of myself as a poet in training, not exactly. All I knew was that I didn't want to wait an entire, endless week to get back to banging those pots and pans around. So I was up early the next day. Aunt J. was collecting unemployment, but she was also helping out at a friend's boutique. (Not that her paycheck ever made it home; every day now, she brought back a pair of chunky shoes or a beach cover-up she told Mom she "just couldn't resist.") So right after my aunt and my mother left for work? I did, too.

I stashed Nella's photo and lots of paper and pencils in my backpack and walked to the Hendricks' house. Carmen and Rufus greeted me at the door. "She's better than a watchdog," our poet explained. "She ran to the door and scratched the paint off till I opened it."

I took a deep breath and smiled down at the furry monster twined around Rufus's legs. She did not smile back.

It didn't matter. Not after I watched Rufus pull a small table alongside that modern desk he'd been using. His new desk had no drawers, and just as the last time I'd seen it, it was buried in a snow of paper. He reached into that mess and came out with a lined tablet, which he put, along with one of the tin pencil cups, on top of the table. My heart did a funny roll-over trick in my chest when I saw how that made a tagalong writing desk, a work space right beside his.

After he'd poured a cup of coffee for me (black, no cream, on account of the dairy), I opened my backpack and showed him Nella's picture. The expression on his face, when he looked at that creased photo, was one I'd never seen him wear before. It was as if he were staring at an old-fashioned valentine, something sad and beautiful at once. And when he spoke, his voice sounded different, too. It was trembling and so tired it scared me.

"Where did you get this?" he asked.

That was when I told him everything: the way I'd walked past his family's old summer place, week after week; how I'd made up names for all the photos, the perfect boys and girls, perfect college graduates, and perfect babies—on walls, end tables, bookshelves, and on the old-fashioned desk where Nella had held court. And of course, I told him about Nella: that I knew she was his daughter; that I'd saved her smile from the fire without even remembering what I'd done; and that I was uselessly, terribly sorry about the crease through the middle of it.

"Her name wasn't Nella." Rufus looked up from her face to mine. "It was Jesse."

I waited.

"This photograph was taken before you were born," he told me. "If she were still alive, this lovely girl would be old enough to be your grandmother."

"She's *dead?*" I'd always thought of Nella as my sister, kept her frozen at the same age she was when her picture was taken.

"No doctor would agree, of course." Rufus wasn't looking at me or at the girl in the picture now. He was staring straight ahead, at something I couldn't see. "But I sometimes think her heart attack was no accident. It was her way of bowing out gracefully, of leaving her famous husband to his misadventures."

"Husband?" Nella wasn't at all who I'd thought she was. My brain was waiting for my heart to catch up. Nella. The family, the marshmallows, everything I thought I knew about her was unraveling. "You two were married?"

"Yes." Rufus looked at me and then at the photo in his hands. "Jesse had the questionable honor of being not my daughter, but my wedded wife, my life partner. She was also a long-suffering bit player whenever one of my endless tours took center stage.

"There were no curtain calls, no lines she could practice. And certainly, there was no applause." As if it were a magnet, the photograph drew him back. "But Jesse was a tragic heroine all the same.

"Oh, she tried to tell me what it was like, how it felt to be left behind year after year, all the seasons of our lives. But each time I promised I'd help raise our family, that we'd make a real, normal home together, I took off for one more trip." He was adding it up, counting those years as if they were a math problem. "After a while, I guess, she just stopped hoping."

The *Great* One—had he been the *Thoughtless* One, too?

"She died without me, Sarah."

Apparently, it was easier to tell the photo than to say it to me. "I was with someone else when Jesse's heart gave out and up. Someone whose name I can't even remember."

In the silence that followed, I tried to imagine Rufus less than loving, less than kind. It was too hard to do, like picturing Fry without his electric smile. His take-charge style.

"That was a long time ago," I told him, not caring what was right or wrong in all of this. I needed to bring him back to here and now, to the time and place where he'd done nothing but good, been nothing but kind.

"Or it was only yesterday," he said. "If missing's any measure."

"Things change. People change." I looked for the words, a way to tell him that I knew Nella, even if I hadn't ever met Jesse. And I knew that lovely girl was past pain now. Past blame or guilt.

Rufus must have seen my confusion. Or else he saw the time. "Look how late it's gotten," he told me now. "If we don't get started, we'll have nothing to show for ourselves." He stood up, started clearing away the coffee cups. "I didn't mean to burden you with my past," he said. "It's just that seeing that photo was a bit of a shock. Like Scrooge meeting Christmas Past." He paused, shook his head. "I wasn't good to her, Sarah. Not nearly as good as she deserved."

I traced the photo's crease with my finger, then raised my face to his. "Last week, you forgave a whole roomful of kids for making a big, dangerous mistake."

Rufus nodded.

"And you forgave me just the other day, when I didn't see how anyone could." I remembered looking in the mirror. I remembered trying so hard to love what I saw.

Our poet nodded again, more slowly this time.

"Maybe it's time to forgive yourself?"

After the coffee cups were washed and put away, after we'd slipped Nella's photo behind the last page of a dictionary to flatten her crease, it happened: *Rufus and Sarah, sitting in a tree, W-R-I-T-I-N-G!!!* He told me that what we'd write, though, wasn't poetry; it was a warm-up. It was like stretching before you run, pliés before you dance. "Put down anything at all, Sarah," he said. "Something that makes you glad to be alive. Or sorry you ever got out of bed—a feeling, a crack in the wall, a muscle cramp. It's all fair game, and it's all yours. You don't have to share it with anyone."

At first, I couldn't get Nella out of my mind. Stay-at-home Nella. Sad Nella. Nella, withering like the flowers all around us. I sat still, waiting for her face to fade.

Rufus noticed. "Keep your pencil moving," he told me. "No erasing, no stopping, no telling yourself it isn't good enough."

I picked up my pencil, determined to write about the first thing I laid eyes on. As it happened, it was one of the bouquets, moldering in its vase. I could almost smell the damp doneness, the rot. It seemed poetic and symbolic, that mass of dying flowers, and I had actually started writing away when I felt something tough and bony, something very insistent, scrubbing my legs. I looked down to find Carmen brushing herself against me. Cautiously, as if I were dipping my hand into a pot of hot water, I gave her an exploratory pat.

My fingers didn't get bitten off! So I kept stroking her. Which set off a rumbling, a sort of electronic hum like a bullfrog on autopilot.

That purr of Carmen's, that grudging tribute, filled me up. Strangely, miraculously, it filled up my page, too. I forgot about Nella and the dead flowers; I wrote, instead, about how grateful that crusty old cat had made me feel, how happy tears had started up, how I had heard the word behind her purr: *Stay.*

But one thing I couldn't forget, as we scribbled away together, was who was sitting right beside me: Every few minutes, I'd lift my head from my tablet to peek at Rufus, to say to myself, *Are you dreaming? Did you really just have coffee with the greatest poet in the Western world? Can you possibly be writing with the man who drew peace and inspiration from Whale Point's picturesque streets and friendly residents?*

After we'd written pages and pages (before I knew it), Rufus said we could go poem hunting, looking for something in what we'd written that might be turned into a sonnet or a sestina or a haiku. I didn't know what most of those were, so Rufus said I should just find a part of my scribbles that felt like the words to a song and write them down.

I tried to turn the dead flowers into a sad song, but it felt preachy, silly. So I used Mega Cat's purr, the bullfrog thrum that had opened my heart, instead. I knew I wouldn't have to read what I wrote, so I kind of had fun rearranging things, trying to make a whole poem that sounded like Carmen. I don't know exactly how it happened, but soon our poet and I were reading to each other. He made sharing so easy, so natural, that I just fell into it.

First Rufus looked up, smiled, read me a line, and asked me what I thought. I told him, and that made me brave enough to read him something of my own that felt good. He nodded as I read, told me I was on the right track. And we kept on throwing each other lines, bits and pieces. "That's a keeper," he'd say. Or, "Who wishes they'd written that?" And he'd raise his own hand, grinning.

But not always. Once I decided to read him one of my fancy scribbles about the dying flowers. Those lines had sounded lyrical and tragic, after all, more like real poetry than a purr ever could. But he shook his head when he heard them. "Kill your darlings, Sarah," he told me. "If you think the whole poem is different without them, take them out. They're holding a place for something else, something that won't stand out, something that will feel like home."

So I went back to the page, and I played with the shapes and music there, banging on pots and pans. It got so I could hear when things fell into place, an almost noiseless whisper that said the words in my head nanoseconds before I found them. I'd write them down, and then I'd read them again, changing, shifting. Until mail dropped through the front door slot. Or Rufus's chair squeaked. And I looked up. That's when I'd remember who sat just a few feet from me, his fingers at his temples, his white head lowered over a poem. A poem that would probably be put in a book and memorized by kids like me all over the country.

Yes, I walked to Rufus's place again the next morning. And the next. And the next. I wrote and I listened and I watched. I watched a lot: I studied the way Rufus sat, the way he held his pencil. (He never used pens, he said they "stopped the flow.") I thought, *This is the way a genius sits.* I thought, *See how his thumb wraps under his finger?* I'd scratch my head like he did, try to hold my pencil (I took an oath to give all my pens to Mom and Jocelyn) the same way he did. And then I'd ask myself again, *Are you dreaming this?*

Most of my writing didn't become poetry, but some of it did. I found the best poems started like burrs, things and feelings I couldn't get rid of. Things that haunted and pricked until I gave them a shape, a place to be. Of course, my pages weren't anything like Rufus's, whose least little scribble came out sounding like a ready-made poem.

It was hard to believe, how they poured out of him. When I was little, a lady who raised butterflies put a newly hatched one on my hand. No one had to teach it to fly. In no time at all, it simply opened its wings and flew away. That's what I thought of every time Rufus made a poem. He didn't hem and haw, just spoke it through from beginning to end. It came out with full-size wings and just took off.

The only butterfly I hatched was a poem about Sarah Bernhardt, and about the feeling I got when I went out onstage. "Bravo," Rufus told me, when I'd read it to him. "Let's not fiddle with this one, Sarah. Sometimes it happens on the first try."

Did I tell Fry and H about morning pages? Would you? If I had, H would have insisted on going along, and I would have had to share our poet with him. Worse, I would have been forced to listen to more of the lines that had nearly managed to turn me off sea and sand. As for Fry, well, you can guess how he would have responded to my taking private lessons at our teacher's house.

Besides, I didn't want to ruin a good thing—no, a *great* thing. Choosing dinner with Rufus over an evening with my boyfriend, it turned out, made said boyfriend more attentive than ever. Apparently, I wasn't the only one who had decided to fight for love. Now, every day meant a trip to the beach. Morning pages, after all, didn't stop me from spending afternoons with Fry, making up and making out.

Except for poetry school, we were on vacation and the sun was finally out. So whenever I didn't have to prep at Mamselle's, we headed for the waves. There was nothing like the way Fry met a wave, and nothing like the joy on his face after riding in on a perfect A-frame. It was like studying Rufus at his desk, to watch that boy cut back toward the barrel of a giant wave. Every move was worth studying. Every second was precious.

Naturally, I couldn't handle the mad waves Fry loved, but sometimes he'd paddle me out on his board. We'd come in together, horizontal, holding tight. Laughing. In between swims, the dunes made a perfect nest, breaking the wind but letting us listen to it rustling the sea grass. I don't know if there have been studies done, but I can testify that salt definitely makes skin and lips taste better. Wilder:

SAND CRAB

(*Burrowing in sand under our towel*)

Scrrrrrrrtchtchtchtch. Sccccrrrrrtchtchtch.
ScrrrrIIIIITTTCCCCHHHHHHH.

FRY

C'mere.

ME

(*Pointing to one corner of our towel*)

Listen.

FRY

(*Leaning close*)

What?

TWO SAND CRABS

(Digging together now)

ScrrrrrSCRITCHHHchhhhhh.

Sccccccc. Scurrrrr. SCRITCHHHHHHHHHHH.

SCRITCH? Scritch?

Scriiiiiiiiiiiiiiitch. SCerch. CLERRRRCHHHHHH.

ME

(Pointing again)

There! Hear?

FRY

(Smiling, pulling me to him)

C'mere.

The only break in this chain of luscious days by the sea came with the second Saturday cleanup. As usual, the guys wielded hammers and spread spackle in one room, and most of the girls (except Cathi with an *i*, who turned out to be a shop major and very handy with a jigsaw) used Lysol and bleach in another. Just as Mr. Shettle had promised, this week was all about nailing and hammering, and Fry got to strap on a belt with two pockets, each bristling with pencils and wrenches and pliers. So it was no shock that the Secret Society of Power Tools kind of swallowed my prince up. It was hours before he and Thatcher and H stopped talking about the proper weight for a claw hammer and which was the best brand of cordless drill.

But once we'd hammered and scrubbed separately, Fry made it his business, for the whole next week, to bring us *very* close together. He was more thoughtful, more affectionate, and more sexy than ever. He still didn't talk like a poet, or act like one, either. And he made me promise not to mention his poem in front of H. Which was all pretty confusing. But whenever he put his arms around me, I forgot to feel confused. And he put his arms around me a *lot*. Sure, I still had to pull his hands back to where there was no chance of forgetting what had happened with my mother and Shepherd. But there were also plenty of times where he seemed okay with just holding hands, with lying on the beach, warm and sun drugged, skin to skin.

It felt almost too good to be true: Starting each morning by sharing poems with someone so smart, so funny, so kind that he made me feel like a real artist. Then, as soon as I'd said good-bye to one poet, I met another on the beach. And if the second poet wasn't interested in our writing together, there were plenty of other things he wanted to share with me.

Okay, with me and H: We still went most places with Fry's second-in-command, especially if we wanted to drive to Ocean Beach, which was farther away but lots more secluded and had the best surf. Our constant companion's heart, although he wasn't the poet Fry had turned out to be, was definitely in the right place. "You know what?" H asked, on a day as bright as all the others. "Even if Julie never reads my poems, she's started something here." He tapped his skinny chest, grabbed his notebook, and opened a page across his beach towel. "I just can't stop the flow, man."

Fry was not exactly glowing with enthusiasm about his friend's expanding poetry collection: "Kinney hasn't got enough student papers to read?"

H didn't notice. Or he didn't care. He held up the notebook he now carried everywhere. "The problem is, I don't think I can give all these poems to her at once." He sounded as if he were parceling out ball gowns or major appliances. "I need to figure out which will make the best first impression, you know?"

"How do you know she hasn't got a boyfriend?" Had Fry forgotten how much this meant to his friend? "I saw some guy in a uniform pick her up from school last week."

"People have brothers, you know," H told us. "And cousins and friends." I guessed it didn't matter what Fry said. H wasn't listening to anything except his own thumping heart.

"It's not like the end of the world," Fry observed. He turned, frowned at a lone surfer in the waves as if the guy were doing it all wrong. "They're just poems, just words."

"Wait a minute." H removed the pencil he now sported behind one ear, clearly a new-poet accessory. "Words can win fair ladies. You said so yourself."

For a minute, the whole day felt like a dish someone had put much too close to the edge of the table. I checked out the slice of Fry's profile I could see. I remembered how I'd felt about H and his Hallmark verse. The way the gulls had circled and circled as I tried to think of something good to say. I touched my guy's shoulders, but he didn't turn around. "It's okay," I told him. "As long as *we* know what's real."

"And do we, Sarah?" Fry was finally looking at me, but his eyes wore their low lids like shields. "What's behind the words? Do you even know who I am?"

I wanted to laugh out loud. He'd just given me the gift of himself, just let me in farther than he ever had. I held up my phone with his poem front and center. "What more do I need to know?"

Fry winced as if a no-see-um had blustered its way onto the beach and bitten him. "Do you like football?"

"What's football got to do with this, Fry?"

"Or NASCAR, Sarah? Do you like those races we go to at all?"

"Well, sure," I lied. "A little."

Fry turned silent, but H, who'd heard NASCAR mentioned, looked up from his writing. "Hey, man," he contributed. "There's no reason you can't like NASCAR *and* poetry. I do."

And just like that, H had pushed the dish back from the edge of the table and saved the day. Because now he thumbed through his notebook, which was filled mostly with poems for Miss Kinney, but also included lyrics on shoelaces, sunrise, and selected power tools. "This one's called 'Last Lap.' It's an ode to Dale Earnhardt. Want to hear it?"

"NOOOO!" Fry and I said it together, as if it were a synchronized routine we'd practiced, as if we'd just been waiting for H to ask. But our budding poet took the rebuff in stride. He grinned, sipped, and in an unconscious tribute to his *jefe*, told us just what Fry would have. "Your loss," he said, and resumed his inspired scribbling.

If being a threesome provided comic relief, it also made it harder to deliver the dinner invitation I was determined to give Fry. I ended up whispering it under a beach towel. In between kisses. And I guess I was glad the way it turned out, because I didn't have to fight for love, after all. At least not with my mother.

Fry's RSVP was hardly formal, but it was perfectly clear. "Hell, no!"

He was close to yelling, and he nearly upset the careful towel tent I'd constructed over our heads.

He helped me rebuild our cover, then in a lower voice informed me that I should not expect his presence at 328 High Court on Thursday evening. "Eating food I don't recognize," he said, "is not my idea of a good time." He closed in for the kiss I'd interrupted with my invitation. "And neither is waiting for your mom and the happy rhymester to catch me using the wrong fork."

Why was I surprised? I should have known Fry wouldn't want to get dressed up and dust off his manners. Any more than he'd want to sit around talking about poetry. He insisted he got his inspiration from one place and one place only—me. And baking on that beach towel, haunch to haunch with my real-life poet prince, who cared about whether he sipped his soup? Or knew a sonnet from a sestina? Who cared about anything but making sure he had all the inspiration he needed?

So yes. Fry and I spent a lot more time kissing than talking. But in between kisses, I could hear the lines he'd texted me, could whisper them in my head: *half-closed eyes, heartful sighs.* And I could make him promise there would be more where those came from: *your name on my lips, still and still.* When there was nothing but sand between his bare right leg and my bare left one, when both of us had forgotten about prying eyes and all we could hear were each other's heartbeats, I asked for a second installment.

"Another poem?" Fry's lips brushed mine, teasing, and I could see his white teeth, his sly grin. "Sure, provided the next kiss meets my rigorous standards."

"Rigorous standards?" I laughed at the words that sounded more like a contract than romance.

"Yep," he told me. "That's what cars have to meet. So why not girls?" Another grin, and warm fingers creeping from my hairline to the strap of my bathing suit.

I felt dizzy. Faint. "Okay," I said, because I couldn't say anything else. Not with his hand where it was, not with his lips covering mine.

Even Mamselle's was bearable now. Better than bearable. Shepherd was out of harassment mode and into something almost as embarrassing but a lot easier to take: He was trying to act like a father. The emphasis here, of course, was on trying. But since he was probably making it all up as he went along, working without a real-life model, I had to give him credit. Sure, he still lost his temper, and he still swore a blue streak, but he was an equal-opportunity yeller now. He took stuff out on everybody, not just me. In fact, not so much on me.

"Sarah," he asked me Saturday night, "how'd the cleanup go? Got the roof on yet?"

I was headed into the kitchen with an order for a party of five (a party of FIVE!). I didn't really have time to chat. "Not yet," I told him. "We're still picking up the pieces inside."

"I know Sid down at Midtown Lumber," he told me. "If you need some cheap timber or a good deal on shingles, let me know, okay?"

I remembered the Great Shingles Debate, but decided materials weren't what Shepherd was really talking about. "Thanks," I told him. "I'll let our shop teacher know."

Little things like that. Things that told me my father was thinking about what I was up to even when I wasn't at Mamselle's, breaking dishes. Things like the way he rolled his eyes now when the crockery hit the floor. Which, trust me, was a lot better than the tantrumation I was used to. Expecting Shepherd to lose it and finding that he didn't, at least not always, might not sound like a major breakthrough to you. But you have to realize that if you've been living on an island with cannibals, meeting someone who doesn't want you for breakfast feels right next door to a miracle.

Before I walk onstage, leave the safe
dark for that distant pool of light inside
a one-walled room, I want to be sick.
Bathed in sweat, I'm sure I'll forget
what I've learned or say it too fast,
embarrass myself and the rest of the cast.

But then comes my cue, a word on which
so much depends (who stays, who goes),
and thoughtless, I am swept by someone
else's needs. I believe in the door that leads
nowhere, the empty glass, the dummy book.
If someone points up a painted hill, I look.

Secondhand words fill my heart, but my
body knows them as mine. A will-less toy
boat carried by the wind, what have I
truly seen? Who have I really been?
In the end, I'm nothing you can speak of,
a sort of go-between, a messenger of love.

A Mighty Fall

When poetry class came around again, I looked forward to a double helping of Rufus Baylor. Because yes, our poet said I was more than welcome to come for morning pages even on the day of Naughty Kids School. Although I should have been used to seeing those two desks side by side, it still gave me an adrenaline rush, a pinch-me-this-can't-be-real thrill each time I rang the Hendricks' hideous symphonic doorbell and saw our shared writing space waiting.

"Have you had breakfast?" Rufus met me at the door with Carmen and a plate of cookies. "Remember madeleines?"

"Memory cookies?"

He glanced at the tray. "Yep. I talked the bakery into whipping up a batch." He smiled at me over the indecently heaped plateful of pastries. "I go through a box a week at home, even without company."

"I can't wait to taste them," I told him. I reached down to stroke Carmen, who sort of took me for granted now, even arched her head under my hand. "Rufus?"

"Yes?"

"I have something to tell you." I remembered how long it had taken me to work up to "sorry," and I didn't want it to be so long before "thank you." "It's about my father. Shepherd?"

"I remember your father. He's extremely hard to forget." Rufus carried the cookies to the table in front of the couch. Our coffee mugs were already waiting for us there.

"And extremely *different*." I sat across from him on a plum-colored wing chair, studied him as I sipped. "Because of *you*."

His smile broadened, those spring-blue eyes lit. "Is that good?"

"It's amazing. He stands up for me now. He talks to me about stuff besides work." (Hard as it was to believe, Shepherd had even called me at home the day before to give me the name of his friend at the lumberyard, to ask awkwardly, "So how's everything else going?")

"He's doing what he's always wanted to, Sarah."

"Really?"

Rufus nodded. "Sometimes a person does the wrong thing. And it can be years before he gets a chance to do the right one."

I thought about the cowboy pajamas. About Shepherd pawing through the sale rack, his eye caught by lassoes and mustangs.

"If he gets a chance at all." Rufus looked sadder, more serious. Were we still talking about Shepherd?

"Well, one thing's for sure," I told him. "My father is not the same since you talked to him." I wanted that smile back. "Thanks."

"*I* didn't change, *he* did." Rufus took a cookie, dipped it in his coffee. "But you're welcome."

My first madeleine was not my last. They weren't fussy cookies, even though they looked dainty and elegant. They were not too sweet, soft enough to crumble in your mouth, but strong enough to stand up to the coffee bath I gave them after I watched Rufus. Maybe it was the cookies or maybe it was because we were going to have class later that afternoon; but the two of us did a lot more talking and remembering that morning than we did writing. In fact, I ended up telling Rufus more than almost anyone else knew about me.

I learned a lot about him, too. Because, just like in class, he never asked me any questions he wasn't willing to answer himself. So our memories and families and wishes got all jumbled together, nuzzling each other the way friends' lives do. And I don't mean history, facts, dates. I mean worst nightmares, favorite colors, first time we hated someone, last time we were jealous, what we were afraid of but made ourselves do. What always, always made us laugh, what made us cry. I almost wished Fry could hear us, could listen to the way we circled around each other, coming closer and closer, safer and safer. I knew, you see, if my boyfriend could have eavesdropped on Rufus and me that morning, he would have been forced to take back every last mean remark, every crude joke he'd ever made about young girls and dirty old men. We'd nearly run out of cookies when Rufus mentioned his children. "That beach towel?" He pulled a photo frame from behind one of the coffee table vases and handed it to me. Inside the frame was a picture of a little boy on the beach. "It was my youngest son's first purchase."

I studied the boy in the photo, but he was too far away to pick out much beyond his coppery hair and a huge smile-for-the-camera grin. The towel he stood on looked like one of the big, cheap ones the ocean-front stores still sold: Splashed across its face was a very large Bugs

Bunny and a very small Tweety, each wearing sunglasses and carrying a life preserver.

I remembered those other bright-faced kids, the ones patting puppies, playing ball, posing in graduation caps—all the pictures I'd spied on in the cottage. Now, thanks to poetry.com, I'd learned more about them than I wanted to know. I'd discovered that most of them had two dates after their names. One when they were born, and one when they died.

"He said he wanted to buy it himself, so we couldn't make him share it with his brothers." Rufus looked at the photo over my shoulder. "He wouldn't let anyone else near it."

I tried to change the subject. I asked him about haiku. About Asheville. Even about our homework. But always, he came back to his boys. "I'm a survivor," he told me at last. "I've outlived all three of my sons, a distinction I'd gladly forfeit if those great trampers and talkers could be here with you, instead."

I thought of the poem he'd written about staying up with a sick child. That child was dead now. Had Rufus changed his mind about God being right?

"I lost my boys when each of them was older than Jesse when she died." His voice wasn't sad, just hard, the words like stones. "I suppose there's some consolation in that." Rufus closed the box top on the two madeleines neither of us wanted anymore. "I don't think Jesse could have stood to let her three warriors go."

This sad story over our empty mugs felt all wrong. I wanted to sweep the crumbs off the table, to go back to talking about poetry. If a word wasn't right, you could fix it. But if a life broke . . .

I knew how they'd died, you see, those boys of his. I knew from following link after link on a long, winding cyber hunt that took me where I didn't really want to go. To the car accident that had taken two of their lives; to the cancer that had slowly, cruelly killed the other. I knew all this, and that's what made it worse. Knowing the end of a story, especially if it's sad, makes listening to it really hard. Thankfully, Carmen began to complain loudly. I don't know whether, somewhere in that prima donna brain of hers, that fur-muffled heart, she sensed her human friend's somber mood, or whether she'd simply gotten tired of being in sight but out of patting range. I do know I was relieved when she leaped onto the couch and insinuated herself under one of Rufus's big hands.

Now, with a sleepy midmorning light filtering through the juniper and fern pines outside, with Carmen rubbing stubbornly against his hand, Rufus jumped the sad track he'd started down:

"Did you know I proposed to Jesse four times?"

My half-smiling Nella had said no to Rufus Baylor?! That hadn't been included in any of the websites I'd checked. "Were you famous then?" I asked.

"Nope." He smiled at something small and far away. "Just full of myself. And she knew it. Three times she had the good sense to turn me down flat."

It wasn't as if the suitor Nella had rejected was as old as Rufus, either. I knew how full-throttle gorgeous our poet had been as a young man—and I had a photo to prove it. It was right there in the book I always carried with me now, the one I'd been reading every night before bed.

"You don't believe me?" Rufus smiled for real now, shook his head.

"Flatter than flat, three times in a row. I believe the phrase 'over my dead body' figured prominently each time."

The mood felt lighter. Because I hoped it would stay that way, I jumped up and retrieved my backpack from the coat hook by the door. I must have moved too suddenly, because for the first time in a week, Carmen hissed at me.

I ignored her, grabbed *Poems for Sale*, and hurried it back to Rufus. "Are you trying to tell me," I asked him, setting the volume in front of him, opening it to the author photo, "that Nella—I mean Jesse—said no to *this?*"

Together, we looked at the handsome face staring up at us. Rufus wasn't really young in the photo, probably in his forties. But those impossible eyes, glancing at us sideways from under ringlets of auburn hair, and a wide, pouting mouth made him look like a movie star. A movie star who only half knew how hot he was.

"I don't think I fooled Jess for a minute." Rufus examined his younger self, as if he were a riddle, a puzzle he'd solved long ago. "I think she knew just what she was signing on for—the strutting that passed for confidence, the neediness that passed for love." He pushed the book away. "But in the end, she signed on, anyway."

For a few seconds, I studied the film star in the book, then turned back to the weathered, craggy face I trusted more. "Did you ever want a little girl?" I asked.

"After three sons?" He looked at me and smiled. "Who wouldn't?" He looked deeper now, as if he were measuring my eyes. Or my heart. "None of my boys wrote poetry. They loved to walk and climb and bike. But none of them stopped to listen to the world the way you do."

Somewhere in front of the house, perhaps in the branches of that giant magnolia, a bird called. "Tou-eee, tou-eeee," it sang. In response, Carmen uttered an immediate and decidedly unfriendly challenge, "Arrhrwhaaaaaaaaaa! Aaarhwhaaaahhhhhhhhhh!"

Rufus didn't seem to hear any of it. "And if Jesse and I had made the kind of love that makes for girls"—he took one of my hands in his—"who's to say she wouldn't have turned out like Sarah, not Sarai?" I could feel someone's pulse—mine or his?—jumping between us. "Who's to say she wouldn't write splendid poetry? Who's to say she wouldn't have a saucy tongue and be the possessor of a stout, unshakable heart?"

He shook his head, not at me but at himself. "By rights, I don't deserve a second chance." Then he was looking back at me, taking his hand from mine to touch my cheek. "But here you are."

I had no more room for feeling sad or sorry or anything but full to the brim. How he looked at me! How he smiled when he did! It wasn't a father's smile. Or a boyfriend's. It was deeper, sweeter. As if we shared that grin between us. As if he started it and I finished it. Which I did, smiling right back at my poet. Yes, he was *my* poet now, and I knew this sad, sweet moment would stay with me forever. Memories trapped in a lemon drop.

When someone knows who you really are, and likes you, anyway, there's nothing you can't tell them. I'm not usually much of a talker, but suddenly, you couldn't shut me up. I told Rufus about Grandma and Grandpa dying before I was born, and how, because the fuzzy photo Mom showed me looked nothing like her, I'd sometimes complain about my mother to my dead grandmother. But once, when I protested that Grandma would never have been as mean to me as she was, Mom had laughed right out loud. "You're right," she told me. "She'd be *twice* as mean!"

Then, at the risk of dashing any illusions he might have about girls and ruffles, I also told my first-ever adult BFF how I wanted to play Hamlet like Sarah Bernhardt had, and how, after we read *Frankenstein* in junior high, I started collecting monsters, posing them on my bookcase and window seat, gluing speech bubbles to their mouths, notes that made them roar things like "Homework is for weaklings" or "Don't forget gym shorts!"

Finally, I told him about banging the pots on the kitchen floor when I was three, and about how no one in my family ever really looked at each other. And because I was on a roll, and because his eyes were such a safe place, I told my poet something I'd never told anyone else: It wasn't just the pots and pans that made music for me. It was trees and birds, waves and wind, crabs tunneling through the sand. "It's not a language I understand, exactly," I explained. "Nothing I can translate. But everything talks, everything there is."

"That's what I mean about listening to the world, Sarah," Rufus told me. "Children and poets know it's all alive, every part of it." He found my hand again. "Myself? I can't play an instrument, and I can't carry a tune." He squinted into the sun. "But I hear music whenever people talk. The way animals move in the world, the way leaves fall, that's my song."

He sat back now. Far enough to take a picture. Even though it was too bright, even though he had no camera. He looked at me without speaking at first, and then he said, "I'm glad to know there will be someone around to listen to things after I'm gone. I think they need the attention."

After he was gone? I thought of what Rufus had said last class, how he had more memories behind him than ahead. But I didn't want to think about some sorrowful day-after-tomorrow. I wanted to talk about here and now, about poems and plays and the summer that was simmering all around us, breaking in through windows and filling us up.

Which, I guess, is what made me ask about the music. Was he ready to play the songs we'd picked out for class? Did he need me to show him about the player one more time? And I suppose it was the music, too loud at first, that upset Carmen, that set her to howling and meowing until we turned it off. Until Rufus tried to soothe her and then decided she might want breakfast.

I heard the crash from where I sat. It happened so fast there was no time to think at all. Only time to put down the player and run into the kitchen. To see a pair of familiar feet sticking out from behind the counter, to find Rufus sprawled on the floor, the cat food can, unopened, halfway across the room.

He looked all wrong there, like someone who was never meant to be horizontal. It was as if I'd come in and found an oak or a sycamore lying in the middle of the kitchen. He was shaking, just a little. But what I noticed most, when I stooped beside him, when I took his hand, was that he was so pale. His face wasn't white, exactly, but blanched; as if someone had squeezed the color, the juice, out of him. His humor, though, was intact. "Not the most dignified position I've ever found myself in," he told me, looking up, wincing and smiling at the same time.

I put my arm around his great shoulders, and slowly, slowly, like someone who wasn't sure he remembered how, he sat up. "But I'd say my leg hurts more than my ego."

"What happened?" I kept my arm around him, afraid that if I let go, he might fall down again.

"A dictionary and phone book do not a ladder make." He nodded toward the two books, the ones he must have tried to stand on, tumbled together near the cat dish, their pages open to nothing that mattered. "Carmen prefers top-shelf flavors."

Hearing her name, Mega Cat, frightened away by the noise and the fall, sauntered back into the kitchen and right up to Rufus. Overjoyed to find him so close to hand, she rubbed against him, begging loudly for a pat.

"Can you wiggle your toes?" Who knows why I said that? But it seemed like a question I'd heard a first responder ask in one of those action films Fry loved. So I suppose they were good for something, after all.

Rufus looked at his shoes and I saw him wince again. "No," he told me. "Not on the foot that hurts." He leaned back against the sink cabinet, closed his eyes. "This feels like a break." He shivered. "I'm sorry."

Rufus was sorry?! It was me who should have been sorry. Sorry for not knowing what to do next. For not being able to muster a more productive response than wringing my hands, princess-style. I took a deep breath, then went back to the living room and slipped a Mexican blanket with tiny, flat-headed sheep running up and down its borders, off the couch. I wrapped it around him, and then I called Fry. It didn't matter anymore whether my boyfriend found out about morning pages. It didn't matter whether he thought Rufus was a dirty old man. What counted now was getting help for my poet, and I knew I could never lift him by myself.

But the prince never got a chance to ride to the rescue. Clearly, he was riding the waves, instead. The phone rang five times and then went to his default message. "Sorry," his not-very-sorry voice announced. "I'm in the water. Call you back when I'm high and dry."

So I called 911, instead. And then I called my father. I didn't get two sentences out before Shepherd told me he'd be right over. And we didn't wait five minutes before he was. He got there before the ambulance, and I was surprised at how he took charge, how he knew just what to do.

"Rufus." Shepherd shooed Carmen away, then knelt beside my poet and slipped an arm around his waist. "I've seen you looking better."

I don't know what it cost him, but Rufus grinned, shook his head. "You've only seen me once," he said.

Shepherd asked me to get a pillow from the couch, ice from the freezer, and a plastic freezer bag (which I found on a shelf in the Hendricks' neatly organized pantry). Then he went to work: "Lean on me," he told Rufus. In one deft move, he lifted the older man, cradled like an oversize baby, and laid a pillow under his legs. "It looks like it might be a break," he agreed with Rufus. "But we'll let the docs figure that out, huh?"

He filled the Ziploc with ice, wrapped it in a dishcloth, then held it against my poet's left shin, the place Rufus said hurt every time he breathed or moved. Finally, my father asked me to get a glass of water, and when I brought it, he scooped his hand under Rufus's head and helped him drink.

I wasn't much use after that, but I hovered. Just like Carmen, I prowled the perimeter, watching Shepherd's every move. For one thing, I wanted to make sure Rufus kept talking, kept, I don't know, *breathing.*

For another, I couldn't tear myself away from the new, totally improved version of my father I saw in front of me. I remembered all the names Mom had called him over the years—deadbeat, no-good, barbarian, embarrassment—and I couldn't make a single one of those ugly labels fit the man who'd just raced to Rufus's rescue.

It's funny, the people who reach out when you need it. By the time I got hold of Fry, both he and H were on the beach, waiting for me. But it was H who gave up a day in the sun and rushed to Whale Point General as soon as he heard what had happened. Fry, who hated hospitals, texted me that he was glad we had everything covered and he was sorry "the old guy took such a bad fall."

So it was just the three of us, Shepherd, me, and H, reading magazines and talking nervously in the ER waiting room. Rufus had been right, it was a break, not a sprain; he came home with a cast and crutches. Which meant H was a big help, because it turned out two shoulders were better to lean on than one. I just stood back and let my father and H ease my poet in and out, up and down. Doors and chairs, cars and elevators—all of them took careful planning and gentle support. Clearly, Rufus wouldn't be able to cook or clean for himself once he got home.

So guess who used his restaurant experience to fix our poet's meals from then on? And guess who Shepherd nominated to be his sous-chef? "Hell," he told me, as soon as he and H had settled Rufus on the couch, "we're used to working in the kitchen together, right?"

I didn't know if my father remembered our togetherness the same way I did. But I was not real eager to relive it. Still, we were both free during the day, and I had to admit that Shepherd deserved a second chance. And Rufus? He deserved all the help we could give him.

"I'll plan and you prep," Shepherd offered before lunch. "We'll do fine."

And we did. We resurrected one of Manny's best sandwiches, his avocado and hummus with chutney. We didn't use focaccia, but the toasted rye worked just fine. Rufus ate more than any of us, and H, who must have used up all his adjectives in his homework, was reduced to repeating, "Hmmmm, hmmmm, hmmmm," every other bite. He even tried to win Carmen over by sharing a crust with her. She backed away hissing, though, and Shepherd took it personally. "I went too heavy on the horseradish," he told us. "I don't know why I always do that."

H hung around because, skinny as he was, he was a lot more help than I could be when it came to lifting and toting. Not to mention that once he got his foot in his literary idol's door, there was no getting him out. And actually? It didn't hurt to have one more vote against my poet when he started talking nonsense. "I think we should go ahead with class," Rufus told us after lunch. H and Shepherd had settled him in a chair by the window, and he seemed easy there, almost comfortable. "Long as I don't put weight on my feet or get the cast wet."

H looked as though Rufus had suggested a quick trip to the moon. "I'd say, with all due respect, sir, that would be a mistake. You broke a bone this morning." He turned to Shepherd and me for support. "Why would you want to get in a car again this afternoon?"

"The doc said stay off it for a week, didn't he?" Shepherd was studying Rufus, like he was trying to figure out where he got his stamina, his fight. "Your body's had a shock; no point in giving it another one."

"Sarah?" Rufus checked in with me, as if I were his last hope.

But I had to disappoint him. I remembered him splayed across the kitchen floor, his white face, his shivering. "I can't see how a car ride makes any sense," I told him. "Not for you, not for anyone with a broken a leg."

Carmen obviously agreed. She crouched like a tiger, then hurled herself up from the floor onto his knees, where she proceeded to yowl . . . and yowl. The noise she made was halfway between a whine and a shriek, and no one in the room knew how to stop it. Except Rufus, who stroked her head, patted and soothed, until she metamorphosed from tiger to house cat, and curled into a docile, marmalade ball.

I couldn't help feeling angry at that spoiled feline who had, after all, caused Rufus's accident in the first place. But my poet didn't care. Over and over, regular as waves, his big hand slipped behind her ears, then down her neck and spine. Over and over, until her raspy engine started up and she fell asleep in his lap.

Second Chance

Before you grow away from
me and find us lost in time,
I should tell you who it is
that's working by my side.

There's no oracle here,
no practice made perfection,
or wisdom born of age,
you glow without direction.

But what a light you cast,
as mine fades out of sight!
What grace falls on tired fields
as day sinks down to night!

Why shouldn't this old dog
learn tricks from someone new?
And drought give way to rain,
as I cede my page to you.

All the poems I never wrote,
the things I've left undone,
will find a chance to shine
in your unrisen sun.

The Fourth Class

"But what if I didn't have to get in the car?" Reaching over Carmen's inert but sizable form, my poet picked up one of his crutches. "What if we held the class right here, and all I had to do was master these devilish contraptions?"

"You're kidding, right?" I checked in with Shepherd. He was shaking his head.

"I could stay at home, teach, and convalesce all at the same time." Again, Rufus looked to me for support. But it was H who caught the insanity.

"Why not?" he asked. "Why couldn't I go over to the college right now and tell the prof we're switching classrooms?" He looked around the living room. "I could even bring back some folding chairs from the auditorium."

Rufus was beaming. He was also much too enthusiastic for Carmen. Woken from her nap, she jumped to the floor and prowled off purposefully, as if she had important cat matters to attend to.

"Now, if someone would just give me a hand here." Rufus tried to stand, so Shepherd helped him to his feet and slipped a crutch under each shoulder.

"Nothing to it," my poet told us, proceeding to swing that long body of his between the aluminum braces. He maneuvered his way around the room, back and forth, back and forth. He got pretty good pretty fast, and finally even Shepherd was satisfied. "You're a natural, Rufus," he told our poet. "That just leaves bed, bath, and breakfast."

Rufus shifted onto one crutch, then let himself drop heavily back into the chair. "The doctor wanted to send someone over from the hospital," he told us. "Someone to nursemaid the invalid." He sighed, laid the crutches against the arm of his chair. "I told him I didn't think that would be necessary. I don't like being fussed over." He reached for the drink I'd put on the table next to him, and must have reached too far. One of the crutches clattered to the floor.

"Not necessary, huh?" Shepherd stooped to pick up the crutch, handed it back. "What do you say I camp out here for a few days, just till you get the hang of things?" He gave Rufus a look that was halfway between a smile and a challenge. "I'm not the fussing type."

And *I* wasn't the fainting type, but I came close. Shepherd staying with Rufus? Shepherd cooking and cleaning up after someone else? Rufus letting him? Well, maybe not that last, since my poet was clearly uncomfortable accepting help. He didn't argue with Shepherd, not exactly, but he wasn't going to agree to a roommate sitting down. He rose up in that chair on one elbow, grimacing when his hips shifted. "As much as I appreciate the offer," he told my father, "I'm not going to let you—"

Shepherd stepped forward now and slipped his own arm through my poet's, then pointed to the narrow hall that led to the back of the house. "Let's discuss this in your room, okay?" He didn't need to say more, he just let the prospect of navigating bed, toilet, shower, speak for itself.

Rufus seemed to realize what he was up against. He fell silent, probably considering the long walk, the thumping and bumping, between here and there.

"Now, if Sarah and Hector will excuse us," Shepherd announced, taking charge, "I'll bet we can find something in your closet, so you can get dressed for class."

For a few seconds I was too surprised to move, to speak. I simply stood there and watched the two of them, the silver-haired poet, his face turned to look up at Shepherd, and my slender, darker father, leaning over him. Even as I headed into the kitchen with H, I couldn't take my eyes off them, couldn't stop marveling at how Rufus leaned into Shepherd, how he let him lift, cradle, adjust, until the two of them were vertical. Until their heads were so close that, against the light streaming from the window, they looked almost like one person.

The text came in while Rufus and Shepherd were in the bedroom. So I had time to read Fry's new poem alone. It was just four lines long, but when you put the first letter of each together, they spelled the word "LOVE." They were printed in capitals so I couldn't miss it, but it didn't matter. Each line said love all by itself.

Like a scent in the wide air,
Of deeper deep I never knew,
Vines knocking on melancholy doors,
Even if I didn't love you, I would love the blueness of your eyes.

Fire and ice. Oil and water. The boy who had chosen the beach over Rufus. The person who'd written this love poem. How could you reconcile those two? How did they even coexist?

If I could have hugged my phone without starting up at least three apps I didn't need, I might have. This poem wasn't as long as the other Fry had sent, but it was just as beautiful. I knew I would copy it into my notebook. I knew I would treasure every line. And I knew that anyone who didn't love being loved by the boy who'd written them would have to be crazy.

I wasn't exactly proud of what I did next. But I couldn't help it. I needed to make sure that the friend who'd let me down this morning was the same one who'd written me this afternoon. That the accomplice who'd helped H concoct the Worst Poem in History had actually felt this Best of All Poems into being. So yes, I put Fry to the test. Right there, waiting for H to get back with the chairs for class, I Googled those lines to make sure they didn't belong to someone else. And guess what? They didn't. Fry was innocent of stealing beauty, guilty of making it all on his own. The way he'd acted this morning left a lot to be desired, but what he'd written on that screen? Well, it was as righteous as a kiss and as splendid as a new start.

When Fry called a minute later, I was crying and smiling all at once. *Vines knocking on melancholy doors.*

"You got the poem?"

He must have known the answer to his own question. I mean, it was hard to miss that I'd turned into a speechless mess.

"I'm glad you think it's okay."

"Okay?" I asked. I wiped away a tear. "Okay?! That poem is so much more than okay. It's nothing short of—"

"Shhhhh." Fry was soothing me, as if I were a dog. A nice dog, but one that jumped on company. "Let's keep this on the down low, Sar. I don't like sharing the way I feel about you with . . ." He paused. "Who's there, anyway. Where *are* you?"

Right on cue, H banged through the front door, four metal folding chairs in tow. Carmen tore off toward the back of the house, and H took a second look at my teary face. "You okay, Sarah?"

I looked up, sniffed. "Sure," I said. "I just got some good news from a friend." I stared at my cell. *Even if I didn't love you . . .* "I have to go," I told Fry. I explained about Rufus's broken leg, about the way he insisted on teaching right where he was.

"Really?!" Fry sounded just the slightest bit impressed. "Oh, well. Guess I didn't get the memo." He chuckled. "But tell me how it goes, huh?"

"You're not coming?" I asked. Not visiting the hospital was one thing, but missing class twice in a row was another.

"Hey, I'm finished jumping through hoops, Sar. I'm taking the summer off."

"You can't cut again. You'll start a stampede and land us all back in court."

"I feel a pretty bad headache coming on." He didn't sound sick, but he did sound borderline furious. "Maybe I'm allergic to twisted."

"What do you mean?" This wasn't poetry. And it didn't sound much like love, either.

"I mean, everyone's making jokes. I mean, it's getting old, Sarah—you and the Reverend Baylor."

The words stung, but I didn't have time to process them. Rufus was sorting through papers on the couch, and Shepherd and H were setting up chairs all around me. Carmen's barbed-wire howl had started up, and I knew we'd have to lock her in the bedroom before class.

"Fry," I told the cell. "You're wrong. You know you're wrong, and I really have to go." I pressed end, turned the sound off, and tucked the phone in my jeans pocket.

It took longer than usual for the class to settle. Meeting in a normal beach house instead of that stuffy classroom kind of went to everyone's head. Not to mention, someone came up with the idea that we should all sign my poet's cast. You should have seen it after we finished—it looked like a bunch of crazed kindergartners had attacked it—there were crooked smiley faces, lopsided stick figures, and one scary cartoon ghost that someone insisted was their muse. There was red and purple and yellow and green, and by the time all the kids had signed, I don't think there was a square quarter inch that wasn't colored in.

In between those smiley faces, though, while everyone else was fussing over Rufus, I heard Fry's voice again, his hurt. *Everyone's making jokes.* Did some of the kids right there in that room think Rufus was a dirty old man? Was the boy who drew a dragon with a broken wing on the toe of the cast one of the kids who joked about us to Fry?

Right up to the last, I kept hoping he'd join us. Hoping I wouldn't have to fabricate some illness, some heartrending emergency, that could plausibly keep him from class for the second time in a row. But he didn't. And I couldn't. I decided that my guy was a grown-up and that he was perfectly capable of making his own excuses. Love or no love, poetry or not, that wasn't part of my job description.

When it was finally time to start and people had gotten out paper and pencils, I offered to take over the music. But Rufus insisted it was his leg, not his arm, that was broken. He brushed that mop of hair off his forehead, took a deep breath, and tried to swipe the player the way I'd shown him. That's when I wished we'd gone full immersion. Because although I thought he'd watched me closely, it was clear that Rufus H. Baylor and the twenty-first century weren't fully acquainted. If we were learning poetry, then he was learning touch screens.

I knew he hadn't sabotaged our playlist, but the music that started up was hundreds of years too old and way too slow. He looked at me, helpless, as the swells of an organ billowed around us. Most of the kids in the room were polite . . . at first. But it was only a minute before they started rolling their eyes, shaking their heads.

As for Rufus, his eyes seemed to grow wider with each thunderous chord, and he tapped the player again and again. Which made things worse, since the classical music now alternated with an ancient playlist of mine, a BF selection that included some madrigals Wanda had insisted I'd love. Between the lutes and the organ, and the laughter breaking out everywhere, Rufus hardly knew where to start. Or end. He gave up, and finally asked for help. "Sarah," he said. "I'm afraid I, er, that is . . . would you . . ."

I rushed to his side, checked the player, found he was playing by artist, not album, in random order, not sequentially, and finally started the song we'd agreed on. I've told you how Rufus's smile lights you up, right? He looked at me now as if I'd saved the day, his life, and maybe the entire planet. I took that pride back to my seat with me. I ignored the smirks from Thatcher's crowd and listened, instead, to the music. It was a relief when the laughter died down and high fives spread around the room.

But suddenly, after just a few more minutes, Rufus turned the player off. Now there were more surprised looks, more heads shaking.

I wondered if I'd picked the wrong piece, if our teacher had decided his idea wouldn't work, after all. But it wasn't that. "I like watching people listen to music," he explained to us. "I can usually tell who's letting it in."

I wasn't sure what he was getting at, but one thing was clear: He was looking over all our heads to the back of the room. "Some people snap their fingers," he went on. "Some people sway, others sing along." He smiled, and I turned around to see who'd gotten his attention. "Only one person in this room closed his eyes. Only one person fell in."

Are you ready? That one person was Shepherd! I guess I half expected that my father would have gone out for a break. Or spent our class in Rufus's bedroom. But there he was, lounging against the back wall. Flushed, even under his tan, but playing it cool. I thought of all the old tapes he kept in the glove compartment of the Mustang. Of how he always made everyone in the car be quiet when the radio played a song he loved. Of how once he'd even pulled over to the side of the road, closed his eyes and tapped his fingers all the way through.

"Can you tell us why you shut your eyes?" Rufus was still looking at Shepherd, and Shepherd was still looking embarrassed. After centuries, he shook his head.

"I guess to give the music room," my father said, studying his hands as if they might help him answer. "Space of its own, you know?" He spoke slowly, reluctantly, as if every word were being dragged out of him. "A place it doesn't have to share."

Dialogue over. Rufus got the message. He went back to talking to the rest of us: "How you listen, what you feel, changes the music itself. Without you, it's nothing. Nine-tenths you, one-tenth the notes, right?

"I'd like y'all to make sure to close your eyes this time, too. And let the music make pictures in your head. Not words, mind. Just pictures."

He turned the player back on, and, mercifully, he got it right this time. The same music started up, and like a roomful of giant baby dolls, we all blinked our eyes shut and kept them that way. When he turned the music off (okay, when I heard him struggling with the player, and opened my eyes to help him out), Rufus looked at Dr. Fenshaw. "Get any pictures, Charles?"

"It went a little fast for me, sir," the prof told him. Fenshaw looked awkward, folded into that gym chair, his small poetry book on his knees. "I couldn't think of anything." He wasn't wearing a jacket tonight, and he even had his shirtsleeves rolled up. He seemed younger, but not more relaxed.

"Whatever you do, Charles, don't *think*." Rufus turned to all of us now, only half smiling. "I mean it," he said. "The thing about music? It reaches you without whys and wherefores. So you need to come at it with your heart before it gets to your brain."

"Stones," someone said from the back of the room. We all turned around, and saw how flushed, how shy, Margaret looked. "The bass made me feel like someone was dropping stones on wet leaves." She paused. "Is there a word for that?"

Rufus let his smile graduate to a grin. "Now that's just what I mean," he said. "This young lady heard a picture. She didn't stop to ask if it made sense, she just heard it."

Margaret glanced quickly at us, then lowered her head.

"This time"—our poet turned the player back on himself, smiling proudly at me when he got it right—"if you see a picture in your head, just stay with it. Ride it like a wave, okay?"

The violins were my favorite part. They were like a light thread woven through the darker, sturdier percussion. And suddenly, Fry's ugly words, his wounded tone, vanished, and I pictured children, little kids running suddenly into a roomful of adults. Under my closed lids, I let them scamper around the grown-ups' party, chasing each other, knocking over tables of food, laughing, and not caring at all what kind of trouble they got into.

When Rufus stopped the player a second time, the kids in my head froze, as if they were playing musical chairs. Then, when the music didn't come back, they just folded their arms, put their heads down, and went to sleep. It made me kind of sad, all that fun and energy sucked into quiet, into nothing. They weren't even real, those little devil-angels, but I didn't want to let them go. I wanted to give them permission to keep right on playing forever.

"Okay," Rufus told us. "Let's keep those pictures by turning them into words. Write down what you can. No full sentences, just quick notes, like catching a dream when you wake up." He grinned. "Write fast before it fades away."

We scribbled for a few minutes and then he played more music and we made more pictures. Then we did it again. And again. (Rufus had passed Technology 101, and was swiping almost gently now!) Sometimes, as I wrote, the hard words got in the way: *Maybe I'm allergic to twisted.* Sometimes they threatened to stop the pictures, break the flow. But almost always, like those little kids on a rumpus, I wrote right through them.

Our poet went around the room, asking us what we'd seen and felt. I told him about my wild children, and he nodded. "I like that a lot. But then you always take me by surprise, Sarah."

H, who was sitting close enough to hear, pumped his fist and grinned at me. Behind him, though, I couldn't help but see Thatcher. Our resident moose smiled; correction, he leered. And did something I didn't even want to think about with his tongue. I turned away, remembered Fry telling me kids were talking. *It's getting old, Sarah.*

When class was over, we'd all written down four pictures, four word sketches we could use for a poem. We talked about how we might stitch them together, and how some of them might make a whole poem all by themselves. "I'd like to make a book of these," Rufus told us.

"I've been reading the poems y'all have given me so far. And I want to go through the rest, put them together for us to remember."

"Do you mean an actual published book?" Coral Ann Levin, who wasn't easily impressed, was taking notice. "As in a real, copyrighted, library-type book?"

Rufus laughed. He leaned back in the couch, relaxed and easy in a way he hadn't been since before the accident. "Well, that might come later," he told Coral Ann. "For now, I just mean a book for us. I've been trying to think of a title."

I raised my hand. "How about *Good Poems from Bad Kids?*" I asked.

Now everyone in the room laughed, especially Rufus. He said he thought it was one of the best titles he'd ever heard, and he brushed away little laugh-tears with the sleeve of his shirt. "We've got only two more classes," he reminded us. "So if we want to get this book in shape, you'll need to do another assignment for me."

We knew the drill, and by now we also knew it wouldn't hurt.

"This one's about touch," Rufus told us. He fumbled in the pocket of the sweatshirt Shepherd had helped him put on. He pulled out one of the black, silky blindfolds we'd used last class. "So the blinkers have to go back on."

I don't know how many people heard Thatcher's stage whisper about touching in the dark, but almost everyone looked at the clock. It was way past time to leave.

"Now?" someone asked, and then our poet caught on.

"Course not," he said. "Y'all choose the time and the place. But I want you to be at home, somewhere familiar. Could be your room.

"Cover your eyes and touch all the things you think you know by heart." (A not-so-quiet laugh, probably from the Vogel Neanderthal again.) "Your wall, maybe. Your desk or your rug. Even your floor. One at a time, go wherever those things take you. Each texture will put you in a different country, a different geography, of touch."

"Should we give these countries names?" one girl asked. I couldn't tell if her question was serious, but Rufus treated it that way.

"Sure, why not?" he said. "In fact, you might use those country names to title your poems. Write as few or as many as you want. But here's the catch: Keep your eyes covered while you write."

"Do we have to use pencils? Can't we type?"

Someone almost always asked that, and Rufus usually said no. But this time was different.

"Yep. Just keep your eyes closed."

"Type with our eyes closed?!!"

"Think you can't do it? I'm here to tell you that you can." The patented grin. "If y'all don't believe me, go on and sneak those blindfolds off. Take a peek every ten minutes or so."

"Got to love it," I heard a kid behind me whisper. "A teacher who gives you permission to cheat."

Jumping, jiving, wiggling free
gyrating, migrating everywhere
are little kids freer than big ones?
Are big ones scared to let go?
Pull it out like taffy, man,
spin it out like glass

go tell your momma, go tell your ~~papa~~ dad
laughing music makes ~~them~~ us giggle
good music makes ~~them~~ us bad
trays are breaking, babies waking
mommies getting mad, mad, mad

don't want to stop,
don't want to go to bed
keep that singsong going

don't want to be down, down down
ashes ashes we all fall down
slow, so slow, no, no no!
I'm not sleepy, mommy
one more drink, one more word,
one more life, please, please, please

Wanda Meets Her Idol and Forgets Her Name

The first one to leave, same as every class, was Thatcher Vogel. Which was fine with me, since I didn't relish fielding questions about Fry, or dealing with the hulk's R-rated sign language and dirty looks. By the time we'd all turned in our poems and Dr. Fenshaw, who'd taken to staying late and asking question after question after question after—well, you get the idea—by the time even the prof had left, there was Shepherd, still watching from the back of the room. "Were you there the whole time?" Maybe I sounded like a rude brat, but I was shocked that my father might have sat (or stood) still for a whole poetry lesson!

"Figured I'd like to see what all the fuss was about." Shepherd leaned close, whispered. "I'm kind of hoping this will stay between us, though, Sarah." He grinned. "I've got a rep, you know?"

I laughed. I could just imagine what my mother would think of Shepherd in poetry school. And that was when I remembered my mother's dinner party! (I would have bet my Sarah Bernhardt posters that she was calling it a soirée when she told people about it.

And I would have bet my program from *Les Mis* that she was telling *everyone*.)

I'd forgotten all about my mother's plans. And about inviting Wanda to join us. But Rufus's day had been too long as it was. Someone would have to phone Wanda and tell her she'd need to wait to meet the Great One. Worse, someone would have to tell my mother to unset the table. And worst of all, class, that someone was *me*.

I explained to Shepherd and Rufus about the dinner that wouldn't be. About how I had to walk home right away and soothe ruffled feathers. My father understood. He said he had everything under control, he was planning on making an omelet for supper. Rufus, who looked grateful (and finally, very tired), said he loved omelets.

I made sure they liberated Carmen, who came tearing out of the bedroom and then refused to pay attention to anyone. I'd said goodbye and closed the door before I wished I could turn around and go right back in: Thatcher hadn't actually left yet. He was standing beside his T-top, back braced against the passenger door. A group of his thug friends were with him, and unless I opted to turn around and walk the wrong way, I'd have to run the gauntlet.

I wasn't ashamed that the Great One was my friend as well as my teacher. Even then, I knew it was something I'd probably tell my kids and grandkids about one day. But I couldn't help being sorry that Thatcher was always within earshot when Rufus singled me out or asked for help. I was even sorrier that, as I walked by him now, Mr. Brawn for Brains was patting his butt again and giving me that smile that was three-quarters leer. "Hey, Sarah," he told me. "Way to snow the old fart."

Now, looking at that smirking mutant, it all made sense. Thatcher and Fry, their matching tool belts at cleanup. Their consultations about hammers and crowbars and things that go bump, that tear and claw. Who would be in a better position to whisper filth into Fry's ear? Who would be so callous, so stupid?

Okay. So Rufus wasn't the only one who'd had a long day. A picture of my poet lying on the kitchen floor flashed in my head or heart or maybe it was my stomach: I felt like I'd lived on a steady diet of fear and worry from first thing that morning to right this minute, when four grinning apes were pushing me to the limit.

"What old fart?" I asked Thatcher. I felt the anger, like a rush of adrenaline. "You mean the man who's famous and loved by people in places you can't even spell?"

Thatcher was still smiling broadly, still processing what I'd just said. I figured that dumb grin was the same one he'd worn when he spread rumors about Rufus and me.

"You mean the man who's won four Pulitzers and will be remembered after you and your whole family are feeding worms?"

"Hey, wait a minute—"

"I guess you mean the man who feels and thinks more in one poem than you ever will in your entire pathetic life?"

Thatcher's smile had faded, and there was just a line down the middle of that wide, thought-free brow. I didn't usually—okay, I *never* talked like this. The moose and his friends were probably all in shock, and so was I. It was as if someone else had taken over my body and my mouth; someone stronger, someone you wouldn't want to cross. I walked past those boys now, one by one. None of them said anything, not a single word. So I kept right on walking. I felt a little nasty. A little mean. And a whole lot better!

My mother was, as predicted, deeply disappointed. But a broken bone is a broken bone, and even she didn't feel we had thwarted her on purpose. If Rufus couldn't come to her house, she decided she would go to his. She and Aunt J. would fix a dinner and bring it over to him whichever night he chose. He chose Sunday.

Which gave me only a few more beach days before the big night. The sun was on my side, and the waves, too. Between us, we convinced my love interest to mellow out, not to listen to morons. Fry, tanner and leaner than he'd been all year, gloried in the water and in surfing for the clusters of tourists that had begun to form whenever he took to the waves. Between the kisses and the pepperoni slices; between toweling him off when he came out of the water, and cheering him on when he went in, all was eventually forgiven. Yes, I was spending more time with Rufus than I'd reported; and yes, some evolutionarily challenged throwbacks were talking. But when push came to touch and touch and touch, we still had a good thing going. And if we stayed away from conversational hot buttons like poetry, poets, and my mother, Fry and I both knew it. We agreed to disagree. "It's a lot more fun fighting with you," Fry told my left ear under our beach towel, "than being angry by myself."

Which may explain why we got so much work done at our third cleanup. Fry and H opted to join the painting team with Margaret and me instead of setting pavement stones with Thatcher and his goon squad. You know by now that I'm not a Home Depot, do-it-yourself fan, but even I was proud of how the house looked after we'd finished the last interior coats. Nothing fancy, no Dark Melon or Burnt Umber, no sponge patterns or swirls. We settled for pale-lemon and off-white walls, and it made the rooms look larger, softer. I wasn't sure whether we were supposed to show Rufus our handiwork, but I knew he'd like what we'd done.

Of course, I still didn't mention morning pages to Fry. And neither did H. Yes, there were two of us keeping that secret now. Because Rufus, who insisted on writing every morning, "hell or high water, one leg or two," invited H to join us. In fact, he invited anyone in class who wanted, to walk right into the house without knocking (or setting off that symphonic doorbell) each morning at eight o'clock. Granted, a lot of my classmates felt the way Fry did about voluntary visits with a teacher, no matter how famous, not to mention getting up with the sun. But I knew Margaret would come, and judging from the way she beamed when Rufus issued his invitation, I was afraid there'd be no keeping Coral Ann Levin away.

Sure enough, I usually had plenty of company at morning pages from then on. Carmen met everyone with the same surly discontent, and more often than not, got banished to the bedroom.

Those mornings always began with Shepherd's coffee. He made it stronger and hotter than Rufus . . . or anyone, for that matter. He always added a pinch of salt and, don't ask me why, it changed everything. The coffee was foamier, less bitter, and the aroma? It was nutty. Deep. Like sniffing toast and late-afternoon sun.

We kept the extra chairs H had picked up at the college, and sometimes sat in them to write. Mostly, though, people took their mugs and their tablets outside in the garden or (if Carmen was in exile) found a comfortable place inside on the floor. We worked silently and freely, letting ideas and feelings rush us, for half an hour. Rufus wrote right along with us, his leg propped up on a cushion, his tablet catching the sun from the window behind the couch.

Sometimes I'd finish a poem, sometimes not. But I usually came away with a secret high, a moist, new beginning. I wasn't sure it would ever become a poem; sometimes it was more like a curtain going up, an opening, a way in. I hate to admit it, but H said it best. "I always feel like I'm surfacing from a dive," he told me one day. "Like I've been somewhere secret, you know?"

I knew.

"Sunday is wonderful!" Wanda was, no surprise, free on the day that Rufus had chosen for dinner. It could have been any day of the week, of course, and any time: I could just as easily have invited her to join us for a midnight snack or a 4 a.m. breakfast—it was all the same to her, so long as she got to meet her idol.

My mother and Aunt J. arrived promptly at six, which meant Shepherd left promptly at five thirty. Before she did anything else, Mom insisted that Carmen, who had greeted her none too politely, be "put where she can't spoil the party." Next, she presented Rufus with the small silver-plated dinner bell she kept in a curio cabinet in our living room. "Now, you're not to move a muscle," she told him sternly. "You just ring if you need the least little thing, you hear?"

Rufus, who had been making great progress and was already maneuvering his crutches like a master, just smiled. "Thank you, Katherine," he told her. "I can't say I'm much at home in the role of helpless invalid. Who knows? Perhaps persnickety overlord will suit me better."

Once Mom had stuffed too many pillows behind her host, so that he looked like a rather uncomfortable sultan, and after she'd placed a tall glass beside him, insisting that "Those also serve who only drink sweet tea," we got to work. I helped her set the table, and Aunt J. filled the cottage's tiny stove to bursting with casseroles and pans. Jocelyn and I had just succeeded in persuading my mother that five guests did not require place cards, when the doorbell rang. In order to cut short the symphony and put Carmen out of her misery (she howled each time the bell rang), I raced into the living room and opened the door on our very excited, very overdressed guest.

Wanda's bright hair was an electric halo, and her yellow silk tee shimmered with sequins. She wore a snake-shaped arm bracelet and peacock feather earrings, exotic notes that didn't quite fit her wide, little-girl smile.

"Oh, thank goodness," she said, racing ahead of me to the couch, where she held out her hand to Rufus and got swept into a double handshake. "If I had to wait a minute longer, I would have expired on the spot."

"Well, if you had, young lady," Rufus told her as if they'd known each other forever, "you would have missed what promises to be a deeply satisfying meal."

Wanda, who refused to give up either one of her host's hands, held them both and continued pumping, up and down, faster and faster. "Oh, Mr. Baylor"—shake, shake—"you can't imagine how much I admire your work." Shake, shake. "I mean, your recording of 'The Sorrowful Villanelles'? I could listen to it forever! Of course, I know I'm not the first person who's told you that." Shake, shake. "And not the last, wouldn't you say?"

"And who would I say that *to*?" My poet grinned at me, then at the way Wanda had persisted in holding his hands. "I'm assuming you're a friend of Sarah's?"

Yes, redheads *do* blush brighter than the rest of us. "Oh, golly, I'm sorry." Wanda took one of her hands away to put it over her mouth. "I completely forgot." She looked down at Rufus with adoring-groupie eyes. "It's just that, well, I know who *you* are, of course. But it never occurred to me you don't know *me*, I mean . . . you know . . ." She stopped chattering to giggle. "How dumb can you be?"

"A lot dumber than you, I'll bet." Rufus outsmiled her, rescuing one of his hands to sip his tea. "I'm pleased to meet you, . . ."

"Wanda, sir." My friend sat down in the chair I brought over, but managed to keep hold of my poet's other hand. "Wanda Slater." The hand pumping had stopped, but the worshipful gaze had not. "Wanda Elizabeth Slater."

As if she had radar, an internal warning device that allowed her to sense when someone else was the center of attention, my mother hurried in from the kitchen. "Rufus!" She practically sang his name, as if he were her dearest friend, as if they hadn't seen each other in years, instead of minutes. "Why didn't you ring? Your tea glass is empty!"

"I'm afraid our captive"—my poet nodded toward the bedroom in which we'd locked Carmen—"responds rather badly to bells." Rufus adjusted the sea of cushions behind him. "Besides, I'm saving room. Whatever you and your sister are concocting in that kitchen, Katherine, smells like paradise."

"It's Kate, Rufus." My mother was smiling as if her face didn't know how to do anything else. "And I hope your appetite is up to the task. I won't allow you to eat less than everything, you know!" Her drawl got longer and more flirtatious with each step she took toward the couch. And yes, she perched beside my poet there, like a preschooler, the cocktail plates she'd been carrying nested in her lap.

Finally, she turned to Wanda and me. "I see you've brought a friend, Sarah." As though I hadn't told her Wanda was coming. As though I hadn't assured her my friend had the smallest appetite on the planet, and promised I'd take extra-tiny portions myself.

Mom smiled the briefest of smiles at Wanda, before turning back to the guest of honor. "We're ready when you are, Rufus. I told Jocelyn to tuck those crab rolls right back in the oven until you give us the high sign." She laughed as if she'd said something incredibly amusing, then placed one of the dainty plates in front of each of us. Which meant she wanted us to linger over what did, indeed, smell like heaven in the kitchen.

Rufus took my mother's hands in his. "Well, let the crabs roll," he told her. "I'm not sure how much more torture our olfactory nerves can be expected to endure."

When Aunt Jocelyn joined us, she had a tray in her hands. It was piled high with flattened hot dog buns rolled into pancakes and wrapped around crab salad. Like a cartoon, Rufus raised his head, his nose leading. "Ambrosia!" he said. "Pure ambrosia."

We waited, holding our breath, watching my poet take his first taste. "This has to be stone crab," he said, after he'd nearly devoured a whole roll in one bite. "Wherever did you find stone crab?"

"How did you know?" Jocelyn's smile matched my poet's, and we all took bites of our own.

"I can always tell stone crab from blue." Rufus shook his head, licked his fingers. "It tastes like lobster—soft and sweet and beyond compare."

"I have a little place I go," Jocelyn confided. "It's a bit of a drive, but I think it's worth it." She smiled at Rufus, at my mother, even at me and Wanda.

I'd watched Rufus during morning pages, seen how expert he'd become at moving around on his crutches. Adjourning to the dining room, then, so Mom could show off the table she'd set, was no problem. And neither was finishing the four courses Aunt J. had cooked. It was over the second, a consommé with sherry and shrimp, that Mom asked Rufus the question she hadn't asked me in the whole month I'd been taking classes with him. "So," she said, putting the tips of her fingers together, a church roof over her jellied soup, "what have you and your budding poets been working on?"

Even though she'd looked at Rufus when she asked, I answered. "We wrote to music last class," I reported. "Remember? I told you how Mr. Bay—I mean, Rufus and I picked the CDs out?"

Rufus nodded, but Mom laughed right out loud. "Oh, my," she said, patting our poet's arm in sympathy. "I guess with inexperienced writers, you really need bells and whistles." She stopped, heard what she'd said. "As it were," she added, smiling at her own accidental joke.

"You should have been there, Kate." Had our poet missed my mother's mean-spirited point? Or was he just ignoring it? "Thanks to Sarah's high-tech lessons for this low-tech learner"—he winked at me—"our words danced."

By the time dinner was finished, Rufus had deflected at least two more of Mom's not-so-subtle suggestions that he was working with a bunch of juvenile illiterates. It must have required considerable energy to cut her off at the pass, because he fueled himself with extra helpings of everything, including Jocelyn's Temptation Torte, a dessert of her own invention that involved more chocolate than should be legal in any one recipe.

It wasn't until we were back in the living room that Rufus got the chance to talk to Wanda. While my mother and aunt were in the kitchen, pouring coffee into the tiny cups Mom had insisted on bringing with her for the occasion, Rufus turned to my friend. "So, Miss Slater," he said, "I'm curious to know what sort of poetry you write."

"Well, sir." Wanda lowered her voice, as if she were telling a dirty joke. "I've written thirty-six poems about my bed." She looked amused and embarrassed at the same time. "And twenty-seven about the cove."

"The cove?"

"Yes, sir." Wanda held her fingers in a circle. "It's a little piece of ocean that gets caught behind some rocks off Dingman's Island. The water there is a whole different color."

"It sounds like a poemworthy spot," Rufus told her. "And now that two poets have joined us tonight, perhaps I should include you both in an invitation to see a play by one of the greatest poets who ever lived."

Wanda and I looked at each other. Thrilled. Curious.

"It seems your local theater company is staging my favorite Shakespeare play next week," Rufus explained. "I've probably seen *The Tempest* thirty times," he told us. "But I'd love to make it thirty-one." He propped himself up with one of his crutches, reached into his pocket, and took out a white envelope. "It seems they've sent me three tickets for Wednesday night," he said, holding them up for us to see. "It's fate, ladies. What do you say?"

Wanda lit up, her hands clasped in an unconscious imitation of Miss Kinney. And me? The perennial auditioner? The stagestruck wannabe? Why wouldn't I kill (or at least, maim) to watch Shakespeare with Rufus and my best friend? A tiny shoot of happiness started to sprout, but then I pushed it down. My mother and Jocelyn arrived with the coffee, and that's when I knew how much one person in the room would be disappointed by Rufus's invitation, would feel cheated, left out.

Wanda was bubbling, chattering about the play. Suddenly, Mom was plunking down our coffee cups, clinking and clanking too loudly, too fiercely. There was hurt in every move she made, and I could feel it across the room. So, apparently, could Rufus, who put one hand on my mother's arm when she brought him his cup. "Kate," he said, "I've asked these two young ladies to accompany me to the theater for a midweek performance. I'd be honored if you and your sister would join us."

My mother stopped clanking and sat down. She put on her coy, flirty face, a demure look that said she'd have to think about it, would have to sort through the countless other offers she'd received. And then, before she could answer, a minor miracle occurred.

"We can't." Jocelyn looked blankly, matter-of-factly at the rest of us. "Kendall and I are taking Kate to the Bluegrass Ramblers."

"What?" Mom, who had obviously been on the verge of graciously accepting Rufus's invitation, looked stunned.

"Don't you remember, Kate? That's the night the Ramblers are playing at the Steakhouse." My aunt paused, her face suddenly earnest. "Kendall says it isn't every day you get to see a group like the Ramblers live." *And it isn't every day,* her spoiled-baby-sister voice told my mother, *that you'll have a chance to get to know my boyfriend, and if you don't do this, I'll pout and possibly hate you forever.*

"There are other plays in the season," Rufus told Mom. "Perhaps we can find a time later."

My mother looked uncertain. She took a survey of the room: Rufus, easygoing, conciliatory in his pillow nest; Jocelyn, threatening a tantrum; Wanda, on the verge of euphoria; me, holding my breath. Then, perhaps because changing the subject was the only way to wrest control of her soirée from its guests, she turned to my poet. "Now, Rufus," she said, apropos of absolutely nothing. "Why don't you tell us what it was like to read at the president's inauguration? I know Jocelyn is dying to hear what they served at the White House dinner."

The Play's the Thing

Slowly but surely, I was adding to my stock of Edward (which was Fry's actual name, the one I was sure he'd publish under someday) Reynolds's poetry. Each time I asked for a new poem, he sighed and shook his head as if I'd asked him to swim the Channel or give up beer. He always told me that *I* was a poem, that he could never write one that came close. But each time, a few hours later, I'd find another text on my phone. One that made me wonder how Rufus could have used the word "talent" about someone like me, when people like Fry inhabited the planet. People who could write, "your body's silent music," or, "sweet rain of whispered words."

But the more I thought about it, the more convinced I was the world would love Fry's poetry as much as I did. That maybe I was being selfish and small, treating his poems like my own personal property, like a signature scent I didn't want anyone else to wear. Which was why, two days after my mother's dinner for Rufus, on our walk home from the beach, with no ride but plenty of privacy, I told him how I felt. "You should really and truly publish these." I pressed my cell phone to my chest, like a heroine in an old-fashioned romance, hugging a bundle of love letters. "Don't you dare laugh," I added. I put a finger over his mouth. "I want you to show them to Rufus. I'm positive he'd help, you know, get them out there."

"I didn't write those poems for Rufus Baylor." Fry wasn't laughing anymore. He took my phone away, as if it were a toy I didn't deserve. "I wrote them for you." He aimed dark, dead-serious eyes at mine. "*Only* for you." And now he grabbed the finger I'd placed on his lips and turned it back on me like a trigger. "Understand?"

I nodded, took my phone back. But I didn't get it at all, not really. How could someone, especially someone who wrote such flat-out gorgeous poems, not want to reach other people with them? How could an artist who made such heavenly word music settle for playing it to an audience of one?

"Got to give props to the fossil, though," Fry told me. "Teaching class with a broken leg." H and I, careful to avoid the topic of morning pages, had talked up my poet's quick recovery after the accident. If we couldn't praise the poetry, we could praise the man.

"He's pretty tough," I said, trying to find an adjective Fry would approve. I considered and rejected "brave," "heroic," and "amazing."

H was relieving Shepherd at Rufus's, so it was just the two of us when we got to Fry's. Correction: just the two of us and Mrs. Reynolds, who was watching TV upstairs. Which meant hugs. And kisses. But no more.

Right after we'd turned up the volume on our set to drown out hers, Fry's cell beeped and he checked a text message. His whole face lit up.

"Guess where we're going tomorrow?" he asked, as soon as he'd read it. He was too excited even to wait for an answer. "I'll give you a hint"—bursting to get the good news out—"H got passes to the school bus races at the speedway!"

Honestly, you should have seen that boy's face. He looked as if he were surprising me with a trip to Disneyland. Europe. Cancún. But truth be told? A three-hour ride in the Taurus with *no* air-conditioning and one window permanently shut since the crank handle had fallen off was not something I was anxious to experience. All to watch lumbering, decades-old school buses race each other around a quarter-mile track. And if you think a bus is way too large to make the turns on such a small course, you're right.

Apparently, though, that was the whole point. "Motorized mayhem," Fry called it, and he and H couldn't get enough of the smashing and splintering, the spilled radiators, the slides, the rear-wheeling, and of course, the crashes. But no matter how differently I felt, no matter how hard I'd have to try to share their enthusiasm, this princess would have hiked up her ball gown and gone with them; she would have been a good sport and laughed at the upended buses with her prince . . . *if* she didn't have a date already.

"I'm sorry," I told Fry, as gently, as casually, as I could. "I'm busy tomorrow." But when he asked what I was doing and I told him about going to the theater with Rufus and Wanda, the casual, gentle thing kind of went out the window:

"You've got to be kidding!" Fry didn't seem to care that his mother was home. He was practically shouting. "You just had dinner with Wilma, right? And what is it with you and Baylor, anyway?"

"It's Wanda," I told him.

Dueling TVs or not, his mom couldn't have missed what he yelled next. "Don't you get it, Sarah? That old perv is putting the moves on you."

It was as if I'd just closed the door on summer and opened it to find bare branches and snow everywhere. I sat, stunned, trying to get used to the chill. "You're wrong, Fry."

Fosdick, roused from his dog siesta by the noise, sniffed first at Fry, then at me. I threw his dog toy as far as I could, but it bounced off Fry's weight bench and came right back to us. "You don't know what Rufus is like," I told Fry. What more was there to say? Rufus wasn't on trial. "You don't even go to class." Why did I need to defend the dearest, kindest person I knew?

ME

(*Hurt, fuming*)

FRY

So? What? Did he tell you your work needs special attention?

OUR TV

Now for more about this story, here's our reporter in L.A. Lauren, what's . . .

ME

Not that it matters. But he says I've got talent.

FRY

I'll bet. And he wants to develop it, right?

FRY'S MOM'S TV

. . . stressed once again that he will not be seeking a second . . .

ME

(Angry, standing)

I've got to go.

FOSDICK

(Looking for his toy under the couch)

RHWRooooom?

OUR TV

. . . by someone who knew the victim well, that there was no . . .

FRY

(Yelling again)

Under the sheets, Sarah. That's where he wants to develop your talent. Under the goddamn—

FRY'S MOM

(At the door)

Is everything all right in here?

* * * *

I don't know if he realized how ridiculous, how like a child throwing a fit, he'd sounded. Or if he just decided that he trusted me more than he trusted Rufus. But Fry made up with a poem. He texted it first thing the next morning, and I read it over and over. Each time, it got better. Like all Fry's poems, this one amazed me with how deep he could go, how his writing voice turned everything he said softer, more tender:

> You—you—
> Your shadow is sunlight on a plate of silver.

How would you feel if you went to bed angry and woke up to that? Did I hear you say confused? Crazy? Sad?

Morning pages, beach afternoons. They were two separate worlds, and I was learning to make sure I kept them apart. But that afternoon at the beach, Fry almost crossed the border: He was funny and warm and said he hoped I wouldn't come back from my "date" expecting him and H to spout Shakespeare. "Methinks thou shouldst think again," he joked. "And tights? By my butt, we will never don that gay apparel."

He even offered, at the last minute, to give up the bus races and drive all three of us to the theater that night. He would borrow H's Taurus, he texted me. Twice. But my newly zealous father put his foot down as soon as I got to Rufus's. "He just got his permit," Shepherd reminded me. "And besides, have you seen the tires on that heap?"

It wasn't just the car, though. "I'm not trying to lead your life for you, Sarah," Shepherd told me once he'd set out clothes for Rufus. (My poet was practicing dressing on his own now, so my father and I were waiting for him in the kitchen.) "But frankly? I think you deserve a lot more in the boyfriend department."

I told him he sounded like Mom, and he told me that, sometimes, my mother had a point. "Just because he's crazy about you," he said, all deep-voiced and stern, "doesn't make him a contender, you know." He slowed, looked at me long and hard. "There will be lots of boys who are crazy about you."

I didn't show him Fry's poem. I wasn't even sure he'd know how good it was. So I just slipped my cell into my pocket and listened to him drone on. He'd just come to the part about the importance of "common interests," which seemed like a phrase he'd picked up from my mother, when my ringtone interrupted.

It was Wanda. She was crying. And sick. "I was hoping I'd get better," she told me. "My mother promised if my temperature got within two degrees of normal, I could still go.

"Oh, Sarah! This is the most hideous day of my life." She sniffed and reined in a sob. Or tried to. "And it was supposed to be the best."

Wanda's misery was "writ large," as Miss Kinney loved to say. It was just as big, just as dramatic, as her happiness usually was. I didn't know what to say, so I just nodded (even though she couldn't see me) and listened.

"I was looking forward to this so much," she wailed. "I told everyone, simply everyone, that I was going out with you and Rufus." She sobbed again or hiccuped or both. "I was just getting used to calling him that—oh, Sarah! This is the sort of thing that happens once in a lifetime. If I live to be a hundred, I'll never have another chance to spend an entire evening with someone so famous, so generous, so . . ."

"... late?" I finished for her. Rufus had called a cab, and it was waiting at the top of the driveway when I looked out the window. "I am *so* sorry, Wanda. The taxi's here." I'd been counting on sharing this outing with her, too. "I wish you were coming with us, you know I do. My two best poetry buds, it would have been so ..."

Rufus hobbled in, sporting his one and only jacket with a dark-green tee I'd never seen before. INNER SPACE, it said right over his heart.

"I have to go," I told Wanda. "But I'll give you a full report."

Wanda sniffed. "Everything?" she asked. "Every single detail?"

"Promise."

By the time Shepherd hustled us out to the cab, I was right—we were late. Luckily, it was midweek, so there wasn't much traffic, and only one or two of the horse-drawn carriages that summer people loved to ride around in. We got to town before curtain, but once we arrived at the theater, it really hit home that this was my poet's first full outing without Shepherd to help. We moved a lot slower than we would have with my father along. Rufus, of course, had asked him to join us, but Shepherd had declined. "Listening to music is one thing," he'd told us, "but sitting still for a whole goddamn play is another." (Which, in the language of Shepherd, probably meant he understood how much I wanted this night to be just me and my poet. I was getting pretty good at translating!)

But if we weren't exactly setting speed records, we made it in the end. Rufus did just fine, stumbling only once when he got out of the taxi. He hauled himself up the theater steps and into the main hall, where we worked our way down the middle aisle to the orchestra section. My poet covered ground by hopping like a wounded bird, a looping, broken gait that, if it didn't look very graceful, got him where he needed to go. An usher handed me two programs just as a tiny orchestra began playing in front of the stage. That's when a second usher, the one who was supposed to seat us, spotted Rufus's crutches. And voilà! An upgrade: He moved us to the first two seats in the very front row!

Which is why it felt as if we were right on the deck of a storm-tossed ship when the play started. And right on the shore of a magical island, watching the same shipwreck in the second scene. The two characters who watched with us were a wise old magician named Prospero and his daughter, Miranda. They had been marooned on the island for twelve years, with only Prospero's books and each other to keep them company. (Unless, of course, you counted a whole cast of spirits and sprites created by the magician's awesome powers.)

The actor who played Prospero had a mop of silver hair, and he was a big man, like Rufus. So when he talked about all the time he'd spent teaching his daughter on their deserted island, I couldn't help but think about those first morning pages, when I'd had my poet all to myself; when we'd stayed in and played with words, just the two of us.

The Tempest, it turned out, had everything—amazing costumes and sets, storms, shipwrecks, duels, ghostly pageants, nonstop special effects. And the characters? I wanted to play every one of those roles! I'd never read the play because Bernhardt had never acted in it. But now, in the middle of all that magic, I did a little casting after the fact: Even while I watched a local college student, hoisted up on wires, "fly" across the stage,

I pictured the Divine Sarah herself as a charming, mischievous version of Ariel, the fairy who helps Prospero with his magic—Tinker Bell, minus the schmaltz and the Disney costume.

But my favorite character of all that night was Caliban, the island's resident monster. He looked just like my collectible Hulk, only a lot bigger. He was a huge misfit who didn't know his own strength, crude and ugly and thick as a post. But I couldn't help feeling sorry for the way Prospero treated him—the same way some people behave with their dogs, as if it doesn't matter what you do or say to them. Granted, Caliban wasn't pretty to look at, but he had a poet's instincts. Or at least, just like me and Rufus, he heard things talking all the time. Voices everywhere.

Which is why I was glad that as part of the happy ending, Prospero gave the whole island back to Caliban when he and Miranda were rescued. He knew that his daughter had her own life to live beyond his books and spells. So he decided to perform just enough magic to get them back to the real world, and then to bury his wand and spell book forever.

When the applause and the curtain calls (four!) were over, and the house lights went up, Rufus and I barely had a chance to stand up before people who'd recognized him walked over to shake hands. First, there was a couple, about Aunt J.'s age, who'd been reading Rufus's poetry for years. In fact, the man confided, he'd proposed to his wife ten years before, by reciting a love poem from *The Wait-a-Minute Bush*. "She said yes," he told my poet, doing the double handshake and reporting something we'd pretty much already guessed. "Now our third grader, Timmy Wayne, has gone and memorized six of your poems."

(Fortunately, this prodigy had not come to the play with his parents and couldn't treat us to a recitation.)

Next, there was a woman who'd read about what Rufus was doing with "those poor, lost children." She had a long, earnest face, and clutched his arm when she told him he was the best example they could possibly have. Finally, there was an English teacher from one of the middle schools who felt the same way, and oh, also, would Rufus have time to read a few things she'd written?

My poet was generous and attentive with them all. He shook their hands, he answered questions about his cast, he signed their programs, though he wanted it clear, he said, that he hadn't been around when the play was written. And yes, I had the same feeling I'd had in class—Rufus seemed to need these groupies as much as they needed him. Which is probably why he promised the English teacher he would read her poems. But the best news, the sweetest news, was that my poet introduced me to each one of these autograph hounds, not as a member of his Bad Kids Class, but as "my friend Sarah." And then he added, "She's been sharing some of her work with me," or, "We're revisiting Shakespeare together."

It was late when the cab dropped us back at the Hendricks'. Shepherd was already asleep on the couch in the living room. We tiptoed into the kitchen, Carmen padding along with us, winding between our legs and begging for a late-night snack. "I loved it all, every minute," I whispered to Rufus. "Thank you so much!"

"Well, I was delighted to have your company," my poet told me. While I found the cat food (which my smart father had moved to a *bottom* shelf), Rufus rummaged through the cupboards, brought out two cups and a package of coffee filters. "Besides," he added, fitting the filter into the coffee machine, "I had an ulterior motive." I could see his smile, even in that unlit room. "I'm hoping, Sarah, that the play we saw tonight has left you eager to keep writing."

I emptied a whole envelope of Tender Kitten into Carmen's bowl. Ungluing herself from my legs, she hunkered down beside it, throwing each bite back deep in her mouth, as if she were afraid it might escape before she could swallow it. Maybe Rufus had been serious about her having no teeth?

"I don't know about writing," I told my poet. "But tonight certainly made me want to get back onstage." I helped him with his crutches, and we both sat at the counter, waiting for the coffee brewer to finish humming and hissing.

"Really?" Rufus looked grave, surprised. "Wouldn't you rather write the script than mouth someone else's words?" He fixed me with that trigger finger. "Remember your poem? I believe 'secondhand words' was the way you put it."

"It's just that no one would ever play Miranda the same way I would." Carmen's sandpapery tongue scrubbed my leg, and I leaned down to pet her. "Or Ariel. Or yes, even Prospero." I turned the trigger finger back at him.

"When you play a part you love," I explained, "it's like a glove that fits perfectly." The rustling of sheets on the couch told me I was speaking too loudly. "No dangling fingertips," I added, whispering again. "No thumbhole you can't squeeze into. It's just right."

Rufus nodded. "You have a way with words, Miss Wheeler." The coffee machine had stopped, and he watched as I filled the two mugs he'd found. One was decorated with a snowman, the other featured a drowsy baby with a cartoon bubble over its head. "I liked what I heard from you in morning pages today," he said. "It's a comforting thought that the line might go on."

"The line?" I remembered what Rufus had told me about his sons not having a poetic bone in their bodies. Was that why I was suddenly Miss Wheeler, instead of Sarah?

"Don't look so worried," he said. "Just because you're elected, doesn't mean you have to take office right away."

"Office?" ONE CUP, the speech bubble on my coffee mug said, AND I'M OUT LIKE A LIGHT.

"Oh, Sarah." Thank heaven I was back to Sarah and he was smiling again. "What I'm saying is how very talented I think you are. And how good, how deeply good, it feels after all these years to have someone I can share this work with. Someone to whom it means more than anything else."

Was poetry more important to me than anything? I wasn't sure. But I wanted to make Rufus happy, so I smiled, too. "Let's not tell my mother I'm going to be a poet just yet," I said. "She has this thing about my becoming a doctor."

My poet nodded again. "So I've observed." He took a sip from the snowman mug, then gave me another grin, bigger this time. "But perhaps she'd settle for your accepting an interim appointment, as my amanuensis."

"Amanu . . . ?"

"It means secretary." Rufus winced. "Actually, the Latin root means "slave." But that's not quite what I have in mind. You see, once I'm back on my feet, I'm determined to be writing regularly. Religiously, you might say."

That was good. That was very good.

"And I'm going to need an assistant. I'm hoping you'll consider it an internship, a way to help me and train at the same time."

Why did this feel like another road map to the future? Not the same as my mother's plans, not exactly. Still it was clear Rufus had done a whole lot of thinking about this without even asking me. "It's just that I love acting, too. Those voices I hear?" I tried to explain. "When everything talks?" My poet said nothing. "I get to try them all out when I'm onstage. I can do anything, be anything."

I took a sip of coffee, but hardly tasted it. "Bernhardt made sculpture," I told him, not sure if I was helping or making things worse. My mouth was on autopilot, my heart blindsided by this new scheme of his. "She wrote books and poetry, too."

"Divide and conquer may work in war," Rufus told me, sternly. "But it doesn't make much sense in art."

I didn't know what to say. What did this have to do with war?

"You can't live up to your gift without caring, my dear Miss Wheeler." He sounded as though he were behind a podium. "And there's not as much time as you think. Before you know it . . ." He stopped, looked toward the window, the velvet shadows outside. "Before you know it," he started again, "you'll be old and you'll find you're leaving nothing behind."

"I'm so proud you like what I write," I told him. *Proud? More like ecstatic, more like saved.* "But I'm pretty sure I need to give acting a try before I make up my mind to be a poet."

Rufus didn't seem to be listening.

"It's like a living thing." I tried again. "The dialogue, I mean. The talk-talk-talking. It never stops." I opened my hands, let the noises of the night fill them: the glass-dampened throb of crickets, the rush of a plane overhead, the deep breath of the ocean behind it all.

"I love poetry, honestly I do." I swam in those marble eyes. "But I want more, too. I want to walk out onstage and feel a fresh start, a scary, jumped-up new beginning every time." Those eyes, how kindly they met mine. "I want to be Sarah, not Sarai."

That's when I noticed he was crying. Just a little, just enough that I saw the shine in the moonlight from the window. "It seems," he told me, "I've fallen into the parent trap." He peered into the dim living room, where Shepherd's bedcovers on the couch stirred, rose up like nervous wings, then settled again. "It seems I owe you an apology."

If you lined up all the things *I* had to be sorry about, they would probably have made a large intestine or a moon shot. But Rufus? He hadn't done anything except make things one bejillion percent better. "What on earth for?" I asked.

"For trying to live your life. For pushing you into a future you may not even want." Another glance toward the couch. "If you were my own daughter, I couldn't have handled it worse.

"I've been so busy turning you into a poet, I never stopped to ask whether you wanted to be one. I was trying to keep you locked up on our magic island." He sighed. "But I forgot that you've got a great deal more life ahead of you than I do."

I wished the ghost on the couch would push off its sheets and sit up. I was sure Shepherd could put an end to this sad talk. But he'd buried his head under one arm and was snoring.

"The truth is, I'm afraid, Sarah."

"Afraid?"

"There's that face again." A thin smile now, a sliver. "No, not of dying. Of not finishing."

I waited.

"I have hundreds of poems up here." Rufus tapped his head. "And I don't want my life to end before I get them onto paper."

And *I* didn't want to talk about this. It felt like ashes and faded photographs. I folded my arms, remained silent.

"But when I heard myself just now? When I looked at you, hiding from me behind that cup?" Rufus shook his head. "I remembered what it's like to be at the beginning. To have choices."

I uncrossed my arms.

"I want you to know," he told me, "that I plan on being in the front row for your next play." Shepherd turned in his sleep, an owl hooted outside the window, and I suddenly noticed how good my coffee smelled.

"It may only be a walk-on," I warned him. "But I'll take what I can get."

"So will I, Sarah." Rufus made a toast, clinking his snowman against my sleepy baby. "So will I."

CALIBAN

(*To servants from the wrecked ship*)

Be not afeard; the isle is full of noises,
Sounds and sweet airs, that give delight and hurt not.
Sometimes a thousand twangling instruments
Will hum about mine ears; and sometime voices,

That, if I then had waked after long sleep,
Will make me sleep again: and then, in dreaming,
The clouds methought would open, and show riches
Ready to drop upon me; that, when I waked,
I cried to dream again.

—*The Tempest*, Act 3, Scene 2

Good-Bye, Sweet Prince

No poetry. At vets with Margrt. Dog is ok.

I'd stayed up after the play doing poetry homework, wearing a blindfold I hardly needed, wandering around in the dark. I thought maybe if I read H's text message over, it would make more sense. But it didn't. I knew H had been driving Margaret to our early writing sessions, but I didn't have any idea what dog he was talking about. Did Margaret's family own a dog? Had they hit a dog on the way over? Only one thing was clear: Morning pages would be minus at least two regulars.

As I walked to the Hendricks', the sky darkened, threatening rain, which probably explained why, when I reached the little house, no one else had shown up, either. H's text said the dog was going to be okay: good. And now it seemed I would have all morning alone with Rufus: better!

"Even your father has deserted us," Rufus told me when I relayed H's message. "He had to go to the restaurant, but he left us with coffee." He nodded at the cups and a plate of rolls set out on the table in front of the couch. "I think it's a plot to wean me. He says I'm nearly ready to manage on my own."

"How much longer for the cast?" I walked with him to the couch, watched him drop heavily into the cushions, then prop his colorful, autographed leg on a stool. The early sun, filtered through clouds, threw soft, fuzzy shadows over everything—his shoulders, the tabletop, the rug.

"I'm told I can stop showering with a plastic bag over my leg in six more weeks." Rufus leaned his crutches against the couch. "That, I can assure you, will be a day to celebrate."

We chatted awhile, and I assumed that, after small talk and coffee, we would do what we always had: write, side by side. Just like always, I would watch as much as I wrote, taking mental notes on how he sat (leaning forward, like he might dive into the page), how he sharpened his pencil (not too sharp, otherwise it would break just when you needed it most), how often he tapped the skin between his nose and his left eye (as if he could jiggle just the right combination of words out of his head).

Later, Rufus would catch my eye and ask me if I'd mind listening to something. Mind? Each time he asked, I wondered if he was joking. Did he truly have no idea how the music he wrote made me shiver? How I could never hear too much?

But none of that happened. I didn't hear any of his work. In fact, neither of us wrote a single word. All because, in between sips of coffee, I kept taking peeks at my cell. I'd put all Fry's poems together in a special folder right on the phone's home screen. And sometimes, like sneaking a piece of candy, I glanced at one. I'm afraid I wasn't nearly as good at undercover reading and texting as Fry. We'd been sitting there only a few minutes before He Who Didn't Miss a Trick and Had Finally Graduated from Technology 101 got wise to me.

"What's that you're so caught up in, Sarah? Is everything all right?"

I guess I'd always known I would tell Rufus about Fry's poetry. Because who else but another poet could understand how those texted lines made me feel? How they'd changed everything? How even when I was angry at my prince, or feeling galaxies apart from him, one look at his poems would bring us back together? I didn't need that feeble, cloud-fighting sun, or even my cell's backlight, to read Rufus the short poem Fry had texted me before the play, the one about my shadow being his sunlight. I knew it by heart.

When I'd finished reciting, I let the words hang in the air between us, like a whispered gift. At first, I thought Rufus felt the same way I did about what I'd shared, because he sat a long while without speaking. But then he said, "That boy must love you a lot, Sarah, to steal a poem for you."

I didn't, couldn't, say anything. But Rufus saw the question on my face, leaned toward me across the couch. "That's from a semifamous poem, you know. It's by someone who might not have minded your sweetheart borrowing it. Someone named Amy Lowell."

Sweetheart. What an old-fashioned word Rufus had used. I was suddenly cold and sad and somehow not too surprised. I had made Fry up, after all. Behind the muscles and guy talk, I'd pretended a valentine, a greeting-card soul mate. Sure, I'd Googled those first poems, but I'd never asked Fry why he forgot his verses as soon as he sent them to me. Why he hated to talk about poems if he loved to write them.

That was when I showed Rufus the rest of the poetry I'd been hoarding, savoring. I opened the Fry folder and read everything there, one poem after another. And though none of them was a direct copy, my poet recognized parts of each one. They were all bits and pieces of stolen property, words cobbled together; snippets from different poems bumping up against one another, getting cozy in a way they'd never been before. Each was just short enough, just changed enough, to fool a search engine. But not Rufus.

One by one, he named the poets whose poems Fry had plundered to make those counterfeit love texts: "That's from Dylan Thomas," he'd say. Or, "If you change the color, that phrase is from 'The Waste Land.'" "Make that door a window, and those four words are Sara Teasdale's." "Marianne Moore wrote that in a different tense." "A widely read young man, that friend of yours," was all he said when I'd finished. Though I knew from class that plagiarism was something he couldn't abide. "Theft is theft," he'd told us several times. I remembered thinking that he seemed to take less kindly to word thievery than he did to arson.

With the sun fighting the rain and my poet's hand covering mine, the hurt came—without anyone shaking their finger at me, without "I told you so" playing in the background. I was used to being disappointed by my mother. She was so busy planning my life, she never even stopped to take a good look at me. But Fry? Fry was different, because I had believed in him. In us. In Love with a capital *L*. And all along, all the time, I was believing in a cheat. Was there any other word for someone who pretended to be what he wasn't? Rufus had called him my sweetheart, but what he'd done was anything but sweet.

I pushed against the pain now; I took its measure and sat, wordless, while the fairy tale melted away. The tears started, and I let them come, in a way I would never have been able to do at home. Or even with Wanda. Finally, just as the storm that had been trying to happen all morning started up and we heard rain against the roof, Rufus gathered me up and held me against that poetry tee of his. I wept so hard I thought I'd never stop. When I was finished, I piled our plates and dishes, then carried everything back to the kitchen. While Carmen stalked my every move, I set the dishes in the sink and ran water over them.

Rufus insisted on "walking" me to the door. Which meant he was listing to the side, leaning heavily on one crutch, when my tears started up again. Not noisy like last time, they were stealth tears, and they sneaked down my face before I even knew it. Rufus spotted them, though, and cradled his right crutch under his arm. He reached out and brushed one away. "Long ago, before you and even before me," he said, "my grandmother would have made lemon balm tea to cure heartache. But I'm afraid I don't have the recipe. I hope this will do instead." Then he leaned over and kissed me on the forehead. No one had ever done that before, and it felt much better than those daddy kisses I'd watched in movies and on TV. I nursed that good feeling all the way home, even in between calls and texts to Fry, who didn't answer any of them. Every word my boyfriend had stolen, every broken piece of someone else's feelings, kept running through my mind. But what stayed with me the longest? What felt like a blessing was Rufus's kiss, right where I parted my hair.

Against all reason, through the middle of my hurt, I guess I still hoped Fry could make it right, could put us back together again. Which is why

I kept texting him. Walking in the rain, which had gotten worse, not better, I held my cell under my tee and sent him message after message, asking him to call. Finally, right outside my own front door, his ringtone made the phone leap in my hand. I stood just inside our hall, gulping air like a beached fish, then said hello. Fry, who had no idea what had happened, sounded giddy, charged up.

"The surf is amazing!"

"You're at the beach?" The rain hadn't slowed. It was still hammering on the skylight above my head. "In this?!"

"There's no lightning, just glassed-up waves." Fry had that kid sound, that look-at-me voice. "You should see it, Sarah! I just caught a monster, rode it forever!"

"Fry," I told him, "I need to—"

"You've got to come out here, Sarah. You *have* to see this!"

I *could* see it: Fry's tanned face, spray covered, happy. I knew that happy, I'd seen it every time he rode a wave. "I've got class in a few hours," I told him. "I have work to do."

"Last night wasn't enough high culture for you?" Fry sounded exasperated. "You need a double dose of stuffed shirts?"

"Fry, listen." And suddenly, it was harder than I'd thought it would be. There was this little boy playing on the beach, and I had to force him to grow up. "You didn't write those poems." What was the point of small talk? Nothing else mattered. I sank to the floor in the hall, watching the rain slam against the glass overhead.

"What?"

I told him how I'd read his poems to Rufus. How the last one he'd sent was by Amy Lowell.

"Amy who?"

"Fry." I almost cried his name. "It was all a lie. You didn't write any of the beautiful words you sent."

Silence. That's all I heard for a long time, so long that I thought he might have hung up. Then, when he finally spoke, his Fry cool was back. "I told you, Sarah. They were only words. What's the big deal?"

"Where did you get them?"

"I found this app called Sonnet Snitch. You input the kind of poem you want—hair color, eyes, you know. Then it puts together stuff from other poems. Not whole sentences or anything, but patterns, words. Pretty good, huh?"

Now it was my turn to be quiet. I said nothing. I listened to my own even breathing and, overhead, the rain.

"It changes just enough, you know? Brown to green. Chin to face. That kind of thing." The boy actually sounded proud!

"Come on, Sarah. You're not going to throw what we've got away over a stupid app, are you?"

"What have we got?"

"Jeez, Sarah!"

The rain was constant, steady, on and on.

"Oh, for crying out loud. It's that old guy, isn't it? He's spoiling this because he's all dried up, right?"

The rain, again and again. Washing everything away.

"Listen, Sarah. This is no good. We have to talk in person. I have to see you."

Arms, heat, holding. *Stay.*

"Just promise me that, Sar. You won't go ruining everything without giving me a chance. Okay? Just one hour? One lousy hour? Is that so much to ask?"

I said nothing. What was there to say?

"Look, Sarah, I can explain."

"Explain what?"

"Everything. Why I'm not a world-class poet." He stopped. "Okay, why I'm not a poet at all. Just give me a chance, will you?"

I hadn't thought there were any tears left, but one found its way down to my nose. I brushed it away.

"Tomorrow, okay? I'll call you. And Sarah?"

No words left. Only the rain. And one last tear.

"Just because I'm not a poet doesn't mean I can't love someone."

He hung up before I realized that was the first time he'd ever said the word "love" to me. At least the first time he'd ever said it without plagiarizing.

The sky stopped looking bruised and swollen, and the sun came out just before class. When he saw the chairs we'd unfolded, Rufus announced that we might want to fold them back up and put them away; we were going to hold our next-to-last class ("penultimate," he called it, which sounded elegant but still kind of sad) outside. H, obliging as ever, started snapping chairs closed with a flourish. If anything, he was more cheerful than usual. And, watching Margaret, working beside him, I had a suspicion I knew why.

"So," I asked him, "what's this about the vet's?"

The two of them, grinning like happy fools and finishing each other's sentences, explained that Margaret's dog, Falafel, had swallowed her owner's earrings. "I named her Falafel because she'll eat anything," Margaret said. "But I didn't think that included jewelry!"

"Those hoops were this big," H told me, joining his thumbs and forefingers to make circles, then reconsidering, opening his fingers wide, wide, wider.

"She started whining just before Hector picked me up this morning." Margaret touched H's arm the same way Miss Kinney had. "He was so great. He said poetry was important, but not as important as making sure Falafel was okay."

They had spent two and a half hours in the waiting room. By that time, Falafel was out of the woods, the earrings were retrieved, and Margaret and H? Well, it was clear they were a couple now. "We wrote morning pages while we waited," H told me. "You should see the ideas this woman"—he smiled at Margaret—"comes up with." Another smile, this time right into a matching one from Margaret. "She could write a poem about her refrigerator and make it sound great." He paused. "Come to think of it, she *did*!"

"Listen to this guy." Margaret's laugh was a lot softer than I remembered it. "I've still got chills from what he wrote about the sea at night."

"Wait!" It felt as though I'd come in just as the credits were rolling. I looked at H. "No more odes to Miss K.?"

Latino toughs aren't big on blushing. But newborn poets apparently are. H rode through his embarrassment in the sweetest way, though. He didn't look at his hands or his feet or the last of the chairs that needed putting away. Instead, he just grinned at Margaret. "Guess a crush can last just so long," he said. "Eventually, you have to find someone who feels like home."

I'd like to say that I was instantly and completely happy for those brand-new lovebirds. But I have to be honest: Watching those two, I was jealous. With only a few words, H had just said more to Margaret about the way he felt than Fry had said to me all year. Not counting his poems. Well, not *his*, actually. You know what I mean.

Of course, I was thrilled that H had found someone at last—someone he liked who liked him back. But that happiness bumped up against the empty feeling I'd been carrying, and suddenly, I wasn't so sure I'd used up all my tears. Each time H bent to whisper something to Margaret, and each time she leaned into him, easy and natural, the spillover feeling built behind my eyes. Why hadn't Fry ever acted like that? How had everything between us ended up like my poet's cottage, empty and ruined?

So I was glad when Shepherd, who'd been helping Rufus put Carmen in exile (i.e., locking her up in the bedroom with food, water, and a large cat toy shaped like a dog), joined us. "That blindfold stuff work?" he asked.

It still shocked me how interested my father was in our class. How he kept up with what we were doing. H, naturally, couldn't wait to fill Shepherd in on the latest chapter in the artistic life and times of his favorite poet, Hector Losada. "I don't believe it," he told us. "I may have to wear gloves from now on." He waved the fingers of both hands, as if he were playing an air piano. "My hands keep sending me messages, even when I don't want them to. It's like I've got eyes in my fingers!"

I was excited in spite of myself. "I know," I told him. "My doorknob took me one place, but my sneakers sent me another. I mean, I'd already written a poem about a poster in my bedroom. I was all set to bring that to class, and then I—"

"Then you got inspired all over again." H snapped the last chair shut, looked at me over the edge of his sunglasses. "I know. I guess that's what happens to sensitive types. We find poems everywhere."

If anyone had told me a month before that I'd *ever* be discussing the sense of touch with H and my father, I would have thought they were living in a different dimension. One where the rules of logic, common sense, and probability didn't apply. But, of course, that was BR. Before Rufus.

"And typing blind?" H pushed his shades back and grinned. "My mom walked in on me, and even though I tried to explain, I think she's still worried about my mental health."

I remembered the way it felt to be alone in the dark with the pictures in my head. I was glad I'd done the homework before this morning. Before the End. BE. If I closed my eyes now, I'd go right back to misery, to wondering how Fry could have lied to me, and how I could have believed him. But BE, I could fall into the concrete world around me, take it back to my desk, keep it fresh while the blindfold kept everything else out. I could type a few lines and remove the blindfold, and guess what? I could actually read what I'd written. "I kind of gave up on capital letters, though," I told H and Margaret. "But who needs them, really?"

We were still talking shop when Shepherd had to leave. "Anselmo is hemorrhaging," he explained. "He says he needs me to go over the accounts." I'd met Mamselle's owner only once, but I'd never forgotten the way that rotund little man depended on my father for everything. The way he didn't take a step, hardly even spoke, until he'd turned to Shepherd and asked, "So what do you think?"

"I'm sorry you'll miss class," I told my father. And I meant it.

"The good news is, Rufus is about to graduate Gimp School. There's almost nothing he can't handle." Shepherd wore an odd, proud-daddy smile, as if he'd taught my poet to walk and talk. "Besides," he added, giving H a shoulder punch, "Hector's here."

A few weeks back, I might have wondered how one skinny eighteen-year-old could be of much help when it came to supporting or moving a senior citizen who outweighed him by at least fifty pounds. But now? Well, I'd seen H in action, and I knew that, between us, we would manage just fine. Besides, a few minutes later, we had backup: The whole class arrived.

Tonight, I lived on a magic island,
watched as it filled with monsters,
wizards, soaring sprites. I cried and
laughed as they suffered and danced.
Tense in my seat, I wanted what
they did, I dreamt their dream.

Later I hold the playbill, close my
eyes to bring it all back. But my
fingers meet only the glossy cold
of dry facts, and the stapled pages
shuffle like dead leaves, faerie
revels flown, magic undone.

The Fifth Class

"We are not at the mercy of electronics today," Rufus told us. "Let's get some fresh air." He pointed to a bulky canvas bag on the couch, even bigger than the baggy briefcase he usually brought to class. "Charles," he asked our prof, who was sporting rolled-up sleeves again, and looking much more at ease than he had last week, "would you do the honors?"

Fenshaw, proud of his role, strode to the couch, hoisted up the bag. Then, after everyone had left their assignments on the coffee table, my poet led us out into the backyard. Although "led" might not be the right word, since he had to entrust his crutches to H while he swung his way down the steps and out onto the patio. By the time he achieved that feat, most of the class had beaten him there and were lounging in deck chairs, waiting for instructions.

"Don't worry about our state bird," he told everyone. "I've brought weapons." He asked Fenshaw to open the bag and hand out four small bottles of mosquito repellent.

"So how did it go?" Rufus stood and watched as we passed the bottles around, rubbing the spray on our arms and legs. "Was blind typing as hard as y'all figured?"

Like me, most people agreed they'd been surprised at how well they'd managed. "It was like being in a cave," Margaret said. "Only the cave was your own head."

"Exactly," H agreed. "Skull Mansion!"

The two of them high-fived, H grinning as if they'd simultaneously stumbled on the theory of everything.

That was when I felt my phone vibrate, and right away I was out of class and into my head. It was Fry: *We have to talk.* I didn't answer. Not that text. Or the next. Or the next. I didn't need to. All my answers would have been the same: *There's nothing to say.*

So while the others described their maiden voyages with blind typing, I was in a skull cave of my own. Over and over, I checked myself for damage. Over and over, I felt the missing dream. The hurt. The why, why, why?

"I can't wait to read your homework," Rufus was saying. "And to show y'all how grateful I am for the way you're feeding our book, I'm going to ask you to write more."

"Here?" Coral Ann asked.

"Here and now," our poet said. Then he did what everyone had been waiting for. He had the prof dig into that mysterious bag again and take out . . . *embroidery hoops.* I turned my phone off and watched as Rufus grabbed a single crutch for support; then, one by one, he handed a hoop to each of us. Some were made of wood, others were metal that caught the light. A few of the boys laughed as they took theirs, and one of them muttered something about knitting needles. My poet ignored them, passing out all the hoops except one. He held on to that last hoop, and looked around the class.

"It's not easy to send these things very far," he told us, "so I need someone with firepower." His eyes landed on the biggest boy of all—guess who? "Mr. Vogel, will you help?"

And yes, Thatcher the Moose went and stood beside my poet. "Think you can launch this to the end of the yard?" Rufus asked.

Thatcher studied the lawn, which, in fact, had to be one of the biggest on the street. He nodded, but chose a wooden hoop instead of the metal one Rufus tried to hand him. "Don't want to overshoot," he said, without a trace of arrogance. It was clear that, unlike Caliban, this monster knew his own strength.

He pivoted, swept the hoop behind his back, and then hurled it like a Frisbee out across the grass. It landed at least sixty feet away, near a patch of weeds by the fence at the end of the yard.

"When you write a poem," Rufus told us now, limping toward the fallen hoop, "you make your own world." We followed him, watched him stand just over the hoop. "It's only a little piece of the bigger world, mind. But it's complete just as it is." He leaned on one crutch, studying the grassy pie shape the wooden circle framed where it lay. "Everything you need is right inside." He grinned. "And everything your reader needs, too."

He asked us to get down on the grass, tell him what we saw in the hoop. Of course, most people said, "Grass," and of course, Rufus asked them, "What else?"

After we'd found an ant, a brown cancer or growth on a grass blade, a clover bud, a yellow stone, and a small piece of string, he asked us to take out our own hoops and walk as far as we wanted, then hurl them away from us. "Wherever it lands," he instructed, "make a world."

For the next half hour, we each sat right where our hoop had landed and wrote a poem about what was inside it. Except for one couple who hooked their hoops together and threw them both at once, everyone was on their own. By now you know that Rufus had a way of getting people to get down and get real, right? This time wasn't any different: The poems that came from drops of dew and dead moths and dry, dusty footprints were special to write, amazing to hear. As I watched a beetle nuzzle a fallen wisteria blossom lying just inside my hoop—and later, as Margaret described the secret, indecipherable letters her hoop had scratched in the sandy soil; as H rhapsodized about the twin star-shaped holes he'd found in a fallen leaf; and as our Eagle Scout prof read about a rock that grew moss on top and a nest of baby spiders underneath—I felt something like a poem or a prayer well up inside me. It was half gratitude, half grasping. I loved what was happening, and I didn't want it to stop.

Part of that feeling, of course, came from knowing that there were no more love poems waiting for me. From knowing, instead, that when class was over and I went home, I'd be alone. More alone than I'd been for months and months. I wished I could stop feeling sorry for myself. Rufus had called it heartache, and that's just how it felt: a sore, bruised place in my chest. This was no metaphor, no greeting-card sadness I could analyze and find new words for; it was a sharp, physical pain that reminded me almost every time I breathed that something big, something serious, was missing. It felt like I'd run a hundred miles uphill. And like I still had a hundred left to go.

The last poem of the day did nothing to lift my spirits. But I guess you could say it put a temporary end to my pity party, and made the sadness about someone besides me, me, me. It was Rufus himself who read just before class broke up. I don't think he'd intended to write a poem at all, not until that bumblebee found our embroidery hoops. It was a bedraggled-looking thing, with a click instead of a buzz and a torn wing in the bargain. My poet spotted it first and put one finger by his mouth. "Shhh!" he said. "Look there."

We watched the one-winged wonder limping over the metal clasps on the mound of hoops we'd given back. (Thatcher had piled them up for the prof to put into the bag, as if he always helped out, as if he were nearly human.) Well, most of us watched the bee. But *I* watched Rufus. And I saw something in his face change. I saw the same half frown he'd worn when he asked me to get serious about my poetry. *There's not as much time as you think.* He studied that flightless creature inching its way toward who knew where, and he seemed a lot more than interested. It wasn't just attention he was paying the bee; it was respect.

"There's a poem in that old fellow," he told us. "He can't fly anymore, but it's not always about the doing." He looked at the bee, then at us. "Sometimes it's just about the yearning."

He took out his shabby notebook and, propped on his crutches, scribbled in its pages. He didn't stop writing, didn't pause to make changes or turn his pencil over to erase. He just kept scrawling while the rest of us held our breath. When he finally looked up from the notebook, it was as if he was lighter, freer. As if he'd put down something he was tired of carrying.

"I kept thinking," he told us, "about what's going to happen to this wounded veteran in a few months." He watched the bee inspect a low-hanging hydrangea branch. Painfully, the tiny traveler crawled onto it, lured by the generous, floppy-headed flowers. "Wings or no wings, fall will finish him off."

The poem Rufus read us then was short. Just long enough to put anyone who was listening, really listening, inside the body of a broken bee. Or an old man. It was hard to watch his face. It was easier to look at the grass.

As we put the hoops into the bag and walked back to the house, my poet took one last look at the bee, which had dragged its way to the center of the hydrangea bush. When it disappeared into the wide mouth of a sky-colored flower, he turned back toward the rest of us without a word. He handed his crutches to H, hauled himself up the steps, then made his way to the front door, where everyone had begun to line up for their double handshake. When my turn came, we both held on extra long.

Her after-class dinner with my poet wasn't something my mother was about to give up. Rufus insisted he didn't want "another fuss," so she promised to keep it simple. "Jocelyn and I will just throw together a few little nothings," she told him. "Basic paper-plate fare, subsistence-level nourishment."

Which is how I got corralled into helping my aunt and mom bring over at least a half dozen casseroles, promptly at six. There was vegetable bread pudding, tomato cobbler, baked chicken risotto, butternut spoon bread, and green beans. And last but not least, a lemon soufflé with raspberry sauce.

An hour, countless texts from Fry (as soon as I turned my phone back on, it started thumping away, regular as a heartbeat), and six empty oven dishes later, Rufus had been sweet-talked into doing an interview for *Her*. While our little dessert plates lay on the drain board, crusted with the remains of Aunt J.'s soufflé, and the dinner plates and glasses soaked in soapy water, we all sat in the living room and listened to Mom's big plans for my poet.

"The entire staff of *Her* is salivating," she confided, as flushed and happy as a girl talking about her prom. "I'm not sure the office will be big enough to hold all your admirers, Rufus." She bubbled away, covering all five Ws. But as always with Mom, what, when, why, and where took a backseat to who: who would photograph Rufus; who would be invited to the magazine offices; who would get complimentary copies for promotion; and who would come home next week to join us for Rufus's final dinner chez Wheeler. "Now that you're able to navigate, Rufus, you simply mustn't deprive me of this last hurrah," was how she put it.

I've said I was used to Mom letting me down, right? But on top of what Fry had done, it was especially hard to hear her description of our final dinner. I couldn't picture H and Margaret fitting in with the who's who she was determined to invite to that party. In fact, it was hard to imagine Wanda or me or any of my friends breaking bread with magazine editors, the writer in residence at every college within a fifty-mile radius, and Whale Point's chamber of commerce, town council, and mayor. I had no idea how my mother even planned to squeeze everyone into our house, much less around the dining-room table.

I think it was right after she mentioned the mayor that Rufus spoke up. "Kate," he told her, "if we're going to celebrate before I leave, we've left some very important guests off your list."

Mom laughed. "Of course, Rufus, how silly of me." The prom queen smiled graciously at her date. "I'll bet you've managed to make some friends here, despite the shameless way I've been monopolizing you." She picked up the tablet from the coffee table. "We can always squeeze in one or two more."

"I *have* made some friends. Seventeen of them. Eighteen if you include Charles, the instructor at the community college. And I'd like to count him among them."

"I don't understand, Rufus." My mother's hand was at her throat.

"I'm talking about my students, Katherine. I'd like to say good-bye to them all." His smile was completely without apology. "Not with a whimper, but a bang."

"Rufus, I don't think—"

"I understand your lovely home is hardly big enough to accommodate a farewell of the dimensions I'm imagining." Now my poet looked at me, a no-holds-barred, beaming smile. "But I happen to know someone in the restaurant business, and I'll see what I can do."

"But I—"

"I'd be glad to meet with your magazine people, my dear." Rufus sounded as if he were talking to a child, an enthusiastic youngster he needed to calm and settle. "And feel free to invite anyone you like to my good-bye party. But I want you and your sister to be guests of honor there, not chief cook and bottle washer."

Someone in the restaurant business. That could mean only one person.

"As for my students, I doubt there'll be any objections to holding our last class at a restaurant." He turned to me. "I think the felons deserve a break. And dinner out. Do you concur, Sarah?"

I did! I did! Rufus had bailed all of us out. It wasn't easy to find bright spots in a day that included discovering your boyfriend was a fake. But the thought of our final class as a banquet definitely helped. Still, I hoped Rufus wasn't being overly optimistic about his restaurant connection. After all, if what he'd hinted at was true, the glorious last hurrah he'd just described depended on a single, not-always-reliable individual—Shepherd Ryan, a.k.a. my *father*.

December Emissary

I am a bee of winter,
A stumbling, tufted drone.
Am I the last of my kind?
If feelings can be trusted,
I am deep alone.

I no longer climb the air,
but glad for morning's chill,
dread night's darker cold
as I weave my way
along the sill.

I know better than to test
bright, implacable glass,
but crawl slowly backward
toward the sweetness
of the past.

Wanda Asks About Mermaids and I Raise the Roof

Fry called six times that night. Once during the casseroles, twice during the soufflé, and three times after I'd helped Mom and Aunt J. carry everything home and we'd started putting the dishes away. I didn't pick up; I couldn't. First, I just wasn't ready to face what I knew was coming next: When a princess finally realizes that her joust-happy prince isn't, despite his 10-and-0 record, a winner, there's only one kind of ending waiting up ahead. And it isn't happy.

The other reason I let Fry's ringtone ("We Are the Champions") play until I couldn't stand it anymore, until I put my phone on silent and slipped it into its case backward so I didn't have to look at his picture, was more complicated, kinder maybe. It would just be too hard, you see, to listen to my formerly confident, can-do boyfriend try to talk his way out of a dead end. Why put him through that? He couldn't be someone he wasn't. He'd already tried, and all it did was hurt us both.

After I'd gone upstairs, after I'd let the last of Fry's calls go to my log and deleted about ten texts (mostly from Fry, one from H raving about alliteration, along with a homegrown example that featured nothing but *M* words—yes, "Margaret" came first and last), I called Wanda. I owed her a report on the play. And besides, it would feel good to relive that special night at *The Tempest,* that BE happiness, by telling her all about it. Which I did, from beginning to end: from Rufus's kindness to his fans, to the whispered talk with my poet at the end of the evening. The talk where he'd told me I was talented. And that he hoped I'd keep writing. When I got to that part, Wanda was sweetly, deliriously thrilled for me. "He said what?!!!" That hair of hers, those wide eyes—I could see them, even on the phone. "Oh, Sarah! Just think, you're a protégé!"

"A what?"

"You know, a promising student. An heir apparent. The next in line."

The line might go on. Isn't that what Rufus had told me?

"You've been working side by side with the most famous poet in the world." Wanda gasped, as if she'd put a hand over her mouth. "Why, you might even inspire a poem!"

I pictured Rufus's face when he'd talked about his dead wife and sons. "I think his inspiration is gone," I said. I already told you I'd been online by now, right? Which means I'd learned a lot about the way people (critics, readers, other writers) treat giants. When you're a celebrity, especially one whose fame lasts longer than a few days or years, people think they own you. They take you apart and then they put you back together again, over and over. In some stories, Rufus was a villain, one who used and abused, who never learned to care about anyone but himself. In others, he was a Southern gentleman, a man of the land, misunderstood and alone. "He's lost his whole family, you know."

Wanda wasn't even listening. "Because of you, he may start writing all over again." A drawn-out groupie sigh. "Think of it! A whole series of elegies to Sarah!" She paused, thought for a moment. "Oh, wait. An elegy's for someone who's dead! The Sarah sonnets, how's that?"

I laughed, but her mistake stuck in my mind. I remembered how Rufus had told me he didn't have much time. What if my writing with him was as important to him as it was to me? Could I actually inspire someone? Someone who didn't grade my kisses?

"We need to talk," I told her. I wanted to make up for missing her birthday. I wanted to ask her advice—about Fry, about Rufus, about everything. "Let's meet for high tea the way we used to. Can you walk into town tomorrow?"

Wanda didn't answer, and I knew why. There was something between us. Or *someone*. Finally, cautiously, she said:

"Won't you be with . . . ?"

"No," I told her. "Fry and I—oh, Wanda, he was sending me these poems, and—"

"Rufus Baylor?"

"No, Fry," I explained. "See, he started texting me these incredible, beautiful poems, but—"

"I know." Wanda sounded impressed. "Muscles *and* metaphors. I'm happy for you, Sarah. And just a little bit jealous, too. Is that okay?"

"You don't need to be, Wan. It turns out . . . listen, can you come tomorrow?"

She could. And I hung up feeling a little less lonely than when I'd called. I couldn't wait to have a best friend again. To spend all afternoon, the way we used to, at one of the Carousel's tea tables, devouring cupcakes and sharing . . . well, *everything*.

* * * *

Next afternoon, we met in the small tearoom behind the glass shelves heaped with pies, cakes, and rows of tiny chocolate truffles decorated like flowers. We sat at a café table, downing glass after glass of sweet tea, along with two spice cupcakes covered with caramel frosting. I'd forgotten how Wanda and I almost always ordered the same thing when we went out.

And we talked the way we used to—about school and life and the bizarre questions only Wanda could come up with and worry about: Who invented fingerprints? Will the last person on Earth be lonelier than the first one was? Why do so many people believe in fairies, and so few believe in mermaids?

"Maybe," I told her, licking caramel off one finger, "it's because people think fairies will grant them wishes. Who ever heard of a mermaid lending a helping hand?"

"Hmmm." Wanda was thinking and chewing at once. "Plus," she decided when her plate was empty, "wings are a lot prettier than scales."

"Or maybe it just takes a while to see the advantages of mermaids." I'd finished my tea, my cupcake, and my stalling. "I used to believe in princesses," I told her now. "But I think I'm switching to mermaids. They don't have to sit on the sidelines at jousts, and they don't have to pick anchovies off pizza."

"Huh?"

And then I told her everything. I told her how sorry I was I'd let her slip out of my life. How I had believed in Fry. And in his poetry. How it was all a fairy tale. How I wasn't sure what was supposed to happen next, but that I knew I wanted her around to share it.

Wanda sat so still for such a long time, I didn't think she'd heard what I'd said. For a few seconds, I wondered if I'd ignored her too much, snubbed her so often that she could never forgive me. But then, as if she'd been feeling a happy pressure build, she exploded out of her seat. She gave a little-kid squeal and, running around the table and the remains of our high tea, gave me a hug it felt like I'd been waiting for forever.

It wasn't just the cupcakes, then, that tasted scrumptious and illicit. I'd been hungry for this closeness, this fun, for a long time. So when Wanda suggested I hang out with some of the Untouchables over the weekend, I said yes before she'd even told me when or where. We made a pledge to meet the next day at the cove and sealed the oath with frosting, instead of blood, on each of our wrists. (Yes, that meant ordering more cupcakes, and no, we didn't worry about the calories. Mermaids, we decided, didn't count them.)

I hadn't laughed so hard in way too long. It felt heady and free—like the beach after school or biking downhill or the first run-through of a play where you don't need your script. I don't know about Wanda, but I think I could have stayed there forever, sipping sweet tea and sniffing rising dough. The only reason I figured out how late it had gotten was that the Carousel's owner, Kitty Hodge, kept sweeping up. After her third pass around our table, the plump, frazzled woman was breathing heavily and we finally got the message: She wanted us to leave so she could go home.

Just outside the bakery, we ran into Lisa Santone, the girl from the beach patrol. The one who was home for the summer to do open-air theater. I introduced her to Wanda, and the three of us talked about how hot it was (very), about birthday cakes (Lisa needed to buy one for her sister), and about acting (Lisa had been in three off-off-Broadway productions since she'd started going to theater school in New York).

And that's when it happened, something little, almost accidental, that I kept inside, like a seed I'd swallowed and hoped might grow: "You know what?" Lisa told me, just as we were saying good-bye. "You should really apply to Tisch next year, Sarah. The city is great, and hey, I'm learning about breathing and memory and motivation—things I never even knew mattered before Tisch."

"Really?" I asked her. "You think I'm good enough to get in?"

"I don't know. I only saw you in that walk-on you did in *Our Town*." Lisa was being honest, and I appreciated it. "I remember you had something about you, though. Something that made me look at you, even when I should have been focused on the lead."

"Thanks," I said. "I think."

"You'll have to audition, just like I did. And it wouldn't hurt to land a role with the Players next year."

"Sure," I said. "Sure." As if it were a done deal. No problem.

After she'd walked away, I turned to Wanda. "You think I could do it?" I asked her.

"Get a part?"

"Go to theater school."

"Is that what you want?" she asked.

"Well, of course," I told her, surprising myself. "It's exactly what I want!"

Fry kept texting and calling. Which meant my usual clown act at Mamselle's was especially painful that night. Not only did I have to juggle all those wrong orders with my apron on inside out, but I also had to keep my cool with a cell phone vibrating nearly nonstop in my pocket. Even when I turned it off, I obsessed about turning it back on. And when I did, the texts and calls poured in, and my juggling turned into fumbling and then into a hopeless meltdown.

Shepherd and his customers had every right to yell at the dumb mistakes I made. But they didn't. I played the it's-my-first-day card over and over with the out-of-towners, and most people were pretty patient. Of course, I couldn't sell that story to Shepherd or to the regulars, but even without it, he put up with a lot. I could see him working toward a big blowup, slapping his head, muttering choice swearwords under his breath. He was like a covered pot on medium high, its top rattling and steam coming out from underneath. But he didn't boil over.

At last, though, when I'd tripped over myself for the millionth time and made the kind of mistakes I hadn't made since my first weeks at the restaurant, he lost it. Not in a giant, twister-landing kind of way, though. It was more low key than his usual approach, and it featured some pretty impressive mind reading:

SHEPHERD

Jesus, Sarah.

(*Slaps head*)

Where is your brain?

(*Shakes head*)

Hell, I'd settle for half a brain right now. What's wrong with you, anyway?

ME

(*Waiting for explosion*)

LAYNELLE

(*Whispering to me, so Shepherd can't hear*)

Honey, that deuce in the corner says they ordered fish, not ravioli.

SHEPHERD

School-school is over, poetry school is going fine. So it must be love.

(*Leans closer*)

Is it love?

ME

(*Still waiting*)

INNOCENT DINER-VICTIM AT NEARBY TABLE

(*Waves me over*)

Miss, I ordered the trout, not the ravioli.

SHEPHERD

(*Steps between me and diner, sweeps away the offending pasta*)

Of course you did, ma'am. Everyone makes mistakes—

INNOCENT DINER-VICTIM

Oh, I didn't mean—

SHEPHERD

—but ours shouldn't cost you. Your trout dinner is on Mamselle's.

INNOCENT DINER-VICTIM

(*Smiling*)

Well, thank you. That's real nice.

SHEPHERD

You're welcome, ma'am. And now if you'll excuse me, I need to talk to your server for a minute.

(*Pulling me aside*)

You already know what I think of that guy, right? So let me tell you what I think of *you*.

ME

(*Waiting*)

SHEPHERD

I think you're way too smart to let someone like him make you clear from the left!

I'd hoped, in a fervent, intense way that came pretty close to praying, that it would rain hard enough for our last cleanup to be postponed. But Saturday morning the sun was so bright it woke me up. And started me worrying: I'd never promised Fry a chance to "explain." Would he try to do that in the middle of hammering and pounding? Would I be able to face him? Could I call in sick?

Pretty immature, right? And pretty shortsighted, too. I'd have to deal with Fry sooner or later, after all. So, finally, setting a record for Slowest Toothbrushing and Longest Shower Ever, I got dressed and found Margaret, H, and Fry waiting curbside. Today, after all, was the day we were going to literally raise the roof at the Baylor cottage. After the hard work we'd put in, no one wanted to miss the big finish.

Given his passion for plywood and power tools, I should have known Fry would be almost as anxious as I was to see that little cottage good as new. That was one thing, maybe the only thing, we could see through together.

My throat and stomach had forgotten Fry and I were over, and they went through their whole jump/tighten routine as soon as I saw him. He was wearing a shop apron, and his shoulders were wider in real life than in my memory. He looked every inch a prince, except for his eyes, which wore a frightened, animal look. "Hi," he told me, climbing into the car, sitting where he always did, beside me in the backseat. But those animal eyes didn't look at me, they stayed hidden, dark.

"Hi," I said.

"Hey!" Margaret turned from the front seat, giving us both a victory sign. "Today's the day!"

And that's how the whole ride went, Fry and I almost wordless, the lovebirds chatty bordering on manic, and totally unaware of what was happening in the backseat. But when we got to the cottage, before the great boy-girl divide could push us farther apart than we already were, I pulled Fry aside. "I'm sorry I didn't call you back," I told him.

"We can't talk here, Sarah," he told me, sounding almost relieved. "I'll see you this afternoon, okay?"

I was going to meet the Untouchables. "I can't." I knew who my real friends were. Finally.

"Sunday, then. Can I come over Sunday?"

"No." Mom and Aunt J. would be home.

"Next week." He looked down. Around. His eyes still hiding. "Come on, Sarah. Give me a chance?" And then it rushed out, whispered, almost too soft to hear: "Please?"

Before I could answer, H and Margaret were beside us, breaking up our one-liners again, forcing us both to smile, to pretend. "Hey, man," H told Fry, "we need you topside." That was when my ex-prince and his friend joined the roofing crew, and Margaret and I got to work tiling the backsplash in the kitchen.

Thanks chiefly to Fry, who knew his way around ladders and shingles, the roof went on quickly. After we'd finished inside, Margaret and I went outside to help put in a stone pathway to the front door and to watch the final shingles being laid on the roof. You couldn't help but pick Fry out from the rest of the crew working up there. Thatcher was the biggest, that's for sure. But Fry had that smooth, easy gait that cute guys do, when they know they're good at something. Everyone followed his lead, asked him questions, even Mr. Shettle. "Hey, Reynolds," the little man would yell, cupping his hands to reach Fry on top of the roof. "You think we need sealer there?"

As if he walked in the sky every day, his silhouette dark against the sun, Fry would come to the edge of the roof, swing one foot over the ladder. He'd confer, perched there, with the shop teacher, then climb back to work. I know I wasn't the only one watching him move like some gorgeous airborne hero across the top of my old/new dollhouse. From down below, he was the perfect fantasy figure, brave and strong and every girl's dream.

Once the gutter was in place and Fry had come back to Earth, we all wolfed down those tiny sandwiches and took photos. Margaret showed me the one she'd caught of the three of us before H forced her to get in the picture, too: Fry was in the middle, of course, and he had one arm around H and one around me. His face was hot and tired and almost happy.

People were still taking photos of the house, the new porch, the front steps, the garden. Even the guy from the county, the one who took roll, was posing with kids, and Fry was moving from group to group. Laughing. Taking bows. That was when I slipped out my cell and texted a poem about the cottage. And about fresh starts. I knew I wouldn't send it to Fry. But maybe Wanda would like it. And maybe, with two or three more passes, it would even be good enough to show Rufus.

Then, when the tools were put away and most of the food was cleaned up, Mr. Shettle clapped Fry on the back. He held up his paper cup, looked at the rest of us. "Want to say something to these folks?" he asked his star workman. "Kind of bring things to a close here?"

"Yeah," Fry said. He faced the crowd of kids who'd worked so hard to put that dollhouse back together. I thought maybe he'd talk about Rufus, about why we were all here. Instead, he raised his cup high and just shouted, "We got her done!"

Everyone cheered.

The dollhouse is finished, time to put
mother and father on the sofa,
the kids in their chairs.

They're still wearing their old clothes,
thinking their old thoughts.
Shouldn't we let them know?

Everything's different, they need to
tell the truth now, they need to
hug their kids.

The Herd Gathers

I was single again. But I still didn't believe it. I was functioning, instead, in a kind of suspension, a place where I moved through thick air, blurred conversations. I was a hit-and-run victim walking, and I was in shock.

Yes, Fry kept texting, and I guess that didn't help. What did, though, was shutting the phone off before I left for the cove that afternoon. As I got closer to the sea, the tang in the air and the cheerful, wordless hum of voices behind the dunes lifted my spirits. It was summer, after all. I had survived trigonometry and not getting a lead in our school play. I had weathered the bash and, now, losing Fry. Best of all, I was sort of friends with one of the most famous poets on Earth, and my beloved Untouchables were together again.

Well, most of us were together: Brett and Thea had weekend jobs, but all the rest were at the cove when I rounded the bend and found them, spread out like jewels on the rocks: Alicia in her mango-colored swimsuit; Marcia, her tattoos and nose stones making her look exotic, even in a sweatshirt and jean shorts; George, quiet and brilliant and utterly hopeless in his adoration of Wanda; my beautiful, flaming Wanda, who would never feel more than friendship for George, but who let him follow her everywhere; and of course, crazy Eli. . . .

Even though the water in the cove was only wading depth, Eli looked as though he'd signed on for a diving expedition. While the rest of us wore bathing suits and shorts, he was sporting a full-body wet suit, complete with a snorkel mask pushed off his face and buried in his dark curls. "Sarah doesn't return to the fold every day," he said. "This is a special occasion, and I wanted to dress for it."

I laughed. "I'm deeply honored," I told him. "But I hope you don't scare the fish." I grinned at the crazy friend I'd missed more than I knew. "Maybe you should have worn tails?"

Eli shook his head at my horrible pun, then slapped one rubber thigh. "She's back," he said. "She's definitely back."

The cove was just as I remembered it, certainly not deep enough for diving, but full of echoes and magic. The coral covering the rocks facing the sea was pink and gray above the water, but underneath, it turned purple or orange. The larger boulders that formed the horseshoe in which we sat were full of cracks and crevices, so at high tide, the ocean would poke its wavy fingers through the holes and make soft, swishing sounds. I couldn't believe how much I loved being there, and I couldn't believe how long I'd stayed away.

Naturally, everyone wanted to know about the course. And about Rufus. I studied the drops of water on my bare arms, my toes under the water, white and glabrous as minnows. I thought about what I really wanted to tell each one of these friends—how much I'd missed them, how sorry I was to have sold them short, to have left them to the not-very-tender mercies of the cool kids. But it was hard to go back, harder to explain how busy I'd been, how wrong.

So I told them about Rufus, instead. I shared what I knew they'd never guess, things about my poet that surprised them and made them wish they'd been hauled into court, too. No, I didn't mention Rufus's dead sons. That was something that felt private. But I talked about our class in the garden, how there wasn't a plant or an animal he didn't know by name; I told them he was the best teacher I'd ever had, the only one who made me feel changed for having listened, looked, tasted, and touched. I described the way he'd opened H's locked car, the way he held both your hands in his, the way he made your memories and your feelings matter.

"It's true, it's all true." Wanda opened her arms wide, hoping the right words would fall in her lap. "Rufus Baylor is, well, he's dear and awesome at the same time. He's like a king disguised as a commoner." She shrugged, helpless to explain. "Like when he talks? You have the feeling he's giving you all these presents, but you don't have a big enough place to put them."

"You two sound like you're on drugs," Marcia told us. "A Rufus Baylor trip." She grinned at Wanda and me. "You should see your faces when you talk about him."

Wanda and I smiled at each other like groupies. Groupies who shared the same delicious secret. Of course, I told them about the new poem Rufus had written just for our class. But even though it was short, I couldn't recite it when George begged me to. I remembered some of the words and all of the feeling. Still, I knew getting even one word wrong would change everything, and I didn't want to spoil it. Rufus had lots of words to choose from, we all do. But he'd chosen the ones that sang his kind of music. And that, as he would have said, made all the difference.

It turned out, though, it didn't really matter. George and Wanda knew a lot of Rufus's old poems by heart, especially the famous mountain odes. They were dying for an excuse to trot them out, and it was thrilling to hear them. Even if Wanda put her hand on her chest and sounded too much like Miss Kinney when she recited.

There was one poem they tried to teach us. It was short, and it used the same lines over and over on purpose. Only they were shuffled around till they became a sort of bell, like the one our class had made on that first day with Rufus.

Or they *should* have made a bell. And if we'd each been able to say our lines at the right time, they *would* have. But somehow we always managed to get things in the wrong order, so they made no sense at all. One of the words that kept repeating was "Fall! Fall!" And finally, that's what we did. Eli started it. Whenever Wanda pointed to him, he didn't even try to remember the line he'd been assigned. He just clamored to the top of the rock he'd chosen as a seat and jumped off, gasping, "Fall! Fall!" as he went.

Soon everyone was parachuting off whatever height they could find, screaming, "Fall! Fall!" as they plunged down. And even though I scraped my knee on my last jump, and even though we never *did* learn our lines, I knew one thing as I watched us dive-bombing and shouting Rufus's poem: He would have *loved* it. I could imagine him there with us, conducting our leaps, fine-tuning our lines—right up until high tide, when the water filled the cove and chased us out.

* * * *

That night, when I walked to Mamselle's, Shepherd was waiting for me. Menu in hand. "What do you think?" He handed me a list of special table d'hôte options on elegant card stock. "Manny worked his buns off on this. Kind of good, huh?"

I pulled off my sweatshirt, scanned the menu. It wasn't just good; it was amazing. Under Mamselle's logo and a design of cresting waves were the words "The Last Verse: A Celebration of Sentences Well Served." And below that was the description of a meal that made my mouth water just reading it: There was a choice of caprese salad with artichokes or mini shrimp kabobs in mango marinade; the entrées were basil-crusted mahimahi with sweet potato flan and roasted vegetable couscous, or filet mignon with asparagus and blue cheese topping served with garlic and rosemary mashed potatoes and spinach-stuffed baked tomatoes gratiné. For dessert? A flaming baked Alaska at each table.

"This is incredible," I told Shepherd. "Has Rufus seen it?"

"I read it to him this morning over the phone. He said to ask you what the kids would think."

"What will they think?" I asked. "They'll think crime pays!" I studied the oversize card again. "This has got to be the best menu I've ever seen." And then it hit me. "Wait," I told Shepherd, "there's something missing." My father might not have been to college, but he was nobody's fool. "You forgot the *price*."

Shepherd wouldn't look at me. He focused on the menu, instead. Could he really have made such a giant slip?

"I didn't forget," he said at last, finally finding my face. "Hey, how often does my daughter graduate from poetry school?"

This was a present from Shepherd? A present that would cost him at least a month's salary? I thought of those cowboy pajamas. I thought of Shepherd, who left home at fifteen. And then I thought of our talk at Shake It Baby: *I've got your back.*

"Thanks," I said. And I meant it. "Thanks a lot."

I'm not sure why, but I held out both hands, just like Rufus. And sure enough, we did the double-handshake thing, only Shepherd didn't let go. He just stood there, looking at my hands in his. "We're going to do better, you and me," he said at last. Then he smiled. Not the way he smiled at regulars. Or even at Manny. It was only for me, that smile, and I'm glad somebody dropped something really heavy in the kitchen just then. Otherwise, I would probably have turned into a soggy mess.

I knew Shepherd's plans for the party were going to be less than a hit with my mother. And I didn't want to have to break the news to her by myself. Which is why, for the first time in forever, I asked Shepherd to come in when he dropped me at home after work.

Given the fact that he wasn't any more inclined to confrontations than he was to Hallmark moments, I might have been pushing my luck. But when I asked him to help me tell Mom where Rufus's good-bye dinner would be held, he didn't say a word. He just sighed, turned off the ignition, and walked me right up to our front door.

So it was the two of us who sat in chairs on each side of my mother as she stared at the menu, which Shepherd laid on the coffee table beside the latest copy of *Her.* And it was the two of us who watched her go to that quiet, throat-clutching place she went whenever she was upset.

"It'll be fun, Mom," I told her, feeling half sorry for the way we'd sprung this on her. "Besides, Mamselle's is the only place in town big enough. Shepherd's going to set up microphones and everything."

"We'll be closed to the public," Shepherd said. "And Rufus asked me to make sure there's room for anyone you want to invite."

I don't know if it was me and Shepherd teaming up, or Shepherd calling our poet Rufus, but my mother was quiet for a really long time. She just sat there, all alone on the couch, looking much smaller than I'd thought possible.

"Mom?" I didn't know what to say, so I said something dumb. "I'm sorry."

It was as if she hadn't heard me. She didn't move. Aunt J. must have been out, because there was no noise from the kitchen and no TV sounds from upstairs. Nobody was going to save us with a dropped pot or a loud commercial.

"Kate," Shepherd said at last. "I need your help with the seating. You know, which muckety-muck goes where?"

My mother, the statue, wasn't even looking at the menu. It was as if she were staring *through* it at something much farther away.

"I was thinking I'd put all the kids at the head table with Rufus," Shepherd went on. "He said he wants to do some kind of poetry thing with them."

Silence. If my mother blinked, I didn't see it.

"Then I was going to put the mayor with some of the newspaper people—"

"You can't do that." Mom's eyes focused on the menu, then on Shepherd. "They just did an op-ed against his decision to run again."

"See what I mean?" Shepherd grinned at me. "Next thing you know,

I'd be mixing the commoners with the royalty." He shrugged, sounded serious. "I really need you to sort things out, Kate."

"And you'll have to split the magazine into two tables. The board needs to be with editorial, but production has to be with art."

"You're talking to the wrong guy," Shepherd said. "You know I'm no good at spit and polish."

My father is not, as I've said before, a dummy. My mother was awake now, looking around the room like someone released from a spell. "I'll need a seating chart," she said.

"I can get you one."

"And what about flowers?"

"Oh, jeez. Can't we just use our regular table vases?"

"Let's not cut corners on this, Shepherd."

Shepherd, a.k.a. My Brilliant Father, turned to me. "What did I tell you, Sarah?" he said. "Thank goodness we got a little class going for us here." He plucked the menu off the coffee table and handed it to Mom. "Kate, choose whatever you think works with this theme, and with the food."

My mother straightened the magazines on the table, then studied the menu again. "It will take time," she told him. "I mean, there are three florists in town. I'd have to see what's in season."

Shepherd looked at her, then at the menu. "You're the boss," he told her.

My mother was livelier now, calculating again. "I'm thinking orchids," she mused. "Purple for the head table, navy for the rest."

"Orchids!?" Shepherd shook his head. "Now, hold on, Kate. You think I'm made of money?"

My mother gave him her Katherine Wheeler look. "Are you putting a price on elegance?" She studied him pointedly, that eyebrow raised. "On good taste?"

Shepherd winced, sucked in his breath. "Listen, Kate," he said, "you can push me just so far. I only got so much blood."

"Orchids or nothing." She folded her arms, waited. There was the shadow of a smile at the corners of her mouth.

"What can I say?" My father bowed his head, like a gladiator conceding a match. "You've got me over a barrel. I need this done right."

"It will be." My mother stood, still holding back a smile. She was good at that. "We should probably throw some dahlias into the mix. A touch of mauve."

Shepherd stood, too. "I'll call you tomorrow from the restaurant," he said, already running for daylight. "We'll order whatever you want."

At the door, Shepherd gave me a conspirator's grin, then turned and said just loud enough to carry back to the living room, "Your mother's got a knack, Sarah. A real knack."

So do you, Dad, I told him in my head. *So do you.*

Linville Gorge

On the lip of joy,
I hear the rude hawks
calling, "Fall! Fall!"
above a sun-flecked stream.

I hear the rude hawks,
yearning, god-eyed

above a sun-flecked stream
coasted with pale cliffs.

Yearning, god-eyed,
I spot from my safe perch,
coasted with pale cliffs,
the distant promise of love.

I spot from my safe perch
on the lip of joy,
the distant promise of love
calling, "Fall! Fall!"

My Mother and I Go Head-to-Head, and I Kiss a Fairy Tale Good-Bye

Friday, while I'd been having tea with Wanda, Rufus had been going through the third degree at *Her*. Apparently, he'd not only survived his interview there, but had helped to cement Mom's position with the magazine and fluff up her ego till it was harder than ever to have a conversation with her that didn't involve the fascinating adventures of Katherine Wheeler, Budding Journalist and Talent to Watch. By Tuesday, she had proofs of the article, and there was no stopping the flow: "If I do say so," she told me as soon as I got home, "this is one of the best features we've ever done." I'd spent the afternoon not answering Fry's texts and watching a remake of *The Great Gatsby* with Wanda and George at the Beaux Arts matinee. I'd hardly walked in the door, when she opened the magazine, magically as always, to the right page, the first of five in the huge article she'd helped plan.

So there I was, after spending two hours in Gatsby's palatial mansion, sitting on the same couch in the same living room I'd grown up in. With the same handsome mother talk-talk-talking. But somehow the couch seemed smaller, its colors faded, the seams pulled nearly to bursting in places. The whole room, in fact, was a little worse for wear and designery in a desperate way I'd never noticed before.

Mom, though, saw nothing but the magazine in her hand. Finally, when she parted with it long enough to let me leaf through the pages, I realized she had every reason to be proud: It was a terrific section, with a double-page photo of the boat launching Rufus had attended when he first arrived in Whale Point, and a beautiful close-up of my poet that would make it clear to the world he was both alive and well. He held his head to one side, as if he'd thought about, given himself wholly to, whatever the photographer had asked.

And the interview? It was full of juicy Rufus quotes, things I would have liked to paste on my wall or stick behind my mirror. For a few minutes, leafing through page after page of Rufus, it was almost like being alone with him. Until it wasn't:

"We're going to get a big response to this," Mom enthused. "I'm sending it absolutely everywhere, to anyone who matters." It was amazing how young she got, how lit up, when she talked about her work. "I'm thinking we might even include copies in your college applications."

"What?!"

"Just to show them the rare educational opportunity you've had." My mother smiled, ingenuous, innocent of her own scheming.

"Mom! I was *sentenced* to that educational opportunity"—I couldn't fathom how the course she'd been humiliated by was now something to boast about—"in a court of law!"

"Well, that wasn't actually mentioned in the article, Sarah." My mother pointed to the first page. "See where it says Rufus is working with a select group of local youngsters?" She was like a child showing off a drawing or a clay figure, totally proud of herself.

I couldn't help it. I laughed out loud. And then, when it stopped being funny, I said I had poetry homework to do. Which was half true and gave me only a temporary reprieve from what I knew was coming.

After Aunt J. came home, and after she'd oohed and aahed over the proofs, the three of us had dinner together. We talked about the banquet, we talked about the new line of peekaboo tops at the boutique where Jocelyn worked, and my aunt even asked about the movie I'd seen with Wanda—maybe because she was interested or maybe because she'd rather talk about anything besides the brilliant doings at *Her*.

But after we'd cleared the table, Mom and I did the dishes together, so it was just the two of us again. She picked up right where she'd left off: "Now that your sentence is nearly served," she told me, handing me a dish towel, "and vacation's half over, we can get down to work."

She sounded as if the "work" we were going to get down to was something she couldn't wait to tackle. In fact, she'd already started. And trapped on the wrong side of the steamy window over the kitchen sink, I had to hear all about it: She'd called the guidance office at school to make sure I would fit in more AP science credits my last year of high school. She'd rounded up a list of tutors just in case any of these courses threatened to lower my GPA. And of course, she was arranging endless visits to the colleges with the best undergrad admissions to med school.

I dried the precious china pieces she wouldn't allow in the dishwasher, and I listened. And listened. And listened.

You know what I heard? Each time Mom lifted a dish or a tray out of the sudsy water, each time she described my certain admission to med school and my glorious future as a doctor, I heard a Technicolor dream. A dream that starred me, instead of her. And for the first time, I wondered about Mom's own dreams, the ones she'd had before her parents died. Before there was no one left to tell her, "I'm proud of you." Or even, "I've got your back."

It made me angry, this secondhand dream. But it made me sad, too. So sad and so tired, I couldn't argue with her. I just nodded and yawned and wiped. And finally, escaped to bed.

Next morning, I waited, as usual, till Mom and Aunt J. left the house, and then I walked to Rufus's for morning pages. Margaret and H were there, and two kids from Shore High. We did less writing than talking, though. Everyone was looking forward to our last class, and when I told them about my mother's plans and my father's menu, sonnets kind of lost out to side dishes. You'd think we were condemned prisoners and all we could talk about was our last meal. When I got so hungry I couldn't stand it, and Rufus had been whisked off to be guest of honor at a Rotary luncheon, I went home to eat. Unfortunately, so did my mother.

Mom *never* came home for lunch. First of all, the office was too far away to leave much time to both breathe and eat; she had to choose one or the other. Second, she loved being with her friends and colleagues too much to shorten her workday on the off chance she'd spend a few minutes with her nearest and dearest: Jocelyn and me.

"What are *you* doing here?" It was the first thing I said. And I didn't mean it to sound as rude as it came out.

My mother didn't seem to mind the inquisition. "I wanted to check on the floral arrangements for tomorrow," she told me. There was a nanosecond while she focused on the banquet, instead of the surprise of my having just walked in the door. Then it was over. She looked at me sharply. "What were you doing *not* here?"

She knew I was a late sleeper, a slow starter, to say the least. And no, I hadn't told her about morning pages. Maybe you think I was silly, but every sinew in my body knew better; knew she would not take kindly to my putting in extra time with what, even though she adored Rufus, she continued to view as one more "distraction." *Poetry is no way to make a living, young lady.*

But the jig was definitely up. And besides, there wouldn't be any more morning pages after the last class. I'd been so thrilled with all our preparations that I hadn't thought of how I'd miss those writing sessions. Now I wondered how I'd manage without my daily walk to Rufus's house. Without writing there. Without talking there. Without Rufus.

Since there was nothing to lose, and since part of me, the little-girl-who-needs-her-mommy-to-be-proud-of-her part, wanted to share, I told her. I explained what I'd been doing, where I'd been going for weeks now. That Rufus had invited us to come and work with him, like real artists, real poets.

True to form, Mom was not pleased. She didn't even want to *hear* about what I'd written in my notebook, day after day; and she certainly didn't want to read it. "We simply can't waste any more time, Sarah," she told me.

She laid her briefcase on the couch, took out extra copies of the interview with Rufus. That was good. Then she found what she was looking for and laid it on top of the magazines: a snappy little tome entitled *Careers in Medicine*. That was bad.

"You don't understand, Sarah." She waved the book at me, as if it were a magic wand. As if it would make me see the light. "That man is turning you against medicine." She sounded indignant. Almost angry. "Every time you visit him, he puts ideas in your head. Every poem you write, we lose ground."

I looked at my pretty, clever mother. "Oh, Mom." My mother with a hurt so old she had no one to share it with. "Lose? If I live to be a thousand, I can't pay Rufus back for what I've gained."

"According to this"—still wielding the book—"we've got enough AP credits, so long as you don't drop that second math course next fall."

"Mom." I wanted to defend Rufus. I wanted to set the record straight. And mostly? I wanted to stop pretending. So now, like those crazy tourists who wade right past the HIGH SURF signs, I told my mother the truth: I didn't really want to study medicine. I wasn't even sure I wanted to study poetry. I thought maybe I'd apply to theater school, instead.

"What are you *thinking*?!" Mom sounded as if I'd suggested an expedition to the North Pole. Or the moon. "Do you have any idea what nonsense you're talking?"

She started sputtering about AP credits, about application deadlines. She said I'd better wake up and come to my senses before I threw my future away. I watched her mouth move, but after a while, I didn't hear a word she said. The whole time she was talking, I felt this stillness, this silence, as if I were backstage again. I was behind the curtains, waiting for them to go up. I didn't know what lines I'd speak when they opened. I didn't know what play I'd be in, or where the theater was. I only knew I needed the adrenaline rush, the make-believe, the magic.

It's funny. I always figured there'd be a big blowup, a scene to end all scenes, when I finally stood up to my mom. But instead, all I felt was strong and sure. And all she had to do was take one look at my face to know she couldn't stop me. It was like that poem Rufus showed me by T. S. Eliot, where the world ends, not with a bang, but a whimper.

We went through the motions, though. Like those phony wrestlers who want to give the crowd their money's worth, even though they both know who's going to win. She told me I was ruining a chance most people would give anything for. And I told her it wasn't my dream I was trashing, but hers. "I know what you want, Mom," I said. "It isn't about me being a doctor. It's about being treated like you're somebody. Like you're important."

Katherine Wheeler and Dealer got very quiet. Her hand flew to her neck like a homing pigeon. The book she'd been holding slipped off her lap and onto the floor. She didn't even seem to notice.

"But the thing is? You're *already* important," I told her. "To me. And to Jocelyn."

My mother's eyes still saw the future, the dream. "We've worked so hard." She said it quietly, as if she were in mourning.

I stooped down, picked up the book, and handed it to her. "Not *we*, Mom," I told her, "*you*." It wasn't the two of us who had scrambled and scratched, who had made phone calls and schemed. Pored over the brochures of every premed school in the country. Compared the curricula of med schools in all fifty states (and a few overseas).

The one who'd done all that was my mother. Or rather the lonely girl I knew was sitting on that couch with her: a fifteen-year-old kid who'd hardly gotten the chance to show off for her own parents before she had to become one herself.

"Mom," I told her, "you don't need an MD for a daughter." *You don't need me to major in medicine so you can major in being respectable, in being somebody.*

"But we've come so far." She had laid the book beside her, and her hands were in her lap now, nested, quiet. Hopeless.

"You can put a whole magazine together all by yourself. You're funny and smart and you know just how to handle people." When she raised her glance, I caught it. "Isn't that enough?

"Me? I'm not sure what I want to do after I graduate, but I'm one hundred billion percent sure it isn't what someone else wants. Not you. Not even Rufus."

"But—"

"If I try out for a part in next fall's play, and if I don't get it?" I remembered what Lisa had said about needing some acting credits behind me. "It won't be your fault. It will be mine. And if I apply to theater school and don't get in? That will be all my own doing." I wanted her to understand. "Do you have any idea how *good* that feels?"

If my mom and I had been onstage or in a movie, she might have wept, might have told me about her long-ago doctor. Might have asked me about Fry. That was the happy ending I'd always imagined. Or maybe you could call it a happy beginning. But the truth is? This wasn't a play, and I wasn't writing the script. If my mother was ever going to confide in me, it would be in her own time. All I could do was walk over to her and take her hand. Just for a second. Then kiss her on the cheek.

She stayed there, frozen, the way she gets. She looked at me as if I were a large balloon that had floated into the living room and was pretending to be someone she knew. She didn't move. She didn't even blink. It seemed like a very long time before she recognized me. When she did, she spoke in a small, resigned voice. "Well, if you're going into theater," she said, "at least you'll always have something from wardrobe you can wear out."

He came to the door that afternoon, the same way he used to. Right after my mother went back to the office, there he was, like always. The difference was Fry stayed outside, head down, as if he were waiting for permission to come into the hall. I couldn't bear to talk on Mom's perfectly plumped cushions, so we sat outside on the front steps. I perched beside a big planter filled with carnations and pansies. (As soon as she'd invited Rufus to dinner that first time, my mother had added the carnations, long-stemmed afterthoughts that towered over the tiny pansies.)

That planter took up nearly the whole step where I sat, so Fry had to find a place below me.

"Listen," he said.

"I am," I said.

"Whoo-heooooo," said a dove from the oak tree next door.

"Let's go to the beach," Fry suggested, "where we can talk."

"We can talk here," I told him.

"But H and Margaret are waiting to see you." He nodded toward the Taurus, shuddering on idle across the street. H waved from behind the wheel. Beside him, Margaret was bent over the front seat, wrestling with the cooler. Fry had brought backup.

I studied the pansies' clown faces and thought about Rufus, about second-chance daughters. Second-chance boyfriends.

"Noooo-noooooooo," said the dove, who knew better than I did. I ignored it and went to the beach.

It was good to hear the ocean again, to take my shoes off and walk in the sand. To feel how the sun had worked its way down into the beach. Yes, morning pages with Rufus were still percolating, and everything felt like a poem. And yes, it was good to sit on a towel, watching the water beads dry on everyone's legs after a quick wade. Finally, it was good to have H and Margaret there. To remind me that things didn't have to stay the same. That they could change in the best of all possible ways.

H's crush on Miss Kinney was definitely a thing of the past. The boy who sat beside Margaret now, who laughed and talked in a lower, easier register than before, seemed older, different. And if you can believe it, *quieter*. One thing hadn't changed, though. He insisted on sharing his latest poem.

I was dreading my encounter with Fry and exhausted from my face-off with Mom. The four of us had barely toweled off, and Margaret had just set out a paper plate of olives and deviled eggs. In short, I was not at all ready for one of H's rhyming disasters. But as it turned out, this one was different; it was more than half good. He didn't need to read it, because like Rufus that first day of class, he had it memorized.

It wasn't long and it hardly rhymed at all. But it was true and sweet and it made Margaret close her eyes, then lean over and kiss him, right there on the ratty NASCAR towel he insisted on dragging to the beach even though it had lost so much of its color that Mario Andretti's nose had pretty much disappeared. "That was good," I told him, and I meant it. "That was really good."

I watched H and Margaret then. Studied them, I guess you could say. The way they sat with each other was comfortable, open. Not wrapped around each other, but just touching. As if that was enough. I was pretty sure Margaret didn't go all helpless, shapeless goo inside each time H talked to her. And I was pretty sure H wouldn't have minded telling her just what he was thinking and feeling.

Fry didn't watch what I was watching, though. Instead, he stared at me. Too long and too hard. He drank a sip of beer and then he stared. Drank another sip and stared again. As if he were trying to memorize me. As if he knew he wouldn't see me again. "Come on," he said at last. "Let's go for a walk."

Like the dove, I knew better. But I went. I took his hand, partly out of habit, and partly because, well, the gulls were screeching, the water was sparkling like fireflies, and everything felt like home. The cottages along the shore got farther back and farther apart. Soon there were just dunes on one side of us, water on the other. Halfway to the cove, it happened. There was no talk, no preliminaries. Fry just grabbed me. Held me close. And covered my mouth with his. Me? I pushed him away.

Not want to kiss Fry? Not want to get up close and sweaty with the sexiest guy in school? Like H's poem, this was something no one could have predicted. But everything had changed since our last kiss. For one thing, I was now clear: That had definitely been our last kiss. Rufus had shown me something besides how enjambed lines rush you ahead like a waterfall. He'd shown me what honesty and being there for someone looked like.

"Fry," I said, backing away from him. "There's something I need to tell you."

"How you're sorry you blew me off? How you miss me so much it hurts?" Now there was a smile, but it was huge, exaggerated.

I turned away, started walking back toward the others. Fry grabbed me, too hard. He pushed me toward a dune, a shaggy mountain of sand that blocked out the last of the cottages along the beach. He was breathing hard, as if he were stroking toward a giant wave. "Listen," he said. "We can still make this work."

A SINGLE GULL OVERHEAD

WHEEE-EEEEE. AUKKKKKKKKKK. WHEEEE-eeeeeeeeee.

FRY

(*Not letting go*)

When you kissed me on that empty stage? I fell like a damn fool.

ME

Look, Fry,

(*Trying to get my arm free from his grip*)

things are different now.

GULL

(*Diving into a high-tide wave*)

KRRRREEEEEEE-EEEEEEEEEE-EEEEEEE-eeeeeeeeeeeeeee.

FRY

A fool who maybe took a few shortcuts to get what I wanted.

GULL

(*With a fish in its claws*)

Krauchhhhhh. Chaaaulllllkkkk. KRAAAAAAAAA.

INCOMING TIDE

SHHHHHHH, NOW . . . shhhhhhh, now.
SHHHHHHH, NOW. NOW. NOW.

FRY

(*Letting me go, sinking down against the dune*)

Mom and Mr. Mustache are getting hitched.

ME

What?

(*Shaking my head, sitting beside him*)

Really?!

FRY

Really. They're moving to California. They want me to come with them.

ME

(*Genuinely happy, and yes, a lot relieved*)

Oh, Fry! That's some of the best surfing in the world.

FRY

I won't go if you ask me to stay.

THE TIDE

(*Washing over both of us*)

Shhhhhhhh. SHHHHH.
SHHHHHHHHHHHHHHHHH.
NOOOOOOOOOOOOOOO-
WWWWWWWWWWWWWWW.

"One word, Sarah," Fry told me, leaning in, seeing a future I didn't. "Stay," he said.

I wasn't quiet because I was thinking it over. It was more that I was afraid of how much he wanted something I could never give him.

"It doesn't have to rhyme, Sarah. Forget that moon-spoon crap." He was smiling, holding my hand again, more gently this time. But those chocolate eyes of his were losing light fast. "Just tell me to stay." The animal look was coming back. And the longer I waited, the worse it would be.

"We can still have next year, just like we planned. I'll hang with H and his family, and we can graduate together. There's always California after that." He took my other hand, too, and his voice dropped, then broke as if he were just now growing up. "My girl comes first."

It was like diving into winter waves. "I can't," I told him.

"Why not?"

"Because I need to find out who I am by myself before I can be with anyone else."

Fry looked at me, and he didn't need to say anything. His face was all hurt, all questions.

I glanced out across the horizon and found a faraway dot that must have been the gull making off with its catch. I tracked that steady, determined wingbeat across the sky.

"It isn't you, it's me." I needed to explain. "I already told Rufus I can't be his amenu—his intern. I told him I want to give acting a try." Finally, I said the hardest thing of all: "I'm pretty sure I don't feel the same way about you that Margaret does about H. Or the way your mom does about Mr. Mu—about her fiancé."

Then I talked for a long time. Way too long. I heard myself filling up the awkward space between us, pouring in words. But I was too nervous, too afraid to stop, and I couldn't even meet his eyes. So I told him about listening to the world talk. About being part of that dialogue every time I walked onstage. I chattered on and on, and when I finally ran out of breath and looked up at him, I saw something I'd never expected. Fry was crying.

For Margaret

Some people laugh
ha-ha-ha.
Other people put
their hands on their mouths
he-he-he.
In department stores
Santa laughs
ho-ho-ho.

But this girl I know—
okay, this girl I'm crazy for
laughs like an envelope
tearing open and good stuff
spilling out.

The Last Class

Fry stopped texting and calling. I knew he was probably surfing next day, and wasn't about to come off the beach for the banquet that night. I hoped the ocean was full of brilliant rogue waves, and that the boy I'd just said no to was catching every one of them, perfect ride after perfect ride.

As for me? I was riding a different kind of wave by 6 p.m.—on Mamselle's terrace. It was heart-in-your-throat exciting to be sitting with Margaret and H at the head table, to look out over dozens of other tables, scurrying servers, popping flashbulbs, and reporters, some from national networks. Because, let's face it, it wasn't every day that a group of regular kids got thrown a farewell banquet by a world-famous poet.

My mother and the three florists she'd worked with had outdone themselves. (And spent mounds of Shepherd's money.) Because it was warm enough to be outside, they'd scattered potted plants and twinkling lights everywhere. The usual ferns and palms were supplemented with silver trellises at all four entrances. Wisteria and trumpet vines crawled up each one and hung like gorgeous draped curtains from the top. Tubs of live orchids filled the center of every table; all the napkins were folded into rabbit ears, then wrapped around a small glass vase that held miniature roses and sprigs of honeysuckle. I had to admit, the whole place looked and smelled amazing, like a garden on steroids, one big, gorgeous botanical paradise.

Even Thatcher Vogel showed up, and maybe, I whispered to Margaret, his mother had dressed him, because he wore a plain sport shirt without a single skull or big truck in sight. Everyone from class was there, sitting right up front at the head table. Everyone except Fry, of course. And sure, even in the middle of that crowd, swept up by suspense and excitement, I still got flashbacks; a few sweet moments flooded me, kisses, laughs, poems. But mostly? I felt relief that it was over. Make-believe poetry. Make-believe love.

I studied the others at the long table: the inseparable couple who'd thrown their hoops together; Coral Ann Levin, whose mother had sewn her a dress by hand; Thatcher and his goon crew; the kids from Shore High; Margaret, whose laugh had made me trust her; H, a kindred spirit and a dear friend, after all. We'd all shared something, something big. None of us were in the same place we'd started a few short months ago.

Me? Where had I been Before Rufus? I'd had a prince, I'd been a "popular girl," and I'd no inkling what an iamb was. And now? I'd lost my prince and was doomed, with the start of school, to fall (back) to the bottom of the WPH social ladder. But I had a new-and-improved father who, in his own unpredictable fashion, was there for me. I'd learned about getting out of bed to do something that's more important than staying in it. And most surprising, most wondrous of all, I'd met a great poet who shared the world I'd always felt alone in—the world I heard crackling and whispering, giggling and singing, moaning and roaring all around me. A poet who made me proud of myself and of what I could do, might do yet.

"I hope someone has the guts to teach those kids a lesson." The microphone snapped to life, and I jumped, as if someone had sneaked up behind me. Actually, though, they'd sneaked up right in front of me. I'd been so busy people watching and gossiping with Margaret, I hadn't seen Rufus and our prof join us.

"If they were a year or two older, those punks would be thrown in jail. I say give them a preview of coming attractions!" It was my poet's voice, but not his words. He'd come in, like he always did, without anyone noticing. For a famous guy, he had the strangest way of disappearing sometimes. But there he was, propped on his crutches, his big hands wrapped around the sides of a lectern, reading.

"I really didn't think it was possible that a bunch of teenagers, regular high school students, some of them kids of my neighbors, could deliberately destroy an old man's past."

Everyone at my end of the table gasped. By now, we all recognized the letters from the paper. The ones by outraged citizens. Where had Rufus found them? And why on earth was he reading them at what was supposed to be a *très élégant* event?

I hardly dared look at Mom's table, where she and Aunt J. were eating elbow to elbow with the mayor, the town council, and her boss at the magazine. As Rufus kept reading, though, I sneaked a peek. My mother's hand was at her throat.

"Most things have two sides, Rufus read, "but the kind of desecration that went on in that house last week is just plain wrong. 'Shameful' is another word for it."

I found the table with the principals and teachers from our schools. Miss Kinney was wearing a beautiful white peasant blouse and a confused smile. Beside her, there was a young man in a uniform. A young man who sat very close to her, his arm over her chair.

"If we're raising boys and girls who trample on everything we hold precious, what hope is there for the future?"

When he'd read the worst parts of those angry letters, Rufus stopped and beamed at all of us. I felt sick inside, not so much that he was punishing us for what we'd done, but that he wanted to.

"I've just read you," Rufus told the sea of tables spread across the patio, "what some folks in town think of the young men and women I've been working with this summer." He picked up a book bound in green and turned a few pages. "And now I'd like to read you what those shameful, thoughtless barbarians have written for all of us." He found the place he wanted, and peered from under that sweep of white hair at the diners around him. "It's about a humble weed we all take for granted, something that blooms in the toughest spots." Then, in a voice that was as warm as afternoon sun, Rufus read the poem we'd all made together, the one about *Lamium*.

At first, as I listened, it sounded like a famous poem, something Miss Kinney would probably make us memorize. But the words were ours, and that day in the garden came rushing back: the twilight, the way Rufus had opened everyone like flowers.

"Is there a heartbeat in those purple veins?
Are those embryos or mouths or rosary beads?
The color of my first dress, gathered with love."

I looked around the room, saw the faces of people who'd never shared that class with us, people who might have written some of those angry letters. Everyone was quiet, listening.

"Fairy cups stirred with blades of grass,
Notes clustered on a windy score,
Three blooms, three friends, alas!"

I couldn't help twisting in my seat, turning toward the entrance to the dining room, where Shepherd and Manny were standing. And sure enough, my father nodded, gave me a thumbs-up. Did he understand everything we'd written? I couldn't tell, but he knew it mattered to me. And that was enough.

"Petals small as a child's tears good-bye,
Dropped stitches everywhere
From a blanket the color of sky."

There was a moment, right after my poet read the end of our poem, when no one said a word, when the kitchen and the nesting birds in the trees beyond the terrace made the only sounds you could hear. That's when I checked my mother's table, saw Mom's stunned-rabbit look, her slow smile as the people around her put their hands together.

The clapping was loud and long; it drowned out the birds, the kitchen, everything except Manny's four-finger whistle. And it didn't stop until Rufus grabbed the lectern and raised one hand.

"This book," he told us, "includes poems written by all the miracle workers at this table. It is my gift to Margaret and Shelly." He held out copies of the green book, and Margaret and the girl from Shore stood up the way you do at the Oscars and took them from him. "To Sarah and Hector." He held out two more books, and H and I stood, too. I felt H's pride beside me. This wasn't graduation, but it sure beat marching across a football field.

When Rufus gave me my book, we couldn't do the two-handed shake, but I settled for one. Plus a patented Rufus Baylor grin. Next, Coral Ann and the boy named Adam from Shore High got their books. And yes, Thatcher got one, too. Along with everyone in class, including Charles Fenshaw, who was seated next to our poet and who, as usual, was speechless.

As the books were handed out, Rufus lost his audience, or at least the part of it at our table. We couldn't wait, we started right in, leafing through our copies of *Good Poems from Bad Kids*. They were beautiful, bound in green and decorated with silver lettering and a small picture of purple flowers. Inside, after the title page and the table of contents, was the poem we'd written as a class, and after that so many poems it made your head spin to see them. They were all mixed up, so you had to shuffle through the pages to find yours. And of course, you got stopped along the way, surprised again and again by how good other kids' poems were.

And yes, Rufus had even printed something by a poet no one expected to be included, one Shepherd Ryan. It wasn't exactly a poem, and it was very, very short. But it was on a page all by itself, like a dedication at the very beginning of the book. H smiled when I showed it to him. "Remember?" he asked. "The class where Rufus couldn't work the player?"

I studied the page, and it came back, the question my poet had asked Shepherd. *Can you tell us why you shut your eyes?* And there it was, my father's answer:

> Give the music room,
> space of its own,
> a place it doesn't have to share.

Pretty soon, we were all looking at each other's books, high-fiving and pointing and reading the best lines out loud. Which was when my poet decided we'd forgotten the other people on the patio long enough. He tapped on the mic with his spoon. There was a hideous raw squeal that made everyone hold their ears. "Fellow poets," he announced, once everyone had stopped talking, "this book is worth sharing. As first editions go, it isn't a large run—only about two hundred copies." We could hear the wink in his voice, if we couldn't see it in his eyes. "Course, that only means it will get more valuable as the years go on."

Charles Fenshaw, smug as a magician's assistant, set another huge pile of books on our table. "I think I have enough for everyone," Rufus said, "so if y'all would help me distribute the booty, the rest of us can read along." He held out a book to the boy next to him. "Well, don't just sit there keeping the good stuff to yourselves," he told us. "Let's pass these around."

And we did. Each person at every table on the terrace got one. The teachers, the mayor, the families, even the reporters from the *Whale Point Watch* and the bigger dailies in Charlotte and Raleigh. And yes, the waitstaff and kitchen crew, too. You should have seen Manny's face when I handed him his copy—he wiped his hands on his apron before he took it, and then, well, "beam" doesn't really describe it. I never knew the man had so many teeth.

"I said 'read along,' and that's just what I meant." Rufus wore a look I recognized by now, a look that meant he was going to take us on another adventure. "Poetry is spoken music," he explained. "There's all kinds of music—lyrical, discordant, sorrowful and slow, dizzy and fast, sneaky, lazy, sweet. But there's one kind of music you'll never hear, and that's silent."

He studied the faces around him at the head table. "Poetry is meant to be read aloud. And part of being a poet is reading your work to others. No one, anywhere, knows better than you how it's meant to sound."

You guessed it. The world's most famous poet was inviting us to read our poems. Not to each other, the way we had in class. But right here, right now, *in public.* I know that "butterflies in your stomach" is just a figure of speech, but I can testify that the second I thought about reading my poetry in front of all those people, *something* in mine was fluttering.

Rufus told us that anyone who didn't want to read didn't have to. But he said he hoped we'd take advantage of the mic and the flowers and the audience. "You won't have this chance every day," he said. "Besides, I'm getting tired of the sound of my own voice. I've marked my favorite poem by each of you in my book here, and I can't think of a more splendid good-bye from y'all than hearing them in your own voices."

When he put it that way, of course, I wanted to read. To *him*. But I was still in no hurry to get up in front of parents, duly elected officials, and all the other "important people" my mother had invited. So it was the brave, nervy kids who started it. H was one of the first, and though you might have expected him to ham it up, you'd have been wrong. I don't know if it was the poem Rufus picked or the fact that Margaret was watching him, her chin in both hands, like she was waiting for the secret of life. Whatever the reason, H didn't hog the spotlight. He read his short poem about the smell of coffee with just enough heart, and since it didn't rhyme, it sounded more than all right. And then, while the whole room applauded, before they'd even finished, he sat down.

Why was I so nervous? I'd had more stage experience than most of the kids there, hadn't I? Why was reciting my poetry harder than saying lines? Why did it feel so different when the words were my own? So many kids, even people I thought were terminally shy, were standing up now. Walking to the microphone one by one. Giving Rufus the kind of good-bye that meant the most.

Yes, I finally got up the nerve to read. Right after Margaret. And walking to the head of the table was the hardest part. After that, I mostly forgot about me, me, me. I could have cried when I saw the poem Rufus had marked with a pencil check in the book he handed me. It was the one about Nella, and I'm not sure I read it very well. I didn't imagine the audience naked or take calming breaths before each line; I simply watched my poet listen, head bent, to every word. I don't remember now whether the applause was long or short, loud or soft, because while everyone clapped, I just sat there, swimming in his smile.

Eventually, nearly our whole table, including the Magician's Assistant, had marched up to the mic, and it seemed the crowd on the patio was clapped out. But they weren't, because there was still someone who hadn't read his work. Rufus stood, finally, not exactly smiling, but clearly content. "I wrote one, too," he said. "Y'all want to hear it?"

In the category of silly questions? That one ranked pretty high. Everyone there had come to see Rufus. Oh, they probably liked our poems, but years from now what they'd be telling their kids and grandkids was that they'd heard Rufus H. Baylor read a poem.

"You teachers know that learning goes both ways." Rufus glanced over at the table where Miss Kinney sat, and she nodded, though I think she would have agreed with anything her idol said. "I learned more than I taught this time round, and part of what I learned is that there's no need to give up on life until it's over."

Give up? Is that what he'd been ready to do before he came back to Whale Point? Had he hated growing old? Fading into retirement? I pictured him alone in the mountains, folding up all that love and music, like old clothes in a trunk. Putting them away because he didn't think anyone needed them.

Suddenly, he was grinning at our entire table, as if we'd given him the greatest present in the world. "I hadn't written a poem in over five years when this group got hold of me," he told the audience. "I'm writing again, and I don't plan on stopping until they bury me. School's never out, is it?"

He read a poem then. It wasn't long, but it stayed in your mind and heart after he'd finished. I was glad it was printed at the end of the book, because that way I could find it whenever I wanted to remember that night. Whenever I needed a Rufus fix.

What Have We Learned, Class?

We've learned trees,
their wind-tossed alphabet.
We've studied sunrise
in the throats of birds,
the charity of dew on moss,
the forgiveness of rain.

We've learned hunger
from a dimpled shell
on a wide beach. We've seen
how beauty trips you up,
makes you stoop,
brings you grace.

If we're smart, we'll
play it dumb, never quite
get it, always have to stay after.
On the board, the sea's song,
the language of stars
over and over,
            again and again.

My Poet Goes Home

It was a perfect scheme. Charles Fenshaw would take my father's place as Rufus's right-hand man. He'd travel with my poet to Asheville, and help him hobble around until the cast came off. He was most thrilled about his second job title, though: amanuensis. It turns out he jumped at the chance to fill the position I'd turned down: He would be my poet's literary assistant—he would take dictation, collect Rufus's poems, and help shape all those butterflies into a new book. He took a leave from the college, and for the few days before they left, he followed his idol's every move, a dutiful Rufus shadow. When Rufus stood, so did his new secretary; when the older man sat, so did the younger one. Ditto for laughing, looking stern, sporting a pencil behind one ear, or air-conducting classical music from that album with a lightning bolt on the cover.

Best of all, rather than drive back to Asheville, the two of them decided to fly. Which meant—thanks to some proactive whining on the part of Sarah Who Needs Happy Endings— my father and I would drive the beater out west when my poet needed it again. Which also meant that by Christmas, I'd get to visit the house where Rufus lived. (Not a nursing home, it turned out, but a cottage he'd built with his own hands when his family was new.) I'd finally see the mountains he'd written so many lines about; the deer and pheasant that roamed his backyard; the study where he still planned to work every day, hatching haikus and sonnets and villanelles, and poems there weren't even any names for yet. We'd go on walks together. We'd drive to a valley where seven mountains circled a lake. He'd teach me to call down barred owls and find fox dens. And yes, we'd write together again, desk to desk, side by side.

"So this isn't really good-bye." That's what he told me at the airport, and that's what I believed. Right through the end of summer. Right through the start of school. And I suppose it was true, since we talked on the phone. A *lot*. I fell into a pattern of calling Asheville at least three times a week. I loved getting updates, checking in. Those calls were like life rafts I sent out from my ordinary existence in Whale Point to Rufus's mountaintop home. After a day of mind-numbing differential equations and my new English teacher's lackluster lessons, it was like snuggling into down to curl up on my bed and hear that voice, ocean deep, tumbling and purring at the same time.

As soon as he'd shed his cast, Rufus began taking short walks along the mountain trails that wrapped around his house. Usually, his faithful shadow went with him, though sometimes he managed to steal away by himself. He was full of near poems about those times, unconscious riffs on the busy, natural world he loved tramping through. "The vole finally got that fig tree," he'd say. "But she made me a fair trade, let me see her nestlings, all five of them huddled under the roots." Or, "A deer and I came nose to nose today! Three feet between us, then a twig cracked and it was gone." He sighed. "How must it feel to carry fear around with you all the time like that?"

And of course, he always checked on my work. "What have you been writing, Sarah?" Or, "May I hear the latest poem, Miss Wheeler?" If he called me Miss Wheeler, I usually read him something, even if it wasn't long. Even if I'd written it only because I knew he'd ask.

But if I was just plain Sarah, I could confess that I'd been AWOL from poetry, that I'd had too much homework or too many rehearsals. I told him that I had tried out for the fall play. And that, yes, I'd actually gotten a good part—not the lead, but sixteen lines, and ten of them mattered. I wouldn't die, which would have been perfect, but I would suffer meaningfully!

He laughed his rumbling laugh, and I knew my boring existence was good for something. If you can make someone like Rufus happy, you feel good about yourself. Even if you have to hang up the phone afterward and go down to dinner, sit in your maroon-cushioned chair with a napkin glued to your lap, and listen to your mother and your aunt talk, talk, talk. Even if you have to go back to your room, half do your homework, set your alarm, and repeat everything all over again the next day.

I couldn't wait to break up this hamster-wheel routine with a visit to Asheville. But early in November, my phone rang. At first, I hoped it was Rufus wishing me happy birthday, but as soon as I heard Charles Fenshaw's voice, I knew something was wrong. "He fell again," Charles said. "He asked me not to tell you. But—"

"Is he okay?" I held my breath, as if I were diving into ice water.

FENSHAW

He wouldn't let me contact anyone—not his friends, not his publisher.

(A long pause, too long)

I had to sneak out to call the doctor.

ME

But how?

FENSHAW

He slipped on some ice outside the patio doors.

ME

Ice? It's not even winter yet!

FENSHAW

There's been snow in the mountains for weeks.

SARAH BERNHARDT

(From the poster above my bed)

"Down, thou climbing sorrow! / Thy element's below."

GODZILLA

(From my window seat, beside the rest of the monsters)

REEwoOOOrrrrrrwwwwwww!!

ME

But he was fine last time we talked. Just fine.

FENSHAW

He could hardly move. He was up for three nights before I got the doctor in. That's when they took him to the hospital.

SARAH BERNHARDT

"O sir, you are old. / Nature in you stands on the very verge / Of his confine."

ME

He saw a deer. They were nose to nose.

KING KONG

HMMMMRRRRRRRRRRRRRRR!

FENSHAW

It was pneumonia. It was the second fall. It was . . .

(Almost whispering)

too much.

ME

Wait. Where is he?

(Louder, nearly yelling)

I need to talk to him!

FENSHAW

I'm sorry. I'm so sorry.

THE HULK
NOOOOOOOOOOOOO!!!!

There was a funeral. There were speeches and tributes and obituaries in every newspaper and on every TV station in the country. There was a will. And some money for his "second-chance daughter" to study "whatever she wants, whatever feeds her." There was even a fund for a Whale Point Youth Center, which made the town council extremely happy. (Before they started wrangling over exactly how to spend it.) There will be a final book coming out next year, with all the new work Rufus did after he got home. He'd written every day, sometimes well into the night, according to Charles. As if he were in a hurry, as if he knew there wasn't much time.

And of course, there wasn't. Hadn't my poet told us that in so many words, over and over? Hadn't I pretended it wasn't true? Hadn't I assumed someone so full of life, so important to me, would go on and on?

Of all the things my poet left behind, the one I wish I could make disappear is the hole in my heart, a hole the wind blows through. Every day. Every night. Sometimes I walk to the Hendricks', so I can visit with Carmen. And remember. She puts up with me, so do the Hendricks. But it isn't the same. Unless I pick up a pencil and start to write.

My poetry isn't for showing to anyone. It's just for the two of us. Because yes, it feels as if Rufus and I are still writing together. It just takes a quiet time, my notebook. And maybe, as Emily Dickinson said, "a certain Slant of light." Mornings are best, when the sun is just catching the edges of the pines, lighting them up like a backdrop. That's when I can feel my poet reading over my shoulder. I may change a line three or four times, saying it over and over till the music is right. And then, of course, that means another line needs to be tweaked. And another. And suddenly, in the middle of my frustration, I hear his voice:

Which part feels wrong, Sarah?

I read again the lines that clunk, that don't come close to what my heart wants to say.

Which part feels right?

I sound out the words that sing, that work without effort.

That's good enough to eat!

I sigh, long and theatrical, because I know what's coming next:

Okay, throw them both out.

I groan. I think of the hard way I've come, the missteps, the false starts. The history it took to make what is close, tremblingly near, to being a poem.

Nothing's ever wasted, Sarah. It's always there when you need it.

It's as if, finally, I can read *his* mind. As if he's in my head forever.

Good. Close your eyes. Now start all over.

And I do.

How long would our poem be?
How much would it weigh?
The first verse would be yours, of course—
Age before beauty, you'd say.

You would not rush so much as crest,
a wave that spreads and breaks

across the eyes and ears to fill
some deeper, inner space.

The next verse would be mine,
self-conscious, yes, it's true,
and full of fits and starts
but bits of music, too.

Would we share some lines then,
just we two?
Here's a place for my words;
here, only yours will do.

And would it matter, really,
after all is said and done,
who made which piece of glory?
Who, this moon? Who, that sun?

The pen drops from your hand,
but there's still more to say.
So I must write our final line,
which is simply
stay.

About This Book

The facts: In 2008, some forty-five years after the death of Robert Frost, a group of teenagers broke into the poet's historically preserved summer home in Ripton, Vermont. Nestled in the New England countryside his poetry celebrates, Frost's farmhouse was not elegant or expensively furnished, but apparently, it was the perfect place to drink and smoke, off the main road and far from town. By the time the party was over, the house had been set on fire and left in a shambles. When police discovered the majority of the teens were underage high school students, a resourceful judge sentenced them to take a course in the famous man's poetry.

The fiction: From the time I read about this case, my author's "What If?" machinery kicked into high gear. What if the vandalism happened, not in Vermont, but in North Carolina, where I live? What if the celebrity poet was also from my adopted state, someone who did for the South what Frost had done for the North—made its landscape and people the heart of his work? What if this poetic giant was still alive when his house was destroyed? And what if he decided to teach that course himself?

The characters: I've read and cherished Robrt Frost's poetry for years. So there are a few aspects of Rufus Baylor's aesthetics and history that Frost fans may recognize. But most of his personality and all of his poems are his own. Sarah, of course, is totally my creation, and is based on no one alive, except in my head and heart.

Acknowledgments

My first readers include my daughter, Robin; my son, Marc; Frances Wood; Marjorie Hudson; and Karen Pullen.

My dreamy agent is Ginger Knowlton, who believes in books and readers and me.

After that? It's so much fun to reach the stage in the publishing process where you have fellow travelers, collaborators who make the going less lonely and the final product a lot more compelling. Could anyone be luckier than to find an editor like Karen Wojtyla, who leaves this book better and bigger than she found it? Or a team like art director Michael McCartney and calligrapher Sarah Jane Coleman, who came up with a cover everyone I know wants to frame? Or a copy editor like Erica Stahler, who cares about the sound that sand crabs make? (Really.)

Thank you all. It took a village.